ABOUT THE BOOK

When Detective David Storm loses his only remaining suspect—the one person who might be able to answer the lingering questions about his wife's murder—the nightmares return.

Soon after the revenge killing of Rique Guzman, a kingpin of Rio Drug Cartel, throws a major case he's on with a combined task force of federal and local law enforcement into limbo.

Yet, just when all looks lost, the FBI receives an anonymous tip linking the murder of the man who killed Rique with the murder of Storm's wife.

Accompanied by a mysterious, beautiful woman, Detective Storm follows the trail of clues out of his beloved state of Texas through our nation's capitol and deep into the wilds of South America and Mexico to find the answers to the questions that have haunted him for so long.

This book is the final chapter of the David Storm trilogy. To find out more about what brought Detective Storm to this exciting conclusion, be sure to check out the previous two books in the series, "Charity Kills" and "After the Storm."

STORM'S END

A David Storm Mystery

By Jon Bridgewater

Storm's End
A David Storm Mystery
By Jon Bridgewater

©2016 All Rights Reserved

ISBN: 978-0-9849142-2-7

Published by Boot Hill

Edited by Carolyn Goss

Cover art by Dehanna Bailee
Back cover photo by Daniel Lyons
Special thanks for encouragement and proofreading to Gini Roe, Bill Poston, Julie Richardson, Chris Manly

Book design by EditWriteDesign.com

This book is a work of fiction. While some of its locations are real, the plot and characters are works of the author's imagination. Any similarities to persons either living or dead are purely coincidental.

This book is dedicated to the memory of a close friend, Lieutenant Colonel James Larry Jefferis. Larry was one of those people who encouraged me to continue to write and tell stories. He helped as he could, proofreading my work to catch those mistakes I missed. I will miss him and his friendship.

Larry proudly served his country from 1966 until his retirement in 2006. Larry served in Viet Nam, Germany and other military bases around the United States, ending his career working at the Pentagon. Being a pretty good story teller himself, he told me stories of serving with Elvis in Germany. One of his favorite games, while studying for his Master's in Engineering, and in the company of some anonymous writer, was Trick or Drinking in his neighborhood at Halloween.

I would also like to thank all the men and women of our United States military and all branches of law enforcement, for your service and for protecting our safety.

God Bless You All!

2000

The day had been nothing special for seasoned Homicide Detective David Storm. He had worked one of those inconsequential cases of one illegal immigrant killing another in a dispute over a woman after an afternoon of drinking outside a bodega on Houston's near southwest side. This barrio of Houston was crisscrossed with major city streets and cheap apartment housing where the illegals could gather to look for work. Groups of men standing on the every corner in hopes of being picked up by day labor employers. Houston's rapid expansion and its predilection for being a sanctuary city had made it become a popular destination for the teeming masses swarming across the border from all points south. The oppressive heat and humidity of an August afternoon, combined with alcohol only exacerbated the situation and it was bound to produce fights and killings, which popped up like wide fires on an arid California hillside.

The call had come in just as Storm was about to end his shift. The dispatch officer saw Storm preparing to call it a day and asked him if he would take a routine investigation of a killing, telling him there were street patrol officers already on the scene. The dispatcher went on to inform Storm that the patrol officers were holding a suspect until he could arrive.

Storm grimaced inwardly because he understood regular working hours didn't apply to a homicide cop and the seemingly simple nature of this blip on the radar screen of a so far uneventful day should only take him a couple of hours to resolve.

This day was special; it was the day his wife would be returning from a week long business trip to Venezuela. Angie, his wife of over ten years, had been out of town on business; another of what had become way too many separations from the best thing that happened in his life. Checking his watch, he saw it was only four in the afternoon and she was not expected home until after six, so that should give him enough time to wrap up a simple killing in the barrio.

When Storm arrived at the scene of the stabbing, patrol officers had a suspect handcuffed and sitting in the back seat of their cruiser, they had cordoned off the crime scene with yellow police tape leaving the victim's body where the man had collapsed. Two other patrol cars were parked on the median under the elevated toll road holding the "Looky Lou's" back from the scene and hopefully keeping them from contaminating the investigation. Another uniformed officer was interviewing two men who most likely were witnesses to the stabbing.

Technicians from the Medical Examiner's office were already on the scene and informed Storm the victim had been stabbed with a four-inch blade at least six times to the torso and neck. "One of the wounds had cut the jugular vein and the victim had probably bled out in seconds" one of the techs informed him.

A bloody, well-worn Buck knife lay in close proximity to the corpse; rightfully suspected to be the murder instrument. Crime Scene personnel had photographed the entire scene, taking pictures of the body, the wounds and the bloody knife lying close by. They were now done with their jobs and were loading up to return to their office. Before they left, they picked up the knife wearing surgical gloves and put it in an evidence bag. They would type the blood found on the knife and dust it for fingerprints to nail down the fact that the suspect, now being held was in fact the killer.

Storm saw the suspect in the back seat of the patrol car and he could only hope the officers had followed protocol and bagged the suspect's hands to preserve any blood evidence on them. Procedure called for the officers to make sure the suspect was photographed for the later court hearings. These photographs would show blood splatter, especially from the severing of the jugular vein. Severing a major artery would cause blood to spray everywhere and if the suspect was the killer, there would be no way to avoid being splashed with the victim's blood, the suspect's clothing would be taken in as evidence and the blood on them would be compared to that of the victim.

The officers told Storm that when they arrived the suspect was being held by two other men who had been sitting under the overpass across the way when the stabbing occurred. The officers had followed procedure, cuffing the man and encasing his hands in plastic bags with tie wraps around his wrists, exactly as the police handbook instructed. They had not questioned him as they were waiting for Storm's arrival and the Crime Scene techs to finish their investigation. They also reported that the suspect's clothes were bloody, confirming their suspicions that he had at least been close to the victim when he was stabbed. Collecting evidence was tedious and time consuming if done right, so all the officers could do at this point was wait and interview the onlookers. They had been assured by the Crime Scene techs that they would photograph the man as soon as they had completed work with the body and knife.

Storm's End

Storm asked if the officers had interviewed the suspect and was told they had only asked his name and the suspect so far had been uncooperative. The man sitting in the back seat of their patrol car seemed to be incoherent, babbling on and on in Spanish. The officers had followed protocol to the letter and they knew that interrogation of a murder suspect was a job for Homicide, so they had waited for Storm's arrival. This was also the patrol officers' way of attempting to pass responsibility for the arrest and booking onto Homicide. But, Storm had his own agenda; he was not some dumbass rookie who would bite on that hook. He had plans and booking this guy in was not in them.

Storm opened the back door of the patrol car, fished the man out of the back seat and stood him upright with his back to the fender of the trunk of the car. The man was indeed covered in blood, from head to toe. He stood about 5'6" and looked as if he might weigh about a buck thirty.

The suspect appeared drunk and continually babbled in Spanish about someone being a puta. When questioned by Storm with his rudimentary command of the Spanish language, the suspect again went into a rant about something to do with how the puta was cheating on him and how, as best as Storm could understand, it had been an argument about the victim being with his woman, or at least that is what Storm thought he was saying. When they got him downtown, a Spanish speaking officer would interview the suspect again and try to make more sense of his ravings.

Storm motioned to the Crime Scene tech taking pictures and asked him to take photos of the suspect and add them to the case file. Next, he went to talk to the two men being detained by officers from the other patrol cars. The two men, one of whom spoke better English, were friends. They had observed the attack and had grabbed and held onto the man they saw stab the victim. They too were illegal and were hesitant to talk to police, but they stated they had heard the two men arguing when the suspect pulled a knife and began stabbing the victim.

The witnesses had arrived at the scene at about 4:00 p.m. after working for a landscaper in an upscale neighborhood near Rice University. Both bought tallboy beers from the bodega across street and retreated to the shade of the overpass to chat with other day laborers before going home. After putting in a day's labor and being paid in cash it was a common practice to buy a tallboy beer concealed in a slim tall brown paper bag and sit with compadres in the shade of the overpass to relax before going to, most probably, an apartment they shared with many other day laborers. The scene under the overpass was analogous to meeting ones co-workers and friends for a drink after work. It was the same dynamic of social networking that could be seen in any city or town across America, just done in a less expensive way. Both men said they had gotten involved in the crime investigation because they knew one of the men, the one who had been killed. He had worked with them on odd jobs and had come from the same area of El Salvador as they had come. He had been seen hanging around for over a year now. They gave Storm his name and told Storm they were sure he had always been a nice man. The killer on the other hand had only been around for the past couple of weeks and they didn't know him well, nothing more than his name which was Javier "something or other."

At that point, both men clammed up. They either didn't know anything more or they were too scared of the policia and the probable involvement of ICE to go on. Storm took their names and addresses, which in all likelihood were false. Any chance of either of these men testifying was like the Pickens brothers, Slim and None. That was okay with Storm since this seemed to be an open and shut case. The forensics evidence of the bloody knife and clothes were going to be enough for any of the young lawyers in the District Attorney's office to get a conviction, even the most inexperienced ones.

It was almost 6:00 p.m. when the morgue wagon arrived to collect the body and transport it back to the Medical Examiner's office for an autopsy, although there would be no surprises as to the cause of death. The Crime Scene techs would collect the bloody clothes and get swabs from the suspected killer's hands after he was taken to a holding cell downtown. The patrol officers would be the arresting officers and the following day Storm would help them with their paperwork and be on hand to testify if he was needed. The dispatcher had been right, this was a mundane case and it had only taken a couple of hours out of his day.

Angie Storm was the vice president of sales for her company's offshore rig platforms and her duties often took her to exotic if not unsavory destinations, Angie was hardnosed and good at her job but most importantly, had studied world situations and understood the nuances of being a woman in a male dominated international market that many times relegated her to playing a supporting roles in front of their clients. Behind the scenes, she was the tough negotiator and she set the policies with which her company would comply. She understood the numbers of the deal and knew when to walk away from a deal when the dollars didn't add up to make it financially worthwhile for her employer. She was tall, dark and beautiful and knew how to underplay or use that beauty to her advantage when working in a male dominated world. She could read a situation during negotiations and knew when to sweeten the pot to find a successful conclusion to a deal. Although in the Middle East and most of South America she played her role behind the curtain, it was her plan that would ultimately be put into action.

Angie's plane should have arrived back in Houston at 5:00 p.m. that afternoon and if Storm was lucky and things at the airport went as normal, he still had a chance to beat her home even at this late hour; baggage claim and Customs would add to the snail's pace of coming home and then there would be the Houston traffic. When Angie traveled to international locations, she always used a car service her company provided; it cut down on parking expense and the company always wanted their executives to be taken care of when traveling on their dime.

As Storm turned off of Interstate 10 onto Heights Blvd. just north of downtown Houston, he saw a black stretch limo just leaving 10th Street where he and Angie had bought their home. A quick thought whizzed through his mind as he reckoned this must have been her ride home and a tight knot rose in his chest as he felt a pang of remorse that he had lost the race and not beaten her home. He knew she would tease him about his hours and then tell him all about her trip and the interesting people she would have had contact with, painting him a picture that made him feel he had been with her. Storm enjoyed her word pictures as he had barely ever been out of Texas let alone traveled to exotic locations like Angie did. They had always shared their lives, spending hours talking about her trips and his cases, always including each other in all the aspects of their lives.

The driveway to the garage ran from the street beside the house to the backyard and he had come to always leave his car in the drive next to house allowing her the use of the garage. The house was an old 1930's pier and beam home that they had remodeled after buying it in what now was considered to be a high toned, up and coming neighborhood. It had a front porch and from the street he noticed the door was open and Angie's bag was still sitting on the porch in front of the open door. His first thought was that she hadn't beat him home by much and a smile returned to his face. But in the next instant, he realized that he couldn't see her moving around inside nor was she coming out to greet him. He thought she must have really been in a hurry or really had to use the bathroom to leave the door wide open and her suitcase sitting outside.

It was not until he began to climb the six short steps to the door that he saw that Angie's body appeared to be lying lifeless just inside the door. He rushed to her and found her motionless on her side, her eyes open and not breathing. Storm fell to his knees and lifted her into his arms. As he did so he realized the back of her head was covered in blood and a pool of what was obviously her blood covered the floor where her head had been. He let out an eerie terrorizing scream followed closely by the sounds of doors springing open from neighboring houses. As people emerged from their homes he yelled for someone to call 911 "get an ambulance and the police.

He held Angie in his arms for what seemed to be an eternity looking at her beautiful face in total disbelief. The love of his, his beautiful Angie had been attacked and she was gone, questions and bewilderment filled his every thought. Her open eyes seemed to be asking him why? Why, was the question that would haunt him the rest of his life? It was the image of her eyes that had begged him to find the answers ever since.

CHAPTER 1

The question in her eyes had begged him in his dreams to find the answers... One restless night always followed by another. Each morning the annoying screech from his night stand alarm shook him out of his hallucinations. *The apparitions and the unsettling dreams were back... As soon as his mind cleared it was filled with his busy day ahead at the courthouse.*

He pulled his 6'4" 240 lb. frame to the edge of bed and sat rubbing his eyes. Those nightmares brought on by that night so many years ago and the image of Angie lying dead were still imprinted in his mind. Years ago the gremlins had pushed him to the brink of losing the only job he loved and had almost taken his life from overindulgence as he tried to take the edge off his sleepless nights and private pain. As before, the night sweats and terrors did scare him, but he knew he could survive them with the help of his friends. And this time he knew who the killer had been. So the only question he had left to answer was the "Why?" He still had to find the answer to the pleading in Angie's eyes.

The nightmares had resurfaced only after he had completed possibly the biggest case he had ever worked on, one he knew was a career builder. Detective David Storm had been the lead investigator in the murder of the little brother of one of his best friends. It had been a killing that had led to Storm's playing a role in a combined law enforcement operation that brought down a criminal syndicate plaguing the city of Houston and the state of Texas, with tentacles reaching all the way from the upper Midwest across the entire Gulf Coast area of the United States.

The evidentiary process for a case of this magnitude was taking forever. Computers had been seized along with paper files and co-conspirators from seven states were arrested in what was quite possibly the largest drug and murder related case ever in Texas history. Storm and Sergeant "Pancho" Hernandez, Storm's partner and fellow arresting officer, were included in a multi-jurisdictional team with federal agents from the Federal Bureau of Investigation, the Drug Enforcement Agency and U.S. Department of Immigration and Customs Enforcement. Border Patrol was even called on to make arrests of suspected "coyotes" bringing the illegal aliens and drug mules across the border.

The heady mixture of murder, drugs, Mexican cartels, New Orleans street gangs, and a dirty federal agent could catapult a lawman's career into the stratosphere if that was what a man wanted, but for Storm all that solving the murder of Robbie did was to bring back the night sweats and disturbing dreams he thought he had put behind him.

As he shaved, he thought back to the day in 2005 he had learned there was a connection between Angie's murder and Alisha's brother. Thanksgiving 2005 had been one of most idyllic days Storm could remember in so, so many years. The consumption of a home cooked meal while leisurely sitting on the wrap-around porch of Alisha Johnson's and Ms. Edith's home on a "Houston Chamber of Commerce" day in the company of good friends was a welcome break from chasing bad guys. A day with friends who had become his family followed by an afternoon watching kids play a pickup football game in the street had almost been too perfect.

Perfect, that is, until Alisha had confessed to knowing more about her brother's murderer than she had yet to tell all of them. During her examination of the bullets that had killed her brother and the two illegals found dead on the ship channel, she told her friends that she had discovered in the archives that the weapon had been the same one that had been used to kill Storm's wife, Angie.

The catastrophic effect of her admission was felt by all the occupants of the porch. Storm felt his breath leave him and his 6'4" frame collapsed in the wicker chair as if the earth had opened and was swallowing him. After a momentary pause from shock, Russell Hildebrandt, Storm's best friend, asked, "Are you positive?"

Alisha went on to explain that the results linking the gun they had found on Kate Gilroy, the dirty DEA agent, to Angie's murder was only discovered after the search had been completed against the entire databases housed in the Houston police and FBI. "Initially, I only used only the Houston database for comparison, but a glitch must have occurred because it didn't catch the match until I got permission to use the FBI database."

Both databases then caught the match, she explained. They all knew that since there had been a federal agent involved in the case, Alisha had not been permitted to pass on her findings until Robbie's investigation had been wrapped up.

Christmas that year had come and gone with barely the blink of an eye as the hours of investigation turned into weeks, then months. For the first few months after the initial raid Storm and Hernandez were either studying paper or data files following the complex scheme of the operation now valued in the millions of dollars or in court testifying to the reasons for the arrest of individual members of the criminal syndicate.

Storm's End

Meanwhile, Dr. Alisha Johnson had finally been appointed as the full-time medical examiner for Houston and Harris County and had resumed her duties overseeing her department. Russell Hildebrandt and Grady Johnson had gone back to reporting the weather and participating in their undercover segments for Houston's most watched evening and nightly news.

They had all celebrated Christmas with Ms. Edith, Alisha's mom, and Mr. and Mrs. Hildebrandt at the Hildebrandt home. After the events resulting from the loss of Robbie Johnson, Ms. Edith's only son and Alisha's brother, the totally incongruous gaggle of friends had become, as Ms. Edith put it, the best "family of outlaws" a mom could ask for.

CHAPTER 2

Winter is a nasty time of year in Houston—cold and wet, the kind of cold that seeps into your bones and stays until the warming sun of spring. Street crimes seem to be limited to those people who inhabit the dark and cold alleys of downtown Houston with the homeless and involving fights over blankets or shelter from the wet cold, but seldom do they include killing one another. Hence, the load on the homicide division of the Houston Police Department usually becomes a little lighter.

Detectives Storm, Hernandez, FBI agents Prescott, and Rush had their hands full, anyway, preparing evidence and testimony for the cases involving the horde of arrestees now sitting in county jail cells awaiting trial for their participation in drug trafficking, murder, and intimidation of a city. Agents Prescott and Rush had been teamed with agents from the DEA and the FBI overseeing the prosecution of the Canal Street 40, a New Orleans gang whose members had been arrested for distribution of controlled substances within the city of Houston and the murder of Robbie Johnson. Each of their cases was being prosecuted by the Houston district attorney and his staff of assistants in city court rooms in front of city criminal judges.

Detectives Storm and Hernandez were working with Lead Agent Ralph Higgins of the FBI, Lead Agent Tom Morran of the DEA, and Lead Agent Sam Moore of ICE. This team had the task of evidence preparation and testifying in federal court. Their first trial had been the prosecution of Reggie du Pierre, formerly of New Orleans, as the kingpin of the multistate operation for interstate distribution, sale of controlled narcotics, and the murder of four illegal mules. The case had been airtight, but when Reggie had decided to flip on his employer and testify against Enrique Guzman, the head of the cartel, the death sentence had been taken off the table. Reggie would spend the rest of his life behind bars but he would escape with his life.

His boss Enrique "Rique" Guzman, on the other hand, had hired the best defense lawyer's money could buy and was settled in for what was expected to be a long court battle, determined to let a jury decide his guilt and punishment. Months had gone into the preparation and finally his day in court was approaching after weeks of appeals had been heard and ruled on by the federal judge assigned to his case. Rique would be tried for possession of more than ten tons of marijuana and cocaine, interstate distribution of said drugs, associated Racketeer Influenced and Corrupt Organization Act (RICO) charges. and the murder of a federal agent, Kate Gilroy.

His defense would most certainly allege that the DEA's own agent was an operative for the cartel and had previously committed murder for the cartel in connection with passing sensitive information to the cartel, and that Rique had killed Kate in self-defense while protecting his own life. The defense attorneys would try to disparage her career; they would allege that she was linked to at least three killings in the past year alone. They would smear her with allegations that she had been instrumental in misdirecting DEA and border patrol agents to the exact location of border crossings that allowed illegal drugs to enter the United States. They would attack the prosecution's case, alleging that the information they obtained leading to an illegal drug ring was supplied by this dirty agent. That meant Kate's information was "fruit of the poison tree" and therefore not admissible in court.

Legal positioning and haranguing would require days of testimony from Houston Homicide Detectives David Storm, "Pancho" Hernandez, DEA Special Agent Tom Morran, and FBI Agent Ralph Higgins. Each man would be called to take the stand and required to testify that they had received no information from DEA Agent Kate Gilroy that led them to request an investigation or seek warrants to search the property leased in the names of Enrique Guzman, Noah Benedict, and his wife Rachael. Their testimonies would be the trial before the trial. Indictments had already been issued against all the participants in the sting that netted murderers, drug smugglers, dealers, and street thugs, but this pre-trial wrangling was the chance for the defense attorneys to see the evidence the prosecution would be presenting against their clients and their opportunity to offer the court opposing writs that would claim that their clients' rights had been interfered with and such material should never see the light of day in the court proceedings.

Day after day the prosecution team would be assembled in federal court under the strict supervision of Judge Elaine Ashford. Judge Ashford had been a President Clinton appointee to the bench and although very liberal in her personal beliefs, she was a stickler for the law and had proven harsh on drug trafficking and interstate criminal syndicates. She was a fortyish woman, rather rotund, with glasses that perched on the end of her nose so that she was constantly looking over them. She insisted on strict courtroom decorum, and outbursts or deviation from her directives would be dealt with in haste and to the detriment of the offender.

This was her first murder case as acting in the capacity as a federal judge—most federal judges seldom presided over murder cases since these types were handled in state jurisdictional courts. The most famous decision to try a murder case in federal court was the Timothy McVey case in Oklahoma. Since his heinous crime of blowing up a federal building and killing scores of occupants included some federal employees, the United States Judiciary allowed his murder case to be heard in federal court because federal government employees had suffered death due to the crime.

Judge Ashford had previously stuck down every motion of the defense on the lesser charges of smuggling, drug dealing, and interstate trafficking. Today the cause in front of the Court was a writ to separate the murder charge from the all the others. A change of venue writ would be introduced due to the defense's contention that their client could not and would not get a fair or unbiased jury pool in Houston to judge his guilt or innocence.

The defense's first attack was on DEA Agent Kate Gilroy. They supplied affidavits that described dates and times of meetings between their client and the dirty agent. They provided information showing how she had mislead border agents about illegal border crossings only to allow the mules carrying drugs to cross the border at alternate locations and make their way to Houston. They supplied evidence that the cartel had made monetary payments to accounts alleged to belong to Agent Gilroy. They even used evidence from other cases that Agent Gilroy had been the shooter in at least three other murders, omitting the fact that their client had been the person who had instructed her to carry them out. When confronted with that assertion, they claimed she acted on the instruction of Reginald du Pierre, a man already convicted on numerous murder and drug related charges, who would be testifying for the prosecution on a promise by the state that it would take the death penalty off the table for his crimes. They supplied newspaper clippings, news videos from local TV stations, and recordings of talk radio that they deemed made it impossible to gather a jury pool that would not already be tainted against their client.

Judge Ashford listened to each side make its case and to the testimony of both prosecution witnesses and the defense's jury consultants. She adjourned the court for the day and told both sides they would commence again the next morning at 10:00 a.m., at which time she would make her ruling. With that said, she rapped her gavel and court was over.

As the defense team left the courthouse they were surrounded by cameras from national and local press as talking heads prattled on, asking questions the attorneys could not answer. The story of a criminal syndicate being taken down, the murders of innocent illegals and hometown boys, the prosecution of a Mexican cartel drug king pin made for sensationalized sound bites. For Houston, this case was more unfathomable than the case of the rich oil man who tried to kill his ex-son-in-law after the son-in-law, a doctor, had poisoned his wife, the oil man's only daughter.

Detectives Storm and Hernandez shrank from the spotlight whenever they could. They were cops, not PR men. When dealing with the press, Federal Prosecutor Damien Stuart would take the lead flanked by Special Agents Higgins and Morran. This case was a career maker and Damien had been specifically handpicked and sent down by the U. S. attorney general to prosecute it. The president was, after all, a Texan, and he wanted their best man to throw the book at this defendant and this case.

Damien was a tall, athletically built man who looked as if he had spent his life swimming the pools and running the playing fields of prestigious Ivy League Schools. His dark hair was perfectly cut and his complexion looked as if he had a perennial tan. In fact, he was none of those things; he was a native of Wyoming and he had paid his way through school working manual jobs in the oil fields and applying for every aid grant he heard about. After graduating from the University of Wyoming he had landed a grant to study law at Stanford. While there he had received his law degree *cum laude* and had been president of the *Law Review*. He was smart, dedicated, and put his toil into his job. His good looks and easy manner were like a magnet that attracted people to him like a bee to honey. Rising quickly in his chosen profession of the law, he found himself being offered a job with the Justice Department after meeting the president only twice while on his campaign trips to California.

Christine Chu, the gorgeous, tenacious reporter who had broken the story about Robbie Johnson's murder, the attack at the cemetery, and the bust of the biggest drug cartel to ever hit Houston, had finally been offered a chance to make the jump from local to national news. Christine was half Vietnamese, half Chinese, and a long-time Houston resident. She had graduated from the University of Texas with a degree in Communications when she landed a reporter's job with the station where Storm's best friend Russell Hildebrandt worked. Now she was with the big guys in New York, and her managing editor sent her back to Houston to report on this ongoing story of corruption and murder.

As Damien approached the cameras and microphones, Christine was the first to shout out her question. "Mr. Stuart, do you believe the judge will grant Mr. Guzman a change of venue?"

Damien was not only smart but he was the consummate politician; he looked in Christine's direction, smiled, and replied, "It is all in the hands of the judge now. I'm sure she will see it our way and decide to leave the trial here in Houston where the crime occurred. I also believe the wonderful people of Houston who will be called as potential jurors in the case will judge the case on its merits and will not be led by articles or sound bites from the press. Enrique Guzman will get his fair day in court. Next question." His eyes rose as he scanned the crowd for his next questioner, but before he could choose from the raised hands and high pitched voices, Christine quickly asked a follow-up question.

"Do you expect the cartel will exact revenge if Senor Guzman is convicted and put to death for the killing of Kate Gilroy, a woman that many are saying was a dirty federal agent?" Christine's voice shook a little as she asked this query. She then stopped and held her breath and her microphone held out for her viewers to listen to Damien's answer.

Damien paused for a minute before he answered that question, his mind racing, as he knew things had become more violent on the Texas/Mexico border. He had to fashion his answer in a way that would not alarm the citizenry of Houston but also implied that the federal government would not tolerate such a reprisal. "No, Christine, they know they got caught with their hand in the cookie jar. Even in their world this man crossed the line when he killed a federal agent of the United States of America. We as a nation have improved security at our borders and are hindering the illegal drug trade that comes across into our sovereign nation. Retaliation of any kind at this time would be ill-advised on the part of the cartel. They just need to lick their wounds and chalk it up to bidness gone wrong."

He thought his answer had most likely satisfied the audience and Christine, who had become his lover since the trial had begun. He looked into her beautiful Asian eyes thinking how nice it would be when she came to his rented loft later.

***

Just as he was about to call on his next reporter the sound of gun shots came from the side of the building. Storm and Hernandez, policemen first and responsible for the protection of the people of Houston, pushed their way through the crowd of onlookers as they ducked for cover. With Agents

Morran and Higgins in close pursuit, the quartet rounded the corner of the courthouse and spotted two federal marshals restraining a burly, rough- looking man. Enrique Guzman lay just a few feet away face up on the cold dirty pavement of the alley that led from the holding cells of the courthouse to the vehicles that were there to return him to his cell in county jail. His eyes went blank as large crimson holes dotted his clean white starched shirt. Rique was dead.

A large scruffy man in overalls who appeared to be in his fifties was being held face down on the same pavement by the two federal marshals. The man was well over six feet tall and must have weighted at least two hundred fifty pounds. He had been subdued and what appeared to be a Colt revolver had been taken from his hand. The man was a stranger but Storm had noticed him earlier in the back of the courtroom. He had given him very little thought at the time except for a quick question to himself about the man's manner of dress.

"So what happened?" Hernandez demanded.

One of the marshals explained, "When we brought Guzman out the side door to load him into the jail van to return him to his cell, this man appeared as if out of nowhere and shot Guzman three times in the chest. And then he calmly surrendered himself to us."

Since this was federal territory the marshals and the FBI had jurisdiction and they would lead the questioning of the perp. "Is he dead?" special Agent Morran ask Storm and Pancho.

"As a doornail." Answered Pancho.

Then under his breath but loud enough for the others to hear, he exasperatingly muttered, "Damn, now what else could go wrong in this case?"

CHAPTER 3

Six months earlier Calvin "Big Cully" Gilroy had been notified that his only daughter had been killed in a drug raid on Houston's south side. The exact circumstances of her death had never been released to him or his two sons, only a statement that she had died in the line of duty.

The government had arranged for her body to be transported from Houston to the sleepy little town of Jasper, Texas, located in the middle of a region commonly referred to as the Big Thicket. The area has been well known for its old growth hardwood forest, long needle pines, cypress trees, blackwater swamps, and a population of outlaws that has lived there since before the Civil War. Even today the area is not recognized for its picturesque views or its idyllic national parks. Instead it is thought of as land that is flat, wet, and overpopulated with a collection of venomous snakes, alligators, and yes, even with four varieties of carnivorous plants.

In the early days of Texas's settlement, settlers and explorers avoided the Big Thicket because of the inhospitable, even life-threatening nature of the territory and its sparse population. Pine trees reaching one hundred feet in the air and ages old live oaks could be harvested on the edges of the marshlands without venturing too far into the swamps and facing untold dangers from bears, black panthers, and the occasional hostile human inhabitants of the quagmire. For years before and after Texas became a part of the Union, the land in the Big Thicket that lay around the Sabine River was known as No Man's Land. Its sparse inhabitants were outlaws and families of bandits that waylaid any intrepid explorer foolhardy enough to cross the unkind backwaters.

As railroad lines moved north from the port cities of Galveston and Port Arthur, spurs were laid down to carry the much-needed logs for a burgeoning timber industry. In the wake of this flowering growth of the area, the clannish blackwater folk kept to themselves. They took jobs working as loggers and scouts, sometimes leading unaware timber prospectors to their deaths amongst centuries old cypress knots and letting the varmints clean up their dirty work.

In the early 1900s, more jobs came to the area as paper mills flourished, allowing immigrants and natives alike to secure jobs cutting the trees and rendering the wood pulp into paper. Many of the native citizenry participated in this work force but after work they would return to their blackwater homes, still not trustful of the newcomers they saw as outsiders. Swamp people kept to themselves, seldom allowing their children to attend public school and keeping to their age-old ways. After a time, the blackwater people developed an uneasy relationship with the growing population but they truly never let go of their roots. These people still eked out an existence poaching, brewing moonshine, and pilfering the townsfolks' processions.

Cully Gilroy came from a long line of blackwater people. A baby boomer born of cousins who had married, he had helped his parents run moonshine through their illegal stills and had set poaching traps with his dad. His family had never gained much prosperity living on government handouts and felonious activities, so they clung to the old ways. Cully was a big strong kid and when forced to attend school was better known as a bully and thief than as a student. He had spent time in juvenile facilities and even a two-year stretch in a state "P" (penitentiary) farm. His time away had given him a continuing education, making him a better criminal, instructing him in methods of beating the law, and opening up a world of criminal activities that afforded less chance of being detected.

After the P farm, Cully got a job as a logger and for all outside appearances he changed his ways and settled into the life of a working man. He married a local girl whose roots ran as deep in the blackwater as his and they began to have children. First were his boys, Josh and Billy Ray. They were just a year apart and took after their father, meaner than a country dog. They were constantly being sent home from school for fighting or intimidating other kids out of their lunch money.

Kate came along almost as an afterthought. She was eight years younger than Billy Ray and nine years younger than Josh. Unlike her brothers, she had fair hair and more resembled her mother, who had died in childbirth due to complications of carrying Kate to term. Kate was the bright child; she liked school, books and athletics. She dreamed of getting out of a world she considered the closest thing to hell someone could live in and not actually have died first. Kate was tough, she had to fight for everything she got at home, constantly receiving a split lip from getting in fist fights with her brothers over who might get the last piece of chicken she had had to fry for supper. When Kate began to show signs of becoming a woman things turned uglier; she had to fight off the unwanted advances of her father after a night of drinking and checking poaching traps with his cronies. High school graduation was a godsend. It it gave Kate the opportunity to escape by joining the military. The military was her opening to a new life and she jumped on it like a duck on a June bug

Cully had only seen Kate once since she broke the bonds of backwoods life—the day she had driven back into the yard of the ramshackle house she had come to know as home when she was a child.

The brand new Ford F-150 dual cab pulled in the drive and an attractive young woman in a pantsuit got out. She was wearing those aviator sunglasses that you could see yourself in. At first Cully was sure it was someone from the state police until she took the sunglasses off and he recognized Kate.

Kate just smiled and said, "Hello, Daddy." Cully was sure she was just there to show off that she had made it out of the deplorable life that was only his to offer. She showed him her credentials as an agent working for the DEA and told him if she ever heard of him or her brothers running drugs she would be back and be more than happy to send him to prison. The exchange had been terse, more like a pissing contest, and she had won, but for some inexplicable reason Cully was proud of her.

After that, Cully had not seen Kate again until the government men had come to deliver the news she had been killed and asked if he wanted her body returned to Jasper for burial. They told him the DEA would pay for her interment, including the flag-draped casket, but because of circumstances they didn't or wouldn't explain to him there would be no honor guard or government personnel in attendance.

Kate's body had been returned, and Cully, Josh, and Billy Ray had had the preacher from the Holy Mount Baptist Church of Jasper perform the funeral and graveside memorial for family and high school friends who still lived in the area and remembered Kate. Billy Ray's wife Caryn was the only member of the family who was the least bit computer savvy and she had begun to do research on the Internet to see if they could find more about the particulars of Kate's death. She found news videos of the raid, the shooting, the arrest, and the subsequent trial of the man the videos indicated was involved in the Kate's death.

Cully couldn't get enough information on this wetback. "He killed my baby girl," he told Josh and Billy Ray, who were more than a little surprised when he called her by a nickname they had never heard him use when she was alive. When word came through that the man would be going to court in Houston, Cully made his decision to go. He had experience with going to court and he knew the man would be surrounded by police, but he had seen enough TV to know that a lone man who didn't appear threatening could probably get close enough to put a bullet in the man who killed his baby girl. After all, who would expect an almost sixty-year-old man in overalls to have planned an assassination?

But he did, and he had pulled it off. And having admitted the assassination, Cully sat in a metallic straight-backed chair with his hands cuffed and secured to a ring that protruded through the center of a nondescript three feet by four feet table with a gray flat synthetic top and metal legs that were secured to the floor. His identification had already been taken from him and the contents of his wallet and pockets lay spread out across the table. Cully seemed at ease; he appeared to have given up and now sat with his cuffed hands folded together almost as if praying.

Cully had been read his rights before being placed under arrest and taken to the FBI offices. To make sure he understood his rights, Special Agent Higgins again repeated them to him, recording on camera that the suspect was in full compliance with the proceedings. Since the arrest and his Mirandizing, he had not spoken and the agents had waited until he was moved to an interview room to begin their questioning.

Storm and Hernandez stood watching through the one-way mirror that separated the interviewer and subject from the recording studio of one of the FBI's interrogation rooms as Special Agents Higgins and Long began questioning the suspect.

Picking up Cully's driver's license, Agent Higgins looked at the picture of Cully and asked, "This is your name? You are Calvin Gilroy?"

Cully neither frowned nor smiled, and his attitude seemed to say he didn't care about looking up or not. He seemed to be studying his hand, then in almost a whisper he replied, "Yes, I am Calvin Gilroy, but most just call me Cully."

"Are you any relation to Special Agent Kate Gilroy?" asked Higgins.

"Yessir. She be my daughter," answered Cully, now lifting his eyes to look directly Agent Higgins.

Higgins thought for minute before he asked his next question. "Why were you at the Courthouse today, Mr. Gilroy?"

"I come to see the bastard who kilt her went to jail or be dead," said Cully.

Agent Long broke in, "But you didn't wait to find out if he would be punished for his crimes; you took justice in your hands, didn't you, Mr. Gilroy?"

"You damn right I did." Cully now looked at Agent Long and added, "I would do it again. I would shoot that sumbitch 'til he don't twitch. He kilt my baby girl and no Messican sumbitch gets away with that."

Agents Higgins and Long both cast sideways glances to each other, a signal that the man had confessed. With his confession and eyewitness accounts of the marshal on the scene, there would be no problem running it through a grand jury. Any grand jury would award the state with the ability to prosecute Calvin "Cully" Gilroy with murder, even if the man he killed was a scumbag drug lord and murderer.

As the two detectives stood on the other side of the one-way glass, Hernandez heard Storm mutter something under his breath. "Did you say something, Storm?"

"No, just thinking out loud. I wasn't done with Rique yet. He had a lot more to answer for and now I won't get another chance to question him about Angie."

Another question appeared on Pancho's face before he could ask it. He, too, had been there the day Alisha had told them the gun used to kill her little brother Robbie and the wetbacks was the same gun used to murder Angie, Storm's wife. He had seen the perplexed look on Storm's face when everyone realized that DEA agent Kate Gilroy had almost certainly been the one to kill Angie and probably been ordered to do so by Enrique Guzman, the same man who had killed Kate. Now that Rique was dead, all Storm could do was brood as his only lead to his wife's murder had been killed went to the grave.

"What do we do now?" asked Pancho.

"We do nothing, Pard. We are cops, we work homicide, and God knows we get more than our share of those to solve, so we go back to doing our job." With that, Storm's gaze narrowed as he looked through the mirror at Calvin Gilroy. He understood Cully. He, too, wanted to kill the man responsible for the death of someone he loved, but he also knew the only suspect he had who might have any knowledge of that killing had just died. His brow furrowed, his face turned somber, and his eyes fixed on the man in the other room as if trying to read his thoughts.

Since Rique's assassination had taken place at a federal facility during the trial of a defendant who had been charged with federal crimes, this case would continue to be handled by the FBI. Storm's and Hernandez's involvement in the case against the drug kingpin was over, leaving little to do but verify some paperwork, sign a few legal papers, and wish Agents Higgins and Long good luck. Over the months the men had worked closely together and had become friends and the agents had heard through Hernandez about the connection between this case and Storm's wife's murder. They, too, could see the clouded expression that masked Storm's face and although they said their goodbyes, they made a couple of comments to each other as they left headquarters.

"What's next for Storm?" asked Long. "I really respect the guy."

Higgins answered. "No way to tell. This one's gonna have to play itself out."

Storm's End

CHAPTER 4

The airwaves had been filled by local news outlets with descriptions of the killing of Enrique Guzman, alleged drug smuggler and murderer of a corrupt DEA agent Kate Gilroy. Descriptions of the incident ran from the ridiculous political left of liberalism to the outrageous right of conservatism. Pundits speaking on local television conjectured about how an innocent Mexican citizen had been shot down like a dog on the steps of the federal courthouse where he was being arraigned on unsubstantiated charges of drug smuggling and murder. "His brutal killing came at the hands of white supremacist militia-joining racist members of the East Texas underground movement," announced more than one talking head as if the statement were fact. Although the killer's identity and any political affiliation hadn't been determined, they corrupted the facts to fit their prattle. On the other side, conservative talk show hosts cheered the man that took care of a case that would probably have run on in the courts for months, thereby saving the taxpayers millions of dollars.

Storm thought to himself how wrong both sides were. This was a simple case of revenge and when the facts came out, the truth would be overshadowed by the myth. Christine Chu, the only reporter Storm knew at all well, probably gave the best report on what happened during the shooting. Christine had been there; she had heard the gunshots and saw the man lying dead in the alley. She had also seen the man who was being held by the marshals and had made the correct assumption he was the killer. She spoke of seeing the man dressed in the overalls inside the courtroom but didn't speculate about who the man was or if he had any attachment to the case. Christine has turned into a pretty good reporter, Storm acknowledged to himself.

Local weather forecaster, Russell Hildebrandt, Storm's best friend for over thirty years and silent partner in crime busting, had called Storm to see if he wanted to have dinner and perhaps go over what had happened at the courthouse. Russell knew all about the nightmares Storm was having and how they had come back after the discovery that Kate was Angie's killer. He told Storm to meet him at the Brownstone, a favorite eatery inside the loop. The restaurant was both close to home for Storm and close to the television station so Russell could make his ten o'clock weather report in plenty of time. Alisha Johnson, the recently appointed director of the Harris County and City of Houston Medical Examiner's office, would be joining them. Storm knew this wasn't just a chance dinner to talk about the events of the day; this was also his friends checking up on his well-being and mental state. Although he hated opening himself up to anyone, these were two friends he had come to trust and if he was going to talk to anyone, Russell and Alisha would be his choice.

When Storm arrived at the trendy restaurant that sat just to the south of River Oaks, the richest neighborhood in Houston, he found George, the ever present maître d', manning the door. George welcomed his old familiar customer and escorted him back to a private eating area where Russell and Alisha had apparently already ordered their first drinks. He knew Russell, a consummate ladies' man, had already made his rounds of the restaurant bidding good evening to any patrons who might recognize him and all the female wait staff. He guessed Alisha had arrived just as Russell was finishing his rounds. Storm took a seat at the round table a couple of seats down from Russell and across from Alisha.

"Well, Pard, you've had quite the busy day, haven't you?" chided Russell after standing to give his friend a bear-like embrace.

Alisha just smiled and shook her head watching the two men who had become her best friends as they hugged, waiting her turn to give Storm her sisterly embrace. A quick kiss on his cheek and a hug and she returned to her chair and the glass of chardonnay she had ordered.

"How are you really, David? I can see from the look on your face that you're troubled and need to work things out with people who would listen and offer ideas that might help." She used a name only his mother and Alisha's mother called him. "Were you there when Guzman was shot?"

Storm sat silently for a few seconds, knowing that Russell respected his friend enough to remain silent until Storm had had a chance to gather his thoughts and answer.

"I am fine, Alisha, really, and yes, I was there, but not when the shots were fired. Pancho and I cleared the corner just in time to see Rique slumped on the ground bleeding out. A man in overalls was being subdued by marshals and an automatic pistol was lying on the ground in front of him. He wasn't resisting, he wasn't screaming or fighting, he just stood there with a very satisfied smile on his face while the lawmen handcuffed him."

"Who was he, Pard?" asked Russell. "The media have proffered all kinds of theories; everything from a white supremacist member of a border watch group to a national hero for saving the public a long costly trial." It was apparent that both Russell and Alisha were anxious for an answer.

A slight smile crossed Storm's lips for the first time since the shooting and he finally spoke. "He wasn't some dickhead member of some paramilitary white supremacist group and he is not for God's sake a hero, at least not to me. The answer is much simpler than that and his motive for killing Rique is even simpler. It was revenge." Storm stopped speaking for a minute to watch the reactions of his friends.

Russell and Alisha just looked at each other, both jaws dropping open in disbelief. "Okay, Big Dog, who was he?" asked Russell, still looking for an answer.

"His name is Calvin 'Cully' Gilroy." Again, Storm stopped talking to watch the understanding dawn on his friends.

"Is he related to Kate?" injected Russell.

"Yep, he's her daddy," replied Storm.

"You've got to be kiddin' us! Damn! Her daddy?" exclaimed both Alisha and Russell in a rush of breath.

"He told the FBI that no damn greasy Messican was going to get away with killin' his baby girl," said Storm.

"What do you know about him?" asked Alisha.

"We don't really know a lot about him yet. He comes from over by Jasper; raised his entire life in what has always been called the 'lawless strip' or 'No Man's Land' that runs down the Sabine River between Louisiana and Texas in the Big Thicket piney woods. He was the child of parents who worked in logging camps and grew up with an outlaw mentality. He married the old maid schoolteacher and had three children—two of them boys who like him work sporadically in the paper mills, run coon dogs as they hunted pigs and gators, and each of them had had their occasional run-in with the law, running moonshine and other criminal activities. Then they had a daughter—Kate. She seemed to be the only one with any smarts in the bunch. She finished school and unlike her brothers, saw her way out was to join the army. He told us she came back to visit him a few years ago. She was driving a new Ford F150 and told him she had become a lawyer and was now working for the DEA.

Later, he saw on television that she had been killed and he kept up with things and waited for the trial. When he came to town, his only intention was to kill the man who killed his daughter. It's that simple, no political inducement, just 'an eye for an eye.' He is just a redneck, old school kind of man and seems pleased as punch about what he has done. I know this is going to sound crazy, but I think he was actually proud of her."

"Wow!" Russell exclaimed. The echo of the word hung over the table for what seemed like several minutes.

"What's the FBI going to do with him?" questioned Alisha.

"Looks like they will hold him for the murder of Rique and he will go to federal prison for the rest of his life." Storm looked at his compadres, raised his eyebrows, folded his hands, and sat quietly in thought until the waiter came back to take their dinner order.

Through dinner each member of the party kept things light with conversation about their lives, the length of the time to prepare for Rique's trial, and the latest conquest in Russell's ever-abundant social life. Finally, the conversation turned to what none of them wanted to be the first to broach.

"Pard, are you and Pancho done with this case?" Russell spoke softly in his most deliberate South Texas drawl. "Did you get any answers to the question you had for Rique?"

Storm knew when Russell resorted to this tone of voice he was trying to coax a response without just coming out and asking. "We had to sign off on some documents for the Feebs at Calvin Gilroy's interrogation, but yes, we are done."

"Did you ever get to spend any quality alone time with Rique before he was killed?" asked Alisha, still dancing around the heart of the matter.

"Yes, I was part of the team that questioned him about his operation and his connection to Kate and Reggie. But he didn't say much; in fact his normal response was that he would only talk to his lawyers," said Storm.

Storm's End

"Dammit, Barretta, you know what we are asking. Did you ever get to bruise him a little, ask him about Angie?"

"Only once. The Feebs left me alone in the interrogation room with him for a few minutes and I put my thumb in the palm of his handcuffed hand and pressed down hard causing him some pain. I whispered in his ear that I wanted to know why his assassin killed my wife. He was plainly in some discomfort with me bending his fingers up but he didn't say a word. His only response was, 'Enrosque de la puta.' I wanted to break his fingers but before I got the chance Higgins came back in the room and I had to let him go."

Storm saw Alisha and Russell look at each other for support and he knew what was coming—the question was something everyone wanted to know. Finally, with Russell pushing Alisha's elbow, she spoke up. Pushing Russell's hand away, she said, "Okay, okay, quit pushing! I know it's my turn to ask," said Alisha, giving Russell a "kiss my ass" look and turning to face Storm as he starred at her intently. "Mmmmm, it's over then?"

"Is what over?" Storm looked back, his eyes had gone black, daring her to ask.

With more trepidation, she swallowed before she spoke. "Are you done looking for why Angie was murdered?"

At first Storm didn't answer. He couldn't believe his friends would ask him such an inane question, but they had and he felt he at least give them a plausible answer. "No," he said, and paused again to let that one single word sink in. Then he went on: "A couple of weeks ago Tom Morran—you remember him, he was Kate's supervising agent over at the DEA—came to me and said they had uncovered more information about Kate when they went digging into all her phone records, bank accounts, and safety deposit boxes and did a sweep of her home. They found records showing that she had been involved with the cartels much longer than what appeared on the surface. She was recruited right after she was discharged from the army. The cartel through a phony philanthropic organization had paid for her to go to law school where they had a professor on their payroll, and he suggested to Kate that she join the DEA or some other federal law enforcement agency. He was actually the one to write her recommendation letter. Being a lawyer and law school professor, he made sure anything he did for her recruitment was within the limits of the law. Therefore, he claimed no knowledge of the cartel's nefarious activities and escaped any legal entanglements. Once Kate was hired by the DEA she was confronted by her benefactors and given no choice but to join the cartel and supply them with information they wanted or they would make sure it would come out that the cartel had bought and paid for her education. After joining the DEA, she found she also had another skill the cartel found useful—she was adept at killing. The DEA now has suspicions that Kate was responsible for the deaths of at least eleven people over the past five years. The .22 that killed Angie can be traced to at least that many."

Russell and Alisha sat stunned. Okay, Kate was a killer. She had already killed at least four people they knew of when Storm had made them aware of the case, but now to be told that this agent of the federal government had willingly killed even more people and supplied information to a murderous organization like the Reynosa Cartel?

Storm knew his information was more than they could process right away. He went on. "They found and confiscated more than half million in cash in various bank accounts and safety deposit boxes around Houston and they're getting warrants to seize foreign accounts she had in Panama and Belize. The girl was rich but deadly—just your type." Storm poked Russell, smiling as he teased his friend the ladies' man.

"Not my type! I don't need her money and I sure as hell like waking up in the morning without my throat cut," quipped Russell.

Alisha piped in, "Okay, okay, you two idiots, that still didn't answer my question. You have lost Rique and Kate now. Where does that leave you? You don't have any more leads, nobody to interview, nobody we know of now to question. So what are you going to do to find out why Angie was killed?"

That's the $64,000 question, Storm admitted to himself. He didn't know where to go next; he didn't have a lead. All he had was the nightmares and memories, but he had to let his friends think he could put this behind him, live with the unsolved murder, and move on with his life, or they would pester him and hound him until he uncovered the truth. Right now his best answer was he was going back to work and do his job, knowing he would always look for that key that opened the door to the answers he needed.

CHAPTER 5

Harold Stanton, Vice President of Foreign Acquisitions for Global Underwater Machine Drilling International, was an aristocratic-looking man with salt-and-pepper hair who stood about 6'2" and weighed about 190 pounds. In his early forties, he stayed fit by working out almost every morning playing squash at the racket club housed on the second and third floors of the GUMDI offices located in the Contex Oil Building, a new medium-rise building wrapped in dark glass that sat near the Galleria just off San Felipe Street. He made his home in Tanglewood, an older neighborhood with houses and large lots that were being converted into nouveaux riche mansions. He was married with three children, his wife the consummate show pony who played the perfect partner to a man on his way up and was capable of charming every man she ever met. His family was the impeccable picture of the upwardly mobile WASP family, with ties to the community and charitable involvements, and they were regular attendees and contributors to their church.

Harold was at his desk when news of the shooting at the federal courthouse flashed across the twenty-four

Storm's End

hour news service he always had open in the corner of his computer screen. At first, he only saw the news as it scrolled across the bottom of the window along with a continuous display of commodity futures, which he followed for the oil prices. He saw the announcement and immediately stopped scrutinizing the numbers from the monthly sales reports to click the rolling banner that opened the story about the shooting: "A suspected drug kingpin and killer in one of the largest drug cartel busts to ever happen in South Texas has been shot and killed by an unknown assailant outside the federal courthouse in downtown Houston. Enrique Guzman, who was about to go on trial for the murder of a federal agent, Rique had been shot at least three times and has been pronounced dead at Ben Taub Hospital."

The news story was sketchy and contained very few details, but like every other 24-hour TV news station, the channel on Harold's screen continuously ran pictures of the crowd that had gathered and the reporter interviewed several witnesses. Most were secondhand accounts from people who had only heard the shots, and there was no agreement as to the number they had heard. Between interviews, the station was running a video of a body being put on a gurney and placed in the back of the medical examiner's van, presumably to be taken to the morgue for autopsy.

Still watching the video that was now at least an hour old, Harold unlocked a desk drawer and retrieved a nondescript, untraceable cell phone. He pulled out a little black book containing numbers for people only identified with initials and stars denoting their importance to him. He placed the first call and within three rings, the person on the other end picked up. Before the person could speak he said, "This is Harold, have you seen the news?"

He listened while the person on the other end confirmed and the conversation continued with Harold doing most of the listening. He knew whoever was on the other end of the conversation was someone in charge, and soon the person terminated the call. Harold moved his finger down the page to the next number in the progression of those he needed to inform and made the next call.

After making four individual calls each lasting almost the same amount of time and with the same results, he put the cell phone back in his desk drawer with the little black book and locked his desk. As he sat there his mind raced. Rique being dead was a good thing, wasn't it? This was a hell of a way to find out Rique wouldn't ever talk to the authorities, though. Harold was not high enough up the ladder in this operation to know if his accomplices were responsible for Rique's death. This could have been just a fortunate turn of events that would save the operation time, money, and aggravation in the future, but he knew there would be those who didn't feel the same way.

Harold was deep into the conspiracy now and there was no way of backing out even if he wanted to. When he first became involved it had all been about the money. He had dreams of grandeur and a lifestyle he was in a rush to attain, but he had never thought that murder would ever have anything to do with him. He was only to be the expeditor, making it easy for these men and women to do business and not be caught. The scheme had been foolproof until that bitch Angela Storm had gotten her nose stuck in places it didn't belong. If she would have just not looked at the shipping manifest and seen the irregularities, none of this would have ever gotten close to him.

Harold hadn't killed her, but he had informed the others that she was getting too close to discovering the inconsistencies, and his report about her scrutiny of the books had sealed her fate. He had merely informed Rique of her travel itinerary and Rique had taken care of the rest. He hadn't killed her. He had merely warned them that Angela might have stumbled across the wrong information and it might have involved her husband, who was a cop. But Harold also knew these people didn't care about a life; if she possessed any dangerous knowledge she had to die and the information with her. Rique had had one of his assassins act as Angie's driver when she returned from Venezuela. The assassin did the actual killing and then searched her papers to see if she had made any notes or kept anything that might lead someone to discover the cartel's activities over past few years. Harold took on the search of her office and computer, deleting anything that might lead to his and the others' criminal activities.

That had been over five years ago. Her murder had never been solved and no one had become the wiser. The illegal enterprise went on, the shipments had grown larger, and Harold's cut of the profits had made him a rich man.

When Rique was arrested and charged with murder, drug smuggling, and money laundering, Harold was sure the operation would stop. Once again, he was wrong. All the organization did was replace Rique and move the warehousing and money laundering to New Orleans. New Orleans was rife with graft after Katrina and money flowed through financial institutions like water, often to undisclosed recipients. The organization set up a phony charity to help the poor and displaced of New Orleans, using these accounts to funnel money from their drug trade to contractors, architectural groups, and humanitarian aid organizations set up by the bosses to legitimize the money before transferring it to foreign accounts. Drug money flowed into the accounts in the guise of anonymous donations; it was then laundered, with very little of the funds actually going to rebuild the infrastructure of the beleaguered city.

Harold was about to wrap up his day when he heard the private cell phone ringing in his desk. Although he had been dreading this call all day, this was one call he had to answer. It was Rique's sister and she would expect someone's head to roll. All that was required of him was to listen to her tirade; she was more important to the organization than Rique and whatever she expected to be done would be done without fail or your life was forfeit.

"I want the dirt on the man who killed my brother," she told Harold, and he knew she was not asking. "I want to know who the pendejo is that put him in jail. I want names—names of anyone who helped put Rique in jail. I want to know everything about these pieces of shit—who their families are, anything else."

Harold had only heard dark rumors about her, but he knew she was someone you didn't want to fuck with. She had assigned him his chores and he would carry them out. He promised he would contact Rique's lawyer and a private detective that worked for the organization. "I will get your answers as soon as possible and get back to you." His shaky finger hit the disconnect button and the call ended. He was scared to death, and he didn't mind admitting that to himself.

What Harold didn't know was that he would set in motion the sinister wheels that would reach the people who had custody of the man who had killed her brother. What he did know is that he had been asked to satisfy the sister of a very powerful man and he would fulfill that request or he, too, might have an unfortunate accident. With his new duties understood and the wheels in motion, he went home to his trophy wife and children. It might be a nice time for them to visit the grandparents.

* * *

In the old Heights neighborhood, Jimmy Westlake had been the bartender at the Keyhole Lounge for almost two decades and knew his clientele as if they were family. Most were regulars who supported the place with their evening stops on the way home to down a few drinks either by themselves or with cronies from the neighborhood. The Keyhole was a long narrow saloon with a long bar that ran down one side and high-sided wooden booths positioned against the opposite wall. A patron could come in, find a booth, and hide from the world or find a stool at the bar. His normal drinkers at this time of day were the usual suspects, those who had to drink to find the liquid courage to go home or who hoped to drink enough to keep them from having to go there.

The place was nearly empty; a couple occupied one of the booths sharing drinks and disappointments before stumbling home together later in the evening. Weekdays were slow and the lonely air in the place of it being almost abandoned was nothing new, so when the old face from the past entered the door it was a shock.

The large brooding man took a seat at the bar and ordered a straight shot of Jack Daniels. For what seemed like an eternity, the man just sat and stared at the drink, occasionally turning the glass between his finger and thumb without drinking. Storm sat contemplating the drink, touching and turning the cool shot glass between his fingers as if trying to decide how bad he really wanted it. It had been three years since he had had a drink and everything in him was fighting the demons and telling him to slide it back across the bar and leave. However, the demons were back and if this time was anything like the last, the only way he could push them out of his mind was to drink this one and many more. Drinking would put him in a self-induced coma. If he was lucky, he might get some sleep tonight, but he also knew if he started drinking again, he was done with the things he truly loved to do. Drinking had almost cost him his job five years ago and if he wanted to hang onto what was now his life, pushing the drink away was his only option.

As if by magic, two other men appeared one on either side of him. The one on his right looked over at Jimmy and told him to bring the bottle over and set it in front of them. When Jimmy brought the bottle, Russell Hildebrandt and Lieutenant Vernon Smith, Storm's mentor and retired police academy instructor, each poured themselves a shot and looked over at Storm as if daring him to join them.

Jimmy had seen these men before, too, back when the detective was a regular and he knew they were partly responsible for him losing such a good patron, but he was also the one who had called them to let them know the detective was there. Jimmy was an AA member, too, and he couldn't stand the thought of someone who had been through so much taking the plunge off the wagon now. He had followed Storm's re-emergence and knew he had been vitally involved with closure of two of the biggest cases in HPD history since he had sobered up and he knew that these friends had been the ones who saved his life and career.

"Well, Barretta, you gonna drink that or are you going to just sit and stare at it?" asked Russell.

"No, I think he is trying to absorb it, Russell, kinda like those worms from South America do when they absorb water through their skin out in nature," smirked Smith with a shit-eating grin on his face.

Storm never looked up; his eyes stayed on the drink in front of him, but under his breath he said, "Why don't the two of you go fuck yourselves? I didn't invite you here."

The lieutenant let out a low whistle. "I think we hit a nerve, Russell, what d'ya think?"

"Yeah, he seems a little testy for an ex-drunk. Guess he wants to throw away what he got back in the last five years," replied Russell. "What the hell are you thinking, Storm? You can't tell me you want to fuck up your life again?"

"Who said my life wasn't fucked up now? How do you know what I'm thinking or how I'm feeling? Neither of you live in my skin and right now my skin is crawling and my head can't deal with all the questions that have no answers," railed Storm.

"Pard, do you really think drinkin' will answer any of them?" asked Lt. Smith.

"Shit, no," shaking his head. "I don't know, but at least I might get some sleep tonight," whispered Storm.

"Yeah, maybe tonight, but tomorrow you will wake up feeling like dog shit and you still won't be any closer to the answers. You will just start looking for another bottle to take your mind off what you think are problems. Shit, David, you been down this road before and you know damn well that bottle doesn't help you one bit. It just numbs you so you wouldn't know the answers if they bit you in the ass and I can promise you if you fuck up again I can't save your sorry ass this time. Until you solved these last two big cases the brass was just looking for an excuse to put you on administrative leave and finally fire your ass," said Vernon.

"Well, Big Dog, I think you have a decision to make. You can sit here in this dark smelly dive and we will help you drink yourself into oblivion or we can pay Jimmy for the three shots, go back to my place, order some pizza, and, if you are a good boy, I might even get you some non-alcoholic sparkling cider so you can feel like you had a drink," snickered Russell.

"Fuck you both," was Storm's only reply as he pushed the shot glass across the bar. Russell and Vernon stood, paid for the untouched drinks, and they all left. Tonight they had to have a round table, make some decisions and put together some kind of plan to keep Storm from reliving the trauma of finding Angie dead.

CHAPTER 6

Two weeks had passed since Detective Storm had, with the help of his friends, resisted the temptation to drown his sorrows in Jack Daniels and in that time, some decisions had been made. He put the house in the Heights up for sale, sold off the furniture with only a few exceptions of those items that held special significance, and moved into a new apartment in a mid-rise near his friend Russell's condominium. Russell, Pancho, and Alisha helped him pick out something simple but nice, where he could live and get on with his life without being surrounded by constant reminders of the past. Alisha's mom even volunteered to be his housekeeper. Ms. Edith had adopted her boys after they had solved the case of her murdered son. She had promised nobody would ever hurt her family again and these men had become her family. She wanted to help the detective any way she could. His mind was hurt and she thought knowing someone cared enough to clean his new apartment would help him understand he had family.

The plan they had come up for his life was simple; he would do his job, and with their help, find bad guys and put them away. It was a tentative plan and was up for constant review as he got on with his life, but for now, it worked. Still, questions about Angie's murder clouded his mind, and with Rique's death he had no leads to chase, and no one else he could think of at this time was really worth questioning.

Pancho was working at his desk reviewing pictures and eyewitness accounts of a murder/suicide when the phone rang. He picked it up, stated his name, and began to listen to a man on the other end of the phone. Storm could see the shock on Hernandez's face when he hung up the phone and motioned for Storm to follow him into the break room.

"What's up, Pancho?"

Hernandez hemmed and hawed a few seconds. "That was the county jail. Cully Gilroy was just killed outside his cell in holding."

"You got to be shittin' me!" exclaimed Storm.

"Nope, they said it just happened. Someone shanked him on his way to the showers," said Pancho.

"Damn, they know who stuck him?" asked Storm.

"They got two illegals in custody and they say they got a video of the killing. One held him and the other stuck him," replied Hernandez.

"Why did they call us?" asked Storm.

"It was a jailer I know. He said he knew we had been on this case and although it was a Feeb case, he thought we would want to know." Hernandez stared at Storm, wondering what, if anything, they were going to do.

"I think we better get down to the jail, don't you?" said Storm. With that, they grabbed their guns and jackets and headed down to county.

At county jail, Storm and Hernandez found FBI agents Ralph Higgins and Frank Long already there. They had the two suspects in Cully Gilroy's murder in two separate interrogation rooms sitting on their hands waiting for questioning. Some time in a Spartan room in handcuffs might soften them up, thought Storm, but from the look of them through the one-way glass, it doesn't look too promising.

"What you got, Ralph?" asked Storm.

"Well, look who's here, Frank," smiled Agent Higgins, seeing the two men they had come to know quite well from their earlier work together. "What brings you boys here today?"

"Nuttin' much, just heard you had some desperados in the tank that might have killed Kate's dad," said Pancho.

"Yeah, pretty much," said Agent Long.

"Whadya know 'bout them?" asked Storm.

"They were brought in three days ago for attempted armed robbery of a bodega. Both are in the country illegally. ICE was called and they were brought here for holding until they could get their free ride back to Mexico," replied Agent Higgins.

"They in any way connected to Rique or any of his people?" asked Storm.

"Not that we know of, but we got prints and mug shots and we're having the office run them against all databases, so if they show up we will know," answered Higgins.

"How did you guys find out about this?" questioned Agent Long again.

"Hernandez got a call from one of the jailers he knows. He told him he knew we had worked on this case and thought we might want to know is all. Any problems with us being here?" asked Storm.

"Not at all and any help you boys might be on this is fine with us. With you two we are not territorial, your help is always appreciated," replied Agent Higgins.

"Fact is, we are waiting for an interpreter, so would you mind if Sergeant Hernandez went in with us and helped question these two? Neither of us is very good with Español and we could use some help. That is, if it's okay with you," said Higgins.

"Hell, its fine," said Pancho. "Let's get started."

Hernandez started his questioning by reading the first detainee his rights and explaining he was not going to be deported immediately, but would stand trial for murder in a U. S. federal case. He repeated each portion of his opening in English and Spanish to make certain the man understood. The first suspect sat handcuffed across the table from Hernandez and Agent Higgins, while Detective Storm and Agent Long watched through the one-way glass. The man never uttered a word in response.

"Le pagaban para matar a este hombre? Were you paid to kill this man?" asked Hernandez.

The man just stared at him.

"Por qué matar a este hombre? Why did you kill this man?" asked Pancho. Again, no response.

"Sabía usted a este hombre? Did you know this man?"

The suspect just smiled and remained silent.

"Quién te envía a matar a este hombre? Who sent you to kill this man?" continued Pancho to no avail.

"Te das cuenta de que el asesinato en un caso federal se castiga con la muerte? You do realize that murder in a federal case is punishable by death?" Again, no response.

The questioning went on for over twenty minutes with no response of any kind from suspect number one. The entire process was videotaped and recorded for the record and a copy would be given to the defense attorney when one was appointed or hired by the suspect.

The same process was conducted with the second suspect and the outcome was the same. Neither man was talking. The agents had the video of the murder and it would be used in their trial. The men weren't carrying any ID when arrested, so the Feebs didn't have any more information on the two men other than their names, and the four lawmen felt the names the boys put on their intake papers were probably phony, most likely aliases given to them by whoever hired them.

The lawmen were positive that Cully's death had been a murder for hire. Somebody was getting even with Cully for killing Rique. After the questioning the agents also felt they should notify local law enforcement in Jasper to check on Cully's sons. If this was a vengeance killing and if it followed the pattern of how cartels settled scores, the boys were in danger or already dead.

Calls went out to the Jasper County Sheriff's office, notifying it that a Mr. Cully Gilroy of the Big Thicket area had been killed in the Harris County jail while he was awaiting trial for the murder of one Enrique Guzman. The sheriff was asked to send deputies to the Gilroy boys' homes to notify them of Cully's death. Agent Long suggested to the sheriff that the boys probably should be warned that possibly they were in danger and if the sheriff didn't have the means or facilities to protect them they should be brought to Houston, where the FBI would make sure they were protected in a safe house until those behind their father's murder were caught and arrested.

Two hours later the Jasper County Sheriff's office notified Agent Long that they had gone first to Billy Ray's home and found him shot to death along with his wife. Josh was later found in the barn located on the family place bound in duct tape with two .9 mm slugs in the back of his head. Whoever was behind these murders had been not only thorough but methodical, the sheriff said there was no evidence left behind, no shell casings and no fingerprints were found anywhere, with the exception of the victim.

Agents Long and Higgins believed the sheriff but told him they would be sending a forensics team to investigate the murder scenes, anyway. They asked the sheriff to cordon off the area and to make sure nothing was disturbed until the criminal investigation team arrived. The sheriff agreed and Agent Long headed to Jasper with the team to supervise the investigation himself.

The whole thing had just gotten nastier and there were at least four more dead because Cully had exacted his own kind of backwoods justice on Rique. There was also a strong possibility that there could be others on the list of people to be punished for the loss of the drug business and death of Rique. Everyone who had anything to do with this case would need to remain vigilant until the perpetrators could be identified and dealt with. If the cartel was behind these murders, they had kicked their violence quotient up a few notches. Never before had they sought so much payback on the U.S side of the border. Although they had never gone after a cop or an FBI agent, everyone involved felt they had better watch their backs, as agents from each entity, from HPD to FBI to DEA and others, had testified against Rique, putting each witness behind the eight ball.

CHAPTER 7

Two weeks had passed since the killing of Cully Gilroy and his boys, and with the exception of the two men now being held for killing Cully, no other leads or suspects had been found. The FBI had done a thorough investigation of the home of Billy Ray and his wife and the barn on the home place where Josh's body had been found and they had come up empty, the evidence, which had seemed so promising at first, led them nowhere. Whoever the assassins were, they were professionals and left no trace that could lead to identification... Neighbors had been interviewed, but no new information was turned up; no one had "heard or seen anything."

The people of Jasper County were close mouthed. Normally they had little respect or regard for federal law enforcement. But this had been a killing of some of their own and the FBI found it most valuable to use the local sheriff and his deputies, who had grown up in the area, to do the interviews. Still, nothing new came to light. Many people interviewed made promises to notify the sheriff if they thought of anything and he could pass on the information if he cared to, "It don't make no never mind to me," more than one of them said.

Although not officially working on the case, Storm and Hernandez were kept apprised of any new information that came to the FBI, which in this case was nothing. The suspects in Cully's killing had been assigned a court appointed attorney and were still saying nothing. No fingerprint matches came up in any U. S. databases and nothing had come back from Interpol to link them to outside criminal investigations. It was as if someone had slammed a large steel door on this case. Storm, Hernandez, FBI agents Higgins and Long, and DEA agent Morran were all sure this was a vendetta killing but finding who was behind it and evidence to prove it was something else entirely.

It was in the third week after Cully's murder that they got their first break. Higgins received an anonymous letter containing a piece of common white computer printing paper that could be purchased in any office supply or discount store. The envelope was of the same genre and could be purchased anywhere. The envelope was addressed to:

FBI Agent In Charge of Gilroy Killing
Houston, Texas

The letter had not been mailed and had no postage attached to it. Somehow, the person or persons responsible for the letter had dropped it off in the mail drop box at the FBI headquarters building in Houston.

The letter was one paragraph, which said:

> To whomever is in charge: Calvin Gilroy was murdered in retaliation for the death of Enrique Guzman. I do not know the persons actually responsible for the murder but I believe if you look into the deaths of Calvin Gilroy and Angela Storm you will find the truth behind these crimes.

CHAPTER 8

The move to a new place had brightened Storm's outlook on life and dampened his desire to ever reach for a drink again. His friends had helped him get new furniture, had stocked his new residence with healthy food, and Ms. Edith was coming over to clean what seemed like every other day. Alisha and Ms. Edith had gone with him to buy new linens and picked out frames for photos they had taken at Thanksgiving and Christmas to brighten up the place. "Don't forget, you have all the support you could want if things ever start to go dark again," they told him.

Six months had passed, and work had taken on a mundane cast as most of what he and Pancho were doing now was catching up on paperwork that had been neglected for far too long. Gathering additional evidence on the drug smuggling charges against Enrique and wrapping up Robbie Johnson's murder had occupied much of their time and Lieutenant Flynn was on their backs to tie up the loose ends on all the things that had dropped through the cracks while they were occupied with those cases.

Storm was sitting opposite Pancho, both partially hidden from view behind stacks of files, when he noticed FBI agents

Higgins and Long accompanied by DEA special agent Tom Morran walk through the glass doors of the homicide division of the Houston Police Department headed for the lieutenant's office. Just a few seconds had passed when his desk phone rang and he and Pancho were requested to join them for a powwow.

Entering the lieutenant's office, Storm and Pancho were in jovial moods, even smiling, which Storm had to admit was a rarity for him, especially while being relegated to doing tedious paper work. The expressions on the other men's faces brought them up short; something serious was going on and they didn't have a clue what it could be. After a round of "hellos" and handshakes Detective Storm and Sergeant Hernandez seated themselves with the others around a small conference table that occupied a corner of the lieutenant's office.

"What's going on, guys? Did you find a lead on the murders of the Gilroy boys?" asked Storm.

Sheepishly the lieutenant raised his eyebrows and looked to Agent Higgins for an answer. "Well, kinda, Detective. We got something in the mail and we needed to come here to see you and ask if you can make anything out of it." Agent Higgins removed a piece of paper from a manila envelope and pushed it face up across the table toward Storm.

With Pancho looking over his shoulder, he picked up the letter and quickly read the one paragraph printed on it. The office fell silent as he read and reread the paragraph trying to digest what it said. His mind raced as he stared at the printed words. His synapses were firing but nothing was making sense. Why had someone sent such a cryptic message to the FBI? What did it mean? Could it be true, as it said that the people responsible for killing Angie were the same people behind killing Cully? His hands trembled and he tried to control himself as he laid the sheet of paper back on the table and looked over at Agent Higgins.

"Where did you get this?" was all he could manage to articulate.

"It was dropped in our mail drop at FBI offices with, as you can see, no return address, no letterhead, no stamp or post office mark—just the letter on this sheet of common printer paper in an envelope just as nondescript. We checked it for fingerprints and nothing, nada, zilch," said Higgins.

"What can you make out of it?" asked Agent Long.

"Nothing," said Storm as he picked the piece of paper up and read it again.

"Why would someone tell us we will find Cully's killer if we find your wife's killer?" asked Agent Higgins.

"I don't know, I don't know. How the hell would I know? You know as much as I know about the gun that killed Angie. This comes as a big shock to me as it does to you," ranted Storm.

Pancho reached over and put his hand on his friend's arm as if to calm him down and let him know he had his back. "Listen, guys, you found out the same time as we did that the bullets from Kate's .22 killed Alisha's little brother Robbie and Storm's wife. It was the first time we ever had anything to compare the ballistics to on Storm's wife's murder. I don't know if we can even treat this as a legitimate lead—a letter anonymously dropped off by some asshole."

"Whoa, slow down, fellas. We're not here accusing anyone of anything. We just figured Detective Storm might be able to shed more light on this if we knew everything he knows about his wife's murder and how it might be connected to Cully. It's just strange that two people from such opposite ends of the gene pool might be part of the same scenario. If we can find any connections we might be able to determine who was behind these deaths and why they were killed," replied Agent Higgins.

Flynn asked Storm, "Is there any way your wife would have known Cully Gilroy or anyone from his family or had any dealing with any of them?"

Storm's End

"No, Lieutenant, Angie would have no reason to know him. Hell, I didn't know him 'til the whole Kate thing," answered Storm.

"What did your wife do for a living, Detective?" asked Long.

"She was vice president of Global Underwater Machine Drilling International. She was in charge of sales for all their down hole processes and the head peddler for their products through lower level sales people, distributors, and rep firms across North and South America. Cully was a Piney Woods thug, a moonshiner and thief who sometimes worked for the paper mills. Hell, they should have never crossed paths." Detective Storm was still shocked that the two names would be somehow related, but whomever the sources of the information, they must have known more than he did.

"Tell us about the day she was killed. Tell us everything you can remember, every little detail. You never know when something might jump out, something you didn't think too much about but might strike one of us," said Higgins.

Storm spent the next thirty minutes delving deep into the memories that had caused his nightmares for the last seven years. He had replayed the day and the scene so many times he wasn't sure exactly what was a memory and what was something that had come from his dreams, but he did the best he could. Often the lieutenant or the FBI agents would stop him, asking him further questions about exactly what had happened from moment to moment as he recalled events. At the end of what felt to him like an interrogation, they didn't seem to be any closer to any kind of a connection that might lead them to believe there was any significance to what could just be the ramblings of a demented mind perpetrating a gigantic hoax.

"Okay, Storm, tell us more about Angie's job; what exactly did her company sell? How did they sell it? Where did she travel?" Each of the agents asked him to repeat specific details again, and he tried to be patient, knowing they were still looking for the link.

Storm told them how Angie had gone to work for Global Underwater when Storm and Angie had first come back to Houston after college at Texas Tech. Angie had been an economics major in college and had paid her way through school working part time and as summer help for Global Underwater in shipping and billing. When she graduated they offered her a job working in their sales department as an inside sales person. She answered phones, took orders for mud additives and equipment, and soon made a reputation for herself as the "that girl" who got things done and made sure the orders were shipped on time in the correct amounts. She got so good that many of representatives who sold their materials to drilling companies wanted her to be the one who called on them in person.

This was a good ol' boys network at the time and her bosses were more than just a little concerned that she would be eaten alive by these redneck roughnecks who dominated the world they were about to ask her to venture into. What they didn't know was that Angie was more than capable of handling herself in most situations. She was tall, beautiful, and had a sharp wit, but more important, she could put a man his place with just a few well-chosen words and he would thank her for it. She learned quickly, and the more she made sales calls in the field the more business she won for the company. Talent and drive eventually won out and she was promoted to sales manager.

The year she and Storm were finally sure they would never have children she had made another decision. For a long time, the company had been interested in her taking over management of the entire sales division. She would handle not only domestic sales but she would also coordinate their international reps. This was a big step because it meant she would be traveling for sometimes a week at a time. She

Storm's End

would be going to South America on a regular basis and she knew that though previously she had been the one making the decisions, to the outside world she merely played a supporting role. Most international customers seemed to be chauvinists and would never hold a female executive in high regard. Behind the scenes, she tracked the orders and the increase in sales of additives and equipment while mentoring the sales people in how to close the sale so it was profitable for all concerned.

She was returning from one of these trips when he had found her body in the doorway. She had not been robbed or violated, and it was days later when one of the company big wheels had finally felt he could inquire of Storm if he knew where Angie's computer was, it was then that Storm discovered her briefcase and computer were missing. The company representative had called, using the ruse that they were missing data that the office needed for sales records. Storm had scoured the house thinking that possibly someone had put it away so that it wouldn't be a constant reminder to him of her loss, but he found no briefcase or computer. The police had interviewed everyone at her company, asking if anyone could think of a reason someone would want to harm her. No one ever said they did and they all supported the idea she was a valued employee and would be missed dearly. The owners, the personnel of the company, and many of the reps who were close by attended her funeral and offered their condolences. The owners even paid for her funeral and gave Storm six months of her salary to help pay off the house along with the settlement on the insurance they carried on her.

Flynn asked, "Didn't you say you saw the limo you thought brought her home when you got near the house that night?"

"Yes, I thought I passed it about six blocks from home, why?" answered Storm.

"In the official investigation report one of the secretaries said she had gotten a call the day after the murder from the limo company they had sent to pick her up, reporting that she had been a no show when they got to the airport." The lieutenant was looking down, reading from the crime report filed at the time.

"Could the limo driver have been our killer?" asked Pancho.

"Could have. In fact, we know the shots came from a gun that Kate carried. She became a person of interest in at least six other killings after Alisha ran the ballistics on Kate's .22," answered Flynn.

"And we now know Kate was working for the cartel when she died, but she could have been working for them as long as she was in Houston while supposedly working for us." Tom Morran had kept quiet, but now he saw the connection. Everyone at the table turned and looked at one another. Maybe they were looking at this all wrong. Maybe this wasn't a connection to Cully, but instead a connection to the cartel.

The deaths of Cully Gilroy and his family had to be a revenge killing. They had been eliminated to send a message. Angie's murder could have been for totally different reasons. Maybe she had stumbled into things she had no business knowing.

"Wouldn't they know her husband was a cop?" asked Pancho.

"Maybe not," injected Storm. "The company knew, but how would the cartel know?"

"Okay, I think we have reached a point where we can end this today. It's late and I have plans with my wife tonight. If I'm not home in time to take her to this event she has committed us to I am in deep kimchi. So, let's wrap this up and plan on getting back together tomorrow, if that is okay with all of you," said Lieutenant Flynn.

They all agreed to let it go but they would meet the next morning at nine to look with fresh eyes at where they were. Good nights were said and apologies given by all the agents for putting Storm through the turmoil of reliving the events of Angie's murder, and Storm knew if they could find a lead it might not only solve Angie's murder, it might lead to cartel members much higher up the food chain as well as anybody still working with them to get their drugs into the States.

After the afternoon they had had, Pancho was not letting Storm go home alone, so before Storm got a chance to leave, Pancho had called the rest of the five and told them that they needed to have one of their dinners. Their friend might need help, he certainly needed to talk, and somewhere along the line, they had to develop a plan to figure this out

CHAPTER 9

Confused and not just a little unnerved by the information the FBI had brought over to the office; Storm was making preparations almost by instinct to go home when he was intercepted by Pancho. His partner half dragged him out of the bullpen of the office, put him in the front seat of his Ford Explorer, and drove him to Russell's condominium.

When he asked where they were going, he got the simplest of replies. "We are meeting our compadres for pizza and we are going to discuss the letter and decide what our next step is going to be. Who else you think can put a plan together?" snorted Pancho.

The doorman, already aware that company was coming to Mr. Hildebrandt's home, watched Pancho park the SUV and waved as they pushed their way through the giant walnut doors into the plush lobby. After an elevator ride to the seventeenth floor, they were knocking on Russell's door.

Russell answered the door with his normal huge smile, slapping Storm on the back greeting him with, "Hey, Pard, hear you had quite a day."

Still feeling out of sync at how fast things were happening, Storm gazed absently around the living room to see Grady and Alisha with soft drinks in their hands. His friends were waiting for him and the warmth of that thought relieved a little of the bewilderment he had been suffering since early afternoon when he first saw the letter and the information exchange with the FBI agents that followed.

"Well, we ordered some pizza from Capone's and Mark said he would have them delivered by 7:30. Do you want a coke or anything?" chimed in Alisha.

"Yeah, I'll have a coke," said Storm, but before Alisha could head for the kitchen, Pancho told her he would get it. Russell always had cokes, diet cokes, and bottles of multi-flavored iced teas in the refrigerator.

As they settled back in the living room awaiting the delivery of the pizza, Alisha, Russell, and Grady hesitated about who would be the first to ask about what had happened that day. Pancho's call only informed them that it had been a rough day for Storm, as he had been pushed into reliving the day Angie had been killed. Finally, Pancho broke the ice and began to tell about the FBI visit and the anonymous letter they had received about Cully's murder insinuating that if they looked into Angie's murder they would find the answer to both crimes.

Russell was the first to speak—he had been the only one who had been there with Storm shortly after his discovery of her body. In spite of what he had seen, he looked as puzzled as the others did about what else the agents could possibly hope to uncover. "Pard, what did they want to know?"

Storm began to talk, but as he did so, Pancho jumped in again. "They wanted him to walk through the entire day step by step, from the time he left the crime scene he had been working to when he arrived home. You know—what she was doing, where she had been, did she travel often, how long she was gone, stuff like that. When he finished answering their questions, no one in the room could see any connection to why a woman working for an international oil equipment company would have any dealings with the likes of Cully Gilroy." Pancho took a long drink of his tea and waited for someone else to join the conversation.

"Pard, do you mind going over it again with us? I was there, so maybe if we go over it together I will remember something that you don't remember. It might be something small but it might take us somewhere you didn't go with the Feebs," said Russell.

Once again Storm began the entire tale of that awful day seven years earlier. Step by step, he went through the entire day but nothing was getting him any closer to why or how Cully Gilroy and Angie were linked to each other. The pizza was delivered and everyone moved to the dining room table as Storm continued his account of his discovery of Angie's body and the investigation that followed.

They let him ramble at his own speed, listening intently as he recounted the events of the day and night and what he knew about the ensuing search for a motive and a killer. When he finished, the group asked questions not just of Storm but also of Russell and his recollection of the incident.

Grady looked around the table and said, " Since Alisha determined it was Kate's gun that killed Angie, of course, that makes Kate the most likely killer, right?" looking at the group for assent.

They all nodded and replied softly, "yes."

"So, if we know or assume Kate killed Angie and Kate was then killed by Rique, who was in turn murdered by Kate's father, Cully, we can probably assume Cully's murder was a revenge hit by the cartel. That's pretty obvious, right?" He stopped and looked around the table to see if anyone was on the same page.

Alisha's face lit up. "Okay. . . .I see where you're going with this. You think somehow all of this, including Angie's death, is tied to Kate, Rique, and the cartel."

"Yes, I do, at least that's where the bread crumbs lead," replied Grady with a smile spreading across his face like the smirk on the face of the cat that had just swallowed the canary.

"Storm, think back to that night. I came as soon as you called me and I sat with you until the police arrived and I stayed with you 'til they left. Do you remember them asking you how Angie got home?" Russell was now in the hunt for a link, too, and he had just remembered something.

Storm's eyebrows lifted as he remembered. "Yes, I told them the company always got her a limo when she went of town. The investigators checked and her car was in the garage; the engine was cold so she had not driven it. Now I remember telling them I had seen a limo turn onto Heights Boulevard just as I turned the corner on our street." His expression turned grim as the memories flooded back.

"The killer must have followed her limo home or they were in that car," said Pancho.

"Right. Did the police ever question the limo driver?" asked Alisha.

"Yes, but the driver that was supposed to pick her up didn't bring her home. He told police that he didn't find her at the airport and he had another pickup and couldn't wait any longer. When they questioned his dispatcher, he confirmed that the driver had called in to confirm whether the service had heard anything from her or the company. The dispatcher confirmed they had called Angie's company, but got no response as to her whereabouts and they sent him to his next pickup."

"So the driver of the limo Angie did ride home in could have been anyone, including Kate?" asked Russell.

"I guess. But I only saw the limo; I couldn't see the driver," said Storm.

"Well, knowing what we know it isn't a great leap to think it might have been Kate," said Grady.

"It well might have been, but we will never know since both Angie and Kate are gone," said Storm. "But even at that, what good would it do us to prove it was Kate driving that limo?"

"Look, Barretta, you dumb ass, it's like Grady and Alisha said, we know Kate was tied to the cartel; Rique was the cartel, Rique killed Kate, and Cully killed Rique. It's not a fer stretch, Pard, to assume that Angie's death was somehow linked to the cartel, as well," piped Russell, who sat back waiting for Storm and Pancho to catch up with him, Grady, and Alisha.

"Shit," said Pancho, "if we assume, and yes I know that everyone knows what assuming does, but if we assume you're right, what could Angie have done that made her a threat to the cartel?" He then looked at Storm and asked, "Did she ever say anything to you about running into drug smugglers or anything about drugs?"

"No!" replied Storm loudly. This conversation was taking on the same tone as the one he had had with all the investigators earlier in the day. The only thing that made sense so far was that somehow, Angie had come across something that put her in the sights of the cartel and she was expendable. His mind kept racing, looking for answers and coming up blank. "She never mentioned anything about drugs or about anything out of the ordinary. That kind of talk was more likely to come from me!"

"Okay, okay. Let's slow down and map this out like we did when we solved the rodeo murders," suggested Alisha. "It worked the first time the five of us put the puzzle pieces together. Let's write down what we know or what we suspect, fill in whatever blanks we can, and see where the holes are. Then we can think about how we are going to fill them."

Russell went into his storage closet and brought out the white eraser board they had used in their previous cases along with an easel and started "mapping" what they knew.

First he wrote Angie's name on one side, then Kate's and Cully's, and finally Rique's on the other side, and then he drew connecting lines between them. "Okay, we know Rique killed Kate and we are guessing, because of the ballistics from Kate's gun, she killed Angie."

Looking around the table, everyone was shaking their heads in agreement.

Now that things had become analytical, Storm could bury himself in the work and try to forget that the "Angie" listed on the board was his wife. The "Angie" on the board had to become a faceless crime victim whose death was related to two other murder victims. He spoke up for the first time that evening with real conviction in his voice. "Put the word "cartel" above the three names and draw a line to Rique, Kate and Cully with a dotted line to Angie." The solid lines were factual, but they were guessing on Angie and had to indicate the difference.

"Earlier, I remembered that the driver sent to pick Angie up said he never found her and went on another call, so who would have known when she was coming home outside of me or someone at her company?" asked Storm. "So write down "company" with a question mark and draw a dotted line to it."

"Was anyone at her company ever questioned about her death?" asked Alisha.

"Yes, her assistant, her boss, and her representative in Venezuela, but nobody seemed to know anything, no reason why she didn't meet her limo or why anyone would want to kill her," replied Storm.

"What exactly did she do for the company or maybe more important, what does the company do?" asked Grady.

"She was vice president in charge of sales for domestic and international marketing," said Storm and added, "The company sells drilling equipment and mud additives for the down-hole process."

"Specifically what did she do? Did she make sales or oversee and train sales personnel or both?" asked Alisha.

"Well, kinda. She started out as a sales representative for domestic stuff, but when she moved into the international market, she was more behind the scenes. She could make the numbers work so everybody made money in a very competitive place. Everyone was out to fuck everybody, so she had to work out the payoffs to government officials, make sure her rep made some money, and most important, make sure the company made money on every order," answered Storm.

"Did she have to follow up on orders?" asked Pancho.

"Sure. She was always tracking shipments and time delays. If they were late with mud additives, it would throw the drilling schedule off and cost the driller money, which meant it cost everyone money, so she was always on top of pending orders, shipping dates, and delivery schedules."

Russell had been busy writing things on the board when he stopped and turned around with an "uh-oh" look on his face. "You remember asking me a few days after Angie's death if I had Angie's briefcase somewhere."

"Yeah, why?"

"Do you think maybe it wasn't her they were after but rather something she had in her briefcase?" asked Russell.

"No, but I'm thinking it may have been both—something she had in that briefcase and because she had come across something she wasn't supposed to know or see," said Storm.

Russell added the new thought process to the board. When he finished there were straight lines tying the people who were related to the cartel on one side and a lot of dotted lines on other side where the questions about Angie were listed.

"Okay, fellers, we got a lot of questions on this side," said Russell pointing to the side with Angie's name on it. "How do we find out the answers and find the connection that puts Angie in this mix?"

Back to being a full-time cop, Storm jumped in. "We need to find out who sent that limo to pick her up. Someone had to know something about it and whoever that was has to be connected to her death. We need to find that briefcase or at least find out who wanted it in the company. I have access to all the old files from her death and Pancho and I can go visit the limo company that was supposed to pick her up and retrace what they did or didn't know. We can also go back to the company and ask who would have known her travel schedule and who authorized the change of car services."

"We can also get with our friends in collaboration at the FBI and DEA and fill them in on what we have put together. They might be able to add something to this, but if not, at least in fairness we can show some interdepartmental cooperation," said Pancho, smiling about the cooperation part.

"If you give us the names of the employees at the company, in our spare time Alisha, Grady and I can do some background checks to see who they are." Now it was Russell, Grady's, and Alisha's turn to smile.

They each had things to do and it had grown late, so they broke up and each headed his and her own way. For the first time in days, Storm felt he might be on his way to finding out the answers to questions that had plagued him for years.

CHAPTER 10

Juan Pablo du Tilly sat relaxed behind his desk in the office built into his estancia. His house sat on one hundred acres of heavily wooded land on a foothill of the Sierra Madre Mountains that overlooked the valley of Monterrey, Mexico. Today as on most days, he would play golf in the morning and later read individual accounting reports from his various operations in the afternoon.

Juan, known throughout the drug world as "El Gato" or "Gato Grande," was the head of the organization referred to in FBI and DEA reports as the Monterrey Cartel. Juan was descended from a family of wealth in Mexico City. He was a descendant of French aristocracy from the days of Maximilian in Mexico and even after the fall of the French dynasty, his family had held on to their wealth by serving whoever took power in the Mexican government. His oldest brother had once been considered a contender to take over the role of president of Mexico inside the PRI Institutional Revolutionary Party from President Gustavo Diaz Ordaz, but he fell well short of the support he needed. In the 1990s the line of succession fell apart, the family lost its power and influence, and the government took back many of the family holdings.

Storm's End

Juan was a distinguished looking man in his middle forties with a full head of hair, although speckled with flecks of gray. He was handsome and clean-shaven with a trim build that drew women of all ages into his sphere. He was well educated in economics and business and had studied law at the University of Mexico. When the family lost its wealth, "Gato," as his closest allies called him, embarked on a new career. Though illegal, the venture was lucrative and such legal trivialities were nothing for a man who knew whose hand to shake and who's to grease. Always with the support of his family, he was considered a politician's best friend when it came to contributing to their financial needs when they ran for office.

Juan had started small when he got into the drug trade. Acting as an intermediary working between the producers and traffickers, he would move the product through Mexico, taking a small commission. As the enterprise grew, he started unrelated businesses through which he could launder his money. He surrounded himself with smart, trustworthy people, people on whom he could depend. If it worked out he could not trust someone, that person would be dealt with in the harshest of ways.

Enrique Guzman had been with him for almost the entire fifteen years he had been in the drug business. They had met at the University of Mexico, where they both studied economics. Rique had been from a poor family and was desperately looking for a way to better himself. Together they had grown the business that now employed hundreds of people, from those who worked in the growing fields to those in the processing plants that put out pure product to the gangs that sold the product to an ever-expanding clientele in the United States and Canada. The corporation owned as many as twenty subsidiaries that now were responsible for passing the illegal money through their doors and paying the appropriate taxes, resulting in untold clean wealth.

Gato had also been smart enough to have removed himself from the daily business dealings. His name was only associated with a paper corporation that owned all the other companies. If one business had to be surrendered for illegal activities, he would fold it up and move on. Enrique's death and the discovery of the drugs and money in Houston had been a hiccup, but not one that couldn't be fixed with a simple change of leadership and a new highway for the drugs. Juan had worked his magic and had business models that could show the profitability of one of his operations to within a few thousand dollars. If anyone ever tried to steal from him, they were merely eliminated and someone new was put in their place.

Gato's one rule that never changed was that no one employed in the upper echelon of his businesses could be eliminated without his approval. He would have gone after the pendejo who killed Rique even without the call for revenge he received from Rique's sister. She was another matter altogether; she was smart, beautiful, and ruthless. Rique had brought her into the business a few years after he had started. She had filled a vital role for information and had been responsible for setting up possibly the most efficient method for smuggling drugs into the United States they had ever had. Juan had supplied the hit men to eliminate this Cully person, but it was she who had put together the plan, working with their man in Houston to execute it. Their lawyers would defend the men at trial and try to get them deported back to Mexico, but Juan was sure they would be incarcerated in some prison in the United States for the rest of their lives. Their families would be taken care of and provided with living expenses on a monthly basis as long the men were away.

Now Rique's sister was asking for his help to settle the score with the people she felt had brought Rique down. She wanted the deaths of men from the FBI, DEA, and the Houston Police Department who had brought about her brother's arrest and murder. This undertaking could not be considered lightly. Even Juan knew that killing law enforcement officials in the United States would carry more heat and scrutiny than he was up to handling. For now, he would appease her and make her believe that he would take her need for vengeance into consideration and hopefully with time she would see the foolishness of her request.

The reorganization was taking more time than Juan had imagined. Rique had been with him so long it was hard to fill the position with someone he trusted totally as well as someone with the shrewdness that Rique had embodied. The method of laundering the money would not be interrupted as it would still flow through the printing and publishing business that had been Rique's, but the method of movement to Monterrey would have to change. He would promote the man they already had in Houston to lead and he would find a new avenue of distribution. He was not worried about the latter—gangs were rife in the major cities in the South so finding new distributors was not a problem; all the gangs were hungry to do business.

Juan had already moved the warehouse to New Orleans and the men that worked for Reggie du Pierre were already back in business supplying street dealers across Texas, Arkansas, and Louisiana. His man in Houston would only be in charge long enough to move one of Juan's own to New Orleans to oversee the disposition.

Rique's funeral was kept low profile, as there was no need to offer him or his organization up to any further inspection. Isabella Guzman, Rique's wife, and the rest of his family had been moved back to Monterrey after his death. Juan had purchased an estancia on five acres with an iron fence that ran around the property. Isabella had four small children who would be taken care of as if they were Juan's own. Guards would patrol the fence at night and the latest in security equipment had been installed to protect his closest ally's family. The estancia sat among the trees of the

Sierra Madre foothills overlooking Las Missions Country Club only a short distance away from his own home.

Taking a long drink of the iced tea that sat on his desk, Gato again picked up his reading glasses and began to go over the reams of accounting reports that lay in front of him and to calculate the numbers in his head as to the profits that continued to roll in. Tomorrow he would be headed out to his villa in Playa del Carmen for a week of rest and relaxation. The beach gave him time to renew his color, relax his mind, and perhaps get in some fishing. Evie, his Scandinavian mistress, would already be there and she knew exactly how to make him forget the rigors of the past few months.

***

Back in Houston, Storm and Pancho had already gone to "the tombs" and retrieved all the reports that pertained to the investigation of Angie's death. They poured over every page looking for loose ends that were not followed up on and for clues that were overlooked. They had briefed the lieutenant earlier, telling him what they were up to and asking for his indulgence and permission to use a couple of days to run down anything they might find that would tie Cully's and Angie's deaths together. They had given him their suspicions but they told him they had to dig deeper to be sure if there was a link in the two murders that might lead to something bigger.

"Okay, you two. You know we're understaffed. You have two days. That's it."

They had scoured everything that was in the files, turning over nothing that Storm didn't already know. Investigators had interviewed the car service that was supposed to meet Angie and the driver had reported he never saw her, although he had waited for almost an hour after her plane had arrived. The detective that handled the case reported he had interviewed the driver's next client and sure enough the driver had picked him up and taken him to his hotel at exactly the same time Storm had gone home and found Angie. The dispatcher had been interviewed and he remembered no one calling from Angie's company, GUMDI, to cancel the pickup, and when a man named Mark Hendricks, the person in charge of executive travel for GUMDI, was interviewed he had no knowledge of anyone outside of himself who would have changed the travel plans.

Looking for anyone who might have known why Angie would take a car from another service seemed to be hitting a dead end. Stopping by Elite Car Service and asking questions almost six years later would most likely prove a waste of time, but they both knew this was not an excuse to let any stone go unturned. Storm had also decided he would go back to GUMDI and question those people who had worked with Angie to see if the years had brought anything back to mind.

Larry Dodey still owned the car service, but the driver at the time was long gone. He had worked about another year for Larry but had moved back to his home in the Midwest. Larry remembered Angie and had actually driven her himself a few times before her death. He told Storm she knew Tim the driver and would have been looking for him unless something else had changed her mind. His only suggestion was that there must have been another driver waiting for her with another limo. "Mrs. Storm would have normally passed through Customs, gotten her bags, and met Tim or me outside, as she had a routine. She knew us and there was never a need for a sign. She always came outside to find us and we would pick up her bags, put them and her in back of the car, and head for her house."

"Did she ever vary from that routine?" asked Storm.

"No, she was the best, always pleasant, although often exhausted. She might even nap on the drive back, but she was always cheerful, giving them a nice tip for the lift and for helping her with her bags," answered Larry.

"Any thoughts on what would make her get into another car?" asked Storm.

"The only thing I can think of is someone beat us there and was waiting inside with a placard with her name on it," replied Larry.

"I don't understand how she could not have seen Tim or that he had not seen her," said Storm.

"Detective, I'm sure most times she would have, but she had just arrived from a long flight, was probably exhausted, and saw a driver holding a card with her name on it. What would you do? She might have asked why Tim or I wasn't there, but that's an easy answer. 'I'm a new driver,' and off they go."

"That doesn't explain how Tim would have missed her when she came out the doors, does it?" asked Storm.

"No, but she didn't have to come out the doors where we normally waited for her. She could have been taken to the doors on the other end of the terminal, it's just little longer walk. If your wife thought the person was a new driver she would probably have gone along without thinking about it," said Larry.

Storm sat looking even more confused than he had been before he came to see the owner of the car service, but he was sure Larry was being honest with him and when Larry offered his sincere condolences, Storm knew he meant it.

One last question occurred to Storm before he left and he was amazed he hadn't thought of it long before. He wasn't sure Larry would know the answer but it was worth asking. "Larry, did you always pick her up at the international terminal?"

"No, sometimes she came in on a domestic flight, but the routine was the same." Larry looked a little confused by the question.

"Aren't all entrances and exits in the terminal buildings monitored?" asked the detective.

"Yes, they always have been. It used to be videotape, but now it's all on computer. Why?" replied Larry.

"There has to be a disc somewhere showing her coming out and if a driver met her, it would surely show that, too, wouldn't it?" queried Storm.

"You would think so, Detective, but it's been over six years. Do you think they keep them that long?" asked Larry.

Storm smiled for the first time in the conversation and said, "No idea, Larry, but it's worth checking it out, don't you think?"

"Yessir," he said as they shook hands. "Good luck with that, Detective Storm, and again, I am so sorry for your loss."

With that, Storm left. He then called Pancho and asked him to look in the files to see if any security discs were included and if not, to call the airport police to see if they would have kept them that long.

CHAPTER 11

Harold Stanton had just finished massaging the numbers for his latest sales activity report when he looked through the glass wall of his office that faced the open bullpen where order clerks sat answering their phones taking orders from distributors and drilling end users for mud additives. He was shocked by the sight of a man passing by his office in the general direction of the office of the new vice president of sales. This man was someone he had hoped he would never have to see again—he was the cop who had been married to Angie Storm. David Storm, he thought as his mind cleared; yes, that was his name, Police Detective David Storm. The last time he had seen Storm was at Angie's funeral and the man had seemed a wreck. He had heard later that Storm had become a drunk, although he was still employed by the HPD, an example of another case of bureaucratic inefficiencies at work in our public services. Nevertheless, what was he doing here after all these years? It surely couldn't have anything to do with Angela Storm's death. He was sure that inquiry had been dropped years ago. Could the case have been reopened? The thought made his skin crawl and an icy shiver ran down from his neck all the way to the small of his back.

Storm had not been in this building since Angie's death and even the look of the place made him feel queasy. He was there to see Ted Sloan, Angie's replacement, to see if there was anything that might have come up the past six years that might provide a clue as to why Angie had been killed and, if he got lucky, the connection to a redneck like Cully Gilroy. Ted had been one of Angie's sales managers and, according to Angie, one of her best. It had been no surprise to Storm when he learned that the vice president of sales was now Ted Sloan. When the receptionist asked Storm the nature of his business with Mr. Sloan, Storm told her Sloan was an old friend. Storm said he had found himself in the area and thought he would drop by to see if Ted had time to see him.

When Ted heard who was there to see him he immediately asked the receptionist to tell Storm that his assistant would be right down to escort the detective to his office. Ted's assistant, Clay Martin, had also been Angie's assistant. Clay was a short man with jet-black hair and his girth was as vast as his height. He was from an old Mexican family whose roots in Houston were well established in the early nineteen hundreds, back in the days of early migration from Mexico's border towns into Texas to find a better life. His great great grandfather had changed the family name years ago, thinking that for the family to fit into the greater Houston community it would better for the family to be known as "Martin" rather than "Martinez."

When Clay saw Storm, he wrapped his rotund arms around the man giving him a hug similar to the ones he had always given Angie. "David, it is so nice to see you, it's been way too long," said the cheerful man, still holding the detective by the arms and looking up at him.

"You too, Clay. Much too long. How you been, brother?" asked Storm as he smiled at the man he had always liked.

"I've been well, David. The girls are growing up, the wife is still mean as hell, and I still look forward to getting out of town." The short heavy man paused just for a second and continued, "even if it's with Ted now."

Storm saw the hesitation and figured Clay was hoping his words hadn't stirred up too many memories. He just smiled at this old friend he had lost touch with so many years ago. His mind flashed to the holidays he and Angie had shared with Clay and his family. The man was one of those rare humans who got away with calling Storm by his Christian name. "It's okay, Clay," he said reassuringly, "I've got my shit a lot better in order now than after—" He paused just a quick second and then went on, "well, you know."

Chattering away about the girls and their quinceañeras and how the oldest one was ready to go off to college, Clay held Storm's arm, escorting him to where Ted was standing outside of Angie's old office, which he now occupied. Ted seemed as excited to see Storm as Clay had been, but there was no hug, just a firm handshake and a smile that covered his face. "Well, big time detective, what brings you here to our humble digs?"

When he realized that Storm was staring at him with a peculiar look, Ted added, "Detective, Clay and I have followed you in the news ever since you found the serial killer out at Rodeo. Sorry, I hope that didn't offend. It's just that we've kept up and we're so glad you're doing so well." Clay stood by smiling and shaking his head, all the while patting Storm on the shoulder.

"Oh, well, thanks for that," Storm said uncomfortably, and changing the subject, he went on. "I just dropped by to visit with you two and catch up a little."

"Well if that's all it is, fine and good, but you got a look on your face like you have a purpose," said Ted, smiling.

"I'd forgotten how well we knew each other. Guys, it's been a long time, but something has come up about Angie's murder and I want to talk to the two of you see if there is any memory you have now that might have escaped you at the time. Let me just tell you this has to be kept between us for now and it might be one hell of goose chase anyway. Are you okay with that?" Storm asked.

Both Ted and Clay nodded and Ted asked, "Do you want to sit down in here or would you rather go into Clay's office since this is Angie's old office?"

"No, this is okay. I'm comfortable here if y'all are," said Storm.

With that said Ted pointed to the two chairs in front of his desk and closed the door to keep their conversation private. He took his seat behind the desk and waited.

* * *

Harold Stanton couldn't contain his curiosity and had walked into the bullpen glancing casually over at Ted's office just in time to see Ted close the door and catch a glimpse of the detective and Clay sitting down with their backs to the windows. Harold had no idea what could be bringing Angie's husband here now. Her death had been too long ago for him to be checking on her old benefits, so it had to be something else. Had the two men in jail talked? Had someone from the cartel given him up? Shit! His mind was in overdrive and his paranoia had him grasping at any straw that could mean his downfall. The only thing he could do was call his numbers and inform them that the police detective who had brought Enrique down was there and he was talking to people. He took a deep breath trying to compose himself and went back into his office. He closed the door, unlocked the top drawer of his desk, pulled the untraceable cell phone from it and began to make calls.

On his first call, he was reassured that neither man in the Houston jail would have talked. He was told to let things pass and all would be resolved without a hint he was involved in anything illegal. The next call didn't go as well. It was the bitch, the one who had put the hit out on Cully and now she wanted to put out a hit on everyone who had put her brother in jail in the first place. Harold knew that was not his decision. The people above him would make that decision, and truthfully, it was something he didn't even want to know about.

***

In Ted's office Storm had already made up his mind he wasn't going to tell anyone about the letter that the FBI had gotten insinuating that there was a link between Angie's death and the killing of Cully Gilroy. He was there to go over Angie's last trip: where she had gone, who she had met with, and to ask whether either Clay or Ted had any idea why someone would want to kill her.

"Ted, Clay," he paused, "I'm here to ask you about what was going on with Angie at work just before she was killed. I want to ask you about everything you can think of, no matter how unimportant it may seem or seemed at the time. I know it will open some old wounds, probably more for me than for you, but I have reopened her case. We now know who killed her,"

Both men looked shocked at this revelation. Clay finally spoke up. "Who, David? Who killed her?"

"You both said you had followed my last cases in the papers for the past couple of years, right?" asked Storm.

"Yes, the killer at the Rodeo and this latest one where you busted the cartel people," replied Ted.

"Okay, well, all the news stories reported that Enrique Guzman was the head of the cartel operating in Houston and across the southeastern United States," said Storm.

"Yes, and you were instrumental in bringing him down," said Clay.

"Yes, well me and a few others. Anyway, if you continued to follow the news you know that Enrique was being brought to trial on numerous drug charges and the murder of a federal agent named Kate Gilroy who was with the DEA."

Both Clay and Ted were watching Storm more intently now, and Storm knew they were waiting to see where he was going and how this had anything to do with Angie.

"Although it hadn't been made public yet, it would have come out in court that Kate Gilroy was really working for the cartel, too. She had been recruited a number of years ago to supply inside information to the cartel about where and when any federal agency was going to strike the cartel. She also supplied false information to the border patrol about illegal aliens crossing the border as a decoy for the real drug mules to cross the border somewhere else. However, the big kicker, guys, is when Kate Gilroy's body arrived at the morgue; they found a .22 caliber Smith & Western strapped to her leg. When it was test fired it was found to be the weapon used in three murders in that case as well as in the murder of the medical examiner's little brother. And . . . it was also the gun that killed Angie. When we looked deeper into her background, we found at least a dozen unsolved murders that can be tied to her and her .22."

Storm stopped talking for a minute to let what he had just told them soak in. You could drop a pin on the floor right now and it would sound like thunder, he thought as he watched their faces.

Finally, Clay spoke up. "Jesus H. Christ, David, are you telling us a DEA Agent killed Angie?"

"That's exactly what I am telling you, Clay."

"Why would she kill Angie, Detective?" asked Ted.

"I don't know, Ted, and that's why I'm here. I know who and I know how, but I don't know why and I've got to find out. This is killing me. It's like Angie is walking around in my dreams begging me to find the answers." Storm's head slumped for just a second, but then he looked up and said, "Guys, I need your help. I need to go over everything she was doing before she was killed. It might not seem like anything now or then, but you might know something you forgot, so we have to go over everything you can remember down to what seems like the most inane detail."

"We're right here with you, Detective. Ask us anything and we'll try to remember and if, we can't we will tell you that, too," said Ted.

Storm asked the men about Angie's job, exactly what she did. She had told him many times, but now since Ted held the same position he might be able to better explain it than a wife to a husband, especially a wife like Angie, who Storm had always joked was smarter in some measures than he was. Ted went through the details of the job explaining the negotiations with distributors and end users. Clay explained the travel and how the cars were hired to pick up the executives when they traveled and how they had used Larry's service for years. He went on to say they were always dependable, but that night they had not been able to find Angie at the airport. It had been Clay who had been trying to reach her when he got the call she had been killed.

Storm told them that security tapes showed Angie leaving the airport through another door in the company of a female driver who looked like Kate Gilroy. "What might have Angie been carrying in her briefcase on trips? The briefcase has never been found."

Both men were surprised that Angie's briefcase was still missing, although neither had an answer as to why someone would want it. Clay told him he usually supplied her with all the files she took with her. Ted even opened his briefcase and showed Storm the files he carried with him, as most of them would mirror what Angie would have had with her. It was filled with files on people, their likes and dislikes. He had shipping reports listing deliveries and returns, briefs on new clients, and files on old ones. All pretty regular stuff.

Ted's secretary had tried to interrupt the meeting in his office for two hours, especially since she thought it was merely a visit from a good friend, but she had been summarily told to hold all calls and she would be notified when the meeting was over.

After two hours of exhaustive interviewing Storm thanked them both for their time and their concern in wanting to help him find the answers. Both men now said their goodbyes and Clay walked Storm back to the lobby. Again, Clay grabbed Storm and hugged him, telling him he needed to come to dinner soon as Estella had been asking about him for far too long and the girls would love to see him.

Storm smiled, doubting Clay's teenage girls would care either way, but he said he would like to have dinner with this roly-poly man and his wife and he assured Clay they would do it soon.

CHAPTER 12

Pancho had watched the airport security video for over an hour when he noticed something odd. Each time he watched the surveillance clip he saw the same thing—Kate pulling Angie's bag out the door and heading for the car. He finally realized what had been bothering him. Nothing suspicious about the walk to the car, but it came when they reached the car. The limo driver, who they all knew was Kate now, reached for Angie's briefcase. Angie appeared to refuse to let the Kate take it from her. Earlier in the video the driver's identity had been somewhat obscured by the uniform and hat, but in this segment when she turned to Angie and reached for the briefcase he could see the face was unmistakably Kate Gilroy's. Pancho had missed the exchange the first few times because he was mesmerized by Angie and he couldn't keep his eyes off her. She was a beautiful woman and even as she walked she exhibited a grace he had seen only in a very few magnificent women, one of them being his wife Gloria. Now as he watched the segment again he saw Angie carried the briefcase until they reached the car, then secured it under her arm and got into the backseat. It was then he was sure that Angie must have had something in that case that she didn't want anyone else to get their hands on. Since the case had disappeared and no one knew what it contained, obviously, it was something she felt she had to personally protect.

Pancho's cell phone rang and he saw that it was Storm calling. "Hola, Storm, what's up?"

"Pancho, I am going over to see Ralph Higgins." "After that I need to see you and Russell. Can you call him and set up a meet and then call me back and leave a message with the time and place?" asked Storm.

"No problem, but if it's late I need to go home first, see the wife and kids for dinner then meet y'all. Will that work?" queried Hernandez.

"Damn! I didn't look at the time. Russell will be doing his show." Pancho smiled, knowing how his partner forgot about other people's schedules and time constraints when he was working and how he time and again forgot how much Gloria hated the interruption of their family meals. "Of course. Tell Gloria 'hello' and let me know when you and Russell can meet me and where."

Grinning to himself, Hernandez disconnected the phone call, punched in his address book, found Russell's cell phone number and hit "call."

Russell answered on the third ring.

Pancho relayed the request for the meeting and listened for a few minutes as Russell cussed his best friend. Both men laughed and agreed that since Storm had called this meeting, they would meet at his apartment and drink his iced tea. They set the meeting for 7:00 p.m. at Storm's new apartment. With that, Pancho hung up and called Gloria to tell her he would be home shortly and dinner needed to be ready at 5:30 p.m.—"por favor"—since he had to meet Storm at 7:00.

* * *

Storm looked at his watch, and seeing it was already 4:00 in the afternoon he thought he had better call Higgins before he drove over to his office to make sure he would be there for a few minutes so he could update him on what he had found in his search for connections between Angie and Cully. Ralph assured him he would wait and asked if he should call Tom Morran from DEA. Storm agreed and Ralph told him they would be waiting for him.

The meeting lasted until almost until 6:00 in the evening, with Storm updating them about his interviews with the limo service owners and his meeting with Angie's successor in her job. He gave the limo driver's explanation for missing Angie the afternoon she had come home and told them about the video from the international terminal at the airport, which Pancho had been studying all afternoon. He also told them that Pancho was meeting him later to compare notes on what he had found. The last thing he shared was what he had determined about the contents of Angie's missing briefcase and the files she might have had with her.

"What kind of files would she have been carrying?" asked Tom.

"Pretty bland stuff, you know, reports on customers, sales reports, shipping reports, nothing that someone would want." Storm paused for a minute, guessing he sounded as confused as he had when Ted Sloan had allowed him to look at what he carried.

"Nothing there sounds too ominous, but still there had to something the cartel wanted or they wouldn't have gone to so much trouble to steal it," mused Higgins.

"Pancho and I have sifted through every file and reexamined every report and every interview that was conducted when Angie was murdered and we've found nothing that ties Angie to Cully Gilroy. So far, it's all a big dead end," groused Storm.

"Okay, let's review what we have," said Tom. "We get an anonymous letter that says that your wife's murder and

Storm's End

Cully's execution are somehow related. We know now that Kate Gilroy killed Angie and we further know that Kate was in cahoots with the cartel. We also know that Cully was killed by the cartel, so it only stands to reason the letter is trying to point us to the cartel."

"Shit, we already knew that," said Storm, showing his irritation with the review. "We got nothing, not a fuckin' piece of anything. We know the cartel was behind the murders, but we still don't know what Angie might have been carrying with her or what she knew that connected her to Cully and got her killed and without that info we got bupkis, zilch, nada, nuttin.'"

"True, but we know who killed her, which is more than we had a few months ago. Angie knew something that scared the bejesus out of the cartel and now all we have to do is figure out what that was." Unlike the others, Higgins was smiling and that made the others look at him askance. He had been holding back an additional piece of news he had saved until everything else had been discussed. It wouldn't necessarily rock their world but if they could parse out the meaning, it might move them a little further down the road. He pulled a plain manila envelope from the folder he had laid on the desk in front of him and from it he withdrew another sheet of white typing paper that had only one sentence written on it much like the other from a few days before. This one read, *"Look to the islands in the sea they hold the key."*

"Jesus Christ, Ralph, when did this come in and exactly how long were you going to wait to show it to us?" protested Tom.

"Got it this morning and just like the other one, there's no fingerprints, no return address, and no postage. Also, just like the other one, it was dropped off and placed in the office mail, sorted, and then inspected by our security because it has no postage. When it passed through that rigmarole, it was brought up to me since it had my name on it," answered Higgins.

"Anyone have a clue what it means?" asked Tom.

"Nope. Either of you have any thoughts on what it could mean? What islands in the sea? What sea?" asked Higgins?

"Not me," said Tom, as he looked at Storm to see if there was a glimmer of recognition on his face.

"Me, neither." Storm felt as confused as the two special agents.

"Did your wife ever go to the islands, any islands, anywhere?" asked Higgins.

"Not that I can recall, but that doesn't mean she didn't when she traveled, although I don't remember her ever talking about any," replied Storm.

"Okay, obviously, this message is linked to the first one, so we have another mystery to add to the list, which is getting longer instead of shorter," said Higgins.

With the receipt of a new message that was as cryptic as the first, the men were tired of this game where the pattern of the puzzle kept eluding them. They decided to break for the evening and sleep on it. Looking at his watch, Storm realized he needed to get home before his guests showed up to rehash the day.

Ms. Edith was still at the apartment cleaning and making her adopted son some dinner while she waited for Alisha to come pick her up. She took the bus and walked about three blocks to get to Storm's new apartment and when she was ready to leave, he would either take her home or Alisha would come to get her. Storm had forgotten that it was one of "Ms. Edith's days," but her motherly smile as she greeted him all dressed up in her black skirt, bright blue blouse, and crisp white apron tied neatly around her waist made him smile, too, and he momentarily forgot the confusion and head banging of the day. Ms. Edith enveloped him in one of her infamous "Mom" hugs, which reminded him of his mother. After months of getting used to them, they were something he now secretly enjoyed. As she released him, he asked, "Ms. Edith was I supposed to take you home today?"

"No, David, Alisha is coming to get me. It's your turn next time. Are you okay? You look a little tired and out of sorts."

"No, Mom," he answered, using the name he had learned to call her at her request, "It has just been a rough day. By the way, it's a good thing Alisha is coming to get you tonight. Do you suppose I could impose on you and Alisha to stay for a while? Pancho and Russell are coming over about 7:00 and I have some things to bounce off y'all if you have time."

"David, I didn't make enough for dinner for several people, but I guess I can rustle up some more before they get here." She waited for David's response.

"No, no, that's okay. Pancho was going home to have dinner with his family and Russell is coming from the TV station, so he will have eaten earlier, as well. Why don't we wait for Alisha and the three of us can eat and be done before they get here?" It was more of a statement than a request.

Alisha arrived just a few minutes after Storm and when asked if she would mind staying for dinner and a chat with the guys, she said she would love to and she met her mother in the kitchen to help prepare dinner for three instead of one. Ms. Edith had brought about two pounds of barbecued brisket thinking David would have leftovers for the rest of the week, but now she would warm up the entire batch, put out some coleslaw, potato salad, and sun tea, and the three of them would have dinner. After dinner when her "boys" got there, she would excuse herself, find her new favorite chair in David's living room, and settle in to watch television until Alisha was ready to go.

When Russell and Pancho arrived they were also subjected to Ms. Edith's smiling face and hugs, but they never begrudged Ms. Edith's hugs as she had become like a second mother to them, too. Pancho sat up the laptop and inserted the airport security video disk of the day that Angie had returned home for the last time. It was pretty mundane at first until it got to the place where Angie and the driver exited the east end of the international terminal, which was

Storm's End

about one hundred yards away from where another camera caught the driver from Larry's car service waiting for her. He sped the video up to the point where Angie and driver got to the car. It was then they could all see the driver offer to take the briefcase and Angie's refusal to relinquish it. He played that three or four times so everyone sitting at the table could see exactly what he had seen.

"Okay, everyone saw that, right? It's not just my imagination; she hung onto the briefcase like she was protecting it, right?" asked Hernandez excitedly, as he looked around the table assuring himself the others had seen it that way, too.

"It certainly looks that way to me," said Russell, shocked that he had almost forgotten how beautiful Angie was. Alisha was shaking her head in agreement and trying to stay in the moment. This was the first time she had seen a video of Angie. It was not like the still pictures that she had seen plenty of when they moved Storm. This was something else, and she could see why Storm had fallen so hard for this woman.

"What did she carry in her briefcase?" asked Alisha, looking at Storm and hoping he had some kind of answer.

"I met with Ted Sloan, who replaced her after she died, and Clay Martin, who had been her assistant when she worked there," as he retold the same explanation he had given earlier to the Feds. "Clay told me he packed her briefcase almost every trip and it was always the same things. Ted even opened his briefcase and showed me what he carried as she would have carried many of the same things. She would also have had her laptop and power converter in the briefcase, which was the reason for the oversized nature of the damn thing," said Storm.

"All of that sounds pretty innocuous to me, nothing that would get a body robbed or killed," said Pancho.

"You're right, Pancho, but obviously there was something else in that briefcase that somebody wanted. They could have wanted to make sure she didn't have copies of—maybe, well—something they thought or knew she had or might have discovered and they sure as shit weren't taking any chances," theorized Russell.

"I also met with Ralph Higgins from the FBI and Tom Morran from DEA this afternoon and told them we had the video and Pancho was going over it. They came to the same conclusion. What's more, they also got another anonymous letter like the first one." Storm looked around the room and realized Alisha didn't have any idea what he was talking about, and, actually, Russell hadn't heard very much about it, either. Seeing the question on everyone's faces, he told them about the first letter and how it looked like Cully's murder and Angie's murder could be tied together. "The letter implied Angie and Cully were somehow connected. Pancho and I have gone over everything and I even went back and questioned people she worked with and the car service driver and so far we haven't found a connection."

"What did the second letter say?" asked Hernandez.

Storm produced a legal- sized letter envelope and pulled out copies of both letters, unfolded them, and laid them on the table for everyone's inspection. Each person took a turn looking at the mysterious sentence on each page.

"What the hell do these mean?" asked Alisha a little too loudly as Ms. Edith stuck her head around the corner frowning at Alisha's language. After being put in her place by her mother, Alisha and the group went back to discussing the puzzles of the notes in a more hushed tone.

"I got no friggin' idea, Alisha, and neither did Higgins or Morran. They kept asking me if Angie had done business with people on any islands or if she had visited any of the islands in the Caribbean or off Mexico, Central America, or South America, and I can't remember her ever going to any island," said Storm.

"Well, maybe she was meeting some tall blonde stranger on some island and you being such a stick-in-the-mud,

Storm's End

stay at home cop, she went without you," laughed Russell, knowing that would never happen but trying valiantly to lighten the mood around the table.

"Oh, some 'suave 'n' deboner stud like you?" replied Storm, grinning at Russell while returning the barb. "Do any of the rest of you have any sane ideas?"

"Could the word 'islands' mean something else? What else could be called an island?" asked Hernandez.

Everyone at the table just kept murmuring the word "islands" as if saying it over and over again would flip a switch that turned on some magical insight as to what the writer of the note meant.

"Okay, let's try another angle. Angie worked with oil drillers who purchased products for drilling, right?" said Alisha.

"Yeah. She sold pipe, fittings, drilling mud, and mud additives," said Storm.

"Could islands be rigs, you know, offshore rigs?" asked Alisha.

"It's possible," said Storm, looking at Alisha as if she might be onto something. He could see Russell and Pancho were looking at her the same way.

"Maybe it isn't that she went there, maybe it has to do with the records she was carrying. You said she carried shipping manifests, right?" asked Russell, following Alisha's lead. "If she had sales reports, she would also have known what and when something was shipping to offshore rigs, right?" asked Russell, sounding excited.

"Again, it's possible. I know she was always checking delivery records for their products to make sure the clients got what they wanted when they needed it. It was how she took care of customer service. She always said customer service was the difference in whether you kept a client or lost them to someone with a lower price." Storm had jumped on the same line of thinking as Russell and Alisha.

"We've got to get our hands on the company reports she would have been carrying when she was killed," added Pancho.

"I will have to go back out there and get somebody from the company to give them to us. You know we will never be able to get a warrant for them. That stuff is proprietary and they aren't going to just hand them over to us," mused Storm.

"Then we got to be sneaky, Big Dog, and there is no one at this table who isn't just a little bit larcenous, but I am not sure it's a good idea to go back to the company. Might be better to get that assistant to meet you somewhere," grinned Russell slyly.

"Okay, it's late and I need some sleep. This day has sucked and Ms. Edith is already asleep in 'her' chair," smiled Storm, tiredness making his voice raspy. "Let's get back together tomorrow and see if we can find a way to get those files without raising too many eyebrows, especially ones we don't want raised."

The meeting broke up with Alisha taking her mother home and Russell going back to do the late weather. Hernandez was glad he could surprise Gloria by being home before midnight, unusual when he met with this bunch. After everyone was gone, Storm watched some news and went to bed feeling a bit better that they had accomplished something and even if the message was a red herring, it was a lead—a string to follow and hope it led to something.

CHAPTER 13

Harold Stanton had spent the night at home alone for one of the first times he could recollect. His wife had gone to one of her charity meetings and the kids were visiting friends, so he had the house to himself. He had brought home dinner from the Whole Foods Market, which had ala carte entrees and side dishes. He liked the way you could pick out your meal, take it home, warm it up, and dinner was served.

The Dragon Bitch had called him again today asking what he was doing about the men she held responsible for her brother's death and he had had to tell her that the police detective she wanted killed had been in their offices. After fifteen minutes of having his ass ripped by this pompous bitch, she told him to never mind about the detective, she would take care of that herself. She again pressed him about the whereabouts of the briefcase that had disappeared after his colleague had been killed and he told her there had never been any news as to where it could have gone. He was grinning to himself as he spoke. He knew full well what had happened to the briefcase.

The night Angie was killed it was he who had met the driver of the limo and paid her for her services. The two of them had decided to take the briefcase and he would hide it They had agreed that whatever the briefcase contained it would be best for them if they kept it as added leverage in case things began to go wrong and they needed some bargaining power with authorities to negotiate their own "get out of jail free" card.

Over the past six years he had added information to the briefcase—bits and pieces of recorded telephone conversations with the heads of the cartel and notes about shipments, including the names of vessels carrying them. He had even included the amounts paid to him for his services and in which offshore accounts some of the money could be found. In the event of his murder or arrest, his lawyer had documents that would give his wife the ability to retrieve the money and live her life as she had become accustomed to and/or be able to pay for what he assuredly reasoned would be an expensive defense of his lawlessness.

When Enrique shot Kate, the last link to Stanton had been severed. With her gone, there was no one to know he had the information that could bring down a large part of the cartel's smuggling ring. It had almost been a relief when he saw the news on television recounting the raid on Enrique's warehouse and the accusations that he had killed a federal agent. He also knew about the ransacking of Kate's father's house, the murders of her brothers, and the subsequent searches of their homes. Never leaving a stone unturned or anything to chance, Gato's thugs had plundered her father's shack as well as the houses of her two brothers just to make sure they got to anything incriminating before anyone else did. All the searches had come up blank; nothing had been found. Gato had reasoned that Kate was the one who had withheld information in the case and he deduced that since the feds had seized all her possessions and the information he was sure was in the briefcase had yet to materialize as evidence against them Gato speculated the feds had not yet found the briefcase and he must be safe for the time being.

If they only knew, Stanton thought. Stanton walked into his private library in the house drugs had paid for and opened the safe he had installed behind a magnificent copy of Claude Monet's "Bridge at Argenteuil." His safe held two Glock .40 caliber pistols, his personal supply of gold coins, bearer bonds, and an oversized black Samsonite briefcase. He pulled out the briefcase, opened it, took out his personal journal, and entered today's conversation with the Dragon Bitch in case he or anyone investigating his death needed it. He felt no remorse about any of the deaths he had had a hand in; all that mattered was his way of life, his money, and his early retirement.

* * *

Pancho was already at work when Storm got in that morning and the lieutenant had left word he needed to see them as soon as they arrived. Storm followed Pancho to the break room to get coffee but also to privately ask Pancho if he had any idea why the lieutenant wanted to see them. Pancho said he didn't but he reminded Storm that Lieutenant Flynn had given them two days to come up with something on Angie's death and their two days were up. After filling their mugs, they headed to the lieutenant's office and waited outside his window for him to get off the phone and motion them inside.

The lieutenant started the conversation. "Where are you with the reexamination of your wife's murder?" The lieutenant pointed his question at Storm.

"Well, Lieutenant, not very far." The little hairs on the back of Storm's neck began to rise as he answered, but he also remembered that the lieutenant had only given him and Pancho two days to go back over the files and look for something someone might have missed. "But, we just got back into it, sir. We're going to need more time."

"You don't get more time. As far the HPD is concerned this is a case that belongs in the unsolved archives," said the lieutenant. His answer was not an order or a request; it was simply the way things were.

Storm started to open his mouth to protest what he felt was a cavalier statement of the situation when the lieutenant held up his hand to shut off any further discussion. When he saw that Storm had gotten the message, he continued, "You two will not have any more time to work the case. I just got off the phone with Chief of Ds and you both have been requested to move to the FBI for temporary assignment to Special Agent Ralph Higgins. The assistant director of the FBI in Washington called the chief and he called Chief of D's Young, who called me. You two will be working with the FBI on drug smuggling, specifically how the cartel is still getting their supply of illegal drugs into the southeastern United States. You will report to the FBI office this morning and for the duration of this operation you will take your orders from them and report to work there. Do either of you have a problem with that? C'mon, you two. Don't look so shocked. The looks on your faces would make me laugh if I wasn't so short of personnel and needed you two back on the streets handling murder cases. You know as well as I do that they always increase in direct proportion to the rise in the heat index.

"Sergeant Hernandez and I don't know anything about drugs. We are not from the drug unit. We investigate killings not smuggling. Wh-why would they want us? What can we bring to the table they can't find with their own or with guys from the drug enforcement?" Storm was almost stuttering; this development had caught him off guard.

Hernandez said nothing as he listened to Storm protesting. As Storm paused he asked what Storm was getting ready to ask next. "Are we still going to be HPD or are we being permanently assigned to the FBI? Lieutenant, do we give up our badges here?"

"No, Sergeant, you both will still be on the HPD payroll, but the FBI will be paying the city for your services." The lieutenant looked at both them as if trying to summon confidence, but this was new territory. "The chief explained that the FBI wants you because of your involvement with Enrique Guzman, the cartel, and because of Kate Gilroy. They don't want people from any drug units or the DEA. You two have proven your worthiness and dependability."

Storm thought, he is also aware the FBI knows I have a dog in the fight and they're right. I won't quit until I find some answers.

"Now you two get some boxes and pack up your personal things. You can store them in the storage room until you get back. I am getting two newly appointed detectives (officers who passed their detective test just waiting for an opening to work homicide) and they will use your desks until you return. Don't take any original files with you, but you can take copies of the files you've been working on for the past couple of days. Now get your kits and get out of here. Agent Higgins is waiting for you to report to FBI offices." With that, the lieutenant waved them out of his office. As they walked out, he added, "You two stay in touch and if you need anything, let me know."

One Justice Park Drive, the home of the Federal Bureau of Investigation in Houston, would take some getting used to. Nowhere near downtown, it sat just north of the Northwest Freeway just outside Houston's 610 Loop. A white five story stucco and black glass building, it epitomized the utilitarian visage of the Federal Government. The visitor parking was in front and both Hernandez and Storm found parking places that would serve until they were assigned permanent spaces in the lot behind the building.

They swung open the front doors and went to the lobby reception area to be met by two armed security guards. The guards wore uniforms and carried side arms, but Storm and Pancho knew in reality the guards were employees of a private security group that was hired by the government to guard all federal buildings. Both men were required to state their business and who they were there to see. Then each had to produce picture identification and surrender their service weapons, which would be held in individual locked metal cabinets located under the desk until they left the building. "Once you get your FBI Identification you'll be allowed to carry your weapons past reception and use your ID to access the elevators that will take you to the floor where you'll be working," one of the guards explained.

Special Agent Ralph Higgins came to the lobby, signed the men in, and escorted them to the fourth floor. Although Detective Storm and Sergeant Hernandez kept pressing him for answers as to why they had been chosen to work for the FBI, Agent Higgins just smiled his crooked smile and said nothing until they had entered the conference room used by his division of the bureau's task force.

"Okay, okay, I know you two want to know what you are doing here and I'm going to go into more detail as soon as Special Agent Long gets here. Let me just tell you this while we wait. We know you two have been working on the murder of Detective Storm's wife, and as you know, we have received two anonymous notes—one that linked her death to that of Cully Gilroy and the other telling us to look at the islands in the sea. You have been retracing all the steps taken in the investigation that was conducted at the time of Mrs. Storm's murder. Have you uncovered anything new that might suggest why she was killed since we know who killed her?" asked Higgins.

"No, but we did find something suspicious on the video from the airport the night she came home," said Storm.

"And what was that?" asked Higgins.

"You tell him, Pancho, you were the one who first noticed it," said Storm.

"It was no big deal, really. After watching the video over and over and comparing it to what the driver who was sent to pick her up told us, I saw something that didn't make sense and when Storm saw it he also thought it was kinda out of character for his wife," said Pancho.

"Well, what did you see, Sergeant?" asked Higgins.

"It appeared the detective's wife was waylaid by another driver just like the driver of the original car service suggested. A person dressed as a driver holding a placard with her name on it was waiting for her just outside Customs in order to lure her to go with them instead of following her normal routine. She followed the driver, who took her larger suitcase, and they exited thru a completely different door. When the driver tried to take her briefcase, it got interesting. She didn't give it up; instead, she held on to it. In fact, it looked like she was protecting it. When she got into the back seat she took it with her."

Agent Higgins turned to look at Storm. "You told me yesterday you were going to visit her old company to see if anyone could shed any light on why she might have killed."

"Yes, but as I also told you yesterday, neither her replacement nor her assistant could think of anything she would have had in the case that would have gotten her killed." Storm was trying to guess where Higgins was going with this. At the moment it seemed to be exactly the same direction he, Pancho, Russell, and Alisha had been thinking the night before.

"Last night, Agent Long and I spent some time going over what you had told me and the note we got yesterday and we think they are related. We think your wife had something that could hurt the cartel. We didn't know about her being protective of the case but we figure she had something in that case that could have been detrimental to the way the cartel does business. If you are telling me now she seemed protective of the case I have to assume she had discovered something that didn't add up and she was holding onto the evidence," said Higgins. "Still no sign of the briefcase?"

"No, not at our house, not at her office, and it wasn't logged in among Kate's possessions that were seized after her death," answered Storm.

"Okay. We know Kate was the last person to see your wife alive and we know Kate didn't have it. We also know we didn't find a case of that type in Rique's warehouse or in his home when we searched it. So, that has to mean someone either destroyed it or Kate's accomplice has it." Higgins was on a roll now and both of the HPD men were in agreement.

"Long and I already decided what we need to figure out is what was in the case," said Higgins.

Storm and Pancho looked at each other, and Storm knew his partner was thinking the same thing he was. *Damn right we do.* "We think we may have a plan that might help us with that, but we will have to be really careful about how we execute it," Storm added. "Last night Pancho, Russell Hildebrandt—my friend the TV personality who was beaten by Reggie's boys—and Alisha Johnson, the ME who did the ballistics stuff for you last year during the Rique Guzman affair all met at my house. I filled them in on my meeting with Angie's replacement, Ted Sloan, who used to work for her. Ted's a good guy and I am sure somebody we could trust. But it is not him who I think will be the most help to us, but rather Clay Rodgers, who was Angie's assistant." Storm just realized it was the first time anyone today had said his wife's first name. "Clay is a good man, too, and I think as much as he cared for Angie, he would do anything to help us clear up her murder and make the guilty party or parties go to jail."

"So, what's the plan your group came up with?" asked Higgins.

"We agreed I needed to call Clay at home so there wouldn't be so many ears that might overhear something. We feel the fewer people from Angie's office who know what I'm up to the better. I will ask him as a favor to me, or really to Angie, to help me find copies of the exact documents she would have had in that briefcase the day she was killed, including the files she took with her and any faxes or emails she may have printed out that he can find in any document records still available at Global. We also agreed that for his safety, since there might be somebody at Global watching such things, we would ask him to rendezvous with Grady Anderson, a friend of ours who works with Russell but would not appear to be connected to us. It's not perfect but it's the best we could come up with on short notice."

"I like the plan, but I don't like to involve civilians in our cases. Obviously, we have to involve Angie's assistant in order to get the information from Global, but not this Grady fella. I'm sure he is a good man, but I don't want to put a civilian who could get hurt in harm's way." Higgins was not asking but telling Storm that they had to find a better way of retrieving the files.

Pancho chuckled under his breath and said, "Damn, Grady's gonna be pissed at you. Russell already told him he was in on this."

"Well, Ralph is right—we just have to leave Grady out of this for now." Storm frowned at Pancho, telegraphing the message, "You're right, but so is Higgins."

Just as they finished this conversation, Special Agent Frank Long and Agent Martin Jones came walking through the door of the conference room. Surprising both detectives, there stood the man that Storm had shot with a bean bag while chasing him after the funeral for Alisha's brother. Jones had been working under cover for the FBI and had infiltrated Reggie's crew. He had gotten caught up in the chase, gunfire exchange, and arrests. As a result of that afternoon's events, he had had to disappear. They had heard nothing of his whereabouts since that case.

Storm's End

CHAPTER 14

FBI agent Martin Jones looked much different than the last time Storm and Hernandez had seen him. No longer clad in baggy starched jeans that hung off his butt, new Jordans, and a yellow four sizes too big polo shirt, Martin stood in front of the men in what might be called a typical FBI uniform. His dark suit draped perfectly over his shoulders and buttoned at the waist, his pants had a crease so sharp you could almost shave with it. His crisp white shirt and tie only accented his smile as if he had just seen two old friends.

Storm and Pancho stood as the men entered the room and shook hands with Agent Long. Agent Higgins said, "Detective Storm and Sergeant Hernandez, you remember Agent Martin Jones? I think one of you shot him once." The embarrassment spread like a rash as Storm's face turned red, and he and Pancho shook hands with man who had helped them find the killer of Alisha's little brother Robbie.

"If everyone would remember the total truth of it, Pancho handed me the gun to shoot him with." Storm tried to add some humor to what he and Pancho both knew was an embarrassing situation.

Storm's End

After the lighthearted banter had subsided, Agent Higgins brought the meeting to order, "You two have been wondering why the FBI asked the city of Houston to loan us two of their finest detectives. Well, now, you will find out. The FBI has embarked on a mission that the men in this room felt the two of you would add to greatly."

Looking at Storm and Pancho directly to assure he had their attention, he added, "We have started an operation given the code name 'Anaconda.' It is an FBI operation at the moment, but will most likely become a joint operation with the DEA at a later date. Operation Anaconda will be an effort to put a stranglehold on the illegal drugs entering the United States through our southern borders and southern ports. This will be a "need to know" operation. Agent Jones, Agent Long, the hierarchy in the Washington office, and I will be the only people to be read in. The DOJ has assigned a full- time prosecutor to the operation and he will work only with the people in this room. His name is Theodore Bussard, although most call him Ted. He, like Agent Jones, is from the Gulf Coast and knows many of the current federal prosecutors in Louisiana, Mississippi, Alabama, and Texas. His job will be to get any warrants we find necessary to complete our mission. This operation is almost entirely the brainchild of Agent Jones with some consultation from Agent Long and me. With that, I am going to turn this over to Agent Jones," concluded Higgins.

Storm already knew much of Martin Jones' background. He was probably at least ten years younger than the youngest law enforcement man in the room, but they all knew he had worked, studied, and fine-tuned this plan for the past six months. When his cover had been blown in Houston and he had had to disappear for a few months he had been assigned a desk in Washington, D.C., where he followed the case of Enrique Guzman and the ensuing events. Working the Gulf Coast for the FBI before he came to Houston, he knew that these men may have shut down the warehouse and arrested Rique, but they had not stopped the drugs from entering the United States. He knew there were other methods of smuggling illegal goods and he also knew the cartels were wealthy enough to find other places to receive, store, and distribute them. What he had to do was identify how the cartel was doing it today. The priority of the current operation would not initially be to arrest the criminals, but to find out who the players were and how they were transporting illegal contraband past border security. Once the intelligence was collected, they would bring in more FBI and DEA resources and make the arrests.

Jones explained how Operation Anaconda had begun. The operation as conceived by Agent Jones was accepted by the assistant director with limitations: the team would consist of only himself, Agents Long and Higgins and two local cops; their scope of investigation would only be the Gulf Coast region unless evidence was found they needed to enlarge the area and then Long would need to get the enlarged scope approved. The idea to add Storm and Hernandez had come from Agent Higgins when he had brought Jones up to speed on the past few days' occurrences and they had found the money to pay them from local agency discretionary funds. The A.D. had then called in a favor and asked the chief of Ds to lend him the two detectives.

"Gentlemen, welcome to Operation Anaconda, or as Frank likes to call it, the 'Big Squeeze,' and congratulations on your arrest of Enrique Guzman and Reggie du Pierre. As I am sure you are already aware, Rique's operation was one of the single biggest busts of a criminal organization to take place since the days when President Reagan started the war on drugs. However, as I am also sure, you are aware; those arrests were only the tip of the iceberg. Drugs are still coming across the border and through our ports. With Rique's arrest you disrupted the management of the cartel, but that vacancy will be filled before Rique's body is in the ground. I know I'm probably not telling you

Storm's End

anything you haven't surmised on your own, but let me explain the plan to put the cartel into chaos.

"You are probably questioning why Ralph and the assistant bureau chief wanted you men involved in this. Well, the simple answer is, you are already involved. You were both a significant part of bringing down Rique and the Canal Street drug runners, and Detective Storm; it was your wife who was mentioned in the first note from our anonymous source. You are looking for answers why she was murdered and everyone knows you are a bit of pit bull once you get your teeth into something." Martin was looking directly at Storm as he continued to explain why they were there.

"Sergeant Hernandez, you were chosen for your ability to work with the detective. Since you two have developed a partnership, it is only logical you be included in this operation. You bring language skills none of the rest of us possess. As we identify the players in the cartel we will be putting legal surveillance measures in place which will include, though not be limited to, data taps and communications tapes. Your ability to translate anything being said in Spanish quickly will be of immense benefit to the operation.

"As far as your fellow officers in the HPD will be concerned, the two of you have decided to take accrued vacation time you have earned over the past few years to investigate the death of the detective's wife. We can't have it getting out that the two of you are working with us. This has to remain a closely guarded secret. You two will not report to this building –you will work from your homes. You will have equipment that gives you the ability to communicate with us at any time either via secure cell phones or secure data links installed on new laptop computers we will supply you. With the exception of the list of people I mentioned earlier, nobody will know what information you are gathering. Certainly, people will know you are looking for answers, but not that you are forwarding what you find to us. We will gather the information and set up surveillance on anyone you become suspicious of and report back to you what we find. But as far as the world knows, you two are lone wolves working on your own."

The room suddenly felt cold to Storm. He and Pancho were a part of this and truly not on their own, but it felt like they were. "Okay, exactly what do you want us to do?" he asked.

"We want you to continue digging into the deaths of Angela Storm and Cully Gilmore. We are sure this is about more than one drug lieutenant being shot by a redneck from East Texas. We need to get a list of participants in the drug trade, who the head guy really is, who works for him, and how are they doing it. There have to be people supplying them with information. There has to be somebody opening channels for them to smuggle the drugs into this country. The more names you can find and the more contacts you can uncover, the tighter the noose will be when we spring the trap." Looking at the two men just recruited, Martin continued, "Am I making sense so far?"

Smiling as if trying to lighten the mood of the room, Pancho asked Ralph, "What do I tell my wife and what does Storm tell his?" The room went dead silent as the three agents were shocked that Pancho would allude to Storm's wife, but then when he saw the looks he was getting he added, "You know, Russell Hildebrandt?"

Laughter broke out from all the men but Martin. *He doesn't know about Storm and the relationship I have with my best friend Russell*, Storm realized. When the laughter let up a bit, Storm pretended to be pissed, hitting Pancho in the shoulder and dropping a one-word retort. "Asshole."

"This is a good time to give you new information we have yet to pass on to you two," Ralph said. "Sergeant, how you handle things with your wife is up to you, but I would keep this close to the vest and you might just want to tell her you are helping the detective solve an old crime. Now as for you, Detective, we have something else in mind.

"First," Higgins looked at the other two agents as he spoke, "we like the idea of you using your wife's assistant at GUMDI to get your hands on exactly what your wife might have been carrying in her briefcase and getting him to help you in the future. You mentioned he had a strong bond with your wife and you felt he was a good and honest man who would give you information that would help solve your wife's murder."

"Yes, I'm sure he would do anything to help, but I am not sure how much help he can be." Storm was little shocked they wanted to use a civilian this way and if they did, somebody needed to step up and assure him the FBI would protect Clay Rodgers.

"We want you to go to his house to visit and ask him to help you as a personal favor, but for God's sake don't tell him about the FBI. Figure out a way he can supply you with information without leaving a trail," said Higgins.

"You might want him to put the information on a thumb drive and find a way for the two of you to exchange it. If it is necessary for him to contact you after, you can give him the new cell phone number which will be untraceable," injected Agent Long.

"Now as for your friend Russell, he is another matter altogether." Agent Higgins knew this was going to be the difficult part of the plan to sell Storm. "We want you to include him in your plan to find your wife's killer. In fact, we want you to include your friend the medical examiner and this man Grady you mentioned earlier, as well. You just can't tell them you are working with us and what the real objective of this operation is. Detective, you will need to get help from Mr. Hildebrandt and you will need to make it appear as if you are only looking to find leads about your wife's death," said Higgins as the rest of group looked on to see how Storm would react to their next request.

Stunned, Storm responded, "I need to know more. I need to know why and what you have in mind. How will I ask Russell to do something if I don't know what it is?"

"Give me a minute and I will explain everything. Martin has been doing some investigation of his own while he was in D.C. He has been looking into the departments that oversee international trade for the United States. He's got a feeling, or let's say an 'educated guess,' that the cartels are busy at work inside our government—maybe not overtly breaking the law but using influence to secure the safety of some people who are forming international companies that are no more than fronts for use in smuggling," elaborated Higgins.

"What does that have to do with me and my hunt for information?" asked Storm.

"Your friend's father is very good friends with Senator Rendell. He has always backed him for election. They play golf together, they belong to the same country club, and have been friends for over twenty years," responded Martin.

"Yeah, so what?" Storm realized he was still dumbfounded by the turn in this plan.

At that point, Agent Higgins jumped back into the conversation. "The Honorable Senator Thomas J. Rendell heads the committee that oversees the workings of the United States Trade and Development Agency, commonly referred to the USTDA or Trade Commission. Now we have no suspicions that he or anyone else on that committee knows anything about anything nefarious that could be going on with this agency, but we do have suspicions that if help is being made available to the cartels and their enterprise of smuggling, someone in the agency is helping them. What we want you to do is ask Russell to ask his father to call his friend the senator and get you into the headquarters of the FBI, DEA, and the Trade Commission so you can look for anything that would involve smuggling, the cartels, and your wife's murder," explained Higgins.

"But you are the FBI, and you said I or we were recruited with the help of your assistant director, so why would I need to go there?" queried Storm.

"It is just part of your cover," explained Martin. "You will have a meeting with the assistant director and he will go over what information we have on what might be going on in the USTDA, but it will be more a meeting to put your cover in place. If you skipped meeting with the FBI or the DEA, somebody might get suspicious of your motives. We can't just have you go and only meet with some representative of the USTDA.

"The DEA will meet with you as nothing more than a courtesy and the fact that their director might think you can get information about Kate and Cully Gilroy. But again, what you tell them will be limited to what is common knowledge and that you are focusing on finding answers about your wife's death."

This entire plan was becoming more and more unnerving, but if it helped find out the answers to his questions, Storm was willing to go along with it. "You mean lie to my friend?" asked Storm.

"Well, not lie, exactly," answered Higgins. "If you want, you can tell him the entire plan, but you have to know he has your back and he will not tell his father any more than you think his father needs to know. Example, Storm: You tell them we gave you intel that we believe your wife had information that could have brought down a ring of drug smugglers but that we are not being forthcoming in sharing that information, so you need to pull some strings and get to people higher up the food chain than us and the only way you know how to do that is ask the senator for help, and by 'help' we mean access."

"You're also putting me out there as bait, aren't you?" asked Storm.

"How do you mean?" asked Agent Jones.

"You know as well as I do if there is someone out there helping the cartels, they will get word out and my life won't be worth a plug nickel. Right?"

Storm's End

"There is that risk, but we are going to take all the precautions we can. When you are in Washington, you will be covered by round the clock backup. Agents will have you under surveillance twenty-four hours a day. Your every move and conversation will be watched and listened to the entire time you are gone," added Agent Jones.

"And we have one other little surprise for you," injected Agent Long. With that, he threw what looked like a lead capsule out on the table. It was about half an inch long and no bigger around then the ink cartridge from a ballpoint pen. "This is a GPS chip, which we can implant under your skin at the small of your back and we will be able to track you to within five feet of where you actually are. If something were to happen to you we can find you within minutes and secure your safety."

Pancho whistled and reached over to pick up the tracking device. "Wow! James Bond, eat your heart out, Detective David Storm is about to replace you." Again Pancho had lightened the mood in the room and each man now grinned at the prospect of Storm becoming a super spy.

The meeting was concluded with decisions made that Storm would tell Russell everything but the fact the FBI was involved. He would ask Russell to ask his father to meet with them both and go over why Storm felt it necessary to seek help from the senator. Storm would call Clay to say he would like come over to his house to visit, as it had been too long a time since he had seen Clay's wife and children. When he met with Clay, he would request his help in finding the answers to Angie's murder and discuss how they would transfer information.

The agents had assured him they would always have his back and with his skills as an investigator he would know the right questions to ask, hopefully getting information that would be helpful in squeezing the cartels. If everything worked, he would get the implant the next day at a doctor's office that the FBI used for covert situations. An FBI tech would monitor the surgery and make sure the device was working. Storm would leave for the D.C. the following week.

CHAPTER 15

The next few days were filled with getting Russell, his father, and Alisha on board with what Storm had been given to do. He called Russell on his way home from the FBI and told him he needed to talk to him as soon as possible and that he would meet him at the Brownstone as soon as Russell could get there after his early evening weather forecast. This was no problem for Russell, as Houston's weather in early summer was pretty much the same forecast; heat and humidity and somewhere between a forty or fifty percent chance of rain, which really meant forty to fifty percent of the city would get rain.

Storm then called Alisha and invited her to join them. It was Ms. Edith's day at the hairdresser's and she would be at home after the two-block walk home.

Pancho didn't join them; Storm knew he would have his hands full with his own explanations at home. Gloria would have to be approached gently and purposefully when he told her he was taking vacation leave and yet wasn't really stopping work. Gloria had always wanted to take a long vacation and go somewhere exotic, and now he had to tell her he was using the time to help Storm find the answers to questions regarding his wife's death. Pancho was trying to follow the plan they had discussed with the FBI agents, not telling her he was working for the FBI or that this operation could be dangerous. Storm knew he needed to explain in half-truths, trying very hard not to outright lie to her.

Dinner with Russell and Alisha went off without a hitch. Storm brought them up to speed, saying that although the FBI had dropped another piece of the puzzle in his lap, they were unwilling to help him look into it. He explained that the FBI was looking into government agencies that might be helping the cartels set up legitimate front companies that could be used to smuggle drugs into the USA. He also told them he and Pancho had agreed to use built-up vacation time to investigate this on their own, but they would need the help of Russell and his father.

"Pard, are your father and Senator Rendell still friends? I remember years ago meeting him at your house and what good friends they were then. He's on the USTDA oversight committee, I think." Okay, okay, Storm told himself, that last part isn't exactly true—I just found that out from Ralph Higgins.

Alisha's part in this investigation would be minimal, but she was too close to them not to be included in the conversation. Storm knew if she found out through outside sources that he had taken a leave from the police department and not read her in, there would be hell to pay. She told him if he needed her to do anything, she was there, but she understood this was a quest to find information and didn't require her expertise.

Russell agreed to talk to his father and one of them would get back to Storm as soon as he could. "When do you want to leave for Washington? You know I'd be happy to take a few days off to accompany you."

Storm politely refused the offer, fending him off with intimations that this might just be a giant boondoggle and he didn't want to waste Russell's time. What he didn't tell either of them was that it could be dangerous. The cartel was not above killing anyone who got in their way and there was no way in hell he was going to put any more of his friends in harm's way. He already had Pancho to worry about.

The next morning he called Clay Rodgers and suggested that he would like to drop by to see him, Estella, and the girls. "It's been ages since I've spent time with you. I'm sorry I've lost touch."

Clay was thrilled with the idea that Storm had initiated a get-together. He answered in a shaky voice that sounded to Storm like he was tearing up. "Come over for dinner tonight, OK? We'd love to have you. It's been way too long." Although Storm protested Estella didn't have to make dinner for him, he finally agreed and they planned his arrival for 6:30 p.m. that night.

The detective arrived exactly at the appointed time and was met at the door by Clay, who expressed again how thrilled he was to have Storm over. Estella came out of the kitchen still wearing her apron and gave Storm a huge hug, much like the ones he had been getting from Ms. Edith. Estella was built like Clay, short and what most would consider somewhat rotund, but Storm had always liked Estella, so he had always thought of her as voluptuous and downright attractive.

The four of them had always enjoyed each other's company. Often, Clay and Angie would start talking shop, leaving Estella and Storm to catch up on what the girls had been up to. Storm liked kids and many times he wondered what he and Angie's life might have been as if the Lord had blessed them with children. Just before Angie's death they had been looking into adoption. *It was not meant to be, I guess.*

The girls hung back, all dressed in what appeared to be their Sunday best, with brightly colored aprons, as well. For them it was a special occasion, both a family dinner and a time to enjoy a guest they had not seen in many years. Storm had treated this visit the way Angie would have when they were invited to the Clay's for dinner, and he brought along a small gift for each of the girls. Alisha had come in handy that day—he had told her their ages and together they had gone to the Galleria and she had picked out the perfect gift for each of them.

When offered something to drink, Storm opted for sweet tea as quickly as possible to mitigate Clay's obvious embarrassment at having offered alcohol. Estella scolded Clay with her eyes for the blunder but quickly smoothed things over. "Girls, thank Mr. Storm for the gifts, and finish setting the table," she told them. Estella had made a wonderful meal of chicken *mole* with borracho beans, Spanish rice, and homemade tortillas. The dinner couldn't be considered simple but it was traditional and for Storm, the fact that it was made with Estella's own hands made it that much more delightful. They ate until Storm felt like he was going to burst and finally threw his hands in the air as a sign of surrender before he succumbed to the impulse to take another bite.

As Estella and girls excused Storm and Clay from the table, she and the girls went to work clearing away leftovers and washing the dishes. Storm, carrying his continually full glass of tea, followed Clay outside to the patio. The sun had gone down and there was a cool breeze blowing through the trees and across the yard.

OK, this is it—the time to convince Clay to help me investigate Angie's murder. Although the dinner and conversation had been wonderful, he was ready to reveal the real intent of his visit. After both had settled comfortably, Storm leaned forward and said, "Clay, I must admit I have an ulterior motive for coming to dinner tonight. I have come to ask you for help with something very important to me."

Clay focused on Storm's face. "What is it, David? You know I would do almost anything for you."

"You may remember my telling you that we had determined that a dirty DEA Agent named Kate Gilroy killed Angie.

Kate Gilroy was involved with the Mexican drug cartels, supplying them with information and acting as an assassin for them. It was her gun that was identified by the forensics team in the medical examiner's office as the same gun that had killed at least five people in Houston, one of them being Angie. I have answered a lot of questions I had after Angie died, questions like how she was killed and who did it, but the one question I have not been to answer is 'Why'?"

Clay seemed mesmerized by the things David was telling him, his eyes wide and mouth slightly agape, absorbing all of what he was hearing. Storm continued, "As I also mentioned when I was at your office the other day, a few weeks ago Enrique Guzman, the man who killed Kate Gilroy, was going to trial for her death and for related charges, including heading up one of the largest drug operations ever discovered in Houston. On his way out of the courthouse he was gunned down by Kate Gilroy's father, Cully Gilroy; a vengeance killing as far as we're concerned, but all the same, Enrique might have led us to more of the organization's hierarchy. A few days later, the man who killed Rique was stabbed to death in the county jail. His killers were Mexican nationals and we suspect it was arranged by someone for them to be in the jail with Kate's father to carry out his killing. At the same time Cully Gilroy was being murdered both of his remaining children and their families were murdered in the their homes in East Texas and their homes ransacked as if someone was looking for something. We have no idea who committed those killings, but we surmise it was the same people behind the murder in the jail. We also don't know if they found what they were looking for."

Stunned by what Storm was telling him, Clay sat motionless in his chair listening in shocked silence to what he was being told and staring at Storm in fear. "Clay, the day I came to the office to see you and Ted we talked about the disappearance of Angie's briefcase. You told me you regularly packed her briefcase because the two of you were so close and had worked together so long that you knew what she would want and what to pack. Ted even assured me it was most likely the same kinds of things he took with him when he traveled. What I didn't tell the two of you is that we have seen the airport video of the day Angie returned. It shows a woman who was impersonating the driver sent to drive Angie home. That woman was Kate Gilroy. It shows Angie carrying the briefcase and refusing to let the driver take it from her. She appears to be protecting it for some reason. She takes it into the back of the car with her as if holding onto it for dear life. The briefcase has never been found."

When Storm stopped long enough to take a breath, Clay finally got a chance to ask his question. "David, what can I do to help you with this? I told you I have not seen the briefcase since Angie left for her trip—" Clay paused, seeming to be at a loss as to how he could help.

"Clay, what I need from you is to see if you can find the reports and files Angie would have taken with her on that trip. What did you pack for her? What emails containing what information did you send her that she requested while she was gone? I need you to go back in history and try to reconstruct exactly what she might have had in the briefcase. If at all possible, I need copies of the exact files and reports she would have had. We think she was killed for what she had in her briefcase, so we need to see if there is anything that might lead me to what she was carrying that got her killed." Relief poured over Storm; he had finally gotten it all out and now he needed to convince Clay that for Angie's sake and his, he couldn't say no.

"David that was a long time ago. I don't know that I can. Those reports and files would be old and may have been archived." Clay looked befuddled as to how he would rebuild what Angie had taken with her.

I have to work harder to get Clay to see that he's the only one Angie could count on to help solve this mystery.

"Clay, you told me the other day she always carried most of the same information; it only varied by where she was going. Ted told me he carried most of the same things she would have when he leaves town. All you have to do is look at the dates of that trip and where she was going and reproduce the same information she would have taken with her."

"I guess I could do that. We are required by business practice to retain reports for ten years. But emails might be harder, although they might be found in archived IT Department files." Storm could almost see Clay's mind working a mile minute trying to figure out if he could do this.

Now comes the big factor in whether Clay is going to help or not. "Clay, there's one more thing. I have to ask you to do this without anyone from the company knowing what you are doing."

Now the fear flashed across Clay's face. "Why, David? What do you suspect?"

"Clay, you can call it my gut or intuition or whatever, but I think the cartel has someone inside your company helping them or at least supplying them information."

Storm could see questions cloud Clay's eyes. He had to settle the man down and get him to help. "Someone had to let the cartel know when Angie was coming home. Someone had to know she had something or knew something that could interfere with business. Somebody inside pointed her out to the cartel, and neither of us can take a chance that they might get wind of what we are doing."

"Would I or my family be in danger? David, I can't or won't do anything to put my wife and girls in danger." His face showed he was resolute on this.

"No, Clay, I don't think so as long as you are careful. That is why after tonight I will not be bothering you 'til this is all over. I will not be seen coming to your office or your home again till we solve this. I will make arrangements for someone totally unknown to anyone who might suspect something to pick up the information. I don't want you to print or take reports out. I will give you a thumb drive to download the information on. You can carry it out in your pocket and give it to the person I will send to retrieve it when you are done."

Storm knew he had to convince Clay this could all be done without anyone becoming the wiser. "If something happens that makes you uneasy, I want you to quit right where you are, take no more chances, and forget the entire thing. Is that understood?" Storm knew he had to give his old friend a way out.

Clay shook his head and whispered he understood. "David, I can't tell Estella about this. It would scare her to death and you're right, I don't want you back over here again until this is over. As much as I want to help you and Angie, I've got my family to protect."

With that over, Estella came out of the house and they sat another few minutes before Storm made excuses, thanked them for a lovely time, and went home. All he could do now was hope Clay could come up with the reports. But that was in Clay's hands now. He was sure Clay would try but didn't know if he could find anything.

The decision had already been made that Grady would pick up the thumb drive. All agreed that few would connect him to Storm.

Storm's End

CHAPTER 16

The mornings were starting to come much easier to Detective Storm. The night terrors had relented and he again was focused and had purpose. He usually woke before dawn and when he went to the refrigerator in his sparkling clean kitchen he would find juice, milk, and cereal. Ms. Edith had taken on the chore of stocking his pantry and icebox.

He had received a message from Russell after he returned home the night before. "Hey, Barretta, I talked to my father and he said he was happy to call his friend the senator and arrange for you to have some time with him when you get to Washington. Now let's hope the senator will arrange for you to meet with someone from USDTA."

* * *

Clay had also awakened early that morning, but unlike Storm, he hadn't really slept the entire night before. He had gone over and over in his mind David's request earlier that evening. Although he felt obliged to help, the idea that someone might catch him supplying information to the police to build a case against people who had no compunction about killing an entire family scared him to death, and protecting his family would always trump doing what was right for someone else. He would go to work and see if he could put together what reports Angie might have taken with her, but he wouldn't take any chances with being discovered. Ted was out of town and if Clay was seen going through sales figures and shipping reports it would be no big deal as that was his job.

The archived emails would be something different entirely. He had to be more careful with them. The good news was the people who worked in the IT department were much like him; they had been with the company for years, they were always in the office, and they were invisible to the powers that be, at least until something didn't work. Then they became "those geeks" who came and purged your system of whatever you had been looking at that introduced some malware that caused your terminal to freeze up. Assistants and geeks always got along fine because they all felt undervalued and in most cases, the assistants were the only ones who knew the geeks' names.

* * *

Russell called Storm about nine the next morning, early for Russell. He told Storm he had an appointment with the senator for Thursday morning at the senator's office in D.C. The senator was looking forward to meeting the man who had been instrumental in striking the largest blow to the drug cartels in the history of Houston police work. This amused Storm, since the case had begun as a case of murder, not one involved in the intrigue of a dirty federal agent and the distribution of drugs.

Pancho had been setting up his new FBI computer at the house and working with Storm on how they would communicate with the FBI and with each other. All communication avenues would be encrypted, which should eliminate anyone's eavesdropping. Pancho would ride along with Russell to drop Storm off at the airport on Wednesday and on their drive they would cover all those last minute details that needed to be covered before Storm left town.

Ms. Edith would continue to drop by the detective's house in his absence just to check that things were still in order. The plan was that he would be gone for a week and if that held up, she would come by the day before he was to return and make sure his home was spic-and-span for his homecoming. If he was delayed for some reason, he would contact Alisha, and Ms. Edith could plan to do it another day.

While they were still at headquarters Pancho and Storm video conferenced with Agents Higgins and Jones to verify the Com package was working properly. And then Storm was off to the airport. Flying was not something Storm relished and every time the plane hit an air pocket he wished he still drank. Almost three hours from Houston to Washington D.C., sitting in an aisle seat so he could at least move his legs into the aisle once in a while helped, but a chatty passenger sitting in the window seat only aggravated his reluctance to be inside a long metal tube hurtling through thin air at 500 miles per hour.

He had never understood how Angie had done this at least twice a week for almost their entire marriage. Outside of driving to nearby places such as New Orleans to spend a weekend in The Quarter or to Lubbock to attend his alma mater's home football game, Storm had never been much of anywhere. This trip was a first in more than one way: his first time leaving the state of Texas to investigate wrongdoing and the first time he had ever seen the seat of government for the country of which he was so proud. He wanted to be a tourist and see everything he could, but he also knew he going there on a job and finding answers was more important than taking in the sights.

Arriving at Ronald Reagan Washington National Airport early in the afternoon gave Storm time to take the short taxi ride to the hotel the senator had suggested. The Willard was a popular place for visiting dignitaries to stay and Storm had been told his stay was being taken care by the senator's office so he was not to worry about the bill when he checked out. The place was over the top; it was like a palace compared to anything Storm had stayed in before.

It was nearing 5:00 p.m. by the time Storm checked in and he found a note waiting for him from Agent Jones instructing him to meet him at the foot of Lincoln Memorial at 6:00 p.m. that evening. The desk clerk gave him instructions on how he could walk to the Memorial and added it should take him only a few minutes.

"Is this your first trip to Washington, Mr. Storm?" asked the desk clerk.

"Yes it is." Trying hard not to appear the total Texas redneck many would have thought him, he went on, "Am I close to the monuments and museums?"

"Yessir, you just go out the front doors and look to your right and you will see the Mall. If you follow the reflecting pool west, the path will take you to the Lincoln Memorial. It will be about half an hour's walk if you take your time. If you prefer, you can get a taxi in front of the hotel and they can have you there in only a few minutes," replied the helpful desk clerk.

Storm thanked him for his help and left the hotel via the magnificent lobby and the front doors. A short walk to the corner and he could see the White House. Although he had asked the desk clerk for directions, he had also read his guide book before he arrived and he knew if he walked right to 15th Street then south or left on 15th he would see Constitution Ave. and he could walk west on it down the side of the reflecting pool and find the Lincoln Memorial at the far end. It was a gorgeous afternoon in Washington and he decided he had time to make the walk if he didn't stop too often to see some of the sights he had always heard about and didn't want to miss on what might be the only time he would ever be there.

It was almost 6:00 p.m. when he got to the Lincoln Memorial and sure enough, Agent Jones was waiting at the foot of the steps. "Did you walk all the way here from your hotel in those boots?" asked Jones.

Storm cast a quick look down at the black highly shined Lucchese cowboy boots that had been made for him with a runner's insole for added comfort and simply laughed the comment off. "Yes, I did. I had plenty of time and wanted to take the chance to enjoy what my tax dollars pay for besides your FBI salary."

The joke was not lost on Martin, but he didn't bite, and instead he turned, indicating that Storm should follow him up the steps of the Memorial like all the other tourists, where their nonchalant conversation would appear to be between two friends meeting to see the sights on their first trip to Washington.

"Your tracking device is working well; we've had you '5 by 5' ever since you left Houston," reported Martin.

"You mean this thing is strong enough ya'll can even track me six miles above the ground and moving at five hundred miles an hour?" Storm was amazed the little pill sized device had that kind of range.

"Technology, Detective, technology," answered Martin with a grin. "Did you think we were going to lose you just when we got you working with us?"

Storm smiled. "Anything else you boys can monitor with that thing, like my heart rate or blood pressure?"

"No, but I'm sure there are some medical versions of it that could," answered Martin. "What time is your appointment with the senator tomorrow?"

"Russell left me a message that he's expecting me at 10:00 a.m. at his office in the Hart Senate Office Building," replied Storm.

"Good. That's just down the street from your hotel and you can walk it a lot easier than you walked here. Just go north from your hotel and it will be on the east side of street in the next block after you pass the White House. What are you planning on telling the senator about the purpose of your trip to Washington?"

"Russell and I had a long conversation with his father before he made the call to Senator Rendell's office. What I asked him to tell the senator is that the wife of a lifelong friend of his son Russell was killed a few years back and that Russell and I have never given up the search for answers to as why she was murdered. He told the senator that I had come across information that my wife had been working with USDTA in Latin America for the expansion of her company's products being sold in the Argentina and Venezuela. Since he sits as head of the committee that oversees the USDTA he might be able to steer me to the correct people who could answer some questions about who my wife was meeting with and if there was any reason that could have put her in danger," explained Storm.

"Do you think he will buy that?" asked Martin.

"He has to. It's the truth, even if not totally the truth. I will assure him I am only here to look for threads that might lead to why a Mexican cartel would want to have Angie killed."

"Detective, you are going to have to be very—and I mean *very*—careful about who you talk to while you are here. We don't know who we can trust and who we can't. That is why the DEA is not involved in this case so far. The senator's office staff is there to protect him and if any of them think you are here to find a tie that implicates the senator to smuggling or anything else illegal you will get the door slammed in your face faster than you can spin around. Washington is a bloodthirsty place. You are going in as the hero of a big case back home and for the senator to be seen with you is good for the voters back home, but it doesn't carry squat out here. These people play by their own rules and power is the most important possession they have. So when you are with the senator or any of his staff don't let on you are looking for anything more than the answers to some non-threatening questions and nothing that could possibly have anything to do with the senator. In fact, make it clear that if you do find any answers you will make sure the senator gets credit for facilitating them, You simply want him to introduce you to the people from the USDTA and anyone there that might have known your wife or might have any information on the business dealings she was having with Latin America.

"We won't have you wired, as we can't take a chance that the senate offices security could find a wire on you. The only thing we have is the GPS that we are tracking you with now. We will know where you are, but not what is being said or happening to you, so for God's sake, be careful."

"I will be, Jones. This is not my first rodeo and I do know a little about an investigation. The senator will become my best new friend and he will believe the only thing he is doing is hooking me up with the right people and helping a hometown hero find the answers to some mundane questions." Storm lowered his eyes with an "aw shucks" look and kicked the toe of the shiny boot against the marble floor.

"Good, then I am out of here. If you want to walk back to the hotel and if you're looking for some dinner there are plenty of places that flank the Mall that have outdoor tables and you can catch some of the sights of Washington. Just be careful of the hookers who work 10th street," Martin grinned as he left Storm with that pearl of wisdom. "I will talk to you after you've seen the senator."

Storm took his time walking back to the hotel, as it didn't get dark until around 8:30 at night. He stopped at the Vietnam War Memorial and found the glossary that listed the names of the fallen. He looked up two boys he had known in high school who had perished in that conflict and found their names. The city and monuments were something he had always wanted to see and it would have been idyllic if the noise of the street didn't permeate everything and the homeless didn't seem to occupy every shade tree along the route. He would find one of the restaurants Martin had mentioned, get some dinner and then get to bed, as tomorrow would be a busy day.

Storm's End

CHAPTER 17

Flashes of light broke through the window of Storm's hotel room and he could hear the beat of rain on his window as yet another flash of lightning lit up the room. The clock on the nightstand read 7:15 a.m. It was after the time he normally rose, but the night before the weather had been cooler than back home and the refrigerated air in his room caused him to leave the blankets on, and he slept as he had not slept in years. His appointment with the senator was not until 10:00 a.m., but as he never slept in anymore, he dragged his fifty-year-old frame from the bed, sat his feet down on the carpeted floor, propelled himself upright, and made his way to the bathroom. He went through his morning ritual on instinct as if he was at home, showering, shaving, dressing, and ready to be out the door in less than thirty minutes.

A wet summer storm came off Atlantic across Delaware and seemed to settle over Washington, giving the city a good cleaning. As he looked through the front windows of the hotel, he could see the rain beating down on the street and the windshields of the cars caught in traffic as federal employees fought their way to work. His meeting was not for a couple of hours and there was no sense in trying to leave the hotel to get breakfast, so he decided to try the Café du Parc, as it was the only place serving breakfast inside the hotel. He had looked at the prices in his room the night before and came to the conclusion that this hotel was too ritzy for him to stay in long. The café was about the most inexpensive fare the hotel offered—two eggs, ham, toast and coffee for under twenty dollars.

Just as breakfast arrived, his cell phone began to ring and he saw it was Pancho. "Yo, Pancho, what's up?"

"Hey, Storm, you made it okay? Was the flight okay?" asked Pancho.

"Yeah, fine, got here, checked in, and met Jones over near the Lincoln Memorial." Storm paused. "Surely you didn't call just to see if I got here okay."

"No, Grady got a call from your friend Clay; he said he thought he had everything you wanted him to get from the company."

"Did he say if he had any problems?" asked Storm.

"No, he just called Grady's cell and told him he had it and couldn't wait to get rid of it." Storm could hear Pancho's chuckle as he relayed the news.

"Well, I can't blame him. If he gets caught getting that stuff for us he could be in trouble with the company, let alone what the Pendejos might do to him and his family." Storm knew Clay was no hero and he would owe him big time for taking the chance to help him. "He is going to meet Grady tomorrow and Grady is bringing me the thumb drive so I can get to work on the reports and see if there is anything they could have wanted," said Pancho.

"Is there anything else going on I should know about?' asked Storm.

"Not that I know of; the Feebies gave me the tracking thing on you and I can track you now, too. In fact, I can see you are in the hotel and I can even see you are in the ground level restaurant. Have a good breakfast and I will talk to you after you have seen the senator," Pancho signed off.

Storm's End

When Storm finished his breakfast, the rain was still falling so he decided to take a cab the short four blocks to the Hart Senate Building. Before going through the metal detectors he waited in the lounge. He was an hour early and decided to wait until 9:30 before he went upstairs.

The employees all seemed to have picture identification that could be passed through a sensor showing their clearance and allowing them entry to the floors above. Storm went to the security desk, offered his police ID from Houston, and told the private security guards he was there to see Senator Rendell. The security guard asked, after he saw the police identification, if the detective was in procession of any weapons, at which time Storm produced his service weapon and turned it over to the guard, who assured him he would be given it back as soon as he was leaving the building.

"May I ask your business with the senator?" asked the guard, who took his ID and ran it through a slip screen on his computer checking the authenticity of the card.

"It is a personal visit from one of his constituents and I have an appointment," replied Storm.

A second guard was placing a phone call to the senator's office to confirm that Detective David Storm of the Houston Police Department did, indeed, have an appointment. The guard replaced the phone and said that an aide from the senator's office would be down to meet him soon and sign him in. He then told Storm to wait for the aide in the lobby.

In short order, a stuffy-looking man wearing a bow tie appeared in the lobby and spoke to the guards. They shook their heads and pointed to Detective Storm waiting in the lounge area. He turned on his heels and walked directly over to Storm. "I am Cyril Leggins, First Assistant to the Director of Assistants to Senator Rendell." Cyril held out his hand to shake the detective's hand. "You are early, Detective, and we didn't plan on you being so prompt. The senator is still on the floor of Congress and he will meet you as soon as he returns. You can wait in his office and I know he is very excited to meet you." Cyril was not only stuffy-looking but to Storm also seemed somewhat smug.

The office smelled of old money. What some would call an antechamber was filled with leather chairs and sofas, mahogany end tables and a reception desk. A large portrait of the senator hung on one wall overlooking all who were made to wait before basking in his presence. Under the massive portrait hung an "ego wall" of 8" X 10" photos of the senator shaking hands with the current and past U.S. presidents. This room's décor made sure any visitor was duly impressed with the senator's status and political staying power. To Storm, he was merely a means to an end, but he also knew he would have suck up his own pride and prejudices if he was to get this man's help.

As if by magic Cyril reappeared in reception area. "Detective, would you follow me, please?"

Storm stood and muttered an almost unrecognizable "Sure." He followed Cyril, the assistant to the assistant, past a door through which he glimpsed desks in perfect parallel lines with busy bees behind them filing papers, working on computers, and generally doing the work minions do in political offices. Ahead of them was a large oak door with a simple script sign: "Senator Rendell."

Cyril knocked on the door and then opened it. "Senator, Detective David Storm is here to see you."

A booming voice with a pronounced Texas accent admonished the assistant for standing between the voice and the man he wanted to meet. "Detective David Storm, I take it," said a distinguished looking man with perfectly cut white hair.

As he did with everyone, Storm appraised the man as he prepared to shake his hand. The Senator was trim, so he obviously cared about his image. There was not a wrinkle in what must have been a thousand dollar suit. Over his extended hand was an infectious smile that belied what Storm was sure was a ruthless drive to gain and keep power.

Storm extended his hand and made himself lift the corners of his mouth as he said, "Senator, so nice to meet you. Russell Hildebrandt Sr. has said many nice things about you."

The senator scoffed, "How is the old reprobate?"

"He is doing fine, and asked me to thank you for taking time from what is surely a busy schedule to see me." Storm had already decided to do his best to play the role of someone in awe of a powerful man. "Is it okay if I call you 'Senator,' Senator?" asked Storm.

"That's fine, lad, and by what name do you like to be addressed, 'Detective,' 'David,' or what?" asked the senator.

"'Storm' is what my friends call me, Senator, so I reckon that will work just fine." Again Storm resurrected his almost forgotten smile.

"All right. 'Storm' it is, and I hope we become friends. You know you can never have too many friends, especially when you run for reelection!" *The senator is really putting on the dog now.*

Another knock at the door was followed closely by the door opening, and this time a forty-something man entered. "Storm, this is my aide, Harrison Connolly. Harrison, this is our hero from the biggest drug bust to ever take place in the great State of Texas." The senator waited as the two men shook hands and sized each other up. "Harrison, did you bring the photographer?"

Harrison was tall and sported a hundred-dollar "public official" haircut. With a name like Harrison, he wasn't a Texas boy, probably from some swanky Ivy League school, David suspected. His hands were soft. *I bet his only exercise is riding a stationary bike in latex bike shorts and a Lycra top with some French or Italian bike company logo emblazoned on the back.* This man is not the sort to ever be a friend of mine, and in all reality, probably not someone to turn your back on, either. His attitude is one of someone who thinks he's moving up in the world and the senator is simply a stepping stone.

"Yessir," answered Harrison as a man with two cameras hung around his neck sauntered through the door and started looking for the best place to pose Storm and the senator for a photo.

"Storm, I hope you don't mind, and this will take very little time from what you have come here to discuss, but when we have a man of your caliber and law enforcement reputation visiting here in the Capital, it is an opportune time to get some photos for the hometown papers." As he finished his sentence, the senator shook Storm's hand again, smiling at the camera. Multiple photos were taken from different points of view in the office, including one showing the senator with his arm around Storm's shoulders.

Senator Rendell dismissed the staff photographer and explained to Storm that by the time he got home the photo should have already hit the Houston, Dallas, San Antonio, and Austin papers. "Harrison here will make sure you get a copy for yourself and I will autograph it before it is sent out. Harrison, boy, why don't you excuse yourself and let me and Storm have some time to ourselves? He didn't come all this way to have you underfoot and he and I have some things to discuss, okay?"

With a wave of his hand the senator made it clear that Harrison was no longer wanted in his office. Storm noted the look on Harrison Connolly's face, as he was not so politely told his services were no longer needed and was dismissed back to the hinterland outside the senator's office. Though he tried to hide his displeasure, he didn't quite accomplish the task. His face says it all, Storm reflected.

The senator pulled free of his suit jacket and returned to his desk, settling into his well-padded leather chair as he indicated to Storm he was to take a seat opposite on the other side of the desk. "So really, Storm, how is my old friend Russ doing?"

Storm's End

Storm had never heard anyone except Mrs. Hildebrandt call Russell's father "Russ," so these two men were either really tight or the senator was hoping to persuade Storm they were. "He is just fine. He and Mrs. Hildebrandt are like second parents to me. Of course they are getting older, but Mr. Hildebrandt still takes his fishing and hunting trips to the Gulf and West Texas, just not as often as he used to."

"You played ball with Junior in college at Tech, didn't you?" asked the senator.

"Yessir. We were roommates in school and he became my best friend." Storm had known ahead of time he would have to go through this line of questioning, and even though it was good-natured, he had always hated talking about his friends with people he didn't know.

"You don't seem anything like Junior. As I remember, he was kind of a gadabout, a woman's man and never content with just one of anything." The senator smiled and acted jovial during the questions, but Storm knew he was trying to see why a man he knew very well and respected very much would call and ask a favor for someone not of blood. "You're a widower, aren't you, Detective?" asked the senator, taking a different tack.

Storm felt himself looking down at his hands as he answered the question. He had known that Angie would come up in the conversation, but he had rarely heard anyone call him a widower. "Yessir, my wife was killed a few years back." With that, Storm looked up again to catch a look at the senator's eyes.

"Russ told me you had found her killer; some dirty DEA agent who had been working for the cartel was the murderer and you found that out when you solved the big drug case in Houston. So what is it I can do for you that you haven't already solved?" asked the senator.

This was where Storm knew he had to do the best job of selling something that he had ever done. "Senator, I see that Mr. Hildebrandt has brought you up to speed. Yes, I know how she was killed and who killed her, but I don't know why. I am trying to make sense of it. During the investigation of her death we never came across any connections with the cartels. She most likely didn't even know how they operated, but she must have come across something that led to her death. The cartels are ruthless, but they don't usually kill people for no reason."

"How do you think I can help you?" asked the senator, sounding as if he was truly trying to understand what he could do.

"You are the sitting chairman of the senate committee that oversees the USTDA, correct?" asked Storm.

"Yes, but how do you think they can help you?"

"On my wife's last trip to Latin America, she met a representative of the USTDA. They visited some of the same plants that Angie's company was looking at to work out a trade and manufacturing agreement. I found this out from her notes that were retrieved during the original investigation into her murder. I was hoping that the USTDA rep who was with her on that trip might remember something, anything out of the ordinary that might have occurred on that trip that might lead me to the reason for her murder." I'm really selling now, Storm admitted to himself. Even if I'm lying, it's by omission, not by changing the facts.

"Then all you want to do is talk to the people over at USTDA to see if any of them was with your wife during that trip and if they remember anything that might help you find out why she was killed, correct?" asked the senator.

"Well," hesitated Storm, "maybe a little more than that. If I can find the person who met her down there, of course I'm hoping they can shed some light on this, but if that doesn't pan out, I would like to go down there to see the same companies she saw with someone from the USTDA, so I go down as part of delegation, not as a cop."

"Then you are talking about a federal agency agreeing to let you travel with them under cover! Are you nuts? This will never happen. We can't afford to have someone snooping around in foreign sovereign nations pretending to be part of a trade delegation!" The Senator seemed visibly shaken by Storm's request.

"Senator, maybe it would be better if they let me accompany them as the husband of a woman who loved their country and who wanted to see the last places she visited before she died?" suggested Storm.

The senator sat quietly for what seemed like an eternity before he answered. "I'll tell you what, Storm; there is a reception tonight for the Taiwanese trade delegation, which just happens to be in Washington right now for a meeting with my committee and the USTDA. Why don't you plan to attend as my guest? I will introduce you to some of the members of the committee and the director and some of his staff. I will also set up a meeting for you with the director's deputy for tomorrow and he can pitch the idea to the USTDA hierarchy, but you will be on your own to convince him and anyone he introduces you to. I will not put any pressure on them to help you with this dog and pony show. Are we clear?" The senator had suddenly become very serious and lost his good ol' boy demeanor.

"Yessir. I appreciate that." Then Storm hesitated and decided he had no choice but to ask. "Senator, I only brought along one other suit and one pair of shoes that aren't boots. What will I need to wear to this shindig?" asked Storm.

The senator reached over and pressed a button on his phone. Immediately the door swung open and an impeccably dressed woman entered. "Mrs. Holmes, this is Detective David Storm from Houston. I have invited him to tonight's soirée and he needs some assistance with the appropriate attire. Would you mind helping him with what he will need to join us?"

Having thus been dismissed, Storm rose from his chair, reached across the desk, and thanked the senator for his time and the invitation. "I promise I'll not embarrass you tonight, Senator," he said with a smile.

Mrs. Holmes retreated and led the way to her desk just outside and to the left of Senator Rendell's office. She asked if Storm had brought a tuxedo.

"Ma'am, I don't even own one," Storm admitted. He thought he was being funny but this woman apparently didn't cotton to levity. She asked his sizes right down to his shoes, writing them all down as he told her. She handed him an embossed envelope that read "Quest" on the cover and explained this was the invitation, which he would have to present to get into the reception. Mrs. Holmes asked for his hotel and room number and told him a dinner jacket, black tuxedo pants, shirt, tie and shoes would be delivered to his room in plenty of time for him to dress and make his way to the Top of the Hay, where the reception was being held. If there was a problem with the formal wear, he was to call immediately to the provider and they would rush the correct sizes over.

"Whatever you do, you are not to wait until the last minute to try the things on," she directed him. With that, he was summarily dismissed like a child from class. He returned to the reception area accompanied by Cyril, took up the umbrella he had borrowed from the hotel and made his way back outside, where the rain had let up.

CHAPTER 18

The dick-measuring contest is over for now, Storm acknowledged with relief. Even though Storm had not been totally forthright with the senator, he felt he had given as well as he had received. The invitation to the gala that night came as a surprise and it worried him. His next meeting with the senator would be in a social surrounding and these types of events never made him feel secure. This would have been a better place for Russell, so it was time to call in the cavalry and talk to Russell. In fact, it amused him that he would have to channel Russell and assume his famous affable urbane manner.

Storm had turned his cell phone off while meeting with the senator out of respect and courtesy for his office. As he pressed the "on" button, the device sprung back to life, showing him he had eight messages, three from Pancho, two from Martin, one from Agent Higgins, and two from Russell. He strolled down Constitution Avenue in no hurry, enjoying the gorgeous day after the soggy morning. The rain had disappeared and was replaced with a bright clear blue sky broken only with those white fluffy clouds, remnants of the earlier storm. The calls could wait until he got back to his room where there would little to no chance of his conversations being overheard.

The hotel lobby was immaculate and the staff stood in their positions like soldiers on a parade ground, their polished uniform buttons gleaming. He didn't know when they cleaned this place but it must have been in the dead of night in order to leave the impression that it always looked this way. His room had been cleaned in his absence, the sheets pulled tight on the bed with hospital corners and the corner of the covers turned back as if inviting him to take a nap. Clean towels replaced the ones he used that morning and the mirror sparkled. His grooming products were placed neatly in a line to facilitate their further use.

Pulling his suit jacket off and hanging it on the back of the ergonomic office chair that sat in front of an office-sized walnut desk, he sat down and picked up the phone. He'd call Pancho first to get the latest on what was happening with Clay and Grady and any other new discovery Pancho may have made since they spoke the night before. Next would be Agent Jones and if things worked out with him, Jones would call Agent Higgins, eliminating that call from Storm's list. His last call and probably his most important would be to Russell. He needed to talk to him and get his expertise. Tonight might be a big deal and he needed some of the Hildebrandt charm to rub off on him if he was going to accomplish anything on this trip.

"Hey, Storm, how did the meeting with the senator go?" Hernandez asked

"I guess it went okay, you know, one of those measuring things, both of us trying to size the other one up," answered Storm.

"He gonna help you get into the trade department?"

"Well, funny you brung that up. I got myself invited to a big shindig for the trade commission and a delegation from Taiwan tonight. They even had some lady that works for the senator order me a tux so I would fit in!" Storm laughed.

Storm's End

"A tux as in a tuxedo as in penguin suit?" repeated Pancho as the inevitable chuckle escaped.

"Yes, asshole, black tie and all. I guess. The senator didn't want this hayseed redneck coming to this bash looking like I just fell off a turnip truck. But the big wheels from the trade commission will be there and the senator told me he would introduce me to them and give me a few minutes alone with the director." Storm was almost out of breath by the time he finished that sentence. Then he shut up and listened to Pancho chuckle on the other end of the phone. "It ain't funny, Hernandez."

"Yes, it is. I can just see your heavyweight ass in a tux. I bet you haven't worn one since your wedding."

"You don't want to bet your ass on it, Pancho. Angie made me buy one a long time ago. She was always trying to drag me somewhere you had to wear one, her and Russell. But you know I am a purist; if I can't wear my boots, I don't go."

"You gonna wear your lizards, then?" asked Pancho.

"I might, Okay, enough of this grinnin' and swattin' at my expense. Let's get down to business. Did Grady hear from Clay?" asked Storm.

"Grady heard from him this morning. Seems your friend Clay got everything he could find and put it on the thumb drive yesterday. He is meeting Grady for lunch like they are old long lost pards to pass the drive to him. Grady said he would call me the minute he has it and bring it over to my house so we can look at it together. Grady's purdy good at looking at stuff like numbers and so I'm sure if there is anything there, we can figure it out and I will call you."

"Good. Let me know as soon as you have it," replied Storm.

"I will. Hey, Jones and Higgins called asking if I had heard from you. Did they call you?" asked Pancho.

"Yeah, both of them called—Jones twice, Higgins once. Guess they are next on my list to call," answered Storm.

"Who else you got to call?" asked Pancho.

"Well, I guess since I'm going to whatever you call this thing tonight, I better call Russell and ask him how I should act," grumbled Storm.

"Yeah, probably your best bet. None of the rest of us would have a clue how to act at one of those fancy back-slappins'. Always remember to lift your pinky finger when you drink something; that is what the rich people do." Again Storm could hear Pancho's laugh.

"Oh, shut the fuck up, Messican, this ain't no Cinco de Mayo party." With that Storm pushed the disconnect button knowing he had left Pancho hangin' and grinnin'.

The next calls were quick and to the point. His first call was to Agent Jones, filling him in on the meeting with the senator earlier in the day and the reception coming up that night. "I'll meet you for lunch at Backalley Bistro on 10th Street," Jones offered. "I have a listening device I need to give you."

Storm then called Higgins, passing on similar information. It was nearing the time he was to meet Jones for lunch. Over a high priced burger Jones reinforced what Storm already knew about how the wire would work. They would be tracking him via the GPS embedded under his skin and how the wire he would wear that night could be hidden much like an earpiece to a hearing aid. There would be no obvious telltale sign of the curly cable behind his ear and he could carry on a normal conversation while all could be heard on the other end. If Jones needed to talk to him he could cut off the voice from Storm's end and speak and Storm would hear him.

After lunch he called Russell, who had just arrived at the station. "Hey, Barretta, how's things in our nation's capital?"

"Just fine. Dang, man, I have never stayed in anything like this hotel before. Glad I'm not paying for it," said Storm.

"Nice, huh? Do the taxpayers know they're footin' the bill?"

"Very funny. I doubt it, but hey, I won't tell if you don't."

"How was Senator 'Stick up His Ass'?" asked Russell.

"Just like you described him. He asked about your dad and, of course, he asked if I was a good friend of 'Junior's'," grinned Storm.

"He did not! Tell me he didn't call me 'Junior'! That fucking old reprobate!" Russell muttered.

"Yep, Juniorrrrrrrrr," snickered Storm, smiling to himself, "and he even acted so familiar with your dad he called him 'Russ.' I've never heard anyone call you 'Juniorrrrr' or your dad 'Russ' before. He was trying to make me believe your family is close to him and what he doesn't know is that I know your dad is just a contributor to his campaigns and doesn't consider himself his friend."

"Well, if you see him again tell him 'Juniorrrrr' says to kiss his ass." Russell sounded pissed that this stump-broke hypocrite was calling him 'Junior.'

"I'll be seeing him again tonight and I'll give him your love. He invited me to some kind of reception for the delegates from Taiwan given by the trade commission He even had one of his secretaries get my sizes so they could order me up the appropriate attire to wear to this thing."

"Whoa, doggies! Now would that be a sight worth seeing—Running Bear, the mad Injun, in a tuxedo. They gonna let you wear your boots to this hoedown?"

"No, they told me the tuxedo shop would even be delivering shoes for me," groused Storm.

"How did this all come about?" Asked Russell.

"Well, I asked the senator if he would introduce me to the people at the USDTA so I could ask about who from their agency had traveled with Angie on her last trip to Latin America. That was when things got a little hinky, or maybe I should say 'that is when he got a little more tentative with his offer for assistance,'" Storm explained.

"What got his hackles up?"

"Nothing really out of line, but you know how you can feel someone is questioning your motives more than they were when you first started talking to them?"

"Did he ask you why you wanted to meet these people?"

"Yes, and I told him all about how we knew who had murdered Angie, but (and here is where I put it all on myself), that I was trying to find some answers as to why she was killed. I told him I wanted to talk to the person who was with her to ask where they went and if anything happened that might have been suspicious or out of the ordinary, things like that," answered Storm.

"Did he buy that?" asked Russell.

"He seemed to and that was when he invited me to the party. He told me the director of the agency, a man named Craig Baltazar, would be there and he could introduce me to him. He also said he would set up a meeting with the deputy director tomorrow morning, but then it was up to me to sell my inquiry to get him to set me up with the director and possibly introduce me to whoever it was that was on that trip. The senator seemed all excited to have what he called "a hometown hero" in town and I got the impression I am going to be his show dog tonight. I have a feeling before he is done telling people about me I will have won the war on drugs all by myself," said Storm.

"Well, my brother, be careful around those people. They are all into power and prestige and they would just as soon slip a knife in your back as help you. You will have to go through some glad-handing and suffer conversations with fools that are all hat and no cowboy, but it sounds like you got a chance to get in."

"Let's hope so. I need to get a chance to talk to these people and see if anybody knows anything about Angie. If I can find out where they went and who they saw, I might be able to get a lead on this smuggling, too."

"Well, since you don't drink anymore, you will keep your wits about you and the best advice I can give is if it's a sit down meal, start with the fork on the far left." Russell snickered, and Storm did, too, knowing a formal dinner in Washington D.C. was way out of his comfort zone.

Just then a knock came at Storm's door and he told Russell he had to go and would call him after Russell got home from his late telecast. The bellman stood in the doorway as Storm opened the door, announcing, "I have a delivery from Georgetown Formal Wear for you, Mr. Storm."

The bellman carried a garment bag along with two boxes, one that obviously held shoes and the other a shirt box. Attached to the hanging bag was an oblong box that had to be the bow tie and cumber bund. The bellman entered the room, placed the boxes on the bed, and hung the bag in the closet as Storm watched. He then turned and told Storm that the front desk had signed for packages but handed him the bill. "This is to be charged to your room, sir," he said.

Storm almost passed out when he looked at the bill; it was $220 for the rental of a tuxedo. Obviously, the senator didn't want him showing up in some half-assed suit. Thank God, this, too, would added to the FBI's bill and not his.

The bellman stood off to the side waiting for a tip. Storm felt like telling him, "Here's my tip: Move out of Washington"—but he gave the man a dollar for the service. He was sure he could hear the man mutter something like "cheap" under his breath.

Storm's End

CHAPTER 19

Storm felt like he was going to his first prom. He dressed and stared at the man in the mirror, amazed that it really was him dressed up so grand. Who would have thought that coming to Washington he would wind up in these glad rags just to be able to talk to a man about his help in finding answers to questions about where his murdered wife had been? With luck, maybe I'll even find out why she might have been killed, he hoped.

He checked the bathroom mirror one last time and decided the tie looked straight, his shirt fit right and the studs and cuff links were all in line, but he was still not sure of himself, as dressy formal suits were not his style. The appointed time had come and he had to go if he was to be at the reception at the hour the invitation said he was to arrive. The Hay Adams was near Lafayette Park, and given the distance to the party location, he would have to take a taxi.

The Willard doormen stood at attention, only breaking formation to open car doors for the arriving patrons or summon cabs for those leaving. The doorman asked if Storm needed a cab and upon his affirmative response, the doorman waved his hand and called for the next taxi in the line to approach the front doors.

Storm's End

"Have a good evening, Detective Storm," said the doorman once again, stunning Storm at the number of hotel staff who knew his name.

"Thank you," said Storm somewhat self-consciously as the doorman opened the taxi door and allowed him to seat himself before he closed it and then moved to the next set of waiting patrons.

"Destination, sir?" asked the cab driver.

"The Hay Adams, please," replied Storm.

The trip was only a couple of miles and when they arrived in front of the historic hotel, there was a line of taxis and limos that stretched almost a block down the street. Storm saw couples arriving dressed in their finest, women in designer gowns and men in dashing formal wear.

The hotel was a busy place tonight with its own clientele as well as with those arriving to attend the function being held on the top floor. Signs in the lobby directed him to an express elevator that would take him to the foyer of the reception at The Top of the Hay.

Staffers, some of whom Storm had seen earlier that day in the senator's office, stood at the doors that led to the reception collecting invitations, while uniformed security guards stood by in case there were any problems. Storm spied Mrs. Holmes, the lady who had ordered his tuxedo, and decided he would give her his invitation and enter the room that way.

"Glad to see you made it, Detective," said Mrs. Holmes. "I see we got the sizes right with the tuxedo, but we must have missed with the shoes," as she looked down at Storm's highly polished black lizard boots.

Looking at the ground sheepishly, Storm let a rare smile cross his face. As he looked back up at Mrs. Holmes, he explained, "Well, it's this way, Mrs. Holmes, the shoes were just fine but the pants were about an inch too long, and well, they broke just right over my boots. See they fall exactly at the top of the heel, just where they are supposed to."

Storm's End

Storm could tell Mrs. Holmes recognized she was being played with and that, being a Texan, he probably felt more comfortable in his boots than in a shiny pair of patent leather shoes. She took his invitation, trying not to smile, and said, "The senator is over there with that group of men, probably solving the world's problems, or more likely, discussing how the Redskins will do this fall." Mrs. Holmes then smiled at Storm and waved her hand in the direction of the senator, dismissing him with a good-natured, "Have a good time, Detective."

Storm noticed the senator was involved in what appeared to be a cordial conversation with what were probably members of the Taiwanese delegation and he decided not to interrupt. At that moment one of uniformed waiters asked him if he cared for a drink. Storm answered the man by asking what type of Coke the man had. The waiter snickered under his breath and impolitely asked where Storm was from. Storm smiled, realizing the waiter knew only Texans asked what type of "Coke" they served when they meant "soft drink."

"A club soda and a slice of lime, please," Storm answered. The chastened waiter left to retrieve the drink. Storm had learned long ago to order a glass of soda with a slice of lime or lemon so that people didn't bother him with questions such as, "You don't drink?" Instead, they just assumed you had a highball and let you be.

The waiter returned with his club soda and then he moved over to the group of men where an interpreter was translating what Senator Rendell was saying for the Asian men. Storm thought to himself, how many of the Asian diplomats, who probably speak excellent English, use the assumption of lack of language skills to their diplomatic advantage? The waiter interrupted the men asking if anyone needed a drink as the senator turned to see Storm waiting to be acknowledged. With a wave of his hand he summoned Storm over to join the group in the conversation.

"Gentlemen, this is Detective David Storm from my constituency in Texas. Detective Storm was one of the members of the local law enforcement group that made one of the biggest drug busts in Texas by helping bring down the kingpin of the Rio drug cartel. Because of his work, millions of dollars of illegal drugs, over two million dollars in cash and the murderers of numerous innocents were taken off the streets of Houston. Detective Storm has come to D.C. to see me on other matters but I felt it would be a great opportunity for you gentlemen to meet one of our best and to give him a chance to see how we work in D.C." The senator was on a roll, praising Storm and law enforcement while showing the men with him that he was a man of the people.

The men all shook hands with Storm as they congratulated him on his fine work and some even asked brief questions, at which time the senator excused himself and Detective Storm. "If you'll be kind enough to excuse us, we have some important matters to discuss," he said with a bow of respect. "Director Baltazar, would you please join us?"

Craig Baltazar was tall, slim, and wiry looking, with a precisely trimmed white mustache and pure white hair that was cut perfectly to frame his tan face. He was a career government employee who had graduated from Yale with a master's degree in international business and had parlayed his education into his prestigious position as Director of the USTDA. This man was a survivor on the Hill and when he was asked to join the senator and this detective from Nowhere, Texas, he took another look at Storm, sizing him up. Storm noted the look, thinking Baltazar had learned a long time ago that you do as the senior senator who presides over the committee with oversight of your agency asks you to do, but you never put yourself in a position where something might come back to bite you.

The three men walked out onto the balcony of the Hay as Storm momentarily appreciated its view of the White House. Harrison Connolly, the chief aide to the senator,

Storm's End

followed along but hung back in a blocking position at the doorway so the men would not be intruded upon and their conversation wouldn't be overheard. "Craig," the senator started, "Detective Storm came to Washington looking for my help and I have agreed to assist him if I can.

"About six years ago the detective's wife was killed in Houston. He actually was the one who found her shot to death lying on the front porch of their home. For a long time there was no explanation for her murder. She had no enemies, she was a successful businesswoman, and there was never a suspect found. In the case, the Rio Cartel case I mentioned earlier, more than a dozen murders were solved. In doing the forensics, they discovered that one of the confiscated guns had been used in the murder of the detective's wife and it was also the same gun used to kill at least four other people in the Houston area. The FBI is now running those ballistics against other unsolved murders throughout the United States and the Mexican authorities are using those same ballistics to determine if any of their unsolved cases might be linked to the same weapon. Here is where you come in and here is where I will let Detective Storm explain to you what you might do to help him find out not only who, as we think we know that, but why his wife was killed."

Now it was Storm's turn to convince this high roller to help him. "Director Baltazar, I came to Washington to see the senator to ask him if he would help me get an appointment with you. You see, my wife was a vice president of sales and member of the management team for an international company, Global Underwater Marine in Houston. They supply drilling tools and mud additives to drillers all over the world. On her last business trip she was in Latin America and one of your personnel accompanied her on that trip. The only thing I know is that they visited drilling operations and drilling companies wanting to joint venture with GUMDI. I was hoping I could impose on you to introduce me to the person who was with her on that trip. I know it's a long shot, but they might remember if there was anything suspicious or out of the ordinary about the people they met with or if anyone might have wanted to harm my wife."

Baltazar stood as still as a statue. He hadn't moved since Storm had begun to speak—it seemed not even his eyes had blinked. "What do you possibly think someone who traveled with your wife six years ago might remember, Detective?"

"Director, I don't know. They may not remember anything, but surely it wouldn't be a big waste of their time to spend just an hour with me," said Storm.

"Craig, who was your person in charge of Latin America in those days?" asked Senator Rendell.

"Robert Dacosta," answered the director. "But, Senator, he died nearly five-and-a-half years ago. He had a heart attack and died at home in McLean."

"You replaced him, didn't you?" asked the senator.

"Yessir, Victoria Marcuccio was promoted and took that position."

"Victoria, hmm, Detective, you are indeed fortunate. Vicky is sharp, smart, and knows Latin America like the back of her hand—and she's lovely. Craig, would she still have records going back that far?"

"Yes, most certainly. Some might be archived, but she would have access to them."

"You have any problems getting the detective with Vicky and asking her to show him trip reports and interview notes from that trip?" asked the senator.

Storm read the expression on Baltazar's face. *He knows this is less of a request than it is a statement of fact. He recognizes marching orders and now he is expected to carry them out.*

"Yes, of course, Senator. In fact we could introduce the detective to Victoria tonight. She is supposed to be here already, as she is Harrison's date for the night. I saw her earlier today and she told me she would be meeting

Harrison here at the reception and was looking forward to meeting the delegation."

Storm realized Harrison had overheard the entire conversation. *He's well aware that Victoria filled the position vacated with the death of Dacosta. He doesn't look happy at having to share his precious time with her with some hayseed from Texas like me.* But Storm understood the protocol: Harrison also knew where his bread was buttered and you didn't argue with the senator about such trivial matters.

The senator flicked his hand, indicating he wanted Harrison to join the conversation. "Harrison, is Vicky here yet?"

"No sir, she hasn't arrived yet. You know how she relishes the idea of making an entrance." Harrison smiled as if the remark was offhand but Storm could by the smiles of his companions that they knew what she was like.

"Well, when she arrives, I want you to find me, Craig, and the detective. I want her to understand she is to help this man in any way she can. Understood?" Again, Storm recognized an order, not a request.

"Yes, Senator, as soon as she arrives." Harrison looked downcast. *He can feel his night and his plans to romance the beautiful woman slipping through his hands,* Storm acknowledged silently.

The meeting was over. Harrison left to wait just inside the doors to catch Victoria as soon as she arrived. Director Baltazar mingled with other members of his oversight committee, while the senator took Storm with him to introduce him to other dignitaries and go on *ad nauseam* about the Rio drug case.

* * *

Victoria Marcuccio arrived at exactly the time she had planned, forty-five minutes after the scheduled time for the reception to begin. Her hair was worn down, falling just below the bottom of her neck and draping to each side of her shoulder line, framing her face with bangs that swept to the side just above her eyebrows. Her hair was black and in the fluorescent light shown as if it had a dark purple blue tint to it, much like the wings of a raven. Her eyes sparkled dark brown with small gold flecks that were only visible if you were allowed close enough to see them.

Victoria was the definition of the word *regal*. She was 5'8" and athletic, with a beautiful figure. Although she was tall, she never slouched and always carried herself with all the majesty of a woman sure of her place in the world and in the moment. As she emerged from the elevator, a hush fell over the guests mingling in the foyer. She was the type of woman who was both admired and hated. Men loved her; they were speechless when in her presence and although the women envied her effect on men, they hated her for it, too. The beaded teal blue gown hugged every inch of her body. It was cut low in the front but covered bare skin with a matching modest beaded jacket that gave just a hint of the curves that lay underneath, leaving onlookers wondering just how voluptuous she really was.

When she entered the room, Harrison beamed, his expression telegraphing, "You're here to meet me." He's not yet aware of the fact she's here for no one but herself, Storm realized. As she entered, Harrison offered her his arm and escorted her over to say hello to the senator and director. As the eyes in the room followed this lovely creature, the senator took her hand. "Vicky, it is nice to see you, and as always, you look enchanting."

"Thank you, Senator," said Victoria with a tight smile. She doesn't like being called "Vicky," Storm guessed.

"And might I say you look your usual dignified self?"

Victoria turned and acknowledged the director. "Sir, you look very handsome tonight, as well, and it is nice to see you in a social setting, rather than in the office."

"Victoria, you look stunning, but have your ears been burning?" asked Baltazar.

The senator turned to Harrison. "Harrison, get this lovely lady something to drink, would you? Vicky, what would you like? Whiskey and branch water like me, or would you prefer champagne?"

"Champagne, Harrison, if you don't mind," answered Victoria.

He left the group.

He feels like a schoolboy in more than one way, Storm guessed. First, he's over the moon that Victoria is his date, and on the other hand, the senator has just ordered him about as if he's a fraternity pledge.

"Now what were you saying about my ears ringing, Director?" asked Victoria.

Senator Rendell took charge. "Vicky, this is Detective David Storm from Houston. This boy is a hero in Texas and he needs your help."

* * *

Victoria had seen the man with the senator and director when she had walked up, but she knew the senator would get around to introducing them at his pleasure. She had serendipitously looked the big mustached man with the salt-and-pepper hair up and down before she was introduced and had immediately noticed the cowboy boots, which moved him out of the category of Washington movers and shakers. She knew his name and knew he had been part of the drug bust that had taken down a Mexican cartel, as the sting had even made the Washington papers. Victoria turned her full attention on the man standing beside the senator and extended her hand. "Hello. Do I call you 'Detective' or 'Mr. Storm' or 'David'?"

"Just 'Storm' will be fine, ma'am." She could already tell Storm was like all other men; he was stunned by her.

She knew something about her had affected him like a surge of electricity. Next he'll feel like he's known me forever, she knew.

"Storm, then, what have these two boys told you I might help you with?" asked Victoria, having decided he was as pliable as every other man she had ever met. Before long he, too, would tell her all his secrets.

Before Storm could answer Baltazar interjected, "Are you available tomorrow, Victoria?"

Turning back to the director, she responded, "Yessir. I have a meeting at the Argentine Embassy tomorrow morning and then lunch with the ambassador but I will be back in the office by, let's say, two tomorrow afternoon. Would that be okay with you, David?" she smiled at Storm and continued, "I'm sorry, but the name 'David' just seems to suit you better."

Storm knew he was very much caught in her web. He just smiled and answered, "Yes."

"Okay, then I will see you at 2:00 p.m. tomorrow. Is there anything I will need to prepare to help a policeman from Houston?"

"As a matter of fact, yes. Before you go to Embassy Row tomorrow, could you have one of your assistants pull the files on your predecessor's trip to Latin America from—when was it, Detective? What time of year?" asked the Director.

"September of 2000, sir," answered Storm.

"September of 2000, Victoria."

Harrison had just returned with Victoria's champagne when the senator announced, "Okay that is all taken care of, so why don't we all enjoy the party now? Tomorrow will come soon enough and it will be back to work again."

Questions swirled through Victoria's head as she repeated the conversation for Harrison later.

***

Meanwhile, Storm was having trouble concentrating on anything but the image of this mesmerizing woman. He had no place at this party anymore and decided to leave. He thanked the senator for inviting him and was about to leave when Mrs. Holmes caught his arm. "Beware of the viper, the snake with the long black hair," she whispered. He could only guess what she was alluding to, so he ignored her recommendation.

Storm's End

CHAPTER 20

Martin was sitting across the street from the Hay when he saw Storm come out of the doors. He immediately started the car, pulled a U-turn and caught Storm before the doorman had time to hail him a cab. Looking through the window, Storm recognized Martin and got into the passenger's seat.

"You following me now?" asked Storm.

"Yep, exactly what I'm doin'. As long as you are working with the FBI and you are in D.C., I or someone we trust will be like your shadow. You don't go anywhere without us now," answered Martin.

"Well, all I want to do right now is go back to my hotel and get some rest," said Storm.

"Good. I'm going with you. How did the party go?" asked Martin.

"It was what it was. At home we would call it a "flash and trash" night. Ooooh whee! So many colossal egos and power hungry people, all standing with their backs to the wall to keep from gettin' stuck. But the senator came through and I have an appointment with the woman who took over the job when her predecessor, who was in Latin America with Angie, suddenly died," said Storm.

"Who is she?" asked Martin.

"Her name is Victoria something . . . yeah, her last name is Marcuccio," answered Storm.

"Okay. We need to do a background check on her and see who she is before you go to that meeting. What time is the confab with her tomorrow?"

"Two tomorrow afternoon," Storm said absently, still thinking about Victoria. Something about her stuck in his mind, something that bothered him, not in a suspicious way but how she made him feel. He found himself sitting in the car with Martin unable to concentrate on anything but the image of Victoria Marcuccio.

"What happened to the guy who had the job before her?" asked Martin.

"They said he had a heart attack a few months after that trip," answered Storm.

Storm looked at Martin. He knew Martin's FBI training was kicking in and his mind was beginning to race. "Does that sound a little strange to you? Your wife is murdered by, until now, an unknown assailant and a few months later the man from the trade commission who was with her on her final trip dies of a heart attack?"

"It didn't 'til I heard you say it, but I guess it does sound a little hinky." Storm was lost in his own world and having trouble following Martin's line of thinking.

"Damn, Storm, somebody in there really got you distracted," said Martin, grinning at him.

"What? Me? I'm not distracted." As soon as he answered he admitted to himself that his reaction had been entirely too quick.

"When a man looks like the cat that just ate the canary, it has to be a woman and I'd say it might be this woman you have the meeting with tomorrow. She must really be something," laughed Martin.

When they got back to the hotel Martin went in with Storm and followed him to his room. Storm had two messages on his cell phone from Pancho and they decided they would call him together to see what was up. Since it would be somewhat like a conference call, Storm used the laptop so they could do a secure video call. First they had to call Pancho on the secure cell phone and then both powered up their laptops to use the application the FBI had installed to video and voice conference.

"Pancho, you called? What's up?" Asked Storm, as Pancho's image filled the screen.

"Hey, Storm. I see you have company. Hello, Agent Jones," greeted Pancho.

"Hello, Sergeant."

"Okay, now that we got all that out of the way, what you got?" Storm was tired and needed to move this conference along.

"Grady got your stuff from your buddy Clay," answered Pancho.

"Anything of interest on it?" asked Storm.

"Grady and I looked at it all afternoon, but all we got is a bunch of shipping manifests and some emails from your wife back to the office looking for status reports on the orders and when they would be shipped. One report-looking document talks about some company in Panama that wants to do some sort of partnership with her company, but nothing so far that would tell us anything about why she might have been targeted or anything that points to anything illegal," explained Pancho.

"Keep digging through them, Pancho. There has to be something there. Did Clay think he got everything?" asked Storm.

"From what he told Grady he thought he did, but he said if he found anything more he would leave Grady a message. We got Grady a burn phone so it can't be traced, just in case. He left that number with Clay," answered Pancho.

"Good, what else is going on?" asked Storm.

"FBI got another cryptic letter today," said Pancho.

Storm turned to Martin and he only needed a look to pass on the unspoken question of why Martin had somehow neglected to tell him that yet.

Martin sputtered, "Detective, I was going to tell you. We just got back and immediately got on phone with the Sergeant. I'm tellin' you the truth! It was next on my list of things."

"What did this one say?" asked Storm of Martin.

"Like the others it doesn't make a lot of sense. It said, *'The islands have regular visitors some known, some not recorded.'* That is it. We still don't know what the last one meant by 'islands'," said Martin.

"Pancho, is there anything about islands or Angie going to islands in the stuff Clay gave you?" queried Storm.

"Nothing so far. Did you get a meeting with Trade Commission?" asked Pancho.

"Yep, tomorrow afternoon at two," said Storm.

"Who you meeting with?" asked Pancho

"A woman named Victoria Marcuccio. She replaced the man Angie traveled with that last week in Latin America."

Martin quickly jumped in and added, "She must be something else! Your pard here has had a dreamy look on his face since he came out of that shindig."

They both saw the smile on Pancho's face and the surprise in his eyes. As long as he had been working with the detective he had never seen Storm give any woman a second thought or look. "Damn, Storm, I think Russell is rubbing off on you," Pancho grinned.

"Forget that! Agent Jones is putting thoughts in my head and my mouth, although he did have a thought about something that I didn't catch. The man from the USTDA who traveled with Angie died shortly after he got back, too. They said it was a heart attack. However, Agent Jones thinks that may be a little too convenient. It does seem strange a little coincidental that the man who was on the same trip as Angie died shortly after he got back, as well. They did say it was natural causes, but I think we need to get either the FBI or Alisha to run down the autopsy and see if anything looks suspicious," Storm told Pancho.

"I will talk to Agent Higgins in the morning to see if he thinks it will be easier for them to get the report or if it would cause less suspicion if Alisha called her counterpart in, what county is it in Virginia?" asked Pancho.

"I'm not sure. He lived in McLean, so whatever county that is," answered Storm. "Either way, get the information to Alisha, understood?"

Pancho understood exactly. This was a small team and they all knew they could trust Alisha. "You got it. I will look up the county name tomorrow after I have talked to Higgins."

"Okay. We are done for now, but if something comes up call me immediately." Storm signed off. In fact, let's have a conference call tomorrow to firm up each of our assignments."
"No problem, boss. Get some sleep, you have a date tomorrow." Pancho was grinning as he cut off the video feed.

"Okay, Martin, time for you to get out of here, too. I need some sleep." Storm opened the door to his room, making sure Martin knew it was time to leave. They made arrangements for breakfast in the morning and he was gone.

Storm went to bed feeling like he was cheating on Angie. All he could think about was this woman Victoria and he hated it. The teasing from Martin and Pancho hadn't helped the situation.

**

As office hours began in the Harris County Medical Examiner's office, Alisha was surprised to find she had a call from Hernandez. She had been told that Storm and Pancho were working with the FBI on Angie's murder and looking into Angie's last week of life. She was also aware that Storm was in Washington and hoped something bad had not happened, as she seldom got a call from Pancho.

Relief came minutes later as she talked to Pancho, but she was surprised at what she had just been asked to do. "Meet me at my house. I'm working on something with Grady," he had told her. She gathered her briefcase and signed out as if she was headed down to Police headquarters.

Grady's car was already parked in front of Pancho's home, as was Russell's. Now she was really confused. None of them were to play much of role in this investigation, so why were they all getting together at Pancho's?

Grady saw her pull up and waited with the door open as she entered. Alisha looked at him and asked, "What's got everybody's panties in a knot today?"

"No idea, dear girl, but we are all here and Storm and the Feebees will be on a video conference pretty soon. They've just been waitin' for you to get here." Grady shrugged.

When everyone was seated at Pancho's dining room table, he pointed to the built-in camera so they could place themselves where they could be seen. The laptop spooled a small picture of the four participants at Pancho's along with one of Agents Higgins and Long and finally one of Storm and Martin.

Agent Higgins began. "Welcome, everyone. I know this is very much an unconventional way for us to talk, but due to time and necessity it was the quickest and most secure way to get us all together. This morning after Detective Storm and Agent Jones had time to review some of the information they got last night we felt it was in all of our best interests to hold this meeting and kick around some ideas of how to pursue what we know. Detective, why don't you take it from here?"

"Good morning, everyone. Thank you, Alisha, for coming, and, Russell, I can't believe we got you out of bed this early," grinned Storm.

With his latte in hand, Russell looked at the laptop and said, "I was coming over this morning, anyway. I wanted to look at the stuff Grady got from your friend. Now what is this all about?"

"Last night I went to the reception I told you the senator had invited me to and he again told me to tell 'Juniorrrrr' hello." Storm even amused himself with that as he saw the people at Pancho's looking at Russell and snickering. "While we were talking I picked up some Intel that really didn't sink in 'til Martin questioned it when I repeated it. The man from the USTDA who traveled with Angie on that last trip died within weeks of getting back. Martin thinks, and I agree, that this might be more than a coincidence and we need get our hands on the autopsy. Alisha that is where you come in. However we acquire it, I want you to go over it to see if you find anything out of the ordinary."

"How am I going to get my hands on an autopsy from another jurisdiction?" She looked totally confused.

"Can't you just call the ME out there and request it?" asked Pancho.

"Absolutely not! Do you think I would give out our records to somebody I don't know from Adam? I would want to know who needed them, why and what they were looking for." Alisha just shook her head like that was the dumbest thing she had ever heard. "Can't the FBI get them?" asked Alisha.

"Same thing, Dr. Johnson. If we go into Fairfax, Virginia asking for the autopsy on a guy that died six years ago there will be red flags everywhere. First, we have no jurisdiction. We would need a federal prosecutor to call the county and ask for assistance and you know we have to keep this off the books or someone will find out what we are looking into," responded Agent Higgins looking frustrated.

While Alisha had been listening to his answer she had an idea. "But there is another way, Agent Higgins. The FBI is always in our offices doing audits of procedures. They check records, they look at the handling of evidence, and they check medical records. All you have to do is get your office to pull an unannounced audit of the Fairfax County Medical Examiner's office and you can look at everything."

Storm's End

"Now you're talking! The Director of the FBI knows what we are doing and I'm sure if I go to the assistant director telling him why we want to look into this and do it under the guise of an audit, we can go look at the records and get out without anyone being any the wiser," speculated Martin, excitement on his face.

"Martin, all you have to tell them is you are doing an audit of records and chain of evidentiary custody. The FBI does it all the time. They do it to protect the citizens and as a CYA move. Although you can't remove anything as the records can't be moved during an audit and everything has to be secured unless there are problems, you can find the autopsy you are looking for and photograph the pages. You can then send them to me and I can go over them, looking for misinformation. Of course, if I find something, the problem will be getting a tissue sample if it turns out I need one. If it comes to that, you can't take the whole sample, only a part of it, or someone will know it's gone missing. County MEs are not as trusting as they once were. We will have to run a tight ship or any evidence we turn up can be ruled out as tainted and we'll be right back where we started from with the guilty person going free."

Alisha sounded stern when she delivered that news, but they all knew she had been through having her records checked and the chain of custody reviewed and it had not been fun. That was what had gotten her predecessor fired, leaving the job open for her. Now nothing left her office without tracking papers filed in triplicate.

"What was the dead guy's name?" asked Pancho.

"Dacosta, Frank Dacosta," answered Storm.

"Okay, thank you, agents, and thank you, Russell, Grady, Pancho, and especially you, Alisha. I will be home soon and fill you all in on my big trip to D.C." With that, Storm cut the video feed knowing Martin had a job to do. The sooner the better.

CHAPTER 21

Back in Houston, Clay Martin sat at his desk filing reports and keeping up with his paper. After a day of intrigue the day before he was relieved that he had completed the favor that Detective Storm had asked of him. Ted Sloan, Clay's boss, was out of town on one of the many trips the VP of Sales had to make and his empty office left Clay to his own devices to fulfill his job responsibilities. Clay had no real desire to be anything more than the man who helped his boss do the best job he could. He had adored Angie and she had told him he was her right arm. She had depended on him to keep her on the right track and now he did the same thing for Ted. Ted too, was a good boss, but there had never been the connection between them there had been between he and Angie. Ted was not Angie—he was more distant and the relationship was more employee and boss, which was okay with Clay; it worked well for both of them.

Clay was just finishing the daily shipment totals and status reports when he got an instant message on his personal cell phone. It read, "*Found another of those herrings you were asking about the other day. You can pick up central market.*" Instant messages were ways underlings in the company could pass information along to each other without using the main computer server and they weren't traceable if management asked to see records of intercompany communication. It was simple really; most of the tech savvy employees had personal cell phones and most had billing plans that allowed them to access the Internet via those phones. If someone wanted to pass a message, they would simply go online via phone, tap into their social network and send a message. Only trusted colleagues knew of this system and the number of people involved was kept small for security reasons. Usually the information passed was about office rumors or plans for gatherings after work for the inner circle. At these social gatherings they would discuss the rumors and facts, trying to stay ahead of anything management have had in mind to change with the company.

This message was different; the herring reference was for him only and Clay immediately knew it had something to do with the information he had requested Clive Beasley, an archival clerk in the IT department, to be on the lookout for. The "central market" referred to the company mailroom where there were individual mailboxes for the employees. The boxes usually contained copies of orders, tracking printouts, and letters from clients and vendors. Even though this was the "data age," management had a hard time not using hard copies for anything less than a year old. Many times management preferred holding a hard copy of a document rather than seeing it on a screen. It had always been Clay's function to pick up those documents after they were printed to catalog them for Ted's perusal in case he wanted to see them. What Clive was sending him would be mixed in with current documents so as not to be discovered and Clay would have to wade through them to find the one sent especially for him.

Clay went to central mail room at his regular time, picked up the latest documents and forms, and returned to his desk. He then began the task of time/date stamping each report and sorting them as to function for storage in the appropriate binder. Clay was methodical and his work always showed it. As he worked his way through the pile, he found the document Clive had sent him and the accompanying reports that went with it. It was an email from Angie asking him for a return report and that specific return report was attached.

Clive had found something he had missed and without asking why he had sent it on to Clay. Now it was Clay's turn to try to figure out why she had made the request and what it could possibly mean. Clay smiled thinking of how people called him "a jolly good fellow," but he also knew some of them didn't know he was also a very analytical man. He could look at reports full of numbers, and could add and subtract in his head much like the Rain Man in the popular film. It only took him a few minutes of scanning the report to find the irregularities. He knew he had to call Grady and get this information to him ASAP, as he felt he might have found a clue to the death of one of his best friends.

* * *

Storm had spent most of the morning going over what he knew and didn't know. It was like watching paint dry waiting to get home in the middle of the investigation. Martin had been at the Hay for breakfast but had left to meet with the assistant director of the FBI to fill him in on what they had to do to follow up on a suspicion and get into the Fairfax County medical examiner's records.

Since sitting around the hotel on a beautiful day made no sense to him and since he was not doing anyone any good sitting idle, he decided he would walk the Mall and see some of the monuments he had not already seen. Martin had his cell phone number and he had told Storm that he should be back by lunchtime and would take him to his meeting with, as he laughingly reminded Storm, "that woman who fascinated you." As hard as Storm tried he couldn't get the image of the Victoria Marcuccio out of his head. She had lingered in his mind and he didn't have a clue why. It was something he needed to get past if he was going to do his job.

The Mall was full of tourists who, like him, were looking at the memorials and musing at the history they depicted. After all, this was his nation's capital and the monuments were symbols of the people who had given so much to make the USA the greatest country in the world. His biggest thrill came when he took the guided tour of Arlington Cemetery. The people on the tour were allowed to walk among the graves and read the markers, but what bought him up short was the grave of President John F. Kennedy. He remembered being only a boy when his middle school principle made the announcement that the President had been killed, and in Texas, no less. He remembered children crying and teachers not seeming to know what to tell them. He remembered they were let out of school to stay home and watch the funeral on television, as their teachers and administration knew it was a country-changing moment in history. His parents were still alive then and all he could think of at the time was how devastated he would be if he lost one of them.

The cell phone rang. "Storm."

"Martin," replied Agent Jones. "Where are you?"

"Just about back to the hotel, maybe a couple of blocks," answered Storm.

"Stay there. I will pick you up, we'll go get some lunch and I'll take you over to your meeting."

After returning to the hotel Storm waited outside for Martin. In only a few minutes the nondescript car used by cops and federal agents pulled up in front and Storm got in.

"How did your morning go?" asked Martin.

"Good. Got tired of hangin' around the hotel so went to see some of the sights, 'cause God knows when I will get a chance to come back to this place. How was your visit with the assistant director?" asked Storm.

"Good. We're going to run an unanticipated review of their records. We will get in and get out unless we find something that warrants an investigation and let's hope that doesn't happen. We want to this to be under the radar," answered Martin.

"Great. How long will it take you do that and get out?" asked Storm.

"Just tomorrow, we hope. We will catch them off guard and have another agent acting as lead. She will take care of the ME while I look at the records. I will take pictures and look for samples if there are any left. We will wrap it up when I notify the agent in charge when I've found what we need, and off we go. It's procedure to do these kinds of surprise checks, so our cover should stay intact," answered Martin. "What do you want to eat?"

"Something that don't cost twenty dollars! This is the most expensive place I have ever been. I don't know how people live up here," groused Storm.

"Yep, and figure most of us are living on government paychecks paid for by taxpayers! But, the good news is I know a place with a good burger that will only cost you about eight bucks." Martin smiled at Storm. "I keep forgetting—you've never been out of Texas."

"So what did you find out about this Marcuccio woman?" asked Storm.

"Well, the boss knew who she was. First thing he did was whistle when I said her name and said she was a looker," replied Martin, grinning at him sideways.

"Did he now?" The smile on Storm's face made it obvious he could have told Martin that himself.

"Looks to me like you already knew that, though." Martin grinned.

"Anything else?" asked Storm.

"Yep, she is from a wealthy Italian family who came to Virginia sometime after the Civil War. They were truck garden people raising cash crops who bought up pieces of land nobody else thought were worth the trouble. They sold fruit and vegetables to the steadily growing population of D.C. and Virginia. When a restaurant couldn't pay its bill, the family would take the business. Pretty soon, they owned a nice share of the eatery business in and around D.C. They added more land as it became available and hired people to work their farms. Some of the family worked the restaurants while others ran the farms. That was until Victoria's grandfather saw the opportunity to expand the family business into land development. He developed those vegetable patches closest to D.C. into nice affordable housing for the masses of people moving to the D.C. area. He offered single family homes close enough to the city to commute but far enough away to be considered in the country. He also built apartment housing and commercial space, some of which the family retained for more eateries." Martin was reciting the family history as the assistant director had related it to him.

"Victoria's mother's generation was the first to be included in Virginia society. The family had become quite wealthy but being recent immigrants, they were looked down upon and not included in the social registry. With their growing wealth they were behind the creation of many philanthropic ventures serving the greater D.C. area, Arlington, and Fairfax County.

Constance Marcuccio, Victoria's mother, and her cousins were the first of the family to be raised in privilege. They attended private schools and were afforded the very best in education. During her college years, Constance went to Italy and met and married an Italian count, but the count was killed in an accident while driving a racecar through the Italian Alps. Constance was pregnant when he was killed and soon after her young daughter Victoria was born, she returned with the child to America.

"Victoria became the apple of her grandfather's eye; she wanted for nothing and like her mother, was sent to the best of schools. She was a very smart girl and was accepted to

Georgetown for undergrad, then attended Georgetown Law School. As you can imagine, the family had become quite large now with Victoria having at least thirty cousins all vying for jobs in the family. Victoria was the oddity. She wanted to use her education working in a field that was related to her degree. She applied for a job with USTDA and was immediately accepted. They put her through the typical background check and she came back squeaky clean. She has been with the commission now for twelve years and has risen to the position of regional director for Latin America with her last promotion. She was appointed to her current position on the death of Robert Dacosta.

"She is the heartbreaker of D.C. from what I have heard. She is beautiful, but I can tell you knew that already. Powerful and wealthy men from every country have pursued her and she has yet to marry. She seems a determined woman and whatever her goals are, so far they have not included a man in her life," finished Martin.

"So, she has been regional director for Latin America for the last five years?" asked Storm.

"Yep. She seems to love Central and South America and according to those who know, she's very content to remain where she is for the time being," answered Martin.

"Guess I will get a chance to judge her for myself this afternoon, won't I?" smirked Storm.

"I guess so, and from your dreamy state last night I think she already has you in her web." Martin laughed at the idea that Storm might be smitten, but Storm merely looked at him and mouthed the words, "Bite me."

After lunch, Martin escorted Storm to the USTDA headquarters not far from where Storm had been at Arlington Cemetery that morning. He told him he would wait for him and take him back to his hotel.

If this meeting went well, David planned to go home the next day. He was happy to be headed back and get his feet soundly planted on good ol' Houston Caliches and clay dirt.

Storm's End

CHAPTER 22

Pancho and Grady sat perusing the new sheets Grady had picked up from Clay over lunch. The two had met at a taquería on the edge of the Southwest Loop in an area quickly becoming a barrio. The place was small with tables that people had to share, so when they entered separately and ordered their meals and both happened to sit at the only table available as it would appear nothing more than happenstance. When he got up to leave, Clay left a folded newspaper on the table, so the older man who had been sitting across from him asked if he was through with it. Clay assured him he was done with it and left. Grady glanced at the paper, saw the report sheets had been tucked inside, he refolded the paper, and took it with him after he finished his barbacoa tacos.

The email from Angie to her company's shipping department had been sent just two days before she was to return home. She had requested bills of lading for one particular offshore rig. She wanted copies of all recent and pending shipments for that rig. Pancho and Grady read the email and now concentrated on the reports. So far they looked mundane, but there had to be something there, or why had she asked for them? The longer they studied them the less they felt like they were seeing anything. Pancho told Grady, "We need someone from the oil patch to bounce ideas off of, someone who was familiar with such reports that we can trust."

Grady agreed. "That someone needs to not be associated with the team so he can remain totally anonymous."

Pancho thought a minute. "Before we bring someone new in, we need to clear it with Storm and probably the FBI. It'll have to wait until we can talk to him."

* * *

Victoria had been meeting with the Argentine Agricultural Commission on the possibility of collaborating with more American distributors to increase shipments from Argentine vineyards. Argentine wines had become very popular with American consumers, but they were the target of a growing lobby of wine producing areas of the United States that were calling for a freeze on imported wines from South America and Australia. In her meetings Victoria played more the role of diplomat than one of advocate. She explained to the Argentines that with an ever-growing presence of wine producing states in the United States, congressional representatives and senators from those states were pushing to further reduce the imports from Argentina. The best she could do is work with the powers that be to assure them that the foreign sources could continue to export the amounts already granted them.

The meeting had been somewhat contentious but in the end, the commission knew it was the best she could do. They also knew she had helped many companies participate in commercial ventures that were very important to the growth and stability of Argentina. The head of the commission invited Victoria to lunch afterwards but she declined, as she knew she had to be back in her office to meet with the dark and somewhat intriguing detective from Houston.

Storm's End

After Storm had left the reception the night before Victoria had spent most of the rest of the evening with Harrison working the crowd of the powerful and wannabe powerful. She had subtly questioned Harrison about Detective Storm and what he was looking for. Harrison was as pliable in her hands as PlayDoh® in the hands of a child. She could always get him to tell her anything without his having a clue he was revealing anything important. He told her all about Storm and the fact that he was investigating the death of his wife some five or six years earlier.

"What does he think I can help him with, Harrison?" asked Victoria.

"He has some silly idea her death might have something to do with her last trip out of country," replied Harrison.

"Was she in Latin America?" she asked.

"Yes, in fact, her last trip was with your predecessor," said Harrison.

"Is that right? What did she do?" asked Victoria.

"She was a big wheel for a company out of Houston that manufactures and supplies materials used in drilling platforms, something to do with equipment and additives." She sensed Harrison was becoming bored with her questions about the detective and she realized he was more concerned with showing off to his fellow staffers that he was with the most sought after woman in D.C. Recognizing his tedium with her questions, Victoria surrendered to his vanity and played the role of gracious escort to a man she thought of as nothing more than an empty suit whose only redeeming feature was that he was the assistant to a man she needed because he could share information important to her.

Before the meeting with the Argentines, she had seen her boss and he had informed her of many of the same things Harrison had. He had also told her she would need to get her secretary to go to the tombs and pull the trip reports Dacosta had written the week after the trip he had made with the detective's wife. When Victoria had taken over his job, she had read all his notes and reports to better familiarize herself with the people she would be working with and nothing seemed to jump out as earth shattering. Still, *I need to reread them before my two o'clock with the detective*, she realized.

* * *

Storm was amazed at the proximity of offices to one another when a person was dealing with agencies of the federal government. Whether the weather outside was temperate or not, a person could walk to most appointments. Even going to the other side of river to meet Victoria was no big deal. The drive had taken Martin only ten minutes to traverse the streets from their lunch café, so that he arrived at the USTDA headquarters fifteen minutes before his appointment.

The lobby elevator took him to the eleventh floor and when the doors opened, he was surprised to find an office of gleaming glass and metal supports. Cubicles filled the interior space surrounded by large, presumably executive offices on the outside walls. The director's office and those of a few of his immediate subordinates had blinds on their doors and walls to create at least the illusion of a private office, but most of the others were open so natural light could filter through the entire space, adding to the open feeling.

A reception desk sat behind the doors etched with USTDA in large letters that were the focal point of the floor. The receptionist was the gatekeeper of this agency and to her right or his left was a miniature lobby/waiting area for people who had come here for meetings. As the entry doors opened, the receptionist looked up with her telephone earpiece connected to her ear and asked if she might be of help.

"I'm Detective David Storm here to see Victoria Marcuccio." Storm was studying the woman behind the desk.

She is obviously not some low level minion. This woman is well dressed and very polished. She has the capacity and presumably the authority to grant access or deny it.

"Yes, Detective Storm, I believe your appointment is for two o'clock." She looked down at her computer screen to verify her statement. "Ms. Marcuccio's assistant will be up to get you at the appointed time. Meanwhile, why don't you have seat?" With a faux smile and wave of her hand, she directed him to the small seating area to the right of her desk.

Exactly at the appointed hour, an impeccably dressed woman appeared in the lobby like an apparition. She was tall, almost as tall as Victoria, and dressed in a very proper business suit fitted to her slim lean body. Her skin was very dark but with a pearly luster. Her accent was somewhat clipped as if English was her second language with just a hint of a proper English education.

"Mr. Storm, I am Naomi Ware, Ms. Marcuccio's secretarial assistant. If you'll follow me, please."

Storm stood and extended his hand, "Hello, Miss Ware, it's my pleasure to meet you."

Ms. Ware neither took his hand nor flashed a polite smile; she merely turned on her heel expecting him to follow.

Storm was seated in a guest chair in front of the desk in what was a very nice, very organized office. The few papers on the desk were arranged in exacting small stacks. There was a vase of flowers (from a possible admirer?) and a photograph of Victoria with an older woman he assumed was her mother.

As he looked around the room, he recalled his training in how to read someone's office. This lady was organized and liked to control her environment. She had other photos of friends and family on her wall. One picture showed Victoria halfway down a sheer cliff, hanging from a rappelling rope. So the lady liked adventure, too! If you could really get anything certain out of reading someone's office, Victoria liked organization and control but she also liked people and was comfortable with them while remaining in a leadership role. There were no photos of anyone who looked like a romantic interest, but that could be merely because she knew people would read her surroundings and she wanted to keep that part of her life private.

* * *

Victoria had planned her entry into her office. She always liked to leave a visitor alone in her office for just a couple of minutes. It gave them a chance to become comfortable before she breezed in, her hair following her as if blown by a wind. She flashed her gorgeous smile, extended her hand, and welcomed them into her web.

Storm stood as Victoria entered and took her hand. "Miss Marcuccio, hello! It's good to see you again. I hope you remember our brief meeting last evening."

"Of course I remember you, Detective. You're the man who wears cowboy boots with his tuxedo." Victoria's smile was infectious and her hand seemed to warm his as Storm took it.

Victoria was well aware of the effect she had on men. She had known how to manipulate them from the time she reached puberty. A tall, athletic girl, she had blossomed with the curves of a woman by the time she was fifteen. Boys of all ages wanted her and even some of their fathers. She knew how to be coy and let them all think they had a chance when only she knew none of them did. She was driven by education as a girl. She attended the best of schools and while there took advantage of everything she could learn. In law school, her exceptional memory came in handy. She could read one of her law books and when it came time for testing, she could remember the page, see the writing, and almost read it back to herself as if the book lay open in front of her. She could not only repeat the text but she understood the meaning. The ability to comprehend some of more abstruse interpretations of the law was a very special talent and she had a vast file of such information at hand when she needed it.

"Sit down, Detective." She motioned him back to his seat. "I met with the director this morning and he told me you are here looking for information about a trip to South America my predecessor Mr. Dacosta was on with your wife, is that right?"

"Yes, I was hoping to meet with him but I understand he passed away just a few months after my wife was killed." Storm's face didn't show the pain he still felt, but a hint of it did find its way into his voice.

"Please, David," Victoria paused just a second, "Is it all right if I call you David? After all we did meet in a social situation. Please call me Victoria." Victoria was trying to loosen the man up some, but she was already fully aware of why he was here. She already knew about his wife's death and the circumstances surrounding it. She had asked Ms. Ware to pull the articles from the Houston paper along with the reports from Mr. Dacosta.

Her smile was intoxicating as Storm agreed and he answered, "I would be pleased if you call me David," then he hesitated before saying, "Victoria."

"I had my assistant pull the trip reports from the week Mr. Dacosta spent in Latin America with your wife and they are right here in this stack. Do you mind if I ask what you might hope to find?" Victoria knew she had to cooperate with this man; the agency had been asked to do so by the head of the committee that had oversight for their organization and any hesitancy might be misconstrued.

"I guess if I got to make a wish I would wish there was something in the reports that made your Mr. Dacosta feel like he and my wife might have been in danger. If he was still with us, it would be easier to just ask him. I know how official reports are many times not exactly the same as how a person remembers things."

"Why don't I move around the desk and sit next to you, that way we can look at the reports together and see if we find anything suspicious." Victoria moved her chair next to Storm as they began to look over the report.

There was nothing earth shattering in the reports, much as Storm had expected. They did give a thorough accounting of the week. It listed whom they saw from each company and the principle players for each. It related how many of these companies were looking for a way to partner with Angie's company and become a supplier of tools and additives used in the drilling process. One company seemed very eager and the report recorded how this company had wined and dined them in only the best of restaurants during this trip. Nevertheless, nothing jumped out or even peeked out that would make someone think there was anything dangerous or nefarious about the people they had met with.

Victoria knew many of these companies herself. She told Storm how she had called on all of them and their representatives of the countries in which they resided. Like every company in Latin America, they wanted to do business with American companies. They wanted access to all the money spent on drilling in the Gulf of Mexico and offshore Venezuela. She was sure there were no criminal organizations involved with any of these companies that could have possibly had anything to do with his wife's murder.

"David, we have been looking at the same four or five reports for the last hour and I don't see anything threatening in any of them. I have told you everything I know about these companies and just don't see it leading us anywhere. Do you want to go on?"

"No, Victoria, I don't see anything, either. I knew it was a long shot, but I had to try." He looked down at his hands as he balled them into fists, his hopes fading.

Victoria reached out and laid her hand on his softly, and he immediately let the tension that had been building go.

"David, when do you go back to Houston?"

"Tomorrow," he replied.

"Well, I have to be in Houston next week. Can I be so forward as to ask you to take me to dinner while I'm there?"

"I, I, sure, I would love to take you to dinner while you are there. Will you have time?"

"I will make sure of it. Why don't you give me your card and I can call when the week is planned out, so we can make arrangements to just enjoy each other's company?"

Storm had not even thought of taking another woman out after Angie. He began convincing himself now this was not a date, but rather, just two people planning on seeing each other again to discuss any further information Victoria might uncover. He handed her his card and felt like the boy who had just talked to his first girl, watching her walk away and kicking the dirt with his toe. He thanked her again for her time and left to meet Martin.

Storm's End

Storm's End

CHAPTER 23

Martin had been waiting in the car. Storm had been gone almost exactly an hour when Martin saw him emerge from the building at 1100 Wilson Blvd. He had a feeling before the meeting had ever happened that the five-year-old reports from a man who was now dead wouldn't reveal much of anything, but like Storm, he had to hope. He started the dark blue Ford sedan and pulled to curb to pick the detective up.

After Storm got into car Martin looked over and said, "Anything?"

"No, not really, there were only about five reports in the entire file from that week and all they did was lay out what he and Angie had done that week—who they had met with, companies and people. He listed the dinners they were invited to, where they had eaten, and who had hosted, but nothing that sounded like it would be of concern," answered Storm.

"Did you get the names of the companies and the people?"

"I did."

"Tomorrow while I'm participating in the audit of the Fairfax County Coroner's Office we'll put some people on the companies and personnel and see if anything pops."

"Good idea. Victoria said she still works with most of them, but it won't hurt to see who they are and who is behind them."

Martin smiled as he heard Storm call Ms. Marcuccio by her first name. "If I had to guess, I would opine you were intrigued by this woman." Storm didn't answer.

When they arrived at the hotel Storm made a copy of his notes in the business center and gave the copy to Martin. Martin was returning to FBI headquarters that afternoon and would put in a request to have the companies on the list checked out. He told Storm he would not see him again until sometime back in Houston. He would be leaving the office early tomorrow to spring the unscheduled audit at Fairfax County. Storm would have to take a cab back to airport. The entire process of the audit and running background checks on the companies would take a couple of days. "You're on your own, Storm, from this point on," Martin said as he left.

* * *

Storm decided to check out early and try to catch an earlier flight back to Houston. He was able to make arrangements to leave Washington by 8:00 p.m., getting him home before midnight. He made calls to Pancho and Russell to let them know he was coming back early and to set up a meet the next day to see where things were with what Clay had given them.

Russell told him that the small group was poring over the papers they believed were duplicates of those carried by Angie, but they were getting nowhere. He suggested to Storm it was time to call in someone they could trust who understood a good deal more than they did about how the oil business worked and the information they were studying. "We need someone who could look at the reports with an eye trained to spot any discrepancies that might be contained in the reports and make sense of what's there," Russell suggested.

Why don't you call our old friend David D?" Storm asked.

"You mean the one and only David D? Good idea," Russell wholeheartedly agreed. "If anyone can help us with this it's David D."

David Dubois, or "David D," as they called him, had been a friend since their early bachelor days back in Houston after college. Like Storm and Russell, David was an ex-college football player, but he had played at LSU. He had had to quit football when he tore an anterior cruciate ligament, or ACL, in his right knee. The tear could be repaired but it would never be in a condition that would allow him to play ball again. After leaving LSU he went to work in the oil patch. He worked as a roughneck and a tool man until he found something he really enjoyed. He became a contract operator of underwater ROVs and was the company man on most rigs, doing a shift job that requires the person to be in charge of everything from drilling to the galley. Therefore, he knew the rig game from top to bottom and was the perfect choice to ask for help if he wasn't offshore.

David D was possibly a bigger scoundrel than Russell, Storm knew. He stood as tall as both Russell and Storm and had broad shoulders. He was also thick through the chest after years of toiling in the Oil Patch. He had been married twice, had two grown children, and was a loud, fun man to be around. He was known to drink beer until dawn, get two hours sleep, and be back on the job the next morning. He hunted, fished and, as he put it, chased women with both hands. He was a man's man and fascinated the kind of women who like the outdoor "unsophisticated" type.

He loved Storm and Angie, and had often attended the barbecues the couple gave in their Heights home backyard. David D would spend hours with Angie, regaling her with tales of life on the rig. When Angie died, David D told Storm if it would bring her back, he would carry her coffin on his back by himself. David had been also another of the group of friends who supported Storm when he was drinking. Many times, it was David D who made sure Storm got home safely from a night of drowning his sorrows.

"I'll call David D and see when he can be available to help," Russell promised.

* * *

By 8:00 a.m. the next morning, the team had assembled at Russell's condominium. Monitored by a doorman, security cameras and intrusion alarms, it was the safest place for everyone to meet in case anyone was being followed. Russell had reached David D and he sounded excited to see his old friends after a number of years. The last one to arrive at Russell's, he was not a shrinking violet, so Storm could hear his big booming voice coming from the doorway as Russell opened it. Storm looked around the corner to see David D holding Russell off the ground in one of his infamous bear hugs, laughing and shaking Russell like he was a rag doll.

"Storm, get your ass over here," he yelled, "It's your turn next." Storm tried to put up a defense, but it was useless. Before he could raise his hands to object, the mountain of a man had dropped Russell and picked the detective off the ground in another bear hug.

"Now, tell me, boys, what kind of bullshit you got yourselves into that you need some redneck from Lous-y-anna to fix?" If anything, David D was direct.

Storm started by introducing Grady , Pancho and Alisha and then launched into his explanation. "David, we're trying to piece together the reason for Angie's murder and we need your help."

"Storm, you know I would do anything for that girl or you, so whatchu need?"

Storm went through what they already knew. He told him they were now certain who had killed Angie, but they didn't know why. He told him about the missing briefcase and how they had hopefully reassembled the contents as best they could from what her assistant knew she would be carrying. At that point, Pancho pulled out the shipping reports and the email from Angie asking to see the return manifests from the supply boats.

David D took the reports and spread them out on the table. He then began to arrange them by date. "You know what you got here, right?" he asked.

"Well, we know they are shipping manifests and return authorizations, but they don't make any sense to us," said Pancho.

"Okay, give me a minute to look these over. They look pretty ordinary at first look, but I need to spend a little more time."

"Sure, take all the time you need," Storm responded.

David D may have been a big rowdy man, but he wasn't immune to age, so as innocuously as he could he pulled out a pair of reading glasses. Even if he had pulled that off, the glasses looked too small for his beefy face and the combination of his trying to sneak the glasses past his buds and the way they fit first drew surprise and then stifled giggles from both Storm and Russell. When David D looked up and caught them, he threatened to pick them both up again and not stop shaking them until the laughing ceased. Both men stifled their urges and assured him it wouldn't happen again.

After studying the files for almost half an hour, David D said, "Okay, boys, what we got here are shipping records for a rig called the 'Juniper Four.' It sits in the Diana Field about twenty miles south of New Orleans. Pretty mundane stuff, actually. I take it these reports are from your wife's company?" David D asked Storm.

"Yep, we think these reports were part or maybe even most of what she was carrying in her briefcase when she was killed. Is there anything out of the ordinary in them?"

"Not really," said David D.

"Then we're no closer to an answer then we were weeks ago." Storm glanced at each of his friends, and he could tell each member felt the same emotion as he did—let down.

David D grinned at the team surrounding the table and said, "I said I didn't find anything weird in the reports, but when I read the email from your wife asking for the returns reports I found something odd." Now he had everyone's attention. "She asked to see what was being returned into stock. You see, the company man who has the last word on a rig has to fill out a report or at least sign off on every manifest that comes and goes from a rig. He either personally checks in every shipment or has a clerk who does it, and then he signs off that they have received everything on the manifest. If he is wrong on the counts, the company is still going to have to pay for what the manifest says they received."

David D began to move papers around on the table so everyone could follow along. "You see, here are records of shipments to this rig." David pointed to the different reports, tracing his finger down the columns of numbers and descriptions of products. "Here you see a total of each product shipped, including a description and weight (if it is something shipped by weight); everything is ritecheer. Do y'all see what I'm sayin?" he asked.

The men nodded in concert as they were seeing the totals, although they still had no idea where David was going with it.

"Y'all see this line ritecheer?" he pointed a column titled "Mud Additive." Again the group around the table nodded, following along. "Your wife's company sold mud additives to this rig and they shipped twenty twenty-five-pound bags for which the company man signed ritecheer." He pointed to the executed manifest for the shipment and the men waited to hear what was coming next. "Now two weeks after they received that shipment, the rig sent forty bags back to shore for which they would want credit against further invoices." Every eye in the room was following his finger as he pointed things out and every ear listened intently. "Now here is where the fucked up part comes in." He picked up the last report Angie had asked for before she was killed. "This is the return manifest that was received when the supply boat returned to dock. It shows only twenty twenty-five-pound bags were received back into stock to be sold at a later date. Twenty bags are unaccounted for. Now the fight for the money for those twenty bags would be between Angie's company, the rig, and supply Boat Company."

The men stared at each other as comprehension dawned, and now David D looked confused. "Okay, cut the crap, what the hell just happened? I know you didn't ask me over here to show you were somebody who lost twenty bags of additives, so what am I missing?"

"David, it isn't about twenty missing bags of additives, it is about smuggling drugs. We believe Angie might have been killed because she saw something or found something she shouldn't have. Something that would connect her to the cartel. You just showed us what that was—how some cartel drugs are finding their way into the United States," explained Storm.

"Shit, Storm, ya could've told me that from the beginning and we wouldn't have needed to go through all this bullshit. Are ya going to tell me you think those missing bags were full of drugs?" asked David D.

"That's exactly what we think," replied Storm.

"You know you're talking about five hundred pounds of dope, right?"

The outrageousness of the idea hit everyone else as David D said it. This was big time. This was just one shipment of 500 pounds of drugs. It didn't matter if it was marijuana or coke, it was a big deal. It was millions of dollars of illegal product hitting the streets of American cities. This was the big time—no penny ante crap—and it would definitely involve the kingpins. It was also no stretch to take it one step further, that it also included getting the money back out of the U.S. the same way the drugs were getting in.

"David, what's your thought on getting the money back out? How would they do it?" asked Russell.

"Before you answer that we need to be full out honest with you, David D. By inviting you here we have put you in probable danger. This is bigger than all of us. The FBI is already involved and the DEA will be when we know exactly who we can trust over there," Storm said, looking the huge man in the eye.

"What the fuck have you guys got me into?" David D's glare matched Storm's stare.

"David, we're not exactly sure, but if our suspicions are right and we've found how the drugs are getting into the United States, we can cut the head off one of the biggest cartel operations on two continents. We know they've had people inside the DEA and we suspect they have people inside Customs and Border Protection. Another thing we know is that when we busted Enrique Guzman and his group last year it was just the tip of the iceberg," said Storm.

"We also know who the mole was in the DEA and we know she killed for them. In fact, we also know she was the one who killed Angie," added Russell. "We're also certain they're responsible for other deaths, but just not how many yet. These are bad people and they are very organized and dangerous. If you want out, now is the time to say so and nobody would blame you."

"Damn!" David's voice had lost its normal vibrato, but then his decision was made. "What the hell? I'm here now, so what else can I do to help?"

"Do you have any ideas on the specifics of how they're doing this?" asked Storm.

"You bet your ass! I've got me some pretty solid ideas how they're doing this."

"You da man! But let's not get into it now. We need to get the FBI up to speed and with us so you only have to go over this once," said Storm.

"Fine with me, but are y'all sure you can trust them?"

Storm smiled but he didn't blame his friend for being leery after what they just told him. "That's the good news, the Feebs we're sure of. Now we need to get Higgins and Long over here to Russell's home."

Storm's End

Storm's End

CHAPTER 24

Juan Pablo was relaxing in his study perusing the latest literary addition to his collection of original masterpieces of world literature. The work was a leather-bound, handwritten translation of the famous Cervantes work, *History of the Admirable Don Quixote de La Mancha*. This edition was thought to be an original translation into French by Filleau de Saint-Martin in 1677. In his translation Saint-Martin opted to change Cervantes' original ending, prolonging the ingenious gentleman's life; hence, the change in title.

Juan Pablo's paternal family, the du Tillys, were a wealthy old moneyed family who could trace their roots in Mexico back to the tyrannical days of Maximilian. Juan Pablo was the second son, and although educated in the best of Mexican schools and college in Spain, he stood to inherit nothing from his father. So, like Enrique Guzman, he had nothing, and they had become allies in college, seeing a great opportunity to make their wealth in the illegal drug trade. Banding together to make the acquaintance of coca producers in Colombia, they made third party deals with men willing to take the chance of smuggling the drugs from the producers through Mexico into the United States. After getting paid their small percentage for arranging the deals, they saw the opportunity to cut out the U.S. buyer, purchase the product directly from the producer, and set up their own network of distribution.

The decision paid dividends within the first two years of operation. As greed replaced fear and common sense, they found they could grow their business even faster by eliminating their competition. They hired ex-Special Forces soldiers from the Mexican army to act as their personal security and henchmen. Opposition cartels found that getting in a war with the Rio Cartel organization would cost them product and untold lives, including possibly their own. Therefore, the Rios cartel business flourished.

The loss of his closest ally and friend Enique had pushed Juan Pablo to become more introspective and careful. He now surrounded himself with full-time bodyguards and always traveled in a bulletproof vehicle. The windows in his homes were tempered using polycarbonate, thermoplastic, and layers of laminated glass, allowing the refraction of the windows to appear normal while stopping most rifle and small arms ammunition. Unlike Enrique's sister, Juan Pablo was more prudent about his desire for revenge. He knew time was his ally and with time, he could dispatch those responsible for his friend's death without putting himself or his organization at risk.

As he was admiring his newly acquired possession, his private cell phone rang. "Hola." The call was from two of his men working a special detail for him. "Es todo okay?"

"Es el regreso de Washington, D.C."

"Bueno, Bueno. Donde está ahora?"

"Qué hizo cumplir."

"Está seguro de qué son FBI."

"Sí, continuar a seguirlo."

Juan Pablo pressed the off button to disconnect the call. His men were doing exactly what they were being paid to do.

Storm's End

* * *

Agents Higgins and Long were introduced to the new man everyone else in the room already knew and called "David D." They soon learned he was an old friend of Storm's and Russell's and they had asked him in to look at the rig reports to see if he could figure out why these manifests might be important. Privately, they had questioned Storm about the wisdom of bringing another civilian into the mix, but were assured it was necessary and he was the right man.

"David, you want to show them what you showed us?" asked Storm.

"Sure." David D went through the reports again and the agents had the same questions.

"How does it work?" asked Agent Higgins.

"It is really kinda simple. Let's start with what they need first. They need one of their own on the rig. They need a boss or as we call him, the company man. If you don't have him on your side, then you got to be a bunch more sneaky. The supplier of products sends out the supplies on a boat; let's call it the "Western Breeze," like the boat carrying the supplies on this manifest. They have an invoice and a manifest for two hundred bags of a special additive. The company man signs the manifest agreeing that he has received the two hundred bags. His company now owes the supplier for those bags of material. The Western Breeze leaves and returns to a port somewhere in the United States.

"In the middle of that rotation another ship comes out and delivers twenty more bags of additives. They, too, are flying an American flag, so everyone on the rig passes it off as just another boatload of groceries and supplies. The men working the rig don't care what's in the shipment as long as they don't run out of supplies. But the second supply boat, let's say it is called the "Eastern Breeze," is in reality a Mexican flagged boat out of, let's say, the Port of Tampico. Since they're flying an American flag no one suspects, and even if they were flying a Mexican flag most the crew on the rig wouldn't notice.

"The company man—the cartel employee—stores the twenty new bags of additives with the others, but they have a special mark on them that only he knows what it means. When the shift changes and the new crews come onboard, they load the supply boat up with returns. They don't need all the mud additives, so the company man has forty mud bags sent back to shore for credit. Now he has to write down a number or the shipping company gets suspicious. So he sends back forty bags of additives. But when they reach shore, twenty bags have disappeared. You see where I'm going now?"

"Yeah, so the twenty bags of drugs in the specially marked counterfeit bags end up in the hands of the cartel's people here."

"Exactly."

"So they have to have a company man on board to accomplish this."

"I would think so, but if not, there are other ways."

"Would the supply boats be in on it?" asked Pancho.

"They might be or they might not. If they are held responsible for the twenty bags that disappeared from the manifest I would guess they would. Somebody has to pay for the missing material. I think that's what Storm's wife found," said David D.

"What do you mean 'you think that's what she found?'"

"She asked the home office to send her a return report. When she saw the difference in what was sent back per the manifests and what was delivered back on the return reports, I think she knew something wasn't kosher. I think she knew something was going on."

"Do you think she knew who was behind it?"

"Not necessarily. I'm saying she recognized something was amiss and when she checked she found the disparities between the manifests and the returns.

"Who else might have known what she found out?"

"Somebody or some bodies she worked with. If someone in the home office was covering up the disparities, they also had to know when she started checking the return reports."

"How will we find that out?" Grady wanted to know.

"You're gonna have to look at their records—all of them—old ones and new ones and find a trail to where the changes were made and where the evidence is hidden."

"Okay, but just to cover all our bases. Is there any other way things that could be smuggled from a rig back to the mainland and not go through Customs?" asked Storm.

"Sure. Let's say the company man gets a call from a supply ship and they tell him they have a refrigerator in their galley that has quit working and a sister ship is meeting them at the rig to give them a new one. The company man only needs to ask the crane operator to drop a line down to one ship and move a carton from one to the other. It could be a refrigerator, or it could be a box full of drugs. Remember, if a boat leaves a U.S. port, goes to a rig and returns, they don't go through customs."

"Then what you are telling us is if you have a company man in your pocket, you can send anything back to shore and nobody is any the wiser," commented Russell.

"That is exactly what I'm telling you. Bad actors and not so bad actors on rigs have been smuggling stuff back to shore for years now. It can be as minor as the cooks keeping their left over supplies and sending them back home to feed their families. It is the way of life on the rigs. Anybody who has spent any time on a rig knows that. Company people know that. In fact, most of them do it."

"How will we prove our theory?" asked Storm.

"You'll have to put somebody on a rig and if I were you, I would put them on this rig," answered David D.

"Do you know this rig?" asked Agent Long.

"Yep, I know this rig and no, I ain't gonna go out there and be your bitch. I told you how they do it; now you gotta put some dickhead on it and let him watch. But he better know what he is doing. Rig crews are tight. They don't like spies and they don't like squealers."

"Mr. Dubois, do you have a CHL?" asked Agent Higgins.

"Yes sir, I'm always carryin' and I have a license to keep it hidden," answered David D.

"Good. You need to watch your back. If these people know you've helped us you are in danger."

David D just scowled at the agent. Storm got the uncomfortable impression David D was thinking, I agreed to hang in on this trouble, but from now on I'll be in less of a hurry to help my friends, if they all live.

"Mr. Dubois, did you tell anyone you were coming here to meet Detective Storm?" asked agent Long.

"No, Russell called me last night and asked me to come over and help on something. I'm off work right now so nobody knows I am here. Shit, I didn't know why I was coming here 'til I got here. Why?" answered David D

"It appears Detective Storm has picked up a tail," replied Agent Long.

"I what?" shouted Storm as the men in the room all took a quick breath. "When did I pick up a tail?"

"It appears you had one before you left for Washington or at least we discovered them when you were in Washington. There were two Hispanic men observing you in Washington and the same two men are now sitting across the street in the parking lot of that midrise office building. They have been watching this building since you came in this morning," Agent Long informed everyone.

We all want to go to the windows to check it out, but the windows of Russell's condominium face the Memorial Park, so we can't see the office building from our vantage point.

"Who found them?" asked Storm.

"An agent we had following you and Martin in D.C."

"You were following me, too?"

"Yes, we told you we would have your back and we didn't just mean Martin. When you flew back to Houston, so did both men. When you landed in Houston another agent took over following you and he picked up the same two men. Whoever is behind it has at least four men in the detail; two are on and two off. We've had eyes on them since you got back last night. But it's a warning to all: Somebody is very interested in what we are doing. Mr. Dubois. If you came into the building alone you will leave alone, and for the time being, I don't want you to have any further interaction with your friends."

"What are they driving?" asked Pancho.

"Black Chevy Tahoe with blacked out windows."

"You sure they aren't DEA?"

"We're sure. We've already called Tom Morran and he said they didn't have anyone following Detective Storm. He was a little irritated we haven't included him in this investigation yet. The guys who are following you operate like intelligence types but not from our government. Our best guess is these boys work for the cartel. The SUV is a rental and was leased in the name of Marina Servicio de Tampico, an outfit owned by a succession of shell companies and we haven't run down the true owners yet. It seems this company runs vessels for fishing in the Gulf as well as hauling supplies to non-U.S. registered rigs in the Gulf. That is all we know at this time. When you all leave, leave one at a time, and when the detective leaves we will see if they follow him," said Agent Higgins.

At that point it was decided the group shouldn't get together again unless Storm could shake his tail. David D would leave first, followed by Russell and Grady, when it was time for them to go to the station. The last to go would be Storm. No more meetings would be held at Russell's residence.

Agents Higgins and Long would be in contact with their men, who would follow the men in the black SUV.

They would also make sure no one else leaving the meeting was followed. Storm would have security from now on.

The team decided it was time to bring Tom Morran of the DEA in on what they had found and what they were doing. The added resources would help an already stretched thin front line.

* * *

At 8:00 a.m. East Coast time, the team of auditors from the FBI came through the doors of the Northern Virginia Medical Examiners Building located just off Braddock Road in a wooded area surrounded by other Northern Virginia law enforcement offices. This was what the local medical offices called "an ambush audit." The FBI would halt all but current investigations while they went through the office's chain of custody paperwork and evidence lockers to make sure things were secure and had not been corrupted.

Agent Martin Jones was listed as one of auditors. The supervisor of the audit had already told him where he would find the information they were looking for and promised him they would keep the director of the facility out of his hair long enough to secure the records he hoped to find. Many of the technicians who worked for the State of Virginia would be kept busy with the file reviews, and members of the team would be going over all their procedures and documentation.

After only an hour Martin found the files he needed and photographed them so it wouldn't appear that anything was out of place. The next step was harder. He had to get a tissue sample from the lungs and heart of Robert Dacosta, the former USTDA director. Tissue samples would be kept in refrigeration and referenced by the container numbers he would get from the autopsy report. He would have to open the containers, retrieve samples, and reseal them without anyone becoming the wiser.

Storm's End

By 10:00 a.m., he had everything he had come to get and the supervisor Okayed his leaving. The team would stay and conduct their review as if this was a planned invasion. Martin put the samples in a small insulated box with a piece of dry ice and returned to FBI headquarters, where he prepared to catch an afternoon flight to Houston. Once he arrived in Houston, he would turn over the tissue samples and reports to Alisha to work her magic.

Storm's End

CHAPTER 25

A week had passed since the team's last full-blown get together and not much new information had been discovered. Storm's tails must have lost interest in him as they, too, had disappeared for the last four days. Communication between members of the team was done over secure voice and video feeds using the computers the FBI had supplied them.

David D had gone hunting and if anyone wanted to do him harm his hunting lease would be worst place they could pick. He was a natural outdoorsman and the woods of the Big Piney were like a second home to him. Being a careful man, he kept his wits about him and watched for any sign of treachery. He had promised Storm and Russell he would contact them the minute he got back to assure them of his safety.

Martin had returned to Houston with his reports and tissue samples and Alisha was in the process of determining if she agreed with the local autopsy of Robert Dacosta and the subsequent death of the medical examiner who had performed his autopsy. Keeping her research off the radar, she worked on it when most of employees had left for the day.

The FBI had included the DEA in what they knew about the smuggling and Storm's wife's death being tied to Cully Gilroy. Together they located an agent with experience as a mud engineer. East Texas Drilling now had the contract to supply mud engineers to the platform where the same company man who had been in charge of the rig where Angie had found the discrepancies was now working. Mud engineers were full time employees of ETD but moved from rig to rig on a rotating basis. An unfamiliar face being aboard this rig would not raise any flags for the company man as long as the engineer had a competent working knowledge of his job and responsibilities. This undercover agent should be perfect to work his shift and still keep his eyes open for anything suspicious.

* * *

Russell was back to the mundane days working at the station and doing the weather. Grady was back performing his function as Russell's producer and both men were waiting for something to break so they could get back to what they secretly loved.

Pancho and Storm were running records on the ownership of the companies Angie had met with on her last trip. One such company came to the forefront when Pancho discovered it fell under the ownership of the same shell company that owned Tampico Servicio, the operation that had leased the SUV driven by the men who had been tailing Storm. Collecting records of ownership for offshore companies was painstaking tedious work. Corporate records for companies registered in foreign countries were not as easy to negotiate as American-based corporate entities' records. Determining who the real owners were required the help and cooperation of foreign law enforcement and their agencies that were comparable to the like departments in the United States. Never knowing who they could trust, Storm and Pancho gave the names to the FBI and DEA, who could go through secure channels within the State Department asking for their assistance in getting that information. Working through channels was similar to watching paint dry. The bureaucracy was maddening; you might ask for something and it would require a committee to obtain the information.

It was then the FBI went to Damien Stuart, the federal prosecutor who had been involved in the Enrique Guzman case, to ask if he could put any pressure on the State Department to retrieve the ownership records they required. Damien was more than happy to help, but he did so with the proviso that when this case came together he would be the one to prosecute the offenders and bring this illegal smuggling ring to the public's attention. His request was quickly granted and the multijurisdictional team of investigators had its newest member.

* * *

With the disappearance of the his tail, Storm had begun to relax again, and as his tension eased, all the members of team let out a collective sigh of relief. The team was relaxed enough to actually take a day off and just enjoy one another's company at a football watch party on the big screen Russell had bought specifically for the occasion. With Storm and Russell both being Texas Tech alumni, they had ordered the pay per view of Texas Tech at the University of Nebraska. Since the working relationship with Martin was panning out, they included him in the afternoon of barbecue and football.

It had been more than a week since Storm had returned from Washington, D.C. and his mind had cleared somewhat from the effects of Victoria Marcuccio. Now on this lazy Saturday afternoon his phone rang. Everyone in the room could hear Storm's side of the conversation, but they could also see the shock that registered on his face when he realized who was on the other end of the call.

"Storm," he answered, as the voice on the end began to talk.

"Of course I remember you! How are things in Washington ...Yes, I remember now, but truthfully, it had slipped my mind. . . . This next week? . . . .Yes, I would love to have dinner with you. I'll pick out somewhere nice, maybe invite some friends."

The room had fallen silent; the only sound other than Storm's voice was the announcers calling the play by play. The color of Storm's face had turned a discernable shade of red and only Russell had ever seen his friend in this condition.

" . . . You have my number, just give me a call when you get to town, and we will make plans."

Storm disconnected the call and laid his cell back on the coffee table, avoiding the questioning eyes of his fellow team members. "Did I miss anything?" he asked casually.

Grady, Pancho, Alisha, Ms. Edith, and Martin all stared at the man as if they had just seen an apparition. Russell chuckled under his breath and with as straight a face as possible asked, "Who was that, Storm?"

"Nobody, just someone I met in Washington."

"Bullshit! That was a woman! You met a woman in D.C.!" Russell exclaimed.

"No. . . . Well, yes. . . .she works for the USTDA. She is the one I met with about looking at the call reports from the guy that went with Angie to Latin America."

"Is she hot, Storm?" asked Russell.

That's when Martin jumped in, "Hell, yes, she's hot! She is the heartbreaker of all D.C."

"What do you mean?" Pancho asked Martin.

"I mean she is about the hottest woman working on the Hill."

"So fill us in!!" asked Russell.

"She is tall, dark hair, gorgeous face, and from what I've seen, a body to go with it. She is the belle of D.C. She has every red-blooded boy on the Hill panting after her. Senators, congressmen, staffers, lobbyists, all, married or single, want this woman to belong to them."

"Is she single?" asked Russell.

"Yep, and from what I know, she plans on staying that way. She is all about power and importance. She is career driven and comes from a rich family so she doesn't need what most women with her looks are looking for," replied Martin.

"What would she want with this poor country redneck then?" Russell asked rhetorically.

"And, Storm, you just made a date with her?" asked Pancho.

"No! She is coming to Houston on business and she asked if we might get together for dinner while she is here. I'm sure it is about the reports." The expression on his red face was changing from embarrassment to irritation.

A chorus of "Storm has a date" rose from everyone but Ms. Edith. "Shush, you boys, let David alone. He told you it was not a date, so leave him be." Although she chastised them, Ms. Edith had a big smile on her face, and it broadcast, "My adopted son has been through a lot in last few years, and if he does have a date it's about time. He deserves to be happy."

Never without his laptop, Pancho whistled as the image of Victoria Marcuccio popped up on his screen. He turned the computer around so everyone could see her official picture from the USTDA website. She was stunning. Alisha smiled, but reached over and closed the laptop. Like her mother she was defending Storm from further harassment.

"Where you gonna take her, Storm?" asked Russell.

"I don't know."

"Well take her somewhere nice, maybe even romantic," added Grady.

"No, not romantic, this is a business dinner, right, Storm? Hell, you told her you might invite your friends," Russell said, grinning again.

"None of you are going!" Ms. Edith said emphatically. "This is David's business and when and if he wants all you scalawags to meet her you will be invited, but not on the first date." Damn! The word "date" had slipped out of her mouth, but she had heard his side of the conversation and she, too, thought David had a date.

For now, the conversation about Storm's impending plans to meet up with Victoria for dinner was dropped, but lingered in the back of all the minds of those present. Storm himself couldn't understand why this woman had such an effect on him. He wasn't blind and it was easy to see she was a beautiful woman, but he still loved Angie, so what was causing him so much anxiety?

CHAPTER 26

As usual, Alisha came in Monday faced with having to clean up after the events at the morgue that had taken place over the weekend. Like most other weekends, it had been busy. There had been two murders and two car wreck victims. The district attorney's office was waiting for results of blood tests on the driver from the car wreck to clarify whether alcohol had been involved.

The reports and tissue samples Martin had brought back from Arlington resided in her office; they were for her eyes only. If anyone discovered she was looking into the deaths of two men not in her jurisdiction she and no one else would be held responsible. As time was available over the past week she had been reading and mentally dissecting the tissue samples, and once she had completed the final test sample later in the day, she would be able to give her educated opinion on how both men had died. The chemical and particulate test was running now and with it, she could ascertain if Dacosta had been drugged or if his heart failure had been for real.

Lost in her bookkeeping and reports for the district attorney, she jumped when the alarm on her computer notified her that the mass spectrometer had finished with her sample and a print out now awaited her. Hurrying to the lab, she retrieved the report, cleaned her sample vial, deleted the test from the memory of the machine, and returned to her office. Reviewing this report took precedence over the determination that a drunk had killed himself and another passenger. She had already verbally notified the D.A. that it was positive the driver had been drunk, but the final report would have to wait.

Alisha had been working on a theory, but the analysis of the mass spectrometer had confirmed nothing. There was no indication that there were any drugs in Dacosta's system that would have caused a heart attack. As she read and reread the results the only thing she could think was the test was either incomplete or she was missing something.

As she went over the lack of evidence of wrongdoing, the answer hit her. She checked the results again and found the culprit. She believed she had found how Dacosta had been killed. She picked up the cell phone they were now using to communicate between team members and called Storm. She needed to meet with the team and they needed Martin there because if they bought her hypothesis, he would need to run background checks to verify her suspicions.

* * *

The team planned to meet at Ms. Edith and Alisha's home. It was in the ward, a place where Pancho's, Russell's and Storm's cars were known to the neighbors. None of the residents would question a visit from Ms. Edith's newly adopted sons. Being a black man, Martin would attract less attention, even though the neighbors didn't know him. He could be a relative invited over to dinner with the family.

Martin was the last to arrive and first to ask why they were there. "Martin, if I can convince everyone here I am on the right track you are going to have to do some checking into the financials of the late medical examiner for Fairfax County," said Alisha.

Ms. Edith had been serving sweet tea and sandwiches to the men when Alisha began to talk. When she finished serving, she excused herself from the room, retiring to her bedroom to watch television and leave the investigators to their puzzles.

"What did you find, Alisha?" asked Storm.

"It is easier to tell you what I didn't find. I didn't find any drugs that could have caused a heart attack or made Dacosta's death look like a heart attack." Her answer was disheartening to the team, but she just smiled as she delivered the news.

"Then what are you smiling about? What the hell good does that do us? If you didn't find anything that proves he didn't have a heart attack we don't have any evidence that this was a murder and we have no way to tie his death to the cartel." Storm sounded pissed.

"Whoa, slow down there, bud. You didn't listen to what I said." Now Alisha was taking a tutoring tone with the men. "I said I didn't find any drugs that could have caused a heart attack and, at first, that fact baffled me, too. It was then I began to look at the report more carefully and I feel I can say without reservation or at least with ninety percent surety that his death and the death of the medical examiner were murder."

"If you didn't find evidence of drugs in the Dacosta sample, how can you say he was murdered?" asked Martin.

"The death of Dacosta was the hard one to figure out. It was totally by luck that you extracted the exact right piece of tissue for me to check. The reports from the deceased medical examiner were right on. He made notes that there was no alcohol or drugs in the victim's system and even a trained pathologist would have deemed this an acute myocardial infarction, a simple heart attack. But when I ran the mass spectrometer, it came back clean, too clean. It was then I went back and started looking closer at the results of the test."

"Alisha, dammit, get to point!" Everyone was hanging on each word, but so far, they still didn't know where she was headed.

"The sample Martin retrieved was a piece of the right ventricle; the only heart tissue sample that could give me what I needed! Our man's death was from an arterial gas embolism or "AGE," and that doesn't mean old age. It means his heart's normal ability to pass blood and oxygen to the rest of the body was blocked by an air bubble. Our body tissue stores the residuals of the last particles that come in contact with it before death.

"As you will learn in any high school biology class, the heart pumps blood and oxygen to all the parts of the body. The lungs inhale air and process that air to join the blood, which is pumped to the heart where the heart pumps it to the rest of the body. Waste products or carbon dioxide from the air we breathe are exhaled. The sample taken from the tissue Martin brought back was 21 % oxygen and 78 percent nitrogen with a smattering of other gases. This is the makeup of the same air we breathe to within a few percentage points in every part of the world. There is no way this mixture of gases should be found in the left ventricle unless it was purposely introduced into the body."

"What are you telling us, Alisha?" The men were all nerves.

"I am telling you numbskulls that somebody shot an air bubble in this man's blood stream. It went through the coronary artery where it hit the left ventricle, causing a blockage that in turn caused a heart attack, and our man died."

"Shit, are you sure?"

"I told you it's my best guess, but from the evidence it has to be what happened. There is no other way the mass spec would have given me the reading it did."

"Okay, if this was the hard one, why are you sure the ME was killed?"

"The report said he died when his car went off the road and hit a tree. His head hit the air bag but the accident was so violent his neck was broken and he probably died instantly, right?" asked Alisha.

"Yes," replied Martin.

"Well, that is not true. He died from a broken neck but he didn't die in the car wreck."

"Then how did he die?"

"Now in the case of the ME, the report reads as a terrible vehicular accident. The car and its occupant were found almost one hundred yards off the highway some fifty yards past the tree line, flipped over on its top after careening off numerous old growth pines. The medical examiner's face was pulp from the beating it took in the accident and he had numerous broken bones. His death was ruled accidental, but here is the twist. There was very little blood loss at the scene. With all these cuts and abrasions one would expect to find a huge pool of blood, but that wasn't the case. When I reviewed the postmortem X-rays, I found the neck had been broken in a radial fashion, which is not consistent with an accident like this. A radial break is more consistent with someone snapping the neck; someone like a professional assassin or someone with military training. That assumption, combined with the breaks to his bones and the lacerations and bruising indicates to me the man was dead long before the car left the road. He was murdered somewhere else and the car wreck was staged. I think this is further evidence that the cartel is cleaning up its mess. Even more damning is there was no organopolysiloxane in his nostrils or mouth; if he was alive at the time of the accident, traces of this substance should be somewhere in his respiratory passages."

"What in the hell was that word you said?" asked Storm.

"Organopolysiloxane? It's a coating on all modern vehicle air bags." Alisha looked around to make sure they were all following her. "Over the years different substances have been used, but this is most common now. It is the fine powdery stuff you find on victims of wrecks, usually on their faces and upper bodies where they were exposed to the air bag. If our victim had been alive at the time of the wreck, he would have had some of this 'powder' in his nostrils or inside his mouth. In the case of the ME, there was none, so he had to have been dead before the wreck. When I re-examined the X-rays of his neck, it looks to me like someone broke his neck by twisting his head till it snapped and that indicates specially trained military, foreign police or hired assassins."

"Then from what you found we can assume that the cartel might, and I say 'might' because we don't have any hard proof, have killed these two men in an effort to clean house and get rid of loose ends?" asked Russell.

"That is exactly what she is saying, but how do we prove it?" asked Pancho.

"To begin with, you and Martin dig into their financials to see if there were any big deposits made to either of their accounts; see what they left their families. If you find money, see if you can track down where it came from. The amount of money it would take to falsify records in a medical examiner's office would be substantial, so a large transfer should have set off some red flags somewhere," said Storm.

"We're gonna have to look offshore, too. If they paid big for this they wouldn't be stupid enough to run it through a U.S. bank," added Martin.

"Look in Panama, maybe somewhere in Central America or the Caribbean," rejoined Storm. Great job, Alisha." The men around table agreed and added their congratulations.

"Now, we know these people are not afraid to kill anyone who gets in their way, so I want everyone here to be careful. Grady, I know you and Russell have CHLs and I want you carrying all the time from now on. Martin, does the FBI still have a tail on Pancho and me?" asked Storm.

"Yep, always one and most times two. But they are only watching your backs; do you want us to put someone on Russell, Grady, and Alisha?" asked Martin.

"No, not unless they feel like someone is following them. From now on, they stay back away from this as much as possible. From here on out it's Pancho, me, and your task force. "Okay. Good luck everyone, and Pancho, I will be calling you later to start the trace on the money. I will need to get a warrant, but with Damien on the team now I don't think that will be too hard."

Storm's cell phone rang and it was Victoria calling. He had forgotten that she would be in town and the call caught him off guard as he answered. His face registered the shock as he realized who it was. "Yes, hello, Ms. Marcuccio."

The team grinned at each other and Russell thumped his heart with his hand. It was obvious to everyone at the table that something was up with Storm given the look on his face—he was smitten by this woman.

"Yes, dinner tomorrow night would great! Where are you staying? I know the Omni. I'll pick you up in the lobby at 7:00 p.m. Great! I am looking forward to it, too. Be nice to see you again." With that said, Storm pushed the disconnect button on his phone and the call was over, except for the ribbing he was about to get from his cohorts.

* * *

In the Big Piney, David D was about to call it a day. He had been out in his deer blind twice that day, once early that morning and then back again in the afternoon. The morning hunt had ended with no shots at all; the deer were there and he had seen plenty of does and fawns, all coming to graze in the open pasture in front of where the blind sat hidden away in the trees of the forest that surrounded the hay field. That evening just before he was about to leave he sat tracking a large six point buck with his field glasses, but the trophy was wary and was standing on the other side of the opening. The shot was too long for a bow and his only hope was the deer would venture farther in the open, maybe cross the field directly in front him.

As he studied the deer, he saw the buck lift his head, his eyes fully alert, sniffing toward the south of the hay field, and then the deer bolted in three rapid jumps disappearing back inside the forest. It was then he heard the slight whine of a two-cycle engine. This property was over a thousand acres of unimproved land; the hay field would not even be there if David hadn't cleared it of trees and planted new seed every year. The sound of the engine was coming from one of the old logging roads that ran near where he had set up his camp.

His base camp was an old single bed trailer with a small kitchen and now defunct bathroom, which sat on cement blocks and looked as if it had been abandoned years ago. The only thing that indicated that a live human being might be there was the four-wheel ATV David used to leave his country home and go to the woods to go hunting. The sound seemed to be coming from the old trailer. He heard the engine stop for a couple of minutes, then start again. This time it sounded as if it was headed for the clearing where the buck had just left. He never had visitors to the hunting camp in the middle of the week and if he did, he would have expected them since it was all posted property and he would have had to invite them. This was something else.

His mind quickly went back to the meeting he had with Storm and Russell; he could be in danger, but if he was, he was in his perfect place to make a stand or run, whichever the need demanded. Dressed in total camouflage, his hands covered with camo gloves and his face covered with netting, he lowered himself from the tree stand and sank to the ground. The sound of the ATV grew louder. There were two men riding the four-wheeler and they certainly didn't know much about hunting in the woods of East Texas. They were dressed in black jeans, combat boots, and black jackets. It appeared that neither man carried a long rifle or bow, but the bulge on each of their sides appeared to be a side arm and strapped around their necks were what looked to be Smith & Wesson or Heokler & Koch 9 mm submachine guns.

David D took stock of his situation. His only chance was to somehow skirt these men, get back the trailer, get his ATV or cell phone, and call for the cavalry. To his north, west, and east was nothing but miles of forest in every direction. The only place he could get to that would give him a chance was his trailer. He didn't want to take any man's life, but if it came down to it, his will to live would replace any hesitancy he might have had about killing them.

As the ATV broke into the opening of the hay field, he moved in a circle around it in at the edge of forest. His camo would make him invisible as long as neither of the men saw him moving. The men in black were not taking any precautions as they moved directly across the center of the opening, when one of them noticed the deer blind amongst the trees. They made a quick turn to the left as David tried to distance himself from where he had just been moments earlier. He had to be quick but he had to be unnoticed, too. He had made about a hundred yards when he heard the shots coming from the direction of his blind. The gun shots were wide and high as if shot to elicit some kind of response from him. He froze, keeping a large pine between him and the men he knew now were there to find him and kill him. Peering around the tree, his face still covered, he could see the men scanning the woods looking for him. Now he was sure the shots were to see what they might scare up. The men started the ATV and were now moving around the edge of the forest. If he moved they would spot him and then it would be kill or be killed.

With the skill of the Native Americans who populated this area more than two hundred years before, he notched an arrow in the composite hunting bow and waited silently for the men on the ATV to come into range. At fifty yards, he came from behind the tree and loosed his arrow at the man driving the ATV. The arrow struck him directly in the chest with such impact that it sent him head over heels off the back of the moving ATV, taking the man behind him off in the process.

Burps from the machine gun erupted. The second man started shooting, more as a reflex reaction then as a plan to hit anything. Rolling and scrambling out from under his companion, he took better aim toward the area where he was sure the arrow had come from and fired again, this time emptying the gun's clip.

David D had left the tree from where he had fired the arrow as soon as he saw the shaft hit its target. Retreating deeper into the woods, he kept moving in the direction of the trailer, but farther off the edge of the woods.

The remaining assassin seemed to let his military training take over. He, too, raced for the woods with the knowledge he now had a target who was aware of him and his purpose here. The man who had fired the arrow was like a ghost, neither seen nor heard, so he had to make sure he would not be the next victim of this apparition.

David D carried the bow and a polished steal-barreled .357 magnum when he hunted. The bow would be better if he could get a shot at the second man in the open, but now they were both in trees and his best hope of survival was the get a clear shot with the pistol.

The assassin was good, but he was out of his element. He was trained in open warfare, not hiding in the trees behind logs or under fallen foliage. He was careful but also loud in the underbrush and so the advantage went to David D, the prey.

David D took refuge behind another tree, the base of which was surrounded by low-lying bushes of coastal dog hobble. His nemesis was now no more than thirty feet away from him in a silhouette against the bright hay field on his left. David took aim and slowly squeezed the trigger.

The big gun exploded with a flash from the barrel that momentarily blinded David. When his vision returned to normal and the smoke cleared, he could see the man lying flat on his back with his arms over his head and a large hole in his side. David kept the .357 trained on the man; if he moved he would unload the weapon on the man. When he got closer, he could see the man was torn completely through from where his bullet had struck. The machine gun lay about five feet from the man's outstretched arms, so David picked it up and checked the ammo just in case.

Once he got back to the trailer he poured himself a glass of Jack Daniels and called the number he had for Storm. Storm got directions from David D and immediately called Martin. The FBI would handle this case and he, Martin, and four other agents would meet David D at the camp and take care of removing the bodies. The way they would vanish would leave the cartel wondering what had happened to their men.

Storm's End

Storm's End

CHAPTER 27

The activities of the day before and the long night following only reinforced the fact that people involved with the cartel smuggling investigation, especially those thought to have been essential in the arrest of Enrique Guzman, needed to be extra careful as they went about their regular jobs. David D would be placed in a safe house until arrangements could be made for him to continue his career under an assumed name working in the North Sea until the investigation was completed. He protested this turn of events but given this one attempt to find, extract information, and kill him, the FBI was insistent that he go into witness protection. Shipping him to work as a contract employee with a North Sea drilling company was the best plan they had for his immediate future.

"Listen, coonass, this is the best plan and here, I brought you something." Storm then handed David D a gift-wrapped box. Inside was a pair of wool long johns complete with long sleeved top and a parka with a fur trimmed hoody.

"Screw you, Storm, I ain't made for no damn freezing weather, so you take this stuff and shove it where part of your body ain't seen daylight since you were a baby."

Storm's End

The grin on his face betrayed how he really felt and he knew he had to do this.

The rest of the team was told about the fracas in the woods and now each of them would be under surveillance any time they left their office or home. Each was to keep his or her weapon handy—not that anyone thought they were in an imminent danger, but safe was always better than sorry.

* * *

The flight from Dulles to Houston had taken just a little over two hours and after retrieving her bags and the taking the forty-five-minute drive to the hotel, Victoria was settling into her room at the Omni by noon Houston time. A car had been waiting for her when she arrived in Houston and during the ride from the airport to the hotel she called her office to check messages and let her secretary know she had arrived. There was nothing pressing from her office and it gave her time to call her local contact to let him know she was in town.

"This is Victoria, I'm here now. I will see you tomorrow at our scheduled time." This was not a request but merely a statement of fact.

She went on. "I haven't heard if you have handled our last directive. Has that been taken care of?" Her voice was calm and deliberate as she interrogated the person on the other end of the call. "What do you mean you don't know? You had better find out before I see you tomorrow." Again, this was not a wish—it was a threat. Before the person on the other end of the line could reply, she terminated the communication.

Her next call was to Storm.

* * *

Storm was having lunch with Russell, filling him in on the activities of the day and night before. He related how when they reached David D's hunting camp he took them to where the bodies still lay. The FBI agents loaded the bodies into body bags and then huddled to discuss how they were going to handle the situation with David D. That was when they all decided he'd have to go into witness protection until everyone involved had been arrested and put in jail and this case was over. Storm was just telling Russell how the FBI background checks turned up information that the two dead men were known members of the Rio drug cartel and trained by the Mexican Special Forces, although obviously not well enough to catch David D off guard, when his cell phone began to ring.

"Storm," answered the detective, and the voice on the other end was just loud enough for Russell to make out it was a woman and definitely not Alisha.

"Yes, so you got in okay? Yes, I am looking forward to it. See you at the Omni at 7:00 p.m. sharp. Yes, me, too." Storm pressed the disconnect button.

"Wow, sounds like your girlfriend." Russell was amused at how Storm had turned red when he realized who it was on the phone. "You forgot you had a date tonight, didn't you?"

The shit-eatin' grin on Russell's face alone is worth the price of admission, Storm thought. "It's not a date! Well, dammit, you know it's not a date."

"Sounds like a date to me. You're picking her up at her hotel and taking her somewhere fancy schmancy for dinner, aren't you? So in my book that's a date." Russell wasn't going to let his best friend off the hook that easy and Storm knew he reveled in seeing his bud twist on the hook like the worm he had used fishing as a kid.

The look on Storm's face was not amusement; it was almost a look of terror when he asked Russell, "Where should I take her dinner? The only place I've eaten in years is with you at the Brownstone."

"Thought you said this wasn't a date."

"Dammit, it isn't . . . but she is used to being wined and dined in the big time in D.C. so shut the hell up about me having a date and help me figure out somewhere to take her."

"What do you want to eat or more like what do you think she might want to eat?" And almost as an afterthought Russell asked, "Is she a vegan?"

"A what?" That question had thrown Storm totally off his game.

"A vegan, someone who only eats vegetarian. They don't like eating anything that comes from animals or is even cooked in animal oil."

"You're kidding me, right?"

"No, there are some people who like to eat that way, so you've got to be careful where you take them."

"No, I don't think she is one of them. I saw her eating shrimp at the shindig the senator invited me to."

"Okay, then I bet you will be safe taking her most anywhere nice."

"Okay, but where?"

"How about Arturo's? It's not far from the hotel; nice place, good food, good service, and I will call ahead and make you a reservation."

"You would do that?"

"Sure, no problem. Have a good time on your date. OK, Barretta, I know this isn't supposed to be a date. Comprendo. But there's something in how you talk to this woman that reminds me of someone else you once were infatuated with."

Storm thanked him for his help, but scowled at him about the date comment.

* * *

Sam Pickler was the agent recruited to be the DEA's man to go offshore working as a drilling engineer. Sam was by education a petroleum engineer and had spent much of his youth working on rigs as a roughneck in the summers and then after college for a year as a junior engineer working the Gulf Basin. He knew the workings of a rig and he hadn't forgotten what his job would be while he worked offshore this time. Drilling engineers were usually contract hires working for the drilling company, and a new face among them would not raise any suspicion with the company man running the rig. The twelve-hour days were long, but Sam would not be required to do the heavy lifting, so a twelve-hour day for twelve days would be no hill for a stepper. Sam could play the role he been asked to and if there was some type of confrontation aboard the rig he was man enough to take care of himself.

Sam had joined the Marines after 9/11 and had served two tours in Afghanistan with the forced recon Marines or, as they tongue-in-cheek called themselves, the "Swift, Silent and Surrounded." They worked behind enemy lines gathering information for the troops leading the advances. At six foot, he was not tall but the look on his face and the width of his shoulders told any potential bad guy he was probably someone better left alone.

Sam had been aboard the rig for about a week when he got his first glimpse of the smuggling operation. One day a supply boat, the Southern Breeze, showed up flying an American flag. They unloaded seagoing containers, some of which supposedly held drilling additives, downhole mud, and food. The containers were unloaded and supplies were stowed in bulkheads used for storage below the main deck of the rig in what rig personnel call the "mud room." Groceries were taken to the kitchen and stored in pantries and coolers specifically for galley use.

As part of his duty aboard the rig, Sam had access to the mud room. He counted the bags they had on hand when he arrived at the rig and kept count of all bags used in the drilling process. The new bags were separated and stored still in shrink-wrap on waterproof pallets marked with big signs that said they were not to be opened and were for return. These bags looked exactly like the twenty-five-pound bags of mud additives that were already on board and Sam was sure the Southern Breeze had been an impostor vessel that was really bringing drugs to the rig for return and shipment back to the port and warehouse in Houma, Louisiana.

Communication aboard a rig was difficult and the crew had very little opportunity to contact the mainland unless it was some type of emergency. For his protection the DEA had supplied Sam with a SAT phone (a cell like phone that uses satellites) in case he found something he felt the DEA and FBI needed to know.

Today the Claire Marie, a ship Sam was familiar with, arrived with equipment and pipe to be used in the drilling process. Sam saw the pallets of mud marked for return being moved and loaded on the Clair Marie for return to Houma. When his shift was over he would retrieve the SAT phone, call in his report, and let the land-based agents take the ball from there. Four more days aboard the rig and Sam, too, would be on land and his cover would still be intact. Sam found a few minutes where he was alone and made the call. Men on the other end of the call than began to make arrangements to be in Houma when the Clair Marie returned, and they would follow the false shipment of mud additives to its final destination.

*　*　*

Storm arrived at Victoria's hotel fifteen minutes before the arranged time; tardiness was something he could never abide. Angie would pretend to take forever to get ready when they went somewhere just to watch him squirm. He would pace the floor downstairs waiting for her to finish her makeup, constantly grumbling to himself that they were going to be late. Of course she was always down in plenty of time for them make the trip to wherever the event was taking place in order for them to be at least five minutes early. Storm, on the other hand, felt he was late if he was not at least fifteen to thirty minutes early.

Victoria's hotel sat on the edge of a bayou that ran down the length of the 610 inner loop that surrounded Houston and was only about half a mile from Russell's condominium. It had been built in 80's and was all shiny metal and glass. Pocketed away from main streets, it was surrounded by trees, a lovely pond, and lots of green foliage conveying a serene retreat worthy of the price of its rooms.

The detective had just gone to the reception desk to have them buzz her room when the elevator doors opened and Victoria Marcuccio swept from the interior with an aura that made one feel a bright light had just been turned on in the lobby. She was gorgeous in a blue silk skirt and jacket with an ecru silk blouse set off by a single strand of pearls. The skirt stopped just short of her knees and the black four-inch platform shoes made her look taller and more goddess-like than the first time he had seen her. Her raven hair was worn down and cascaded over her shoulders framing her perfectly blended make up that accented her natural beauty. Storm stood transfixed; stunned not just by her beauty, but the effect she had on him mentally and physically. His mind raced as he tried to formulate an explanation for what was going on with him and so far, he had come to no conclusions. It was almost like he had stopped breathing until she reached out her hand to take his and said "hello" with a radiant smile.

Storm stuttered, but finally managed a feeble "hello."

* * *

Victoria was accustomed to making an entrance; she knew the effect she had on men and women alike, but what gladdened her inner self more was the obvious effect it was having on this man called Storm.

"It's so nice to see you again, Detective." Victoria smiled as she felt him tense when she took his hand. In most ways, this man was like any other, the only difference being that most of the men in Washington liked to believe themselves above her ability to impress them while this man simply showed by his look and mannerisms he was under her spell.

"Shall we go? My car is right outside." Storm retrieved his hand as he guided her through the massive electronic doors to his car.

"Where are we going to dinner, Detective?" Asked Victoria.

"We're going to Arturo's. It's nearby and we'll be there in less than ten minutes," said Storm. He's trying to regain his composure Victoria realized.

"Good, I'm famished. What kind of food do they serve? Am I dressed appropriately?" This was Victoria's way of trying to get the detective to comment on how she looked, not so much for the flattery as to determine if she was succeeding in mentally seducing him.

Even when married to Angie, Storm had never been one for exaggerated flattery, so he answered in his simple way, "You look great!" followed by a seldom seen smile.

Victoria giggled and said, "No, I meant am I overdressed; I see you are not wearing a tie."

Victoria saw Storm's shocked expression and knew she had embarrassed him and so she spoke before he could reply. "Detective, you look wonderful. I like how men in Texas remember their roots and I think you look marvelous in your boots and jeans. I just didn't want to look out of place dressed the way I am if we are going to a BBQ place."

* * *

Storm had not thought of a tie. This was Houston in the new millennium and only a very few restaurants even had dress codes. He never thought of wearing a tie to dinner. He was confused; he had asked Russell what to wear and Russell had told him starched jeans, a nice shirt, his boots, and a black blazer. Did she expect more since she was used to running with the big dogs in Washington? Had he been wrong to listen to Russell? His mind raced and halted, but why was he worried? This was not a date, it was a business dinner.

Storm sucked it up and let out a small laugh, "No, no BBQ tonight. This is a nice place and I am sure you can find something you will like on the menu. My friend Russell frequents it and he made the reservation for me. He promised we would both like it and if I am underdressed you can blame him because he told me what I should wear."

"Will I be meeting your friend Russell?"

"Yes, if you want. I guess I assumed you were going to be here for a couple of days and if you don't have plans every night I thought we might go out again and see some of Houston. I'm pretty sure your business accounts won't take you on a tour and you can meet my friends."

"I have plans for tomorrow night, but I will be here till Friday afternoon and have no plans for Wednesday or Thursday night, so either one is open. Just let me know when."

"By the way, Russell is my friend who set me up with the senator and therefore, how I met you," said Storm.

"So, he is the one I blame for meeting a tall attractive Texas detective, huh? I guess I will have to thank him for that." She laid her hand on Storm's arm as he drove.

It wasn't until they had arrived at Arturo's and the valet had taken the car that Storm's face returned to its normal color after Victoria had touched his arm. "So is Wednesday good then?"

"Why don't you call me tomorrow and confirm? But I think it will be great," said Victoria.

The host seated them right away so they didn't have much time to loiter in the waiting area where the other patrons were obviously starring at the goddess dressed in blue. Dinner was as good as Russell had said it would be and they talked about family and their roots, both with stories interesting to the other. When dinner was over they shared a dessert and Storm took her back to her hotel promising to call her tomorrow.

On the drive home, he couldn't get her image out of his head; not just her looks and poise but how he delighted in her company.

CHAPTER 28

Special Agents Morran and Higgins had brought teams of lawmen to Houma hours before the expected arrival of the Claire Marie. The docks and warehouses where the Claire Marie would come ashore were fenced with entry gates at two points on the property. They gained access and set up a perimeter with agents pretending to be dock workers, forklift operators and roving security guards to keep an eye out for the supply boat's arrival and discharge of the their return shipment.

Each man stayed in touch with the base located in a second floor office overlooking the docks that had access to the warehouses via personal radio. The waiting was always the tedious part of any operation. Every time a boat entered the breakwater men went on alert thinking it was their target, and for the first five or six times, they had to be told to stand down, as it wasn't their vessel.

Just after midnight the Claire Marie was seen entering past the breakwater headed for the mooring it used to load and unload cargo. This time is was not a drill; the agents were alerted to merely watch the unloading, watch for the phony bags of mud additives, and see where they went. This was not going to be a situation where anyone was being arrested. This was fact gathering and observation. They would follow the drugs and see where they ended up. Later they would bring a warrant and seize all the records of the shipping company so they could arrest the people involved in the smuggling.

It was well past 2:00 a.m. by the time the Claire Marie had cleared its hold of the returned cargo and the counterfeit bags of additives were off loaded, freeing the ship to leave the docks. A dockworker hung back and made a radio call to an ally who was driving a forklift and he picked up the tail of the illegal goods. The pallet of phony additives was driven to a warehouse with a sign that read GUMDI. There a large white panel truck stood waiting. The back doors of the panel truck opened and the drugs disappeared inside. Immediately the truck started and headed for the gates.

Noticing the process, Tom Morran notified his mobile teams to be on the lookout and follow the van. Morran and Higgins called their men and returned to their vehicles to follow the teams pursuing the van. They had enough teams in enough vehicles that they could let one follow while the others waited for their turn in the rotation to avoid the chance of the van driver spotting the tail.

This game of car tag continued until 5:00 a.m. when the white van exited the interstate, taking surface streets to a light manufacturing and warehouse area just west of New Orleans. The white van disappeared through the massive doors of one of those warehouses. The agents assumed this was a holding area for the drugs until they were delivered later to street dealers across the south. This operation was eerily familiar to Morran and Higgins, who had been part of the seizure of drugs only a year ago in Houston.

* * *

Clay Martin had come into work early, just as he did every day. A man of habit, he had done this for a lifetime and nothing had changed with Angie's death. He sorted the important reports and scanned them for email to Ted Sloane for later that day. These reports were similar to the ones he had gotten for the detective and his friends, but somehow they seemed antiseptic. He had never been a suspicious person, but after seeing the reports that showed the discrepancies that Angie surely had been carrying, he looked closer at all the paperwork to see if he could find any inaccuracies that might indicate someone was scrubbing the numbers. These reports looked just like all the others and didn't show any irregularities in the amounts shipped, those awaiting shipment, or those products returned.

Ted was out of town on one of his many trips meeting with clients and securing future business, which meant Clay, filled his day doing his job and canoodling with other worker bees who held the company together at the grass roots. Rumors circulated about everything from people leaving to people being promoted to new employees' sexual preferences. Today the instant messages began the minute the receptionist welcomed a woman of extraordinary looks who was there for an appointment with Harold Stanton.

Clay's office was positioned across from Ted's office and just down the hall from where Mr. Stanton, the VP of Marketing, resided. His office had large windows that overlooked the residential neighborhood that surrounded the parking garage. Large floor to ceiling interior windows served as the inside walls to create an open, airy and welcoming atmosphere. Everyone who worked for GUMDI assumed these windows were installed at the direction of Mark Wells, the CEO, and they were appreciative of his thoughtfulness. But Clay had heard Mark speak the truth more than once while he sat in on meetings between Mark and Angie—Mark had confessed he had purposely made the inside walls glass so he could keep an eye on his executives. He also admitted that the many years he had spent in the Middle East and his subsequent appointment as CEO of GUMDI had jaded his outlook about being home in the U. S. of A. He also joked that since he no longer had to put up with looking at women dressed in burkas that covered them from head to toe, he also no longer had to look only at a woman's eyes. He had put up the glass walls so he could look out of his office and see the beautiful women that worked for him. It might be a chauvinistic view of life but he was in charge.

With Clay in the room, Angie had actually inquired if that was why she had been promoted. Mark quickly and emphatically answered no. "You were promoted because you are good at what you do," he said. He admitted she had been hired because she was attractive, but when it came to the work and the job people were rewarded for their minds and their ability to do the job. He waved his hand at the people working outside the glass walls and asked them both which view they would rather have: attractive people or people in burkas. After a good laugh, both Angie and Clay were sworn to secrecy concerning his admission.

When the receptionist announced the beautiful woman's arrival, Clay happened to look up and see her as Harold's assistant escorted her to Mr. Stanton's office. She was gorgeous—and almost every man on the floor was craning his neck to catch a glimpse of the lovely stranger.

Clay's immediate reaction was that he had seen a ghost. He shook his head, closed his eyes for a minute, and looked again. He saw Mark Wells come out of his office headed in the direction of Mr. Stanton's office. Mark saw Clay gawking and waved his hand, indicating Clay should quit staring and return to his seat. Clay smiled, blushed, and returned to his chair as Mark winked back at him. He didn't know who this woman was but he would get the skinny within seconds when he got a response to the message he had just sent the receptionist.

* * *

Harold Stanton stood at his door, holding it open when he saw Mark Wells walking between the bullpen cubicles and headed his way. It was obvious to Stanton that Mark was going to intrude on his meeting with this representative from the USTDA and it pushed his buttons to realize the old perv had to come meet the beautiful woman who was there to talk to him—*to him*, not to Mark.

Stanton's assistant introduced Harold to Ms. Marcuccio and then stepped back to watch as his boss took the beautiful woman's hand in his and shook it. "Ms. Marcuccio, may I also introduce you to our CEO, Mark Wells?" Stanton directed Victoria's attention to the older man now joining them.

"Mr. Wells, it's very nice to meet you. Will you be joining our meeting this morning?" Victoria flashed her million-dollar smile, which brought most men to their knees, and she reached out to shake the older man's hand. He seems to be having a problem letting go, Harold noticed.

Mark Wells invited Victoria inside Harold's office and took one of the two chairs in front of Harold's desk while Harold took his seat behind the desk. "Would you care for some coffee, Ms. Marcuccio?" asked Mark.

"Yes, that would be nice," answered Victoria.

Harold raised his hand and beckoned his assistant to return. "Would you get us some coffee, Chad?"

"Yessir. Would the lady like cream and sugar?"

"Yes, please," replied Victoria.

The three of them settled into small talk while they waited for Chad to return with the coffee. Victoria asked again, "Will you be joining us in our meeting, Mr. Wells?"

"No, but when someone from the government comes to visit us I like to meet them and assure them that if there is anything we can do to assist we stand ready to do so. From your title, I assume you are the representative that is working with Harold on a partnership between us and some Latin American companies who hope to obtain a license to bag some of our products and distribute them in South America."

"Yes, I have been communicating with Mr. Stanton for some weeks now about that prospect. Actually, my predecessor was working with another of your Vice Presidents before I was appointed to his job," responded Victoria.

"I am sure you are thinking of Angela Storm. She was invaluable to the company but she was lost to us in a tragic murder a few years ago," replied Mark.

"I am so sorry for your loss." Victoria's eyes even dropped when she said it, and a quick thought crossed Harold's mind—you are good at playing roles, Victoria.

It was then Chad came back with the coffee and Mark excused himself, thanking Victoria again for her visit and again making her promise if there was anything he could do for her to let him know.

Upon the departure of Mark Wells, who pulled Stanton's door closed, Victoria picked up her cup of coffee and took a small sip before she looked over at Stanton and in a quiet self-assured voice asked him, "Have you received any word from our people sent to take care of the oil man?"

Stanton's eyes betrayed his attempt to keep a poker face. Scared and unsure of how to answer her, he did his best to smile before dropping the corners of his mouth and answering, "No, nothing yet, but nothing out of law enforcement, either. There's been no news about a killing in east Texas and nothing about a possible attack on anyone in the area."

Without dwelling on her apprehensions, Victoria continued, "Have you been cleaning the company records so we don't have another foul-up like you did with the detective's wife?"

"Yes, I have that all under control now. There should never be that kind of problem again. The manifests from the rigs will not show the exact amount of the product being returned ever again. The crews unloading the boats are now being paid to deliver the specified counterfeit bags directly to our people who are delivering the product to New Orleans. A load was delivered last night."

"Have you obtained the names of all the people involved in arresting Rique?"

"Yes, I have the list right here. You can take it with you."

"Has your board of directors approved the licensing of our company in Monterrey to bag your products for distribution in South America?"

"No, but the board meets this week and it is on the agenda. Actually, your visit here today will help that along. Mark was impressed with you and he has the vote you need to push this over the top."

"That dirty old man wasn't impressed with my mind or business savvy. All he wanted was a chance to look up my skirt or down my blouse."

Harold could tell Mark had annoyed Victoria. A woman with her looks would expect ogling from most men but since she represented an American trade agency, she had hopes he might be more interested in her business proposal than her legs, he guessed. "If I might make a suggestion, you might want to take him up on his offer and call him before Thursday and tell him how a positive vote would go a long way in growing his sales while securing favor with the committee that over sees the activity of NAFTA and the U.S. Trade Commission," he told her.

"I will do that. Now I want you to get back on the phone and see if you can find those men. Juan Pablo will be looking for a report from you and you know better than to disappoint him."

***

Victoria knew she scared Stanton, but she knew the threat of Juan Pablo being upset with him was even more dangerous. This man may be vain, unscrupulous and greedy, but he isn't stupid enough to go against Juan Pablo, she assured herself.

When their talk was over Victoria arose from her chair and held out her hand to shake goodbye. She had delivered her message and she felt like she needed a shower after only spending about a half an hour with this snake.

To everyone outside of the office it appeared as if they had had a mutually rewarding session and the woman with the incredible figure and the long black hair was leaving. Still inside the glass walls Victoria was seething and had to impart one last piece of information. "I had dinner with the detective last night."

This revelation came as a shock to the man already fighting to maintain his composure. His glib look was once again replaced with one of apprehension and fear.

"In fact, I'm having dinner with him again tomorrow night and he has made plans for me to meet his friends. I am sure some of those I will meet will be on this list you just gave me."

"Why are you meeting with him?"

"The best way to defeat an enemy is to understand him, how he thinks, how he works, who he is and best of all, the people he considers his friends. You don't go to war without intelligence and I will be gathering it." Concluding the directives to Harold, she met Chad at the door. He escorted her back to the lobby and thanked her for her visit.

Victoria's driver waited with an open door to her car, she sank in the seat and closed her eyes as the driver sped away, congratualating herself with her performance in front of Harold "I was as ruthless as my namesake, the Dragon Lady." She mused.

CHAPTER 29

Storm had called his friends and invited them to dinner to meet Victoria. He had planned this to be a relaxing evening and one in which he could show Victoria a little Texas hospitality. It didn't even cross his mind that he was acting like this was a on date to show off his new girlfriend, but his friends were reading more into it.

Russell and Grady would not be available until 7:00 p.m., so they would meet Pancho, Alisha, Ms. Edith, Storm, and the new woman at the Brownstone restaurant. Storm had already talked to Phillip, the manager, and reserved one of the private rooms large enough to hold his party. He was comfortable there and so were his friends, and although he felt it was not as "high toned" as places Victoria would normally be invited to, it was nice, the food was good, and he hoped the conversation would be just as rewarding.

Phone calls began to percolate between his friends, all with the same conversation. Why was Storm introducing them? Was she his new girlfriend? Was he crazy? He had just met the woman. Could it be he was only trying to make her feel at home in Houston? Did he even have a clue how this appeared? They assumed they would have answers after they had dinner.

Storm's End

* * *

Back at the FBI offices, Martin and Pancho were going through stacks of records that Ted had supplied to them. The ownership of the companies that Angie had visited on her last trip to Latin American was a hodgepodge. Some were straightforward, with ownership easily identifiable, while others were a maze of threads that led from one shell company to another. When they found the corporate owner of one, it would be a dead end. Tracing these companies kept them running back to ask Ted for more information and more requests from the State Department to Mexican authorities in hopes of following a sliver of information that would finally lead them to a real person or persons in control of this web of corporate chicanery.

One such lead was the ownership of Tampico Servicio, a shipping company that supplied material from vendors to the offshore rigs that worked the southern Gulf of Mexico. The first break they got was finding that Tampico Servicio was a solely owned subsidiary of Chichimecas Publicación, whose owners just happened to be the now deceased Enrique Guzman, his wife, and members of a board of trustees. That was when they found the names of the people they were looking for: the board of trustees included Juan Pablo Du Tilly, Rique's sister Isabell Guzman, and the biggest shock of all, Harold Stanton.

Chichimecas Publicación was the company that printed the books and turned out the DVDs for Noah and Rachel Benedict when they were running their fraud across the south. It was later accepted that the Benedicts had most probably not been part of the interstate trade in drugs, which saved them any serious jail time, but did cause them to forfeit all their misbegotten financial gains, leaving them penniless with a record that would follow them the rest of their lives.

Storm's End

Juan Pablo Du Tilly was known to everyone who had anything to do with law enforcement since 1998 when he had parlayed a meager inheritance and ruthless psychotic penchant for doing business into the powerful Rio drug cartel. The body count had never been tallied, but in his wake he left numerous families dead or running for their lives. He resided in Monterrey, Mexico, and according to Mexican Drug Enforcement, he was now fully in charge of the cartel and caring for Enrique's widow and children in a secluded villa near his fortress on a golf course.

Neither man reading the reports had ever heard of Isabella Guzman, nor were they aware that Rique had a sister. She was a total unknown entity. Who she was and how did she fit into the equation this would take further investigation.

Harold Stanton was another deal. The minute Pancho saw his name he remembered it. He was the man from GUMDI who had worked with Storm's wife. He was a vice president of some kind and both Martin and Pancho knew they had found their first real lead as to who was behind the smuggling and quite possibly Angie's death. Storm, Special Agents Higgins and Morran would need to be informed immediately they had important information but how they would use it was a concern above their pay grade. A plan would have to be prepared to trap all the rats at the same time. Pancho would find a way to bring Storm up to speed but reasoned he would wait until tomorrow and with the support of Martin and Agents Higgins and Morran to tell Storm what they had found.

* * *

Victoria was ready and waiting in the lobby of her hotel when Storm arrived to pick her up. He had told her the restaurant was nice, but not fancy and it would perfectly fine for her to dress casually. She wore her hair down cascading over her shoulders, framing her face to let her natural beauty shine. She was the type of woman who could get away with very little makeup unless she was going to some big formal event, where her makeup would have to be as impeccable as her attire. But tonight was not one of those nights and she felt at ease going out for a pleasant relaxed dinner with new people. None of them would know she was sizing them up; nothing they said or did would escape her scrutiny. Her true identity was a closely kept secret with only her mother, her grandfather, and Juan Pablo knowing who she really was.

Storm was early as he had been two nights before, but this time she had prepared early and was waiting. His nondescript police car was not what most of her suitors would have picked her up in, but she had already pegged him as a man who could care less about worldly goods. He seemed bright and very driven but he didn't need luxuries.

The drive to the restaurant was short so they had little time for anything but pleasantries. When they arrived at the eatery, it was obvious the employees knew him; the maître d met them at the door and escorted them to the semiprivate room Storm had reserved. Awaiting them in the room was a Spanish-looking man with an obvious limp, who appeared to be the other policeman described in her intelligence report. Also waiting was a younger black woman sitting beside an older black woman. The younger woman was most likely the medical examiner who had also been described in the detailed report supplied by Harold Stanton as one of the people involved in Rique's arrest and his ultimate death. Who the older woman was she had no idea, but she was sure before the evening had ended she would know about her, too.

Storm put his hand on Victoria's arm, steering her into the room as if showing her off. "Everyone, this is Victoria Marcuccio, she works for the USTDA and has been trying to help us understand the details of Angie's last trip to Latin America and who she might have met with. Victoria, this is Pancho Hernandez, my partner; this is Alisha Johnson, the medical examiner for Harris County and her mother Ms. Edith, who has adopted us all as her children. They're all good friends and people I wanted you to meet."

Each of them shook her hand and welcomed her. Ms. Edith took her by the shoulders and gave her a warm embrace.

After they were seated, Victoria turned to Storm. "I thought there was to be seven of us?"

"There will be; the other two will be here shortly. They had to finish doing the weather at one of our local television stations," replied Storm.

"Oh, they are on TV?"

"Well, not both of them. Russell, Russell Hildebrandt, is the weatherman for Channel 5 and Grady Anderson is his producer and cameraman. They should be here any time."

A waiter had just taken their drink orders when Russell and Grady stepped through the door of the room and Storm went about introducing Victoria to both men.

* * *

Alisha and Pancho both caught the same look from Russell; it was if he had seen an apparition from his past.

Neither Alisha nor Pancho had ever met Storm's wife when she had been alive, but they had seen enough pictures of her to know this woman looked like the reincarnation of Angie. When Russell had regained control of himself and stopped his stuttering, he shook her hand and welcomed her to Houston.

Drinks were served all around, with Storm getting his soda and lemon, giving the appearance that he, too, was having a drink. Ms. Edith chattered away at everyone who sat around the oval family style table, catching up on everyone, their health, and what they had been up too. The conversation was light and amicable among old friends who haven't seen each other in a while. Ms. Edith asked

Victoria where she was from and what life was like living in a city where it seemed everything revolved around politics and politicians.

"It's probably very much the same way life is here; you work, you go home, you try to spend time with your family, if you have a family, and life goes on."

"Do you come from a big family, Victoria?" asked Ms. Edith.

"Well, yes, my mother, my grandfather, grandmother, and enough aunts, uncles and cousins to fill a small stadium."

"Do they live in the area where you do?" asked Alisha.

"Yes. I am a fifth generation Virginian. My great grandparents settled outside of Washington D.C. shortly after the Civil War. They were farmers; they grew vegetables and sold them to the restaurants that opened to feed the growing community that came to Washington after 'the War between the States,' as people in the South refer to it. As the family grew, some went into the restaurant business while others remained in farming, buying land in the Virginia countryside. My grandfather was the one who got them into the real estate business. He developed the farm land into homes, apartment structures and business districts to support the growing expansion in Arlington, Virginia."

"It sounds like you had a lovely childhood then with all that success in the family," said Ms. Edith.

"Oh, I will admit to being spoiled, but I was expected to succeed on my own. Each cousin was pushed to go to school, graduate, and either go to work in one of the family businesses or find their own way. I chose working for the government and since I have a law degree in international business I found a home with USTDA and so far have been very fortunate."

"Great," injected Ms. Edith, launching into the real question everyone had hoped she would ask. "Do you have a boyfriend or significant other?"

Alisha gasped. "Mother!"

Storm exclaimed, "Ms. Edith!" While all the others just laughed in relief. The question was one each of them wanted to ask but didn't have the guts.

After the chuckling subsided Victoria smiled and answered easily without the slightest embarrassment. "Why no, Ms. Edith, I don't, do you have anyone in mind?"

"What about the guy from the senator's office you came to party with?" asked Storm.

"Harrison?" she laughed softly, treating the question as if it might be the most ridiculous thing she had ever heard. "No, Harrison is an acceptable escort to functions and nothing more. He would like a relationship, but he is too snobby for me and too sneaky." Her eyebrows arched as she answered, and then she added, "There are a lot of that kind of people in D.C."

"How is my friend the senator?" asked Russell, changing the subject to get her off the hot seat.

"I guess he's fine. I haven't seen him since the party where I met David, but I'm sure he's fine."

Alisha and Pancho looked at each other again. *She called Storm "David,"* Pancho's expression telegraphed his reaction as. Alisha just rolled her eyes.

"And I'm sure he's still the same old perv he has always been!" Russell looked closely at Victoria to see how she would handle his reproach of an esteemed member of Senate.

"Well, let's just say a girl wants to stay out of reach when around the senator. He may be aging, but he still has fast hands."

"Storm told us you are helping him look into the events of his wife's last week in Latin America," said Pancho.

"Well, I'm not sure I'm much help. As you all probably know, I replaced the man from our office who was with her on that trip. All I've been able to do is go through his reports and supply them to David so he can look to see if there is anything in them that might help explain her death."

"I'm sure he appreciates that."

He can meet the same people his wife met on her trip." Storm looked surprised with this news as she said to him, "That is, if you would still like to go, David."

Caught totally off guard by this turn of events, He looked as if he was at a loss for words. He sat quietly as the others waited for him to reply. Finally he answered, "When would we be going?"

"Next week. I have the trip already planned and today the director approved your accompanying me. So if you want to go, we will need to make your reservations by no later than Friday."

"Can I let you know tomorrow?" he asked.

"Yes. Why don't we have lunch?"

"Great! I will know by then if I can get away."

Everyone at the table chimed in that this was the opportunity of lifetime, and surely, he could get away for a week, especially in such wonderful company. With that said they ordered dinner and continued chatting about life in Washington and Houston, about family, and about their various jobs.

***

As they all chattered on, Victoria kept mental notes of what was said and asked questions to get a better understanding of the people around the table.

CHAPTER 30

Since the attempt on David D's life when the two cartel hit men had been dispatched, the tails on Storm had disappeared. Still, the team members were cautioned to remain vigilant for anything that looked or seemed out of place and each was assured this was not the time to stop carrying their weapons. With his shadows gone, Storm and Pancho decided it was in their best interest to meet at FBI headquarters, where Martin and Pancho would brief him on the latest Intel from the search into companies Angie had visited on her last trip out of the country.

The three men were meeting in the conference room when Agent Higgins came through the door and joined them. He carried files in his hands and he laid them down on the table, leaving them closed for the time being.

"So, gentlemen, what have you found?" he asked.

"Sir, we spent the better part of two weeks running down leads on the ownership of the companies Detective Storm's wife met with the last week of her life." Martin looked over to make sure Storm was okay with the direction of conversation. "Most of them are Mexican-owned corporations and the leadership of the companies is easily verified. About half of the companies are subsidiaries of larger corporate entities with global ownership and investors from as far away as Russia and China. Although we are suspicious that we have foreign traders operating in our backyard, we can find no connection to drug running or cartel operations, with one exception." Martin paused and turned to Pancho, indicating that he should continue with the briefing and inform Storm and Higgins of their one and only problematic discovery.

Pancho shot Martin a look that could kill; he was not any happier about what he was now going to tell the men than Martin seemed to be. "The only company that was hinky was one that supplies offshore rigs with water, foodstuffs, and medical supplies. It is called Tampico Servicio. It says in the notes we got from your friend Victoria that this company wanted to arrange an agreement with Mrs. Storm's company to package mud additives. We looked into the company and initially it seemed to be nothing more than a small shipping company with three supply boats contracted to drilling companies working offshore to bring essentials for everyday operation of the rig. Nowhere could we find that they had any capabilities to make or package products. They are simply a distributor and carrier of supplies. But it appears they are also a shell company." Here Pancho stopped a minute to let what he had just said sink in.

Agent Higgins spoke deliberately and quietly, but with the intention of letting it be known it was time to move on and let the chips fall where they may. "I'm sure there is more to this or you and Martin wouldn't have felt like this was important enough to bring the detective and myself into a face to face meeting, so go on."

Martin and Pancho both winced at the rebuke and Pancho continued, "Yessir, there is more. First, we got in touch with Ted Bussard and asked for his help in tracking down the ownership of this company. It took almost a week for him to go through the state department and for them to inquire of the Mexican government through trusted diplomatic channels for names of the individuals who were listed as the owners and board of directors of Tampico Servicio— " Again Pancho paused.

"For God's sake, Pancho, get on with it! What did you find?" urged Storm.

"Tampico Servicio is solely owned by Chichimecas Publicación out of Monterrey, Mexico. The CEO of Chichimecas Publicación is the one and only Señor Enrique Guzman."

Martin and Pancho both glanced at Storm. He sat motionless as he heard the news but waited to hear what additional information the men had found.

Pancho continued, "Also listed as owners and members of the board of directors are Juan Pablo Du Tilly, now the Guzman estate, Isabella Guzman the sister of the late Enrique, and finally the most interesting member owning ten percent of the company is Mr. Harold Stanton."

"Who?" Shock replaced decorum and Storm's voice became louder. "Did you say 'Harold Stanton,' the same little weasel that works for GUMDI and the same prima donna that worked down the hall from my wife? Are you friggin' kidding me?" Storm was livid; the veins on his neck and head bulged as rage painted his face.

"Easy, Detective, get a hold of yourself." Special Agent Higgins saw the rage flare and knew this was a time for cooler heads to prevail.

"I'm going down and drag that sumbitch out by his neck and kick the shit of him right in front of the rest of that snake pit. He sat in his office and bald-faced lied to me. He lied and y'all know he did. I met with him five years ago and the detectives investigating Angie's murder met with him and he sat there and lied. The sumbitch had to know. He was in bed with the cartel then. He had to know."

"You are not going anywhere and you are not gonna kick the shit out of anyone," responded Higgins, "at least not yet. But believe me, you are going to get your chance."

"If you take things into your own hands right now, you'll blow the case we're developing, and the other conspirators will get away.

"You know we can't go in there hell bent on revenge. This is not the Old West and with all the money and influence these people have, we need to have all of our ducks in a row when we take them down. Then I promise you will be the one who arrests Harold Stanton. Now let's get back to the briefing."

Martin and Pancho just looked at each other. Pancho had known Storm longer, but he had never seen such a violent reaction from his partner or ever even heard of him nearly coming apart like he had just done.

Martin continued his part of the briefing. "We know Guzman was one of the kingpins of the Rio Cartel and we also have Intel from the DEA that Juan Pablo Du Tilly and Guzman had been friends since their college days. Juan Pablo had the political connections and it was once thought that his brother would someday lead Mexico. The DEA and Mexican drug enforcement have always been sure that Guzman was the public face and Du Tilly was the power behind the leadership, although so far nothing has ever been successfully tied to him as a part of the cartel.

"Now, who is this sister, this Isabella Guzman, is, we got nothing. From corporate records, we know she owns twenty percent of Chichimecas, which would make her a twenty percent owner of Tampico Servicio. So far, there have been no records showing that Rique had a sister, yet she is listed on the corporate papers as an owner, board member, and sister," added Martin.

Storm jumped in. "We have the Intel connecting Harold to the cartel, so all we have to do is go over there, pull that asshole out by the hair, arrest him, and let me have him for a few hours. He will tell us all we need to know."

"No, we can't," Martin insisted. "I know you're pissed and you want him bad. We do, too. But we have to have an airtight case before we make a run at these people. If we go in breaking down doors, it will alert them that we are on to them and the rest will slip away. We have to play this by the book."

"Is that all you two have?" asked Higgins.

"Yessir. That's it, but Storm has something—something I think he needs to tell you about," said Pancho.

* * *

Storm looked at Pancho like he had lost his mind. What the hell was he talking about? He didn't have anything new. All he had now was a case of the red ass and he wanted to get hold of Harold Stanton's neck.

"Tell him, Storm; tell him about your invite." Pancho was trying to get Storm back in the discussion.

"What invite?"

"The invite your pretty lady friend made last night." Pancho sounded like he was pushing Storm to think it through. This could be a good deal for the team and the investigation.

"Oh." Storm's mind snapped back into gear, "Yeah, right. Well, last night we were all having dinner with Victoria Marcuccio from the USTDA. She is in town visiting companies here that she tries to marry with foreign companies in cooperative business arrangements. Anyway, she told us last night she had received permission to take me along on her next trip to Latin America to visit the same accounts my wife had been to see on her last trip." Even though he had just told Agents Jones and Higgins about the invite, he was still sorting out in his mind what he making such a trip might do for them and the investigation.

"What did you tell her?" asked Higgins.

"Oh, nothing yet. I told her I would let her know today." Storm didn't really comprehend why Higgins was concerned He hadn't decided whether making the trip was a good idea of more immediate importance was Harold Stanton and he knew where to find him.

"How long would this trip last and how many companies would you be seeing with her?" asked Higgins.

"I don't know. I didn't ask, but I guess the same companies Angie went to see with Ms. Mariucci's predecessor," answered Storm.

"I think you should go," said Higgins.

"Why?" Storm was surprised that Higgins said so quickly he wanted him to go.

"It would give you a chance to see these people in person. You are intuitive, you've been a cop for a long time, and you would see through the fakes and recognize what they might reveal without really knowing they are revealing anything. How would she introduce you? How would she justify you being with her on this trip?" asked Higgins.

"I don't know. I guess she could tell them I was the husband of a late representative from GUMDI and I was just along to see the last places my wife visited." This response was not well thought out on Storm's part because he had not decided on going.

"No, I don't think that is good idea. The Latin mentality would be to offer you their condolences, and any meaningful business conversations would be tabled until you were out of the room. I think we need to go to State, who can go to USTDA and get them to set up the cover story that you are along as personal protection for a female representative of the American government in a foreign land in unsettling times," said Higgins. "In fact, I will make the call to Ted when this meeting breaks up and get back to you as soon as he talks to State and they talk to USTDA. After all, this will be a great show of cooperation between agencies on the Hill. Call Ms. Marcuccio and tell her you are tentatively saying yes if things can be worked out."

"Okay, but Ralph, I don't even have a valid passport," another detail that had not occurred to anyone yet.

"Not a problem. I'm sure our boys at State can get you credentials in time for you to make the trip. It might not be a passport, but it will be papers that will get you out of the USA into any country you want to enter and back into the U.S. Now that that is settled, I have something to add to this briefing," with that, Agent Higgins opened the files he had brought into the room. The first file he extracted, an action report, looked to contain about half a dozen typed pages.

"Gentlemen, your friend Dubose was right. They are smuggling from the rigs. Our man on the rig found exactly what Dubose told us we would find; shipments of supplies came in from Tampico Servicio and were dropped on the rig. The shipment was overseen by the company man. Two days later our agent saw the same pallet of bags being loaded on a supply boat headed back to Houma, Louisiana. There were at least forty bags marked "Mud Additives" still shrink-wrapped in exactly the same way they had been delivered. He called Morran and Morran called me and together we set up surveillance and waited for the supply boat to make shore in Houma. We observed the pallet of additives being unloaded and taken to a warehouse marked "GUMDI" where they were loaded into a white unmarked panel van and were carried to a warehouse outside of New Orleans," Higgins continued to read the report, "We staked out the warehouse and over the next several days we saw numerous small trucks and vans coming and going from what looks like a building abandoned in the aftermath of the ravages of Katrina. Many of the men driving those trucks and vans were members of Reggie's old crew, the Canal Street Boys. It appears even with Reggie in jail and turning state's evidence against Rique and his crew, he is still in the employ of the cartel."

The next thing Agent Higgins pulled from the files was what looked like another of the cryptic messages addressed to "Whomever is in Charge of the Angie Storm case." He tossed copies of the message to each man at the table. The message read, "In the days of Arthur, a knight's biggest concern was the existence of the dragon. Beware of the Dragon Lady."

"What the hell does this mean?" asked Storm.

"Right now we have no idea, but we have figured out the other messages. Those messages led us to the connection of your wife's murder to Gully Gilroy that they were killed on the orders of the same people and those people are tied to the Rio Cartel. We now know the message about the islands wasn't referring to islands in the strictest sense of the word, but rather man-made islands or drilling platforms. Now we just need to figure out who this message is referring to. Whoever it is, the messenger thinks the person is a danger and, of course, it doesn't take a rocket scientist to see it must be a woman.

"But, gentlemen, I have better news for you. We might not have to figure out who the messenger is referring to; we might just be able to ask the messenger." Higgins had a smile on his face that softened even his rugged features.

"What do you mean?" they all asked in unison.

"Before the third message arrived, we had placed a security camera over the mail drop where all the messages have been dropped. We put it on a constant eight-hour loop on the same time frame as when the mail is retrieved from that mail drop since all mail is stamped with a time code showing when it is received in the mail room. We can then go back and look at the previous eight hours of video and see if we see anyone who looks suspicious dropping off what would appears to be the type of envelope the messages come in. With facial recognition software, hopefully we can find our messenger."

"Have you done that yet?" asked Martin.

"Yes, and we have narrowed it down to six subjects observed dropping mail into the box." Agent Higgins took six pictures from the file and threw them on the table.

It took only seconds for Storm to recognize one of the people in the pictures. Of the five men and one woman, it was the photo of the woman that jumped out at him; he recognized her immediately. The shock of his recognition rendered him speechless. The woman was Estella Martin, Clay Martin's wife. When he caught his breath, he spoke softly. "Jesus Christ, Ralph, here's the woman who has been delivering the messages." Storm held up the picture of Estella Martin.

"How do you know?" asked Higgins.

"She's the wife of our insider at GUMDI; that is Clay Martin's wife."

"Why would she be delivering messages that led us here? Why wouldn't her husband just come to you and tell you what he knew?"

"I don't know. The only thing I can think of is they wanted to stay invisible to the people he was leading us to. He was my wife's assistant and they were very close. We used to do things with his family and they used to come to our house. Angie loved him and his family. His kids were like her nieces. The only thing I can think of is they are scared."

"We need to talk to him and we need to talk to him now," said Higgins.

"We've got to be careful with this. If they went to all this trouble to stay out of it we've got to find a way to keep them out of it," said Pancho. "If they are like a lot of other Mexican families living in Texas they have family in Mexico and if it gets out they had anything to do with bringing down an organization like the Rio Cartel, we could put a lot of people in danger. The cartel has no inhibitions about killing family members over what they would consider a betrayal."

"How do you get in touch with him now?" asked Higgins.

"We give him a burner phone and only we have the number. Grady Anderson calls him and sets up lunch. Grady is someone few know has any link to us. He would just be seen as an old man who meets a nodding acquaintance from time to time in the same restaurant having lunch and they shoot the breeze." Pancho hesitated a few seconds. "But I'm not comfortable asking Grady to do this. It will be too dangerous for everyone concerned."

"How do you plan on doing this then?"

"I don't know yet, but whatever we do, it can't lead back to Clay or his family. Obviously, they have been very careful about this and as of right now they are in the clear. Give me twenty-four hours to come up with a plan and I will let you know. In the meantime, whatever you do, don't let any agents approach him or his family. We don't need anything happening to them."

Higgins agreed he would wait for Storm to come up with a plan. Storm would tell Victoria he was going with her and the papers he needed to travel would be complete within the same amount of time as the team expected him to formulate a plan. When the meeting broke up, each man knew what he had to do.

CHAPTER 31

The car ride back to Storm's apartment was quiet, broken only by the occasional outburst of expletives such as "asshole," "sumbitch," and "little piece of shit" as his mind raced to wrap itself around the information that somehow Harold Stanton was involved with the cartel, let alone possibly with the killing of his wife. When they finally arrived, Storm had calmed down and both he and Pancho knew they had to find a way to confront Clay about his or his wife's sending the mystery clues.

Ms. Edith was at Storm's apartment; it was one of the days she came to clean and grocery shop for him, keeping him supplied with healthy food and the home cooked dinners she would make or bring already frozen and stored in his refrigerator until he needed them. She always stayed until Alisha got off work and came to pick her up. Now reclining in her favorite chair that she had long ago claimed as hers, she sat watching her shows on TV. She bolted to her feet in surprise when the door opened. "Oh, my Lordy, David, you gave me a start!" she gasped

"Oh, sorry, Ms. Edith. I forgot today was a day you were here. Are you okay? We didn't mean to scare you."

With a big exhale and with her hand upon her heart, she assured them she would be fine as soon as her blood pressure went back to normal. They all laughed and each got the famous hug from the large black lady who had become like a mother to all of them.

"Can I get you boys something to eat?"

"No, Ms. Edith, we're fine. Just got some stuff to talk over and some decisions to make, but we can talk in the kitchen," said Storm.

"Well, you boys go talk and I'll stay here in the living room watching my shows. You know it is hard to find something to watch when it is not time for Oprah." Ms. Edith was a huge Oprah fan and even followed her reading list. She followed up with, "If you boys change your minds I can make you a sandwich." She smiled and went back to her chair and made herself comfortable, catching up with her soap opera.

Pancho sat at the table in the kitchen and pulled out his computer and a lined tablet. When they made plans, he was usually either looking up information on the computer or using the tablet to keep notes on what they were discussing. "You know, however we get to Clay and his wife, we got to be careful. I know it appears none of us are being shadowed right now, but we can't be too careful and we don't want to put anyone else in harm's way after what happened to your friend David D."

"I know. God forbid we get Clay or Estella hurt in this. So far if it hadn't been for them, we would still be stuck looking for a clue as to why this is all happening." Storm's mind was in high gear. They had to talk to Clay and probably bring his wife in, too, to cover all the bases, but the question was how to do it and not arouse any suspicion with the bad guys.

"We've got to get them to come in and they can't be seen with any of us," said Pancho.

It was as if a light turned on in Storm's mind. He turned in his seat. "Ms. Edith, what time is Alisha coming to pick you up?"

Pancho turned too, seeing Storm grinning; it was like the same switch had turned on in both of their minds at the same time. He knew where Storm was going with this inquiry. "You thinking the same thing I am?" he asked Storm.

The detective just smiled as Ms. Edith answered, "She should be here about five, why?"

"Ms. Edith, could you do me a favor? Could you call her and ask her if she could pick you up a little early?" Storm asked.

Ms. Edith looked confused but got up from her throne and walked to the kitchen to get her cell phone where she had laid it next to her purse. "What is it, David? Do you need to go? I can always catch a bus if I'm in the way."

"No, Mom," Storm assured her, using the name he had come to use when he wanted Ms. Edith to know how much she meant to him, a word that always made her smile. "You don't need to go. We just need to talk to Alisha in person and we need you to stay, because if this is to work, we will need your help, too."

* * *

Alisha received the call from her mom asking her to leave work early and come get her, but it didn't make sense. When she questioned her as to why she needed to come early, her mom replied with a curt, "You just need to come now," and she hung up.

Alarmed at her mother's behavior, she rushed to Storm's apartment worried that something was wrong. At her mother's age you never knew what it could be, and her mom was the only family she had left if she didn't count the men from the team she worked with so closely.

Ms. Edith answered the door after the first knock. "Good, honey, you're here.'

"What's wrong, Mom? Are you okay?"

Storm's End

"I'm fine," Ms. Edith grabbed her daughter and gave her a big hug while she whispered in her ear, "David had me do it this way. I'm sure he can tell you why, although I still have no idea what's going on."

"Storm, what the hell is going on? You just scared the crap of me. I thought something had happened to Mom." She glared at Storm, demanding answers.

"I'm sorry, Alisha, but I knew that would get you over here the fastest way. If somebody at work asked, you could tell them you had an emergency with your mom and had to leave. Nobody would be any the wiser. If we are all still being watched, you're coming to pick your mother up wouldn't make anyone suspicious."

"That still doesn't answer my question."

"Okay, both of you sit down." For the next thirty minutes, Storm and Pancho went over what they had found out that day. They explained how during the search for information on the companies Angie had gone to visit on her last rip they had found a member of the board of one of those holding companies was none other than Rique, and how also on the board was one of biggest known drug traffickers in northern Mexico. Last but certainly not least, so was Harold Stanton, a man Angie had worked with for the last six years before her murder.

After that news had been fully absorbed by the two women, Storm added the part they needed to understand in what had come to him and Pancho at the same time as a budding plan. "The FBI found out who has been leaving them the mysterious messages about this case."

"Who?" asked Alisha.

"They caught Clay Martin's wife Estella on a concealed camera dropping off what looked to be an envelope matching the envelopes containing the messages the FBI has been getting and she was seen dropping it off only an hour before the mail was taken out of the box and delivered to Agent Higgins."

Alisha's mouth dropped open in astonishment, while Ms. Edith remained quiet. They all realized she didn't have all the information. "Why wouldn't he have just come out and told you?"

"I or we are guessing they're afraid. He knows too much and people who know too much disappear around these types of gangsters," said Pancho.

"Who is Clay Martin?" asked Ms. Edith.

Storm took a couple of minutes to bring her up to speed.

"Well, if you have a plan, what do Mom and I have to do with it?"

Storm sat quietly for a minute before he began to speak. "Well, we have to bring them in so we can find out what they know or what Clay knows. I'm not sure Estella knows much at all. I suspect she is just a courier for Clay."

"Okay, now back to what do Mom and I have to do with this?"

"Have you seen anyone tailing you lately or seen anything out of place that just didn't fit?"

"No, nothing."

"Okay, here's the idea. We will have Grady call Clay and tell him they need to meet just like he has in the past. We'll set the meeting for early on Saturday. We will have Russell and Pancho staking out Clay's house, so that when he leaves to meet Grady, we'll know if he is being followed. If someone is watching the house, Agent Higgins and I will also be watching and we'll abort the plan. If there is nothing suspicious, I will buzz Pancho on his phone with the go-ahead and he will go to Clay and Estella's, tell Estella who he is and that he needs her to come with him and bring the kids. If necessary, he will let her believe something has happened to Clay. That way she should come without too much questioning."

"That's a kinda dirty trick, Storm."

"I know, but the less talk, the better, at least 'til we get everyone together."

Storm's End

"What will he do with her once she goes with him?"

"Pancho will drive them to your mom's house."

That woke up Ms. Edith.

"Where will I be?" she asked.

"I don't know. How about visiting a ladies' spa for the day, somewhere safe, where we can keep an eye on you," said Pancho.

Again, the light went on in Storm's head.

"Right!" he said. "How about we treat you and a friend to a day at the spa on the FBI and you can get treated like the queen you are?"

Ms. Edith just smiled but added, "I'm not afraid of these people. I'm an old lady; they won't hurt me."

"You never know, Ms. Edith," said Pancho, shaking his head.

"Mom, you're going. If we use your house you aren't going to be there. No chances." said Alisha adamantly.

Ms. Edith finally accepted the fact she would have to leave for the day and let the conspirators use her home as their meeting place. It was then that Storm's phone rang and he saw that Special Agent Higgins was calling him. He listened for a minute and then told Higgins of the plan he and Pancho had come up with. Higgins must have responded positively and Storm hung up.

"So did he have any new intel?" Pancho asked.

"No. He just called to tell me everything had been worked out with the State Department and my travel documents to accompany Victoria to Latin America as her bodyguard have been approved and are being overnighted to FBI headquarters."

"Then you are going?" asked Alisha.

"Looks that way," answered Storm.

"Now all you need to do is call her and tell her you are going with her," said Pancho.

"First, is everyone okay with the plan?" asked Storm.

"You still need to get Russell and Grady up to speed," stated Pancho.

"I'll do that right after I call Victoria."

* * *

Victoria felt her cell phone begin to vibrate. When she was working, she turned off the sound and relied on the vibration to alert to when she had a call. A quick glance at the display indicated that it was David.

"This is Victoria."

"Hello, Victoria, its Detective Storm from Houston." Victoria could almost see him wincing, because, of course, she knew he was a detective and she knew he was from Houston. *He's probably asking himself, "What am I, an idiot or what?" Bet he's glad I can't see how embarrassed he probably is.*

"Hello, David. I knew it was you; I have your number programmed into my phone so when you call it tells me it is you." Victoria smiled to herself. She knew the man was naïve and she knew she had him caught in her web.

"What can I do for you?" asked Victoria.

"Have you talked to your office today?"

"Yes, and the director told me all about how you might be going with me on my next trip south and that State with pressure from Senator Rendell's office, right?"

"Yes, that's what I was calling to tell you. I'm looking forward to the trip, but everyone concerned thought it better that I go as a bodyguard than as the husband of a woman who was there a few years ago."

"It probably is a good idea. I will be there on business, so no sense in getting them off track with talk of your departed."

"Yep, that's what everyone here thought, too."

"Have you thought about how you will do this? Will you be traveling with me or meet me at the first stop?"

"Actually, Victoria, we haven't gotten that far yet, but I will call you before Monday and let you know. I guess it would be better if I went with you since I am supposed to be your bodyguard."

"This is very exciting. I have never had such an attractive bodyguard. I'm looking forward to this."

With promises to call her as soon as his arrangements were made, he hung up. Victoria had other calls to make and plans of her own to put in motion.

* * *

Storm still needed to call Russell and Grady to fill them in on the plan for Saturday and how they fit into it. Friday after updating Agent Higgins, the plan was changed somewhat. Agent Higgins suggested some modifications to make the pickup of Clay and his wife simpler and less traumatic. Rather than Pancho going to get Estella, Storm would. He already knew her and the kids, so there would probably be less anxiety on Estella's part. Russell would drive Grady to the appointed breakfast meeting with Clay and drive them both to Alisha's home. If Clay needed persuasion to join Grady, Russell would intervene since he, too, already knew Clay from the many social gatherings at Storm and Angie's old home.

Both pickup cars would be tailed. Pancho and Higgins would follow Storm and Frank Morran from the DEA, and Ted Bussard of the attorney general's office would follow Russell. Each tail team would keep their eyes open for anyone who looked like they might be following the parties involved in the pickup. Two other teams of FBI agents would keep what they called "high cover" for all those involved with the pickup. These teams were to be the eyes that oversaw the ultimate safety for the people who would later interview Clay and Estella.

After the interview Clay and his family would be closely monitored to ascertain if they had been discovered talking to law enforcement. If there ever appeared to be an imminent threat to their safety, they would be moved to witness protection until such time as the authorities felt it was safe for them to resume their lives.

Alisha would get her mom out of the house and off to her day at the spa. The FBI had arranged for Ms. Edith and one of her close friends to be picked up by a chauffeur driven limo and escorted to their day of being pampered. In case any problem might arise, the driver was an FBI agent trained in evasive driving and witness protection.

Storm's End

CHAPTER 32

The plan was put into effect early the next morning. While Alisha held down the fort at her house, she received a call from Russell. The pickups of Clay and his wife had gone off without a hitch. Clay had shown some hesitation accompanying Grady and Russell, but with just a little arm-twisting and an assurance everything was okay, he had gone along. Estella, on the other hand, had been scared out of her wits when Storm came to her door. He was a policeman telling her she needed to bring the kids and they needed to go see Clay; her first thought was something terrible had happened to him.

Storm hated that he couldn't tell her the entire truth but they would get to that soon enough.

Alisha had opened the gate that allowed access to the yard from the back alley so the two cars could pull inside the eight-foot high wooden fence, a protection that was de rigueur for every yard in the neighborhood. When Storm arrived in the last car he would close the gate so anyone who drove down the alley wouldn't see the cars parked inside the fence.

Storm's End

The men on high overlook would take up positions at the end of the block where they could see both the entrance to the alley and have a clear view of the street, one car with two agents on each end of the street. If someone suspicious was spotted, they would call in for a license check and keep an eye on the vehicle until it was eliminated as a possible threat.

Storm pulled down the alley and into the yard. When he got out, Ralph Higgins exited the car with Estella and the kids, herding them toward the house as Storm closed the large wooden gate. Alisha met them at the back door with Clay standing behind, surprised to see his wife and kids. Estella rushed past Alisha, grabbing her husband and sobbing into his shoulder as the girls clung to their dad's legs. They were all visibly relieved to see him in good health.

As Storm entered the house, Clay pulled himself free of his family and began to rage at him. "Dave, what the hell is going on? Why was I asked to come here and why have you brought my family? We've done nothing wrong and you are supposed to be our friend."

"Clay, let Alisha, Russell, and Grady take care of the kids. I need you and Estella to come into the dining room. We need to talk." Storm was speaking in a smooth soft voice and motioning them in the direction he needed them to go. With that, Alisha calmed the kids, asking if they would like a cookie and something to drink and telling them Mr. Russell and she were going to entertain them while their parents talked to men in the dining room. With a forced smile on her face, Estella shooed her kids away from their father and told them they would be in next room if they needed either of them.

Neither Clay nor Estella seemed to have any idea why they been lied to and taken away from their home on a Saturday morning and Clay was becoming more impatient to find out why. "Dave, this is cruel. Why have you brought us here?"

Storm's End

The entire assembly of participants was seated at the table when Storm began to explain. "Clay, you've been helpful in getting the papers that you were sure were duplicates of the papers Angie was carrying in her briefcase the day she was killed, and I thank you for that. I know you want to find the people responsible for her death as bad as I do, but you haven't been completely honest with me, have you?" Storm stopped talking and reached for a plain white eight-by-ten-inch envelope and put it on the table. It was an exact duplicate of the envelopes used to deliver the mysterious messages the FBI had been receiving. Clay stiffened and Estella grabbed his arm, but neither said a word.

"Clay, I never told you about the messages the FBI has been getting from an anonymous source for the past few months, did I?" asked Storm.

Clay didn't move but his body language gave him away; his eyes just stared at Storm while Estella looked down at the envelope. Neither spoke.

"After the FBI got the third of what is now four messages, they sat up a surveillance camera on the mailbox where each envelope had been dropped. With that camera, they watched the mailbox hoping to find their mysterious messenger. You see, Clay, when the people who work in the mailroom take the letters and such from that box they time stamp and X-ray them to make sure there are no letter bombs or powder substances in the envelopes and packages that could be a threat to FBI personnel. The box is cleaned out every eight hours and with the time stamp, the men responsible for checking the camera can condense the delivery time to one eight hour period on the camera." Storm stopped speaking for a minute, but there was still no reaction from Clay or Estella.

Storm opened the envelope he had laid on the table and almost whispered as he pulled the contents from inside. "Do you recognize anyone in these pictures?" He asked, as he spread out five shots that were clearly of Estella.

An expression of shame spread across both their faces at the same time, but still neither spoke. "Estella, that is you, isn't it?" Estella held her breath. She knows it, Storm realized. And she knows everyone at the table knows it, too.

Before she could speak, Clay broke the silence with gush of breath. "I sent those messages. I wrote them. I am the one who sent her with them."

"But why, Clay? Why not just come to me and tell me what you knew?" Storm's voice has risen and his face showed he was confused about why his and Angie's friends had held back information that might have solved her murder a long time ago.

"I couldn't, I was scared." Clay's face dropped and his eyes filled with tears.

Then it was Estella who couldn't hold back anymore. With tears in her eyes, she spoke for the first time since sitting down at the table. "David, he was afraid for our lives—me and the kids. He knew the kind of people that were behind it and he knew they don't care who they kill, men, women or children." She stopped talking for a second, took a breath and began again. "David, he was scared for us, don't you understand?" In her eyes Storm could see how strongly she was pleading on behalf of Clay and the girls.

"I understand, Estella, but for five years I have been tortured with why my wife was killed and here sits a man who could have helped with that. He could have told me what he knew. A man who worked with my wife, who supposedly thought the world of her, and who I know she loved, as well, both him and his family. Now we find out you both know something and neither of you came forward. Instead you sent mysterious anonymous notes and we found you, anyway. Now, Clay, it's time to come clean. Tell me what you and Estella know." Storm's last statement was not a request. It was an order.

"David, Estella knows very little of this, she only delivered the messages to the FBI. I wrote them and told her where to take them."

"Why the FBI? Why not me?"

"I couldn't bring what I knew to you, I had to take it to someone else. Everyone knows Angie and I didn't just work together but that we were friends. If all of sudden I started talking to you every day or seeing you very often, someone might catch on that I was helping you find her killer. I wasn't sure at first, but I was scared that I was being watched and I couldn't let anything happen to my family."

"Why would you think someone was watching you? Did anyone make a threat?"

"No, not at first. Everyone at work was told to cooperate with the police working on the crime at the time, but as far as management was concerned, it was just a random thing, a robbery gone bad. But after a while, I began to feel there was something else going on."

"Why did you think that?"

"When the investigators came around asking if anyone had any idea where your wife's briefcase was, it got me to thinking. According to the police, Angie wasn't robbed, so it was not about money, but her briefcase had disappeared so it was only logical that whoever killed her wanted what was in her briefcase." Clay stopped for a minute and asked if he could have a glass of water. His mouth was dry, his hands were shaking, and his voice was cracking. Agent Higgins got him a glass of water and left the questioning to Storm.

"Are you okay now, Clay? Can you go on?" asked Storm.

"Yes, thank you. Well, when you came and talked about the missing briefcase and what she might have in it, I already knew what you were looking for and what Angie must have found. I told you I packed her briefcase with the files she needed for the trip and I updated her when she was out of town with emails. Back then, when the briefcase was first missing I put together the same files she had taken with her. I started reviewing them, looking for anything something, that didn't look right, just like I assume you have been looking since I got you the files. Well, I found something—something that didn't add up, literally didn't add up.

"Angie always followed shipments and returns. She always had a handle on how long things took to get to where they were sent and what was returned after a job was completed. I looked and sure enough, that's where the errors were. More stuff was being returned then we delivered to a job and that's impossible. We have statistics and know the amount of additives that are used and we can predict what might be left over; the numbers didn't match. The other problem was the amounts specified on the manifest were different than the amounts we received back into inventory."

Storm knew this much already. David D. had found the same discrepancies when he went over the reports, but Storm needed Clay to confirm the bogus figures. "Go on."

"Well, not long after I found the errors, the reports changed and product returns were listed on another report. They didn't show up on the shipping reports anymore."

"Where did they go, Clay?" asked Agent Higgins.

"That's the deal; returns now show up on a report that is only given to the vice president of marketing. The shipping manifest that shows returns now falls under Harold Stanton. He is the only one who gets those reports. Management said it was because they hadn't replaced Angie yet and they needed him to oversee that function of the company."

The men around the table didn't even blink. They already knew that Harold Stanton was somehow involved in this and now they were learning more about him. He had influence and as VP, he could scrub the reports and leave out the inflated returns, inserting the real number before anyone else in the company could see them.

"What else can you tell us about the reports, Clay?" asked Pancho. He had been closest to the reports and had a couple of specific questions about them. "Were these errors showing up with returns from more than one rig or job?"

"Yes, when I went back and started looking at paper files Angie had me make copies of, the errors might be from different rigs or jobs, but I also noticed they were always signed off on by the same man, the same company man who ran the rigs and was responsible for all shipments."

"Who was that man?"

"A man named Trevor Dean."

Pancho made a note of the man's name, although they had already seen his name on the manifests and were suspicious of him. David D had had told them there had to be a company man somehow involved in this and the reports they had received from Clay earlier had his name all over them. That was why the DEA had sent their man to the rig Trevor Dean was running.

"What happened then?" asked Storm.

"They promoted Ted and I went to work for him. I kept my mouth shut because I didn't know if I could trust him, and things just went back to the way they had been. I was doing my job and time passed and I didn't think much more about it. Anyway, I was an assistant and it wasn't my job to rock the boat." Clay didn't want to face David when he made the last statement--he knew Storm probably felt like he had betrayed a friend.

"Okay, we have the history out of the way. Now what changed and caused you to feel it necessary to write the notes and have your wife deliver them to us?"

"Nothing more happened until last year. That's when I recognized a man who was always coming and going from Stanton's office."

"Who was he?"

"I didn't know his name. It was never recorded by the receptionist and I never heard it spoken, but last year when you broke up the drug ring in south Houston, I recognized the man's picture in the paper; he was the same man the paper said was the head of a drug ring."

Shock showed on everyone's face. "You're telling me you saw Enrique Guzman in your offices?" asked Pancho.

"Yes, he was in Stanton's office several times in the last couple of years." Clay now had everyone's attention and even his wife was paying closer attention.

"What was he doing there?" asked Storm.

"I don't know, but every time he was there he met with Stanton and after every visit Harold seemed all uptight about things."

"Did Stanton ever say anything?"

"No, he would close his door; lower his blinds and kind of retreat into his cave."

"What made you suspicious?"

"I had pretty much forgotten about things 'til I saw the pieces in the paper about him and your investigation. It listed Agent Higgins and Agent Morran as two of the people behind catching him. That's where I got their names. David, the articles I read said something about Monterrey and that this Guzman was from there, and," he turned to Storm, "I don't know if you remember, but my family is originally from Monterrey." Storm didn't remember, and Clay continued. "Well, anyway, something just kind of clicked in my head. So I called some pretty well-off family I have who still live there. They are business people and I was sure they weren't in the drug business, so I called them and asked them about Guzman."

"What did they say?"

"First they told me if anything was going on with Guzman to stay out of it. They told me he was very dangerous and the people he did business with were even worse."

"But you didn't stay out of it."

"No, but I didn't really know anything. All I knew was this man was meeting with Stanton and Stanton seemed really distracted."

"What happened next?"

"I was keeping up with Guzman's trial when he was killed, killed by the father of the agent he had shot the day of raid. The next day the man who killed Guzman was killed and his whole family was killed. I knew then that somehow Guzman and your wife were connected."

"You mean you had a hunch?'

"Maybe, but no more than that. Everyone was somehow connected to Stanton. Angie was his counterpart at GUMDI. Guzman visited Stanton and he was always unnerved when Guzman left. So maybe it was more than a hunch; I just knew there had to be connection. That is when I came up with the idea of sending the first message."

Clay hesitated a moment but went on. "I wanted to stay out of it and just give you people a clue as to where you might find out who was behind all this and get more drugs off the streets. That was when I asked Estella to deliver the notes. I never thought anyone would look for her or figure out that she was my wife. But I was wrong and you were smarter than I was. Again, I was and am afraid of these people, but I had to help catch the people responsible for killing Angie."

"What about the other messages?"

"When I didn't see anything about you catching the men who killed that man Gilroy and Storm came to see me about the papers in Angie's briefcase, I figured you needed some more help, so I wrote the second one and finally the third. You did figure them out, didn't you? You know the "islands" are man-made; they're rigs that set offshore, don't you?"

"Yes, we did finally figure that out and we also know about some of the ways they are smuggling drugs into the country."

"Good," was all Clay said.

"How much do you know about the organization in Mexico, Clay?"

"Not much, really, just that there are some very powerful people involved in the cartel in Monterrey."

"Is the name Juan Pablo du Tilly a name you recognize?'

"Yes, my uncles told me he was partners with Guzman and his sister."

Again, the room fell silent. They had heard of the sister but they had no idea who she was or where she was.

"What do you know about this sister?'

"Nothing, except she is also a partner in the cartel."

"Do you know her name?"

"No, only that they call her 'the Dragon Lady.' Supposedly, she is the one who put the hit out on Gilroy. She is supposed to be a really bad woman."

"That is why you wrote the fourth message warning us about the Dragon Lady?'

"Yes, that and I think I saw her the other day."

"Where did you see her?"

"She was in our offices; at least I think it was her."

Flabbergasted, the people around the table could not believe what they were hearing. Guzman's sister was in town and she was so far under the radar no one even knew it.

"Why do you think it was her?"

"After this woman left, I heard Stanton ranting on his cell phone in his office and using the name 'Dragon Lady' to describe her."

"What does this woman look like?" asked Storm.

"She's beautiful; she's tall with dark brown hair, well dressed, and . . . really hot." Clay looked at his wife as he described the woman, but she looked too scared to worry about whether her husband had noticed a beautiful woman.

Not a word was said by anyone. Only Pancho seemed to be doing anything, and he was fiddling with his laptop. Pretty soon, he spun the computer around and showed Clay a picture of a woman.

"Is that her?" he asked.

"Yes, yes, that's her."

Russell, Grady and Alisha had been in the other room with the kids, but even they heard the gasp from the other room and came running in to see what was going on. Everyone was looking at the computer screen, and smack dab in the middle was a picture of Victoria Marcuccio.

"Sumbitch! Are you sure that is the woman you saw?" asked Storm.

"Yes, why?"

Stunned, no one knew what to say next. They were all trying to deal with the possibility that Victoria was Rique's sister. Was Victoria the Dragon Lady?

Storm's End

Storm's End

CHAPTER 33

The group of investigators and the Martin family spent the time through early afternoon with Clay going over everything he knew or had learned about Harold Stanton and his relationship with Enrique Guzman, Juan Pablo du Tilly and, of course, the woman they now suspected of being the Dragon Lady, the one and only Victoria Marcuccio.

The family was then discretely dispatched in a blacked out Suburban with bulletproof glass that couldn't be penetrated with small arms fire. First Clay was dropped off behind the restaurant he had left earlier that day, where he retrieved his car and drove to their family church. There he picked up Estella, the kids, and drove home. To any observers it would appear the family had simply attended mass. Agents of the DEA who were familiar with many of the faces of the cartel henchmen followed at a judicious distance, always keeping the family in sight, being careful not to give away they were acting as bodyguards. The agents would be on revolving security duty for the next few days or until they were sure the family had not been compromised and were safe and not under suspicion by the wrong doers.

***

Back at Alisha's all hell was breaking loose. Russell was the first to voice his concern. "You can't possibly think you can go anywhere with that bitch!'

"Whoa, Russell, watch the language!" said Alisha. "Was Clay sure it was the same woman he saw talking to Stanton?'

"Hell, yes, he was," argued Russell, "You heard everyone in the room agree that he said it was Victoria . I'm pissed. Victoria came into our group and tried to pass herself off as one of us. The bitch played us. She sat there at dinner with all of us and acted sweet as can be and who knows? Maybe she was the one who ordered Angie's murder!"

"We don't know that," piped in Agent Higgins.

"Well, we may not know that, but we now know she is Rique's sister and she is part of this whole thing. Nobody can tell me it will be safe for Storm to go somewhere out of the country with this woman." Russell was making his point that he was worried about his compadre.

"Hold on, everyone, before we all run out of here half-cocked we've got to look at this thing from a logical point of view. First, let's say she is Rique's sister, so what? It's better to know the snakes in your bed then to get a surprise later, isn't it?" asked Storm. "Second, we aren't ready to spring the trap on all of this; there are still some loose ends we have to get control of and it could take a hell of a lot of time to get everything in place so we don't lose anyone. Third, she doesn't know I suspect who she is."

"But fourth, you will be out of the country with her and anything can happen to you out there by yourself," countered Alisha.

"Au contraire, mon ami! I will be with a small delegation of people making this trip and Agent Morran has already committed a small armed security detail that will be following me around to watch my back."

"Not only that, but since the detective can't officially carry a weapon into a 'friendly'—Morran made quotations marks in the air with his fingers—"country, we will have our men slip him a weapon when it can be done without anyone's knowledge. The detective will also wear a Kevlar vest the entire time he is out of the country. If he does come under any type of hostile fire, his major organs will be protected and give him an eighty per cent chance of survival." That remark received a round of groans from the entire table.

Russell finally exhaled when he saw the determination on his friend's face. "There is no way of talking you out of this, is there?"

"No, and think about it, if I cancelled now there would red flags going up everywhere. If they are going to try something, why not make it on my terms? Make them think I am the sacrificial lamb. I promise I'm not looking to get myself killed; I just want to punish them and punish them all."

Nothing more was discussed about aborting the trip. Now they had to spend the rest of the afternoon ironing out the plans for the trip and the major operation that was necessary to make the arrests. Timing and planning had to be perfect or they might lose some of the conspirators.

Storm still had the GPS device implanted in the small of his back so the agents tracking him would always have him under surveillance. The trip had been planned with hotels and transportation requirements for the visitors, and everyone had a copy of the rigid itinerary. Any deviations would be considered as a threat to him and his safety team would close in to stop any possible loss of life.

Storm had made arrangements to meet Victoria at their first scheduled hotel in Caracas, Venezuela on Monday afternoon. The schedule called for them to stay the first night at Gran Meliá Caracas and meet the next morning with Sedvedra Drilling, which had been interested in a trade exchange as a distributor for GUMDI products to the nationalized Venezuelan oil business. Tuesday night they would move to the Radisson Decapolis in Panama City, Panama for a Wednesday meeting with Petrolifera Servicio, and finally their last stop would be in Tampico with Tampico Servicio. They would stay at the Camino Real in Tampico for their last stop before heading home on Friday.

The team knew the last stop would most likely be the most dangerous for Storm. Tampico Servicio was the shell company owned by Enrique, his sister, Juan Pablo du Tilly and Harold Stanton. If the cartel was going to take a run at the detective, it would most assuredly be on their home turf.

DEA agents working undercover in each destination city would pick up Storm's security coverage. A plan was in place so that Storm could recognize the security detail and not confuse them with people looking to do him harm. In Venezuela, the agents would act as limo drivers and pick him up at the airport, transporting him to his hotel. On the trip, they would supply him with photos of the other men in the detail so Storm could identify them while moving from city to city.

It was against international law for most Americans to carry a weapon while in a foreign country even if acting as a bodyguard for a high-ranking American delegate from the trade commission. Storm would be unarmed until they reached Mexico. Arrangements had already been made to supply him his favorite weapon, a Walther PPKS 380, a ACP semi-automatic pistol that would be left in his room after he arrived in Tampico. The Walther was easily hidden on his body and would give him some peace knowing he was armed in what everyone considered his most perilous destination.

* * *

The flight to Caracas had been uneventful and as Storm emerged from Venezuelan customs, he was met by a limo driver holding a sign with his name on it. The man escorted him to a car without much fanfare or much in the way of introductions. Another man waited in the car and after getting underway, the two men introduced themselves as DEA agents who worked Venezuela and Columbia. They informed him they would be looking out for him while he stayed in the capital and make sure he got on his plane the next day for his trip to Panama. They also informed him of the identities of those watching his back in Panama City and Tampico. Those men would not contact him unless there appeared to be an imminent threat to his person or his party.

They told him the weapon that would be left for him in Tampico would be hidden in the reservoir of the commode in the bathroom with three clips of ammunition, all wrapped securely in plastic wrap to keep the water out. His cell phone number was already programmed into each agent's phone as well as those of the men who would take the security in each stop of his trip. If anything appeared out of the ordinary, he would get a 911 text, which meant "hit the ground and take appropriate action to save your and Victoria Marccucio's lives."

By the time they had reached the Gran Meliá Caracas the briefing had ended and as he exited the car at the entrance of the hotel Storm tipped the driver as if this ride been just another pickup from the airport to hotel.

* * *

Victoria arrived at the hotel almost an hour after Storm. She checked in at the desk, and being a frequent visitor to the hotel, she quickly completed her reservation and a bellboy carried her bags to her room. She had been informed at the desk that her party was already checked in and had left a message informing her of his room number.

She made a quick call after putting her bags away and told the person on the other end of the phone that she and the detective were both in Caracas and she would soon be touching base with him to take him to dinner that night. In turn, she was informed that a plan was in place for their arrival in Tampico and she would be given the specifics once they arrived. Victoria disconnected the call and picked up the hotel phone to call her traveling companion's room.

"David, I'm so glad you're here. I hope you get some answers from this trip."

"Victoria, nice to hear from you, and me too, but honestly, this may be nothing more than a wild goose chase."

"You may be right, David, but at least I got you out of Houston and maybe you'll enjoy letting me show a part of the world you have never been to before."

"Well, I couldn't have a lovelier guide."

"Should we meet for dinner at say 7:00 in the lobby?"

"That would be great. See you then," Storm answered.

A smile crossed Victoria's lips. She had the Texas bumpkin fooled. Victoria disrobed and got into the shower. She planned to take special care with her looks to keep up the illusion of her personal interest and keep this collaborator in Rique's death off guard until she and Juan Pablo could implement their plan for him in Tampico.

* * *

In his room, Storm wanted to scream. He was not good at role-playing and whether or not Victoria had been directly involved with Angie's killing, she was a part of it and as soon as the timing was right she and her accomplices were going down. He just had to hold it together and keep her convinced he was enamored with her charms.

Victoria met Storm in the lobby dressed to the nines, fashionable but not pretentious, with her hair down over shoulders. What little makeup she wore only accented her natural beauty. If Storm hadn't known what a calculating harpy she most likely was, he admitted to himself that he would have been drawn into her web.

Dinner went well. They ate at a restaurant that Victoria was familiar with near the hotel; it had a nice ambiance and the seafood was wonderful. They spoke quietly about their mutual upbringings and how different Storm's had been from that of a girl raised with all the wealth her family had in Virginia. He told her about Angie, and had to admit Victoria played her role to a T. She even gave him soulful looks when he talked about Angie's death, all, he realized, to make him believe she might really care about him. She even went so far as to take his hand in hers and hold it on the ride back to the hotel.

They rode the elevator up to his floor and she told him they would meet for some breakfast at 8:00 the next morning, when she would fill him in on the company they were seeing that day. Just before he exited the elevator, she again brushed her hand down his arm, telling him she would see him in the morning. After the doors closed, Storm seethed at the mockery.

The meeting with Sedvedra the following day went off smoothly. Since his identification showed he was with the State Department, Storm was allowed to accompany Victoria into her meeting. Although his Spanish was rudimentary, he understood enough to know when they were talking about business and he paid special attention when the officials asked Victoria who the big man with her was and why he was along. Victoria simply explained he had been assigned by State to accompany her as an observer. He would be with her on this trip learning the intricacies of attempting to do business with South American corporations looking to expand American partnerships. After this initial explanation, the meeting was more or less conducted in English for his benefit.

That afternoon's flight to Panama was the without fuss; Victoria sat next to him on the plane and again she asked questions about his childhood and college days. She told him she had not been a big football fan while in college but had learned to appreciate the game while working for Trade. Many of their visitors came in the fall and they liked to attend the Redskins games. There they would talk of the differences between what the Americans called football and the true sport of soccer, which they contested was real football. She had even dated for a short time one of the quarterbacks who had played for the Redskins. "He was nice, but you're much smarter than he was," she said.

There was always just the essence of sexual overtones in the way she spoke to Storm and in the way she would let her hand brush against his, never going so far as to make him think she was interested in more, but always going far enough to make a man curious and smitten as she used the subtle encouragements that would keep an opponent off his game.

That night they left, walking from the Radisson Decapolis to a restaurant nearby that, according to Victoria, served a delicious array of local dishes she knew he would love. This time as they strolled down the brightly lit avenue, she took his hand. Storm wanted to push her away; actually, he wanted to take her lovely neck in his hands and choke the truth out of her, but he had to play along for now. Now was not the time to move, the rest of the team; their plan was not in place and it wouldn't be until next week. For now, he had to suck it up, and as in college, play through the injury, even if this was a mental one.

During their walk he spotted the two DEA operatives, though he was sure Victoria had no idea they were being followed. Even though unarmed, he felt safer about being out on a strange street in a foreign city in the company of a presumed criminal.

The meeting at Petrolifora went off in much the same manner as the previous meeting. Negotiations had taken the same march toward what Storm felt was a never-ending process of conciliatory rhetoric and he wondered how anyone ever got anything accomplished doing business this way.

Storm's End

* * *

They headed to the Panama City airport for the flight to Tampico, and Victoria excused herself while they waited to board. Finally, I can make the phone call I've been waiting to make for the last couple of days, she assured herself. "We are arriving on schedule. Is everything all set on your end?'

"Yes, all arrangements have been made; everything will go as planned on your taxi ride back from dinner tonight," the person on the other end of the call replied.

"I will be wearing a bright blue dress, so make sure those pendejos you've got doing the shooting know to let me get out of the way before they open up."

"Don't worry about that, these are my best men, they won't just spray the car with bullets, but make sure you are on the street side of the taxi and can get out quick."

With some hesitation Victoria replied, "My shoes will be off in the taxi and when I hear the first shot I am out the door." She knew she would be cutting it close but she had to be in the car and seem to be in fear for her life or she could look suspicious.

* * *

The flight to Tampico took them to Mexico City with a change of planes and although she was trying her best to make this leg of the trip seem like the others by continuing her flirtatious manner, she was filled with anxiety for what she knew was going to happen in a few hours.

Storm and Victoria checked into their hotel and each went off to their rooms, agreeing to meet back in the lobby where they would go to the beach for dinner. Storm got to his room and immediately checked the toilet for the gun he had been assured would be left for him. It was right where he had been told it would be a 380 Walther PPKS and three eight shell-clips magazines full of hollow point ammunition. Whoever had left the gun had also left a note warning him if the assasins were going to hit him, it would be most likely tonight. The informant that left the gun apparently didn't know when or where the hit would take place but assured Storm that agents were watching over him and an old friend was with them.

Storm didn't know what the latter meant but he didn't have time to dwell on it as the airplane had been late and if he was going to meet Victoria for dinner, he had to get a move on. He unpacked his ankle holster, secured it to the inside of his left leg, loaded the magazine pumping one shell in the pipe, flipped the safety on and slid the gun in place. Before he left his room, he spit on a piece of thread and put it high on the door from the doorjamb to the face of the door. If anyone entered his room while he was away, they would have to break the thread, and, although precautionary, it would give him a warning to be on the lookout.

Victoria seemed somewhat more distant at dinner, not so conversational, even a little pensive and more reserved about touching him. When he asked if something was wrong, she merely laughed and told him she was sad that this would their last night together for a while. She said that after the meeting tomorrow she would be headed back to Washington while he would be going home to Houston. Storm then did something he didn't think he would ever do again, not with any woman and certainly not with this one. He reached over, took her hand, and told her, "We'll see each other again, I'm sure of it."

"I'm sure we will, too." Victoria smiled.

When dinner was over they asked the maitre d' to hail them a taxi. When it arrived, Victoria slid across the seat of the cab and over by the back right hand door. Storm slid in behind the driver and gave him their destination.

The taxi had just turned off the beach highway lined with beachfront restaurants and fishing wharfs when the men acting as Storm's security noticed the black pickup truck with blacked out windows fall in behind the taxi. They could see two men squatting in the back of the truck with what looked like assault rifles at the ready. One agent hit the emergency button on his cell phone, and almost immediately, Storm's phone started vibrating with the 911 distress message.

Shocked, Storm yelled, "Stop!" He grabbed for Victoria, forcing her down in the seat as bullets began to spray the vehicle. He reached for the door handle and together they tumbled out the door on the opposite side of the taxi that was being raked with bullets.

The surveillance team in the Suburban sprang out, keeping themselves hidden behind the armor-plated doors as they began firing on the pickup. Fearing for their lives, the men in the pickup began to fire wildly, first at the agents and then back again at the taxi. The taxi driver was slumped over the wheel of the taxi, his body riddled with bullets.

With the gunfire now focused between the agents and assassins, Storm took the chance to pull his weapon and fire on the pickup. One man in back was already down and the second was continuing to fire but was panicking and hitting nothing. The passenger window of the pickup came down and another shooter materialized from the opening.

Storm snapped off two quick shots through the window and saw the man slump. The last man firing from the back was hit with at least three separate bullets and fell to the ground. Then the driver tried to put the truck in gear and escape when his window blew out. The engine continued to race leaving a cloud of smoke from the exhaust hanging in the air, but the truck didn't move.

A terrible quiet ensued, broken only by the sound of the racing engine. Then sirens could be heard in the distance. So much weapons fire must have at least alerted the local police, who had taken their time responding. Storm knew local police were not to be trusted so the men in the Suburban had to move fast if their counter plan was to work.

Victoria was shaking but she hadn't said a word; she only uttered a low moan. She didn't appear to be hit, but even though Storm urged her to get up, she remained on the ground in a fetal position that signaled she feared for her life.

Even under the circumstances, Storm was not prepared for what happened next. Martin Jones appeared as if out of nowhere. He put his finger to his lips and motioned for Storm to keep his mouth shut. He fired two shots into Storm's bulletproof vest leaving holes in the shirt and jacket he had worn to dinner that night. Martin grabbed Victoria and gave her an injection from a hypodermic needle filled with a sedative that put her immediately to sleep. He splashed fake blood on Storm's body and fired a firecracker round off at Victoria's abdomen, leaving burns and holes on her dress and small burn marks on her skin. "Lie still and pretend to be dead," he whispered. The agents would load his and Victoria's bodies in the back of the Suburban for transport to a safe hospital, where they would be pronounced dead. Local officials would be supplied photographs and autopsy reports while their bodies were flown home.

Not fully understanding the plan but trusting Martin The agents lifted Storm by the arms and legs and loaded him in the back the of the Suburban, they picked up Victoria's seeming lifeless body and placed it beside Storm to anyone watching they were removing dead bodies. Whatever this plan was, it was now up to Martin and the DEA agents to pull it off.

CHAPTER 34

Mexican photojournalists and television stations with ties to major American networks were on the scene right after the Policía Federal Preventiva, or PF, had shown up. When the PF arrived at the scene, Mexican military police, now saddled with drug intervention, had already blocked off the area where the gun battle had erupted. From the sidelines, people with cameras immortalized the death and mayhem, recounting to news reporters the number of explosions they had heard in the heat of the battle and how when they arrived they saw the dead bodies lying in and out of the pickup truck and taxicab. Those who arrived early at the scene depicted in detail the carnage of bodies everywhere. They described men lying on the ground and great pools of blood surrounding the corpses. Observers also related how those who attacked the taxi were clothed in black pants and shirts with ninja-type wraps around their faces to hide their identity. They went on to say that one man had been seen lying beside the taxi and what they were sure was a woman's body was lying nearby. They both appeared to have been shot in the chest, with blood covering their upper bodies. Neither the man nor the woman showed any signs of life and the observers were sure they, too, had been killed in the melee. Some even showed the news reporters pictures of the bodies they had taken with cell phones when they first arrived.

When asked where the victims were now, the reporters were told by onlookers and police officials that the bodies had been picked up for transport to a local hospital. The men and the single woman were on their way to a holding area in the hospital until their families could be notified and the bodies released to be taken home and interred by grieving family members.

Later outside of military police headquarters, an announcement was made that the bodies of six men and one woman had been identified. Four bodies were those of suspected members of the Rio Cartel. One body was that of José Pedrosa, the owner/operator of the taxi that had certainly been carrying the other victims, Victoria Marcuccio and David Storm, representatives of an American trade delegation. At this time, there was no way of connecting the murdered Americans with the drug cartel and their bodies had been released for return to America.

* * *

Two men lingered outside the emergency entrance to La Virgen de Emaculate Hospital watching and waiting to see what the disposition of the two Americans who had been killed in the beach road shootout would be. A Mexican military police van backed up to the automatic doors leading into the hospital, where no less than a dozen military policemen in full riot gear and weapons surrounded the doors. Two bodies in black body bags were rolled out on gurneys. Four policemen took a corner of each bag and slid the bodies into the back of the transport van. With sirens and flashing lights, a cadre of police vehicles made their way to the Tampico Airport. The witnesses then saw police and what they thought to be American personnel move the bodies with all the respect afforded to the dead from the van to a Cessna Citation business jet. Once the bodies were inside, the American agents boarded the aircraft and it embarked on what the observers were told a flight back to the United States.

A quick cell phone call was made and the undercover American agents melted into the background, resuming their surveillance of reactions to the killings from the military police and international news feeds. This was no ordinary killing; it had taken the lives of two Americans, not just citizens of the United States, but people here from an agency of the American government.

While watching the news on television, Juan Pablo du Tilly took a call that quietly informed him that the bodies had left Mexico. He hung up and made a call to Houston to let the people on the other end know to be on the lookout for anything suspicious.

* * *

On board the aircraft headed back to Houston were the two bodies of the man and woman killed in the ambush in Tampico; both were secured in the black body bags. Martin Jones reached down, unzipped the bag with the man in it, and released Detective David Storm. Storm gasped for a breath of air that didn't smell of plastic and pushed the zipper farther down so he could get his legs out of the bag. He watched as Martin repeated the procedure with the bag that held Victoria Marcuccio.

Victoria was still unconscious and a portable diagnostic monitor placed inside the bag with her was keeping track of her vitals. She had been given another hypodermic before they had left the hospital and should remain knocked out until they reached Houston. Just before touchdown in Houston, a medical specialist would oversee her condition and if needed, she would be given another shot to maintain her appearance of death for anyone who might be snooping around when they unloaded the bodies.

"How's she doing?" asked Storm.

"She's just fine; all her numbers are strong and all she will remember of this trip is a very long nap. When we wake her up she might have one hell of a hangover but she will be fine," the medical specialist said with a bit of sarcasm in his voice.

Looking at Martin, Storm asked, "Don't you think it's about time you filled me on all this? When I left Houston I don't remember any of this being in our plan. Why didn't you warn me about the shots to the chest? They hurt."

"Well, I think I owe you a shot to the chest, don't I?"

Remembering the first time he had seen Martin undercover in hip-hop street clothes, a time during an earlier Houston murder case when he had mistakenly judged Martin as a local thug and had shot him in the chest with a bean bag projectile, Storm grinned and shook his head yes.

Martin took his time before he answered the first question and offered Storm a cup of coffee before he got into the turn of events. "Storm, you know we wanted Victoria alive and we weren't sure the cartel did. After you left on the trip a decision was made by the director of the FBI, the director of the DEA, and Ted that if the two of you weren't killed in this attack it had to appear that you had been. If you had been killed and Victoria got out alive, she would have become a heroine in the American press, making it even harder for us to go after her. If it looked as if the cartel was trying to kill her along with you, our people would be given the task of making sure both of you lived. I was there to make sure she didn't talk before we could get her back to a safe and unknown location for questioning." Martin stopped talking for a minute, letting what he had said so far sink in for Storm.

"So everyone is going to think we are dead?"

"Well, not everyone," Martin hemmed and hawed for a minute then went on. "The public will think the two of you were killed while on a diplomatic mission for the trade department. The only people who will know you are alive are the men who saved you and our team, including Russell, Alisha, Pancho, and Grady. Your police department will think you were killed while investigating the murder of your wife. The trade commission will think Victoria was killed while facilitating your trip. It is imperative we keep people thinking you are both dead. If it appears either of you lived, there could only be two responses from the cartel; they would try again or scurry for darkness like roaches when you turn on the lights."

"Victoria is from a rich family and works for a powerful agency of the US government," Storm protested. "How you gonna keep them at bay long enough to put the rest of the plan in effect? And by the way, what is the rest of the plan?"

"Ted is going to show her agency pictures of her bullet-riddled body and tell them that the department of justice and the FBI are keeping her body temporarily until such time as a complete medical examination can be made to certify her death. We should be able to keep them off our back for a week and that, hopefully, is all we are going to need to put together a task force that can storm the walls of the castle and arrest all the others."

"She's connected, Martin; her family is rich; there is no way Ted can hold them off for long."

"There is going to be all hell to pay when this is over but the ends do outweigh the method."

"God, I hope so. The shit is going to hit the proverbial fan when they find out you kept her as a hostage for a week. I hope Ted has huge brass ones to carry this off." Storm just shook his head as he thought, damn, we are in it now.

Aloud he asked, "What do we do now?"

Martin spent much of the next hour and a half bringing Storm up to date on what was now being called "Anaconda 2.0" and how all the pieces fit. Just before Storm was required to crawl back into his black bag of larceny, he made one final statement. "Martin, I want to be one of the people who questions Victoria. I think I deserve that."

"You will be. Ralph told the director you would be and it was approved."

* * *

In Houston all hell was breaking lose around Russell. Every news organization in the world, including his own network, were clamoring for an interview about the loss of his friend. Although included in the masquerade, he had been sworn to secrecy and knew the lives of a lot of people depended on the ruse being successful. Russell had asked the manager of his station to take off some of the sick days he had accrued over the years. He told the manager he needed time to process the loss of his friend and promised that the station would be the first he made any comment to. He asked that he be allowed to put together a statement and would get back to him in twenty-four hours.

Alisha found herself in the dubious position as being the person in charge of conducting the phony autopsy and hiding the truth about the deaths. According to news outlets, the bodies were to be taken directly from the airport to her morgue. Extra security had been given to her by the FBI and her technicians and staff were screened to prevent any leaks and the charade being discovered. FBI personnel would drive the morgue van and the bags would be switched at the airport for identical bags filled with rubberized forms resembling human bodies. The faux bodies would be delivered and secured in her morgue under lock and key and Storm and Victoria would be secreted away to an undisclosed location where the questioning of Victoria would take place.

Storm's End

* * *

In Washington Senator Rendell held a press conference outside the senate with Harrison Connolly standing to his right and just behind him.

"Ladies and gentlemen, as many of you know, we have just learned of a very unfortunate situation that occurred in Tampico, Mexico last evening. Suspected Mexican drug cartel members operating in northern Mexico just south of the Rio Grande River mistakenly caught two American citizens in an ambush. As many have already seen from photographs aired by the international press, the bullet-torn bodies of a man and woman were found on a beach road where they were cut down when returning from having dinner at a popular seaside restaurant. The man has been identified as Detective David Storm, on loan from the Houston Police Department to the trade department. The woman is very well known to all of us in Washington; she was the strikingly beautiful Regional Director to Latin America for the USTDA, Ms. Victoria Marcuccio."

The senator, always the campaigner and politician, paused for effect before going on. "Ms. Marcuccio will be greatly missed by her family and all of us who knew her well. She was a leader in growth of business development between the United States of America and many of our Latin American allies. Ms. Marcuccio's family has asked for the speedy release of her remains so they may get on with their grieving and put their loved one to rest."

At this point, the senator drew a handkerchief from his pocket and dabbed at his eyes as if restraining a tear. "Ladies and gentlemen, I can assure you a thorough investigation is being conducted by our government and that of Mexico to bring the people behind these heinous murders to justice. Although Detective Storm had no family, I would like to extend my sincere condolences to all of his friends and colleagues in Houston and the Houston Police Department. I send my deepest sympathies to all those who have lost these two singular people."

At that time, the senator left the podium and Harrison replaced him, telling the crowd there would be no questions and all follow-up inquiries should be taken up with the FBI and DOJ.

Across town Craig Baltazar, Director of the USTDA, was conducting a similar press conference, keeping to his talking points and only offering sympathies to the family and friends of the bereaved.

In the senator's office Mrs. Holmes watched the press conference and thought to herself about what a loss it was to know that a man she had only known for a short period of time had lost his life. She also admitted, like many other women in Washington, she would not miss Victoria in the least.

* * *

El Gato, Juan Pablo, had been watching the same news conferences and felt a rush of relief spread over him.

The man who might have caused problems and the woman he didn't want as a partner were now both taken care of. The business was all his now and the wealth would belong to him.

The only people he had to care for now were Enrique's family, as he considered Harold Stanton a nonentity. Rique's wife was happy with her mansion and money and the children were still too young to be any threat in wanting their father's share of the business. If they ever did grow and aspire to run the cartel, he would merely take care of them, too.

* * *

Storm's End

As a dark gray Ford Explorer neared the front of a nondescript warehouse on the northwest side of Houston, Pancho stood poised to open the rolling garage door to allow the SUV admittance to the building. Special Agents Morran and Higgins waited with Pancho on the inside to welcome home Detective Storm and Agent Jones. The door quickly rolled down and Storm and Martin got out with a greatly disheveled Victoria Marcuccio. Her hair was matted to her head as if she had been asleep for several days and sleep lines still creased her face. In actuality, she had still been asleep, although not for days, and was not yet fully conscious. She was aware enough to be feisty, demanding to know what was going on and why she was there, though no one was answering her, let alone giving in to her demands. She was handcuffed and still wearing the same clothes she had donned the night before during the ambush.

The warehouse had been hastily turned into an operations office, with a working area, kitchen, bathrooms, and sleeping areas for all the agents who would be using the facility. A special room had been erected just for holding Victoria. It had four soundproofed walls, a sink, and a shower and toilet, all cordoned off for her privacy. A medical bed sat against one wall and she would be handcuffed to it unless allowed to use the bathroom or taken to questioning.

Agent Higgins approached Victoria and handed her a set of what appeared to be nothing more than medical scrubs, fresh unflattering underwear, socks, and a pair of blue canvas sneakers. "Ms. Marcuccio, this is your room for the time being. These clothes are clean and you may have a bath to freshen up. After you have had time to change clothes, we will begin your questioning regarding the smuggling operations that you are a part of. Although your bath is out of sight of the cameras in your room we will still be able to monitor you, so don't get any silly ideas. Go ahead now; we will give you a few minutes to compose yourself."

Victoria began screaming at the top of her lungs, but her protests fell on deaf ears as she was summarily escorted inside the room. Agent Higgins merely unshackled her wrists, pushed her through the doors, and joined Storm, Pancho, and Morran for a debriefing.

"Somebody watch her to make sure she doesn't do anything to hurt herself," Higgins shouted. He had lied to her about surveillance on the bathroom; it could be seen, and every move she made could be observed.

"How are you feeling, Detective?"

"I'm fine, a little tired and a little confused, but Martin pretty much brought me up to speed."

"Good. We have a lot to do and very little time to carry it off," said Morran, as Higgins brought out a whiteboard with diagrams of how the plan was going to be put into effect.

* * *

Victoria looked for an escape but soon found the room was secure and there was nothing she could use as a weapon or any opening that would precipitate a means to flee the prison she now found herself in. She would resort to her most useful tool, and that was her charm. If these men were no brighter than the other men she had met in life, it was entirely conceivable that one of the mental midgets holding her would fall for her wiles.

She took a quick shower and removed what little makeup she had worn the night before with the only cleansing products she could find, body soap and water. She heard the announcement over the speaker in her room that a man was about to enter and the door opened. She was handcuffed again, taken to a chair at a table in the center of warehouse, and told to be seated.

A table had been set in the middle of the almost vacant warehouse and a single chair sat on one side of the table, while three other chairs sat on the other. She was brought to the table and her handcuffs were taken off one arm and secured to a metal U-bolt attached to the table. She was told to sit and asked if she would like something to drink, water or a soft drink. She declined but everyone could see the fury in her eyes.

"What the hell have you people done to me? I am a representative of federal government and you have no right to hold me or treat me in this manner. I want to call my office, I want the FBI, and I am going to file charges against every one of you." She spoke the words so rapidly they sounded like snarling spit.

"Ms. Marcuccio, I am Special Agent Ralph Higgins. I am with the FBI and you are being held by a joint task force of the FBI, DEA, and DOJ. Last night in Tampico, Mexico, an attempt was made on your life and the life of Detective Storm. We believe you are involved with the Rio Cartel from Mexico and are instrumental in its smuggling and distribution of illegal drugs into the United States of America. We can hold you here as long as we wish or until you begin to cooperate and supply us with the information we need to bring that organization down."

Victoria's eyes went wild with rage but never showed any surrender. She yelled every profanity she knew at the men on the other side of the table, finishing with, and "You can't hold me! People will be looking for me!"

Agent Higgins again began to speak. "That is where you are wrong, Ms. Marcuccio. As far as your agency, your family and, in fact, the whole world knows, you were killed in the attempt made on your life last night. Every news agency in the world carried pictures of the two of you shot up and lying dead in the street in Mexico. News teams witnessed your bodies being taken from a Mexican hospital and put aboard a private aircraft being airlifted back to the United States. There your body was seen being transported to the morgue, where it will be held until a complete and thorough autopsy can be performed and the findings be given to the DOJ and

FBI to investigate your murder. So yes, Ms. Marcuccio, we can hold you indefinitely. To the outside world you are dead."

Victoria's eyes again flashed her hatred of the men sitting across from her but she sat silently.

It was then Storm's turn to speak and he would begin the questioning. "Ms. Marcuccio, did you have anything to do with the murder of my wife Angie Storm?"

"What the hell are you talking about? I don't know anything about your wife's murder and I sure as hell had nothing to do with it. I work for the USTDA and I was on that trip to help you find out answers to questions you had, so screw you and the rest of these assholes. When I get out of here you will all go to jail for kidnapping me and holding me against my will."

Storm seemed to be thinking for a minute before he spoke again. This time it wasn't a question but a statement in the form of a fact. "Maybe I should have addressed you as 'Ms. Isabella Guzman.'"

Storm watched Victoria's face. *I think I got her with that one.* She looked stunned, as if her brain had gone numb. Then she seemed to gather her wits... "What are you talking about? My name is Victoria Marcuccio. My grandfather is a very wealthy and influential man in Virginia and our family has more ties to power people in the government than you bunch of yokels even have inbred relatives. My father was an Italian count who died before I was born, so I'm sure I have no idea what you are talking about."

"Then you have never heard of Enrique Guzman, a man who was the son of Juan Pedro Guzman and your mother's lover the year you were conceived, while your mother was on a trip to Mexico?"

"I have never heard of either man and my mother never had an affair with some wetback." Victoria had regrouped, but Storm and the others guessed she was surprised they knew this much about her. *She knows her best defense is a good offense,* Storm reflected.

"What part do you play in the smuggling of illegal drugs into the United States?" asked Higgins.

"I have no idea what you are talking about. I don't know anything about illegal drugs." Higgins nodded. Storm knew why. Victoria had to maintain her innocence and she knew the best way to do that was to remain silent.

It was obvious to the men in the room that she was still too defiant to get any answers, so for now all they could do was put her back in her room and use a subtler way to wear her down, break her attitude, and get the answers they needed. Victoria was returned to her room and inside the soundproofed chamber they began to play redneck music and metal rock at increasing levels to work on her nerves, never letting her rest or relax.

Storm's End

Storm's End

CHAPTER 35

Victoria remained defiant; these wannabe terroristas would not intimidate her or shake her confidence. She filled her mind with the resolve that people would be looking for her and in no time, these hicks and yokels would have to release her. It would be then she would get her retribution, creating a furor that at a minimum would cause these men to lose their jobs and possibly even go to jail.

Her right wrist was secured to the hospital bed they had supplied for her and brazenly she awaited her imminent rescue. Secure in her knowledge all would end well, she was just about to drift off to sleep when something stirred her; it was a chilly breeze blowing across the crisp sheets she lay on. Then the music started; soft at first but building, becoming louder and louder until it was intolerable. Twangy country music alternated with acid and metal rock, all genres she detested. The room became colder, almost frigid, when she realized she didn't have a blanket. There was nothing on the bed to cover her shaking body with. Shivering from the cold now, she searched the bed for a pillow to cover her head to block the sound when she realized she didn't have a pillow, either. She contorted her body, moving her head to where the one wrist had been secured to the railing of the bed, plugging one ear with a finger while holding the free hand over the other.

Outside the room, the agents monitoring her saw her begin to shiver as they turned the air conditioning to a setting of 65 degrees. The room was soundproofed so the level of the music didn't bother them and the agent at the control kept increasing it until they saw her fighting to cover her ears. If the agent overseeing the process saw her begin to fall asleep, they would barge into the room take her out of the bed and start interrogating her again; always with the same questions: "Who are you working with? Who had Mrs. Storm killed? Are you Enrique Guzman's sister? How many people are involved in the smuggling?"

For hours, they got the same response. She would flash her big brown eyes filled with rage and disgust at them and say nothing, except to threaten them with the loss of their manhood for her treatment.

* * *

In the operations area of the warehouse, Special Agents Higgins, Morran, and Jones went over the plan for the arrest of all those they knew to be involved in the criminal venture. Detective Storm and Sergeant Hernandez followed along as each piece of the plan was explained in detail and they were allowed to make any observations they felt cogent as to the workability of the massive arrest plan outlined on a whiteboard. The plan was simple but contained a plethora of moving parts. To carry this off the combined agencies would need over one hundred men and a variety of cars, boats, and aircraft. Each operation had to go off simultaneously or they risked the chance they could lose some of offenders.

Victoria had been fighting the good fight with day one completed. She wasn't showing any signs of cracking under the constant pressure being applied by the men outside her room. It was like clockwork; every two hours on the nose she would be pulled out of the room and interrogated again. She would be taken food and water, though during the first day she had not only refused to eat it but had used the full plastic water bottle and the bologna sandwich on white bread as projectiles to fling at her tormentors.

The second day as the men made slight modifications to their plan, they saw that Victoria was showing signs of physical and mental distress. Her face no longer was radiant, her eyes no longer shined, but her attitude stayed in place, daring the men to break her.

It was sometime early in the morning of the third day when Storm felt his leg being shaken and awoke to find one of the agents responsible for Victoria's care standing at the end of the cot he had been using as bed.

"Detective, she is all in. She says she is ready to cooperate," said the agent. "But she only wants to talk to you."

Storm rubbed his tired, sleep-filled eyes and rolled into a sitting position on the cot. Slow down and start again, his mind directed him. He was still groggy and trying to make sense of what the agent was saying to him.

"She has broken; it took almost sixty hours but she had finally caved, but she will only talk to you." Storm still remained sitting on the cot. "Get up, Detective; this is what we've been waiting for. She can confirm we are going after all the right people."

"Do you really think she knows everyone involved in this?" The question had been rhetorical, but he asked, anyway.

"Hell, Detective, I don't know, but if you don't hurry up and she gets her bearings, we might never know." He took Storm by the arm and pulled him to his feet.

Storm needed Victoria to talk. He knew she had information about who had murdered Angie that she was the person he wanted to go after. No matter who they brought in during their sweep, he had to be the one to bring in the person responsible for killing his wife.

Victoria sat at the table where she had been questioned repeatedly for the past sixty-some hours. Her eyes were no longer filled with contempt and loathing for the men, but rather appeared to have softened as if she had resigned herself to the fact she had lost.

"Victoria, these agents just told me you are ready to talk, but you want to only talk to me."

"David, can't you help me? I know you liked me; can't you make them stop and let me get some rest. Let me go home to my family?" She was pleading now.

"Victoria, I told you the minute we got here, I, or I mean we, need some answers from you and if you are helpful and answer everything that is asked of you, they will let you get some rest. They will even get you something decent to eat. But until you are truthful with us and tell us everything you know, you will be put back in your room and the treatment will continue."

He watched as her failure to remain strong washed over her. Her eyes dropped as she agreed to answer anything he asked.

"Okay, Victoria, you know my primary question. Did you or someone else decide to have Rique's assassin kill my wife?"

Victoria sat quietly for a few seconds; she looked up with tears swelling at the corners of her eyelids before she answered, "It was Stanton and Rique who did that. Believe me, David; I would have never done that. I would never have ordered the murder of a woman; not someone's wife."

Your feminine wiles haven't completely deserted you yet, Victoria, Storm acknowledged to himself as he watched the tears. Storm didn't know if he should believe her or not, but he had an answer. He also knew Victoria was a treacherous bitch and was now in self-protection mode. He asked, "Why did they need to kill her?"

"She knew too much. Stanton said she was too smart and had found the irregularities in the shipping reports and she was beginning to ask too many questions. He told Rique about her and they decided she needed to go, so Rique had his dirty little blonde bitch do it. It was simple. Stanton knew her schedule and that she used a car service, so they switched out drivers."

"What happened to her briefcase?"

"I have no idea."

"We never found her briefcase. She always had it with her and now we are sure she was carrying the reports that would prove somebody was cooking the books."

"I don't know, David, I really don't. I never heard about it. Either Rique had it or Stanton does. Stanton is a sneaky little prick; I would bet on him."

Storm muttered almost as if to himself, "Stanton must have taken it, because we didn't find it with any of Rique's stuff. All we found was an empty file folder with Angie's name on it." Storm hated even saying his wife's name around this woman, but it just slipped out.

"Who had Cully killed?"

"I did. I wanted revenge for Rique's death, so Juan Pablo hired the men to go to the jail to kill him after they killed his family."

She told him about the entire organization, as she knew it, including where Juan Pablo was most likely to be and what kind of security he would have. She told them about how El Gato and Stanton had to have Dacosta and the medical examiner who did the autopsy in Virginia disposed of to get rid of loose ends.

She explained the new operation and that they now had three men who ran the rigs in their employ to facilitate the smuggling and the changing of Tampico boat flags so they could bring the contraband to the rigs for shipment back to America.

She explained how putting away Reggie had been no more than a blip in their scheme, as thugs and gangs were easy to find in any large troubled city.

Storm's End

The questioning went on for almost four more hours before Victoria collapsed and had to be taken back to her room. This time the air conditioning was adjusted and she was covered with a blanket and given a pillow to sleep on. When she had rested a few hours, other agents would resume her interrogation.

* * *

Agents Jones, Higgins, and Morran joined Storm and Pancho to compare the information Victoria had given up with what they already knew. Most of her testimony only verified their information, but she did fill them in on the fact that the cartel had three company men on three separate rigs working for them and at least two different supply boat companies.

Her information didn't change the overall plan; it only added a couple more details that would need to be calculated in if they were to bring down the cartel all at one time.

They all agreed that Storm would be part of the unit that went for Harold Stanton at his office. They would serve warrants to search his office, his home and all his bank accounts. Ted supplied them with warrants would also be served to freeze financial accounts for all of the other suspects and their holdings.

* * *

In front of his home TV Station later that day Russell came to the podium and the reporters fell silent. These were his first remarks since the reported death of his friend. Behind a single microphone set up by his station, he prepared to give his statement.

"Ladies, gentlemen and fellow reporters, this will be a short comment and I will take only a couple of questions after I have finished my prepared statement. The folks you

Storm's End

see behind me are Dr. Alisha Johnson, the medical examiner for Harris County, and Grady Anderson, my producer here at the station. As many of you already know, the three of us in addition to Police Sergeant Julio Hernandez were part of the team that stopped a serial killer a couple of years ago. We were also there when Detective Storm arrested the killer of Dr. Johnson's little brother and brought a drug cartel determined to flood Houston with illegal drugs to an end.

"Some of you may remember that almost eight years ago Detective Storm's wife was found murdered just inside the door of their home. What many of you don't know or maybe don't remember is that her murder was never solved. Last year when we solved the heinous murder of Dr. Johnson's brother, Dr. Johnson discovered that the same person who murdered her brother was the person who murdered Detective Storm's wife. Detective Storm made this trip to Latin America to retrace his wife's last steps before she was killed. He hoped to find something that might help explain why she had been killed. It appears he must have gotten close and by doing so, he put himself in harm's way and lost his life as well. I have been informed by the Houston Police Department, the FBI, and Mexican police authorities that they will make every effort to find and prosecute those responsible for his death.

Russell motioned to the man and woman behind him. "We were his family. We were his best friends"—he hung his head theatrically—"and we will miss him dearly. The only thing more I have to say is thank you for all your sympathies for our lost friend. We would also like to extend our condolences to the family and friends of the trade department employee who perished with him. Pausing, he scanned the crowd. "I will take only a couple of questions." He looked over the crowd trying to pick the reporter he most wanted to give an opportunity to ask a question.

"Yes, Christine," Russell pointed to Christine Chu, a former colleague and competitor.

"Russell, can you give us the name of the woman whose body was also seen in the ghastly photos of the murder of Detective Storm?"

"Christine, I'm sorry but I can't. I only know it was a female representative of the USTDA."

The crowd was getting louder as Russell picked Clint Swan from Fox News.

"Dr. Johnson, is it true you have the bodies of both Detective Storm and the mystery woman in your morgue? Can you tell us her name?"

Alisha stepped forward but answered with only one word: "No." Then she retreated from the microphone.

Christine jumped in again. "Did the detective find any information about his wife's death?"

"Honestly, Christine, we don't know. The last time any of us spoke to him was the day before he left on the trip." Russell held up his hand and stopped the questioning, thanking the reporters for coming, and then he, Grady, and Alisha left the podium.

* * *

In the warehouse, positioning diagrams lay all over the table and the attack schedule on the whiteboard seemed to change almost every few minutes. Victoria had given up what they thought was most likely all she knew and had been secured in her room. The temperature had been raised and a blanket and pillow provided so she was more comfortable, and the music had been turned off. Now only one agent watched her and she appeared to be sleeping. She had asked for her bags with her own clothing and beauty products, which were still being kept from her.

Special Agents Morran of the DEA and Higgins of the FBI were in charge. They would be the home base for the operation, coordinating all the moving pieces. Agent Morran would oversee his agency's personnel and that of the Coast

Guard. His people would hit the three rigs, arresting the company men who were complicit in the smuggling scheme, while the Coast Guard stopped and boarded all the supply boats used in the activity. DEA agents, with the cooperation of the Mexican Federal Police, would hit Tampico Servicio, taking in everyone suspected of drug smuggling, while seizing all computers and records.

Ted was in charge of making sure all the federal warrants were in place for each arrest and seizure of illegal drugs and any incriminating records and files, while coordinating with the US Department of the Treasury to freeze all Tampico's financial accounts whether domestic or international, as long as the United States had an agreement with that country to do so.

Ted whistled really loud to get the attention of all the men in the room. "Everything is in place, all warrants have been issued, and each of your field operatives should be receiving them as we speak. Give them about thirty minutes and have them report in that the warrants are in hand and we are ready to go."

The men all cheered and clapped. This was going to happen; the operation was going live.

Storm's End

Storm's End

CHAPTER 36

The Black Hawk helicopter was almost silent as it approached from up wind skimming the ground at tree top level. A spotter from the ground was in constant communication with the team inside the Black Hawk, relaying the exact location of their quarry and listening for the tell signs of the helicopter's approach. The team was comprised of two shooters and two rangers who would drop out of the side doors of the chopper attached to high tensile braided nylon cord polysheath rope two hundred feet long. The shooters had to be quick and good; they would have to dart their victims on their first shots from a moving platform, hitting their man and his bodyguards quickly before they had a chance to evade capture and return fire on the helicopter.

At exactly 10:00 a.m. Central Standard Time in Houston a black helicopter rose above the trees of the Las Missiones Country Club. Two agents each took aim and fired air pressured tranquilizer darts filled with Thiopental, a fast acting animal sedative, and Juan Pablo, his playing partner, and two body guards went down. Juan Pablo du Tilly was just about to tee off on the seventh hole when he heard the *thwok* of the blades and turned to find the cause of his annoyance. El Gato felt the slight prick of a pin hit his neck and that was the last thing he felt as he fell unconscious to the ground. His playing partner and the two henchmen hired to protect them fell in unison as if they were dominos.

The rangers were out of the doors before Juan Pablo hit the ground. They lifted his limp body and attached a harness around it. Then one of the rangers secured Juan Pablo to his rigging and motioned for the men in the Black Hawk to begin the lift. The second ranger checked the bodies of the downed men to insure they were still alive and then signaled for his retrieval.

The Black Hawk swung sharply around with its catch still dangling from the ropes and made its escape back over the trees and out of sight, reeling the rangers and their capture back inside. The entire engagement had taken no more than a few seconds and they were up and gone to deliver Juan Pablo to a government aircraft that would carry him back to Houston to stand trial for drug smuggling, conspiracy to commit murder, and murder.

The linchpin for this operation was the arrest of Juan Pablo. Once the Special Ops people had him in custody, word would go out for everyone to move, and the plan was for all of them to move at once. Split-second timing and coordination was imperative. They could not risk the chance that any high-level criminal would be missed in the first sweep and given a chance to escape. All electronic communication devices would be seized and the media would not be notified until they were reasonably sure they had everyone they knew about or wanted in custody.

Once back aboard the chopper they were off to a clandestine airport for transportation back to Houston to execute the warrants they held for Juan Pablo's arrest and detention. The bodyguards left on the ground would awaken in about thirty minutes and the only story they would have to tell would be about the approach of the black helicopter.

Storm's End

* * *

Special Agent Higgins was in charge of most of the domestic arrests. He had men watching the warehouse in Houma to arrest the drug handlers and distribution gang members left over from Reggie's old New Orleans gang. Under his supervision Agent Jones, Detective Storm, and Sergeant Hernandez would arrest Harold Stanton and seize all records being kept in the offices of GUMDI. Another team would serve a warrant on Stanton's wife to search his home.

Higgins ordered his teams to leave the warehouse and set up for their raids. He pulled Storm to the side and said, "This is your arrest. Martin is going with you to get the files and records and Pancho is there to help you handle Stanton as you see fit, but please don't kill him." Higgins was kidding, but only kind of; they needed Stanton alive and needed him to stand trial, no matter how bad Storm might want to wring his neck with his bare hands.

Storm just winked as he put on his flak jacket and crawled into the passenger seat of the blacked out SUV with Martin, Pancho, and three other agents going to GUMDI. Two Suburban's full of men would hit the office, securing the computers while moving the employees of GUMDI away from the their work areas and holding them in the conference room until they could decide which employees could be sent home and which needed to stay for further questioning.

The only thing left to wait for was the snatch of Juan Pablo and even with less than fifteen minutes from the time they left the warehouse the wait seemed like an eternity to Storm.

* * *

Coast Guard cutters and aircraft had been tracking the supply boats used by the cartel since early the day before. Their exact locations were updated in real time with the

Storm's End

cutters standing off at a range so as not to be suspected by the supply boats. The minute word was received from operations that El Gato was in custody they would move at flank speed to intercept the drug boats. Each boat would be secured by Coast Guard personnel and put under the Coast Guard command and returned to Guard stations in Houma, where they would be searched, their crew detained until thorough searches could be completed, and the crews either released or taken to jail for violation of drug laws.

Coast Guard choppers were always exercising impromptu inspections of offshore rigs, so when the choppers appeared on the horizon headed for the three rigs it was no cause for concern. Once on board the rigs, armed officers would make their way to the office of the company man for each rig, where he would be arrested and the team from the chopper would begin a search of the warehouses located below the drilling platform deck. All three company men would then be loaded on the choppers for transport back to shore where they would be turned over to FBI agents.

Simultaneously, Mexican Authorities would assault, Tampico Servicio, while FBI and DEA would secure the supply warehouse in Houma, capturing all personnel, computers and smuggled contraband found on the premises.

* * *

Storm's team had only arrived at GUMDI's office building as they got the word to move. Over the tactical radio, they each heard the announcement, "Go, Go, Go." There was a rush to the elevator. Two agents were left there and at each exit listening on their radios in case anyone from the office tried to flee.

Storm was the first one through the doors. He and the other agents pulled their badges as they spread out, securing the facility. Martin stopped just long enough to tell the receptionist to hang up her phone and remain where she was sitting. He then asked for directions to the chief executive's office and off he went, allowing Pancho and Storm to proceed with the business they were there to do.

Storm saw Clay peering around the corner with his mouth open staring in amazement at the commotion. Clay saw Storm, and he stood and started toward the hallway when Storm motioned with a wave of his hand for him to sit back down and stay put for the time being. Storm burst through the glass doors of Harold Stanton's outer office with Pancho close behind. Pancho quickly shushed the secretary, lifting his fingers to his lips. He motioned for her to hang up her phone and took her by the arm, propelling her into the hallway, telling her to join her fellow employees in the conference room. Then he took a position just outside the inner office entrance, giving Storm the time he needed to conduct his affairs.

Startled by the abruptness of the invasion of his private domain, Harold Stanton jumped to his feet demanding to the know the reason for such an intrusion, but before little more than a gasp could escape his lips he felt his world explode and the lights go out.

Storm had broached the door and saw Stanton rise to his feet and begin to back away. Storm hit him squarely in the nose and watched as the man's eyes rolled back in his head as he slumped back into his chair. Storm had knocked him out, but he wouldn't be out for long. While Stanton struggled to regain consciousness, Storm had already circled his desk and handcuffed his hands behind his back. The man was shaky and not fully aware of what was going on, so the detective waited as he stood over him. Finally Harold Stanton's eyes refocused. He realized the detective had hit him fully in the face and he felt the blood running out of one nostril. "What the hell, Storm? What was that for?"

"For having my wife killed." Storm had reached his calm place and was now just looking at the man still slumped in the chair as if he were no more than a rabid coyote he was about to put down.

"What do you mean 'killing your wife'? I had nothing to do with your wife's death."

"Is that your story? Are you really gonna go that direction?" Storm was becoming more upset with everything this man was saying. The veins on Storm's neck begin to throb as he demanded, "Or are you going to tell me the truth?"

"Honest, I had nothing to do with that; I worked with her, I liked her—"

But before he could finish, Storm slapped him across the face; this time not hard enough to knock him down but rather as a reminder of who was charge at the moment.

"Don't lie to me, Harold. We have Victoria and Juan Pablo in custody." He stopped for just a second letting that information sink in and then went on. "They both have already spilled their guts about your involvement in Angie's death, the drug dealing, the smuggling, and countless other murders and crimes."

Stanton's eyes widened but he said nothing.

"Stanton, if it was up to me, you wouldn't walk out of this room alive, but everyone has already told me it would make me no better than you, a scum-sucking killer, and I know Angie wouldn't want your blood on my hands. So I'm going to read you your rights and take you out of this office and turn you over to the FBI.

"Other agents will go through your office with a fine-tooth comb, confiscating all your files and your computers. Your cell phone will be seized and all communications records reviewed." As a dramatic afterthought Storm said, "And hey, Harold, I already found that burner phone in your desk so yes, don't worry, I already have it. Your bank accounts will be frozen and most likely seized. As we speak, a team of investigators is already at your house searching it, so anything you think you might have squirreled away will be found and used against you. Your wife will be read the charges we are leveling against you and all of this will be on the evening news tonight. Your society friends will desert you like rats off a sinking ship, so don't expect any help from those corners. Basically what I am telling you, Harold, is your ass is mine now, and as long as you live you will not be out of my mind. Now stand up and let's go." Storm grabbed him by the collar, forcing him from his chair, and shoved him into the hallway.

Storm had just turned Harold over to Agent Jones when the call came that he needed to go to the Stanton residence, as the agents searching the house had found something he needed to see.

Agent Jones took Harold and sat him in a chair just outside of Mark Wells' office so the entire staff could see the man as his nose still bled. He was done and everybody would now know he was a murderer and smuggler who had used the company they loved as a front to obtain his own wealth.

Storm walked away down the hall to see Clay. He didn't trust himself not to hurt Stanton further. He kept repeating to himself that Angie would not want him to commit murder as revenge for her death. If karma really did exist, Harold Stanton was a dead man walking, anyway. The new cartel leaders or the men he would spend life in prison with would take care of him and his blood would not be on Storm's hands.

Storm's End

EPILOGUE

At the Stanton residence, Special Agent Long was waiting for Storm and Hernandez to arrive. He greeted them at the door and let them inside.

"David, one of our agents found something we think you should see. They found your wife's briefcase in a vault hidden behind one of Stanton's paintings in his study. I thought you might like to see it again. Inside you will find a necklace; I am hoping you can tell us if it was your wife's. Obviously, for now it will be needed as evidence in the cases against Harold Stanton, Victoria Marcuccio, and Juan Pablo du Tilly for the murder of your wife."

Storm sat down in a chair near the entry and held the briefcase on his lap. He seemed almost afraid to open it and look inside. He kept running his fingers over the familiar item that his wife had carried since he had bought it for her when she was promoted. Finally, he opened the briefcase. Inside lay a small gold necklace with a single diamond hanging from it.

The necklace was Angie's; it had been a gift from his mother, who had left it to Angie when she passed away.

The necklace was never off her neck and he couldn't imagine that in all these years he had missed the fact that it was gone. Finding these things in Stanton's house only solidified the case that he had been behind Angie's death and Storm felt a tingle of anger begin to build again. But when he touched the necklace, it was as if Angie had just touched his shoulder assuring him he wasn't a killer and she was at peace now.

It had taken eight years for him to find her killers. Now all he could do was wait for their conviction. It wasn't over, but he now knew the "who and why" and was finally in a place where he could put it behind him and hopefully, purge himself of all the nightmares and demons that had haunted him.

The only thing he had to do now was let Russell and Grady know they could break the story he was alive and had been instrumental in bringing down a criminal empire.

THE END

REWARDS

When you give of yourself to children and get back a smile, or a hug, the reward belongs to you.

Jon has been a volunteer for over thirty years now with the Houston Livestock Show and Rodeo, an annual event that has as the informal motto, **"It is all about the kids."**

In those years, Jon has had the pleasure of working with children of all ages, but, for the past twelve years, he's worked mostly with the Special Children's Committee, a committee that entertains special needs children and adults.

His favorite event is the Committees' Lil Russler's Rodeo; an occasion where sixty special-needs children get to go down on the floor of the arena to act like they are real cowboys and cowgirls, riding real horses, and racing their chaperone with stick horses around barrels just like the barrel racers of the real rodeo.

Watching the children in this special event, experiencing their joy, excitement, and fun, can pull on the heart strings of even the most callous of committee members and volunteer chaperones.

This year, during the event, a beautiful child was sitting on the floor outside the arena, resting from all the activity she had been involved in, when Jon saw her and went over to ask her and her parents if she'd had a good time.

Her father pointed out to Jon that the little girl was deaf, as were her parents and little brother. He then went on to tell Jon that she could hear a little with the help of the small hearing aids she wore behind each ear. He then told Jon her name was Grace and that she went to deaf school so she was learning to sign and speak somewhat.

Jon knew just enough sign to tell the little girl she was very pretty, so Jon signed to her, "Pretty girl."

Grace looked up smiled and asked Jon if he thought she was pretty, and then held her arms up for him to pick her up. He reached down and picked the little girl up and was lost. She now had become his newest best friend.

The picture on the back of this book is the picture taken by Grace's father of Jon holding Grace. Jon felt that this moment was so special that he had to have it for the back of this book.

For him, this picture represents the rewards someone can get from the giving of oneself to children.

Storm's End

ABOUT THE AUTHOR

After a career in sales and marketing, Jon Bridgewater turned his love of spinning a yarn from an avocation into a vocation. A graduate of University of Nebraska in Communications and English, he took jobs with Xerox, Southwestern Bell and AT&T before finally moving to Houston In 1977.

A thirty-five-year resident of Texas and lover of history, he developed a great respect for writers who applied their craft to the writing of Westerns and mysteries. Pushed and prodded by friends, he went to work on his first novel and, after as many as ten rewrites, published *Charity Kills*, a story about a down-and-out homicide detective who gets a last chance to solve the murder of a young woman who no one else seems to care about.

This was the beginning of the David Storm Mystery Series. *After the Storm* is the second of a trilogy that follows the flawed-yet-determined detective as he turns his life around and strives to solve the murder that matters the most to him, the death of his beloved Angie.

Storm's End

Jon's setting is modern-day Houston and, although the David Storm stories are inventions of his imagination, they are based on actual events and take place in recognizable locations in the city he has come to love.

After the Storm centers around the months after Hurricane Katrina caused many of the people of New Orleans to leave their homes and find refuge in cities across the United States. Many were temporarily housed in the dilapidated dome Houston once called the Eighth Wonder of the World. When a good friend's little brother is killed in a way that appears to be a message from a rival gang, Storm and his band of unlikely investigators begin their hunt for a killer, and what they find is criminal activity much larger than any of them would suspect.

Bridgewater has already written the third book, *Storm's End*, of the David Storm Mystery Series. In the past two years he has moved from his beloved home in Houston to Colorado, to do research on a series of Westerns he hopes to publish in the next few years. The David Storm series will continue with Storm, Russell, Pancho, Alisha, and all the others of his band of characters being called upon to solve cases many others don't want to touch.

Made in the USA
Columbia, SC
18 April 2022